The Blood of Five Rivers

THE BLOOD OF FIVE RIVERS

ARJUN BEDI

Palimpsest Press
1171 Eastlawn Ave.
Windsor, Ontario. N8S 3J1
www.palimpsestpress.ca

Printed and bound in Canada
Cover design and book typography by Ellie Hastings
Edited by Jamie Tennant
Copyedited by Sohini Ghose

Palimpsest Press would like to thank the Canada Council for the Arts and the Ontario Arts Council for their support of our publishing program. We also acknowledge the assistance of the Government of Ontario through the Ontario Book Publishing Tax Credit.

LIBRARY AND ARCHIVES CANADA CATALOGUING IN PUBLICATION

TITLE: The blood of five rivers / Arjun Bedi.
NAMES: Bedi, Arjun, author.
IDENTIFIERS: Canadiana (print) 20230490239
            Canadiana (ebook) 2023049031X

ISBN 9781990293580 (SOFTCOVER)
ISBN 9781990293597 (EPUB)
CLASSIFICATION: LCC PS8603.E42485 B46 2023 | DDC C813/.6—DC23

For my family.

Not in any sense of the word will this narration be reliable. It won't be reliable in the semantic sense because this is a story composed of memories that are not my own, memories excavated with bias, and too much separation from the source fouls the purity of a thing. And neither will it be syntactically reliable, because my mind is constituted by all the voices that have shaped it, all of them diametrically opposed, and they enter and leave as they please, coming and going with all their contradictions, inaccuracies, and idiosyncrasies.

How, then, to shine light on those stolen memories and to harness those voices into a cohesive whole? It's no simple affair, so I'll have to use all the tools at my disposal, all the structures of knowledge I have access to, each a lens offering a unique insight—the world witnessed through my five senses, the testimony of my ancestors, the revered fictions of creased and yellowed novels, and the tangled outcomes of foreign histories. This is the burden I bear—the task of communicating this story by any means necessary.

But even in this I know I will fall short, because the past is not available to us like some vast reservoir. We cannot view it as we do an endless ocean from the shore, to see the high crests of our victories and to peer into the nebulous depths of our failures. Our experience is rather limited. We view the past through peepholes, narrow telescopes that display barely moving vignettes, and we give them colour through the tint of our emotions, but we can never recreate the picture as it truly was. As we look back, we see a world tainted by the transience of our present circumstances. We are voyeurs of things we can hardly understand.

Which brings me to the pressing question: If the task is so near impossible, why bother? Well, for one, because "understanding" has never been the point of remembering. Memories sit stubbornly in the mind not because they are accurate but because they are malleable—shapeshifters ever ready to change their form in service of whatever end we can imagine. And it is because of this that we can use them as raw materials in the construction of a story that offers some feeble fulfillment of that desperate desire for meaning.

Yet, aside from this general and theoretical justification, I am also driven by a more personal motivation. You see, this particular story has become something of an inescapable compulsion for me. It cycles though my head, again and again, and like a disregarded barfly or an old miser abandoned at a retirement home, I find myself rehearsing these lines as if an enigmatic young journalist might sit next to me one day, and ask: "So what's your deal?"

In that sense, perhaps the goal is simply to unburden myself, to objectify these words, like etchings on a tombstone, so they exist outside of me, so they can consecrate the useless remains of something once living. Or maybe there is no point at all, in which case allow me to go forth with a conceited hope—a wilful denial of the presciently obvious—that the purpose of this exercise will be revealed at its conclusion.

In the meantime, I'll turn my attention to something more practical: The beginning. And where else to begin but a birth—not of a child, but something grander and more clearly defined than a human being. For now, we focus our attention on the birth of a nation.

1947

Once upon a time, the world was at peace. At least, where my grandfather was born, where he grew and where he lived, there was peace. But elsewhere, a man sat in a room with a pen and a map, and as my grandfather sat in a relative state of tranquility, a line was drawn across that map. So subtle a thing, surely it should have had no consequence. But peace is fragile, and so easily was it torn apart by that line, and so easily was the fabric of my grandfather's reality torn apart with it.

Once upon a time, my grandfather had sat under the shade of old trees, the sky stark blue and the sun bright, and he watched the labourers laugh and joke as they worked the fields. He would smile shyly at the young women who were young girls when he had been a young boy. He would walk next to his mother, carrying her bag of fresh produce from the market, and listen to her speak about his future—that he would one day oversee those happy workers, that he would one day marry one of those young women, and that he would one day walk through these same markets with his own child.

Once upon a time. It is the correct way to speak of things, because all that is contained within that phrase is no more than childish fantasy, a fairy tale, where futures are certain and lasting peace is structurally built into the universe. But that is not what happens in *our* universe.

Because a line was drawn, the fairy tale evaporates. Because a line was drawn, his mother collapsed next to him as a lead ball with dimmed velocity burst forth from her chest, and he halted for a moment as the crimson mist settled onto his skin. And from her knees she opened her mouth to speak, but only blood welled out.

He ran, the muscles in his legs contracting and expanding of their own volition. Black ash fell, black clouds rose, and flames flickered, diaphanous against the blood-red sky. No laughter and no jokes; the limbs of labourers severed and strewn all around, and dead eyes from broken faces peered up at him, while his legs continued to run.

The fire clawed at his back and singed the tendons of his heels. His mouth was smoke-coated; the smell of burning flesh and noxious gasoline fumes blistered his nostrils and throat. Old trees burned red against the horizon. His home burned.

The market, where fresh produce once lay in neat stacks and stubborn housewives haggled for discounted prices, was a mirage of hell. The mouths of homes, gaping maws that exhaled black air and screams of the dying. The dirt beneath his feet was soaked in blood, a black mud that pulled him downward. His legs continued to run.

A gentle river, once clear and clean, was now crimson and transported the bloated remains of the once living and once laughing—young faces he had smiled at shyly, young faces he had envisioned a future with.

"Pajo!"[1]

Screams and screams. A strangled child hung limp from the arms of a screaming woman.

Carbon erupted, lead flew, and metal clanged.

Everything ached.

Carbon erupted, lead flew, blood soaked into dirt, and a limp child rested next to its limp mother. The screaming stopped.

---

1 Run!

Mouth ached for water untarnished by blood.
Lungs ached for air untarnished by smoke.
Eyes ached for a horizon untarnished by flames.
Heart ached for a home untarnished by death.
But all the world was blood, smoke, and flames.
All the world was tarnished by death.
"Je jena chondeyein, pajo..."[2]

---

2 If you want to live, keep running...

The Darkness After Dawn

1956-1958

Two things conspired to greet the child on the day of his birth: heat and humidity. Of course, this confluence was neither rare nor unique, as both these elements operated blindly in regard to human affairs, and where the child was born, they were both at work daily. Even the midwife, who had walked fourteen kilometres from her village to the east to deliver the boy—and was like many in her country, prone to a fixation with star arrangements and other potential markers of auspicious things—did not consider anything about the day to be rare or unique. While executing her duties, she held the loose assumption that this was nothing more than the birth of yet another unexceptional farmhand.

The boy did not wail or cry as he emerged from the womb, as might be expected, but with large, dark eyes he expressed curiosity, swallowing the world in hungry glances. The child's father, who was outside distributing sweetcakes made from ground sugarcane, was called inside. He looked at the boy and asked, "Eh sidah ah?"[3] The midwife shrugged and slapped the boy on his rear and then he wailed. Her hands, conditioned by the rigours of subsistence living, were rough and calloused, and when he was handed to his mother, he found hers were rougher and more calloused. She held

---

3 Is he stupid?

the child close to her chest, exhausted and still in pain from the delivery. When she had given birth to her first child—a daughter who was being cradled in her father's arms—she had been fortunate enough to be given poppy seeds steeped in milk. This time she was not so fortunate and received only turmeric steeped in milk.

Many villagers could not muster the energy to care about the proceedings at hand. The few who had come to offer their congratulations did not stay long. Fields required tending and cows needed milking. In the heat of the midday sun, many were simply eager simply to find some shade. The humidity stifled the rising dust kicked up by the baba's bicycle tires on the single road out of the village. He arrived that morning from Amritsar to speak with the boy's grandfather, a man with a soft face, features too crowded toward the centre, and a beard that was too easily pierced by the light of the sun. The old man spat on the ground as he spoke to the baba, and it landed on the foot of the Chuhra, who was on his haunches, slicing tall blades of grass with a sickle. Neither man looked down and the Chuhra continued his work, half listening to the conversation, which was not about the newborn, but rather about old grievances.

The father, a predominantly silent man (timid more than stoic), watched the boy tremble in his mother's embrace and raised his voice again. "Eh comjor lagdeh."[4] But the midwife was unable to conjure any sympathy. She dipped her hands in a water basin, the water already tinted pink, and remarked, "Hun tan rab de hath de vich ah."[5] The mother did not concern herself with her husband's worrying. Instead, she cradled her child closely, gently cooing to ease his migration into the world. The midwife collected her payment, a bag of grain which she slumped over her shoulder, and exited the shady room into the oppressive heat. It was a long march back to her village and she aimed to return before dark.

---

4 He looks weak.
5 It's in God's hands now.

The father said nothing more, his features soft like his own father, crowded toward the centre of his face, but with a life still too short for old grievances. The boy had his mother's face, sharp in all aspects: a sharp nose, a sharp chin, and a sharp stare. Though, at the moment, his mother's face was softer—an uncharacteristic sentimentality—and it rested on his face, on his large blinking eyes, and to him alone she said, "Mera Kaka."[6]

Here are some things that must be mentioned. The day of his birth was 23 June 1956. The location of his birth was Ahmedpura, a small village on the outskirts of the farming township of Patti, which is within the municipality of the Sikh religion's spiritual capital, Amritsar, in the state of Punjab. Ahmedpura is eight kilometres to the west of Patti, and Patti is forty-five kilometres south of Amritsar.

Know I include these precise and impersonal details sheerly out of necessity. Such brute specificity is apt to subtract from the sublime nature of occasions such as these. For the romance of myths exists in their obscurity and as much as possible should be done to protect that magic. But it is also true that these events happened in space and in time, and in order to chart the trajectory of our protagonist, we need to mark his point of origin.

Now there is a schism, a rapid alteration and reversal that occurs and is absorbed in the supple preconscious mind of the child called Kaka. The mud hut he was born in was home for as long as it took for him to hold his head aloft, unassisted. Then he was routed from the fertile soils of Punjab to the sun-bleached grey tarmac of the country's capital. Here, the streets did not kick up dust but produced a mystifying haze as the heat arrived and retreated, as so many things did in New Delhi. It distorted the visual spectrum, elongating limbs from a distance, pulling things in and out of focus

---

6 My little baby.

at whim, and in general, offered a wobbly representation of reality.

Here he learned to walk. He yearned, reaching forward with all his being, producing hasty steps that swung his weight wildly from side to side. The sturdy anchor of his mother's finger was there should he have needed it, but his ambition was too great. He waddled, waddled, waddled, and collapsed, falling forward and scraping the soft skin on his knees and palms. The skin would scab and become calloused like the hands of the woman who stood back with her arms folded, waiting for her son to stop wailing and pick himself back up.

The father left in the mornings to his coveted, yet in-glorious job as a maintenance worker for the city's sewage and plumbing system. As he trudged knee-deep through the city's excrement, Kaka waddled above, tugging at the hem of his mother's chunni until she relented and took him to the bustling streets. Kaka breathed the world in and he saw mil-lions of people engaged in millions of tasks. Alleys jut in and out of larger streets, which smelled of burning oils, incense, fried alu, golgappa, and fresh manure from the sacred cows of Hindu and Sikh clerics, who shouted their admonish-ments and proclamations to half listening pedestrians. The impression of a greater world was slowly seared into Kaka's mind, and with it, the axiom that all the wonders such a world might offer can be taken back in an instant.

Trudging knee-deep in the city's excrement did not pay a high enough salary for supporting a family of four. It was naive to believe otherwise. So the fragile dream of the father was shattered by the pressures of the world. The mother, the sister, and little Kaka, who wouldn't stop waddling, were sent back to the pind[7] again.

It was nightfall when the three arrived at the mud hut in Punjab. It sat at the edge of the pind, adjacent to the few acres of land that Kaka's grandfather has secured with

---

7 Village.

his small fortune. Kaka's grandfather was too old, too concerned with old grievances, and too bitter because of them to engage in commerce, so his son's family would have to take the wheat grown on his land and sell it in the markets at the town square. Specifically, this task would fall to the young boy as soon as he became capable of hauling the weight of the harvest through the streets. But none of this was known to Kaka. All he knew is that he could sleep in the dusty corner where his mother pointed her finger. All he knew is he liked the feeling he felt when his legs carried him forward. All he knew is that somewhere out there, something greater awaited.

1991

Are you curious about my birth? Well, you shouldn't be. If the midwife was present at my birth, she would roll her eyes, throw up her hands, and scoff. All the precautions, all the safety and sanitation, the painkillers flowing through translucent tubes, the rubber gloves and plastic goggles to protect the nurses' painted nails and fabricated eyelashes, and the doctors in white coats and nurses in blue smocks, and more fabrics of white and blue draped over everything to conceal the gritty, gruesome, and *red* reality of childbirth. All in all, generally too much mothering of the mother and certainly too much babying of the baby, and none of it auspicious in the least! At least, that's what the midwife would say.

But what does her opinion matter? During this entire episode, I consider myself something of a hero, because I decided to arrive while my mother was delivering newspapers door to door, in the grip of a cold February storm. A saviour was I, from the toils of minimum wage labour, an emancipator of the working class. In those early hours of the morning, when the world was cast in the dark blue glow of Canadian winters, as she squinted her eyes against the flurries of snow and desperately dug her frozen hands into her coat pockets after throwing another paper at another door, I took notice of her anguish and gave her respite the only way I could—by demanding life.

The witnesses of my magnanimity include my brother, the First Man, who steps forward to navigate the rocky and craterous geography of second-generationism before me; my father, who possesses a mysterious infatuation with the nation of Germany (and thus is aptly dubbed Der Vater); his sister and her brood, among whom is present my first cousin, Toucan Sam. This name, along with the others, requires some explanation, I'm sure, but that will have to wait for another time. For this is my day, and all eyes shall remain glued on me.

So, what do I look like? Cradled in my mother's arms under the dim glow of a hospital bed lamp, do I resemble her at all? Perhaps I do, but she does not belong in these pages, so we will not dwell on the particulars of her visage, intelligent and optimistic as they are. Maybe my father, then, whose eyes are dark and deep-set, further darkened from lack of sleep, and who has an impressive stature, heavy arms, broad shoulders, and a subdued presence that somehow manages to fill the room. His features are sharp and angular, inherited from his mother who I should mention is also here in the fray today. She stands at the foot of the bed, arms folded across her lean torso, the wiry muscles of her forearm flexing and relaxing, and the hint of a frown resting on her face. Her husband, however, is regrettably absent. My grandfather, the father of my father, was called in for the dreaded night shift, working security at the international airport, where he is also paid minimum wage to absorb the vitriol of uncooperative motorists who insist on idling in no-idling zones. In all honesty, as a squirmy newborn, I probably resemble him the most as currently my soft, undeveloped features are intolerably crowded toward the centre of my face.

What follows over the course of the next several hours is this: A barrage of advice from the medical professionals that would cause the midwife to throw a fit. A slow car ride through the semi-slippery roads with clean, yellow paint separating the lanes, which drivers are taught to stay in, and—in stark contrast to behaviours displayed at airport no-idling zones—actually abide! They even flash their little blinkers when they switch lanes and move only 10 km/h over the speed limit before calmly re-entering the cruising lane, just as is depicted in the provincial Driver's Handbook. Suffice to say, this is all quite awe-inspiring to me, who like any new arrival to Canada, is witnessing such lawful auto-motoring for the first time.

Then I am taken to the homestead, a lovely little abode Der Vater fell for once he set his eyes on the foreclosure price. As soon as the festering crow corpse was scooped up from the master bedroom en suite, and the pentagram drawn in ominous red paint was scrubbed clean from the basement wall, it was home sweet home. The neighbourhood roads are clean and empty. There are no crops growing nearby, no scent of manure in the air, nor the piercing sound of holy house bells at ungodly hours of the morning. Rather, I experience the bliss of secular silence and the flat and inoffensive odours of a sleepy Canadian suburb. Here, the food is not grown from the ground but arranged neatly in rows, under bright lights with no flies or worms, and in place of sweaty, irritable farmers who swing their scythes at you if you come too close, there are smiling cashiers who wave and tell you to "Have a nice day!"

These places are called "grocery stores" and there is an expensive one and a cheaper one, but they are both owned by the same company to effectively target all potential consumer markets, and to ensure the people who can spend more on their groceries don't have to rub against the dirty elbows of those who can't. We buy our groceries at the cheaper grocery store, and it is in the cereal aisle that Der Vater is struck with the name I am to be called. He sees the box with a cartoon gentleman wearing a crisp, blue naval uniform. The gentleman has a brilliant white moustache, like Guru Nanak, whose portrait is hung in the landing at the top of the stairs at the homestead. And lo and behold, the moustachioed naval officer even holds his right hand up, just like the portrait of Guru Nanak! Boy, that's a nice name, isn't it? Feels good on the palate, has historical and metaphysical panache, is disarmingly simple at first glance, yet has enough ethnic nuance to slip up that charmless Western tongue. If only the midwife had been there to dissuade Der Vater from pursuing such an inauspicious course of action. But she was not, and as an unfortunate result, it is in the cereal aisle of Mark and Linda's No Frills where Der Vater is so inspired by the cartoon mascot Cap'n Crunch that he decides unilaterally, "Han, mein puth da naam Nanak rakhunga!"[8]

---

8 Yes, my son will be named Nanak!

1968

The wind rippled through the endless oceans of wheat, gentle amber waves which imparted a sensation like that of being marooned on an island; a small, insular civilization lost in a sea of its own making. It took less than an hour to walk down every street in this civilization. Kaka's feet had nowhere new to take him, so he roamed the streets again and again, counting the houses. He'd been doing it for years, so there was not an inch of the village that was unfamiliar to him. There are eighty-seven houses, and the largest, a house made of brick with two floors, belonged to his grandfather, Maher. Maher stood on the flat roof of his house and scowled at the world. When facing the direction of the setting sun, he scowled more fiercely, because in that direction there was an empire of fertile soil and thriving wheat crops, which in his mind was where he should have been standing. Cyril Radcliffe moved his pen down the map and fourteen million people lost their homes. Cyril Radcliffe moved his pen down the map and one million people lost their lives. Cyril Radcliffe moved his pen down the map and drew an eternal scowl across Maher's face.

Kaka watched his grandfather on the roof of his house, caressing his most prized possession, an unfired Lee Enfield Mk III rifle, a gift received from a cadre of departing British officers, one of whom (with the strangely Russian name Chekhov) held Maher in higher esteem than the rest of the rabble, "Tally-ho, you're a good chap, Maher, the best of chaps, tally-ho!" Rifles are expensive and they can kill a person, so Kaka watched his grandfather hold what was not just an arbitrary token of superiority. The rifle was a dual symbol of wealth and power and with its practical capacity for violence, it showed those who resided in the other eighty-six houses they were in the presence of an extraordinary person. Just as Cyril Radcliffe was made a Knight Grand Cross of the Order of the British Empire after the drawing of his line, so Maher was made exceptional by the caressing of his rifle.

In the courtyard, the Chuhra constantly moved about, performing various tasks. He had learned well that a body at rest was a body punished. So he kept his body moving. Even if the grass was even and the porch was swept, even when there was no work to be done, he was always engaged in at least a pantomime of activity. "Oye Chuhriya, daru leya!"[9] Maher shouted from the roof, and the Chuhra hurried out to obey the command.

The Punjabi day drags long, so much so that it stresses the limits of most people's ambitions. The young farmers squatted and stood countless times through the day in the endless fields in pursuit of a perfect harvest, and the old farmers leaned against the mud walls, groaning about the aches in their knees, bemoaning the fact that the youngsters didn't heed their advice, even though they never heeded their own elders. The old wives gossiped in hushed voices about the comings and goings of their neighbours as they taught their daughters how to scrub soiled linens with baking soda. The daughters glared enviously at the boys who were given free rein to skip through the streets shirtless, whipping branches at the heels of stray cats and cowardly dogs.

In the evening, the wind blew against the open wheat fields and Kaka climbed the branches of the banyan tree in Maher's field. Beneath the limbs of the tree was Shinda, the son of one of the wealthier families in Ahmedpura. With a house also made of brick, he had few worries on his mind and ample leisure time

---

9 Hey low-caste, bring me some liquor!

to pursue his passions, one of which was to aimlessly throw rocks into the swaying wheat fields. Next to him, the fraternal twins, Gora and Kala, jostled each other to no end and for no gain. They jostled each other in the heat of the womb and now they jostled each other in the heat of the Indian sun. Gora was fair-skinned and tall, and Kala, much darker and much shorter. These differences had resulted in the development of profoundly different worldviews, and jostling one another was the only way to test which was superior. These were Kaka's closest friends, comrades from youth when allegiance is easily granted and brought closer together by the tender age of adolescence, which surreptitiously imposes illusions of heroism and adventure on even the most mundane activities.

The sound of ringing bells brought them all to a halt. But the bells were not from the Gurdwara whose call had already beckoned the pious who sought to hum their hymns to God. These were from cowbells, not accompanied by the mooing of a cow but the neighing of a horse—it was Pinda, the desi daru moonshine merchant. The moment they spotted the daru merchant approaching, the idlers, who lay on weaved cotton munjay[10] and gawked endlessly at everything, perked up like a troop of macaque who sense a predator. But they had no intention of running. They widened their eyes, extended their necks, and smacked their lips. They swarmed the daru merchant as his horse pulled to a stop before them.

Pinda was not a scrupulous man. He made no moral discernments between patrons, whether by age, means, or proclivity towards addiction. When a hand reached forward with rupees, he reached back with daru. The hand with the most notes belonged to the Chuhra, who did not drink but only did the bidding of others. Maher awaited on the roof of his house, caressing his Lee Enfield Mk III. Pinda kept his eyes on the horizon and one hand on the reins of the horse, watching for signs for movement. His desi daru was stored in the retired inner tube of an old automobile, tied to the flank

---

10 Cots.

of the horse. The undistilled liquor contained flakes of barley and industrially sanitary percentages of alcohol. He pumped it out with a thick rubber tube that resisted corrosion. The legality of Pinda's enterprise was not well-defined. He slept soundly enough as long as his horse was able to outpace the bicycles of the local authorities and the feet of families who had recently burned blue-tinted corpses.

Shinda said, "Oye chuhriya, ithe ah!"[11] The Chuhra, who was also employed by Shinda's father, said, "Haan ji, Sardar ji"[12] and scuttled across. Shinda cajoled the Chuhra to relinquish some of the desi daru and the Chuhra, unaccustomed to refusing orders from Jatts or Shimbas or Khatris, relinquished it. He replied, "Haan ji, Sardar ji," and poured a glass full of the stuff for the boys.

The glass spun counterclockwise from Shinda to Kaka to Gora to Kala, again and again, and Kaka's head spun too. The far left of his peripheral vision took centre stage, then the far right, and all the while he stared directly ahead. His proficiency at taking steps degraded and he became like how he was as an infant, too eager as he moved, his weight swinging wildly from side to side. There was laughter, and a cool breeze. He fell backwards and hundreds of stalks of wheat bent and broke and held him. He saw the full moon shake violently in a sea of blinking stars. His legs became still and he could not move them, but it did not matter because he was content. For the first time in his life, he was happy with his legs at rest.

---

11 Hey low-caste, come here!"
12 Yes, sir.

The Meridian of Beatings, or The Evening of Black and Purple in the East

Before daybreak the shoe flew across the room like the crow across the clean sky and hit the boy in the temple and awoke him from a slumber where temporary peace was permitted. The mother stood scowling and said, Uth ja dungara![13] The boy stood and broke his fast with stale water from a cistern, where mosquitoes and blackflies gathered and birthed offspring. The sun had not risen. He left the place where he had found sleep with nothing except the clothes he wore, and he knew it would be long before he found sleep again. He passed the rows of houses, still in darkness with no movement and no villagers. Gradually, the fires began to be stoked from the lazy coals that burned from the night, and the sun broke over the horizon, and pillars of light fell through the cracks of the mud architecture.

He walked on. The bells of Gurdwaras clanged resoundingly and hymns were hummed to God by devout women

---

13 Get up, you lazy ass!

wearing chunnis and salwar kameez, their heads covered in reverence. The roosters clucked and crowed and the cows stared through their coal-like eyes as he walked on. The children of the women who hummed and of the men who were in a drunken stupor sulked and yawned and rubbed their eyes, and he was reminded of his father who was away. He thought about what labours his father would be engaged in and how much effort he was expending toward a better life. He wondered if his father thought of him as much as he thought of his father. He walked on and came to the school, lit by the sun that had now risen higher in the sky, bringing warmth to drive away the cold. The instructor shouted at him, calling him panchode,[14] and struck him with a metre stick made of rosewood.

There was pain but he did not bleed. He was told to go to the back of the class, place his face through the gap between his legs and hold his ears. He sat on his haunches like the small monkeys who sit on their haunches on the battlement of the white alabaster structures adjoining the Golden Temple, who sneer and mock and steal the bananas of the pilgrims who go there. But he was unlike the small monkeys in that they assume their posture through the freedom granted by their simian nature, and freedom of any kind was foreign to him. When the sun was at its highest and no shadows were cast and the cows were not to be bothered to stand in the heat any longer and the howling, starving dogs grew weary of howling, he released his ears. He left the schoolhouse even though classes were on. The starving dogs looked at him hungrily but he walked on because commerce was calling and wheat harvested that morning needed to be taken to the market at the main square and it was miles away and the day would still be long.

He walked on and he approached the home of his grandfather. The iron gate that separated it from the world was inlaid in gold, but the iron itself had accumulated rust from

---

14 Sister-fucker.

the humidity. The Chuhra was on his haunches, culling the tall blades of grass, but he was also unlike the monkeys of the Golden Temple because he was following the command of his master, who did not abide the machinations of nature's grace to proceed as they wished. All men are born to impose their will and if they die with tall grass, they have lived lives that were less than those lived by men with even grass. The grandfather saw the boy approaching and lifted himself from his chair, made of teak wood, made by the hand of the Chuhra, who still kept his eyes down. The boy said, Kush hega vetchun nu?[15] The grandfather raised his hand, which held a bottle of English whisky in which only the dregs remained. The whites of his eyes were stained red from his consumption of liquor, and he pointed to a meagre pile of soggy wheat. The boy said, Hor kush?[16] And the grandfather threw the bottle in his hand and it collided with the ground, hard and dry and red like baked clay but stronger, and the glass shattered, shards lodging themselves in the boy's legs, making him bleed. The grandfather said loudly, Ja duffa ho, kootia![17]

He walked on and he carried the soggy wheat and it became less so because the sun was covetous of moisture, and even he became like the wheat because it had been long since he had drank the water from the cistern and it would be long till he drank from it again. He came to the market in the village that was many miles from his home. Macaques and langurs harassed the fruit vendors, and men slick with sweat and muddy from the dust of the road yelled and shouted, and cows not to be bothered with movement congested the narrow roads. He laid down the wheat, now completely dry, and he called into the market. His voice was dry and weak from the walk and it did not triumph the screeches of apes and the shouts of men. A woman who wore a salwar kameez came to him and looked at his wheat. She raised her hand

---

15 Do you have anything to sell?
16 Anything else?
17 Screw off you lousy dog!

which held a rolled-up paper, held it high like the hand of God who she sang hymns to before the sun rose, and said, Ah ki baqwas vech da hein?[18] He said nothing. The newspaper clapped against his forehead and he fell to his knees.

The sun fell towards the west and cast tendrils of lights through the dying marketplace and the shouts of the men became murmurs and the wheat remained and the boy looked around and he was the only one left with wheat. An old man approached him and said, Mein leh lunga.[19] The boy was relieved because the clang of rupees in his pocket were more righteous than the bells of the Gurdwara. The man took the wheat and pressed the rupees into the small palm of the boy, who looked into his palms and saw less than he was owed and yelled, voice dry and cracked and soft and unyielding. The man struck the boy mightily and he fell to his knees and the wounds from the shards of glass opened and he bled and the soil drank greedily. The man said, Ah ki panchode karda? Kharab kanak vech ke, poora mul mangda? Ja khoo vich dig![20]

The sun was now falling in the red sky. The boy walked on and bled into the red soil and his mouth was dry and, though his stomach ached and growled, he craved only the taste of water. But he felt the metal in his palm and it nourished him and he walked on. He came close to his home and the bell of the Gurdwara was clanging from a distance and the bell of the desi daru seller was clanging closer. When he approached the daru seller, he was cuffed by the merchant who said, Pehlan paisey de.[21] The men on their bamboo and cotton cots, who had drunk heavily, screeched and howled like starving dogs and small apes, but they were worse because the sun was low and it was dark and it betrayed the contents of their souls.

---

18 What is this garbage you're selling?
19 I'll take it.
20 What's this sister-fucker doing? He's selling rotten wheat and wants full payment? Go die in a ditch!
21 You have to pay first.

The boy walked on. The earth was flat and black in front of him and he found more comfort in the darkness for it shielded him against the cruel heart of mankind, which, in the light, finds ample cause to untether its malign desires. He knew the world existed as nothing more than a canvas for the brutal will of humanity to meticulously craft its beautifully violent masterpiece, and one could only weather the violence and isolate within it the element which, when bonded to a single soul, forges it into something stronger and more deserving of adulation. When he returned home, the cistern was empty but the mosquitoes were ravenous, so he bled again. His mother extended her hand and he pressed the rupees into her palm and he was relieved because it was done. She looked down at her palm and held the alms without reverence. Then she closed her hand into a fist and brought it down on the boy and he could not call out because his voice was gone like the sun was gone and she beat him and he bled from his face. Finally, it was done. When she left him, he went into the dark embrace of his home and laid his head and closed his eyes knowing what had happened would happen again the next day.

2015

An iron burns hot. I'm playing pool and drinking Jameson's Irish whisky, double neat. It's my fourth, and the geometry of the game is becoming lucid in my fingertips. The heavy buzz erases my anxieties and opens up avenues for performance enhancement that were dormant in the squishy grey matter of my subconscious. The auto-queued bar playlist appears to be a Jackson-themed one, currently playing the 1969 smash Motown hit, "I want you back." Emil said, "Existence would be quite an impractical enterprise if we stopped granting importance to that which has none." He's right, but he died decades ago and he had no idea who I am. Lindsay H. said, "You're super chill; add me on Kik so we can keep talking!" I was wrong—I had thought she was real for too long and I got my hopes up and started to believe I might be able to put my balls in her holes, or bang against her on a green felt tabletop, or some analogy that makes sense between the act that mustn't be spoken about and pool.

Toucan Sam returns from the bar with three more shots of Jameson's. We take a shot after nearly every game but they drink beers in between and I just sip on more Jameson's. He's called Toucan Sam because he inherited those sharp features from our mutual grandmother, along with the grandiose olfactory system that runs rampant through Arabia. (He's also called that because I'll be damned if I'm the only one whose name was inspired by a breakfast cereal mascot.) French Sinatra is here too, an expatriate from the Quebecois sub-subcontinent, and likely the most beautiful man one might ever have the good fortune to witness. He is one with the majesty of the Khalsa flag, smooth orange complexion like the fertile sands of Punjab, and eyes blue—oh so baby-blue—just like the fleur-de-lys.

The pool table is inactive. The balls are gathered neatly into a triangle at one-third the length of the surface and cues are leaned up against the wall. The energy that might have been employed toward the game is being spent on squabbling; a new argument about old things ensues. "I fucking got it worse than both you pussies," says the Toucan. "I got left at the park one time and had to walk like ten fucking kilometres home, and then I still got my ass whooped." French blinks his baby-blues, unimpressed. "Whatever man, I used to get locked in the garage and chased around with a belt." The bar playlist appears to be eavesdropping on our conversation as the next song it seamlessly transitions into is the 1983 smash pop hit, "Beat it." (A bit on the nose, I think.) I opt to stay silent and sip my Jameson's because the one time I was beaten was by my biji[22], who cracked a turmeric-stained wooden spoon on my knuckles. It was painful, but clearly no contender here. But, again I remember the iron, how it sat upright in between pairs of wrinkled pants, and the waves of heat it produced that distorted the air behind it. How do I explain the way an iron burns?

"Wire coat hangers hurt more than belts if you swing 'em right." Toucan adds, and French replies ominously, "Man, you don't even know…" Maybe I should mention the proclivity in literature to remember notorious horse beaters, like Raskolnikov's dream man, or the dog-thrasher that reminds Yossarian of Raskolnikov's dream, or the ill-treatment of the horses in front of Billy Pilgrim's wagon, or for the more philosophically inclined, the horse beater who precipitated Friedrich's

22 Grandmother

madness in the Piazza Carlo Alberto. Music as well, I should add, for Joe Jackson must also be credited as a notorious horse beater, though his thrashings produced one hell of stallion. But I mention none of this because Toucan doesn't read, and Sinatra only reads basketball stats, and now the point is so tenuous that it's lost even on me. After all, it was a horse who saved the man who stopped by the woods on a snowy evening.

The spoon has reason behind it. It is stained yellow because curries and *subzis* contain great heaps of turmeric, which has an anti-inflammatory property to cool the ache of childbirth and generational traumas. The spoon was cracked against Young Nanak's knuckles because he was responsible for a most heinous crime. Armed with the often-underused wire stripper attachment of a Swiss Army knife, he assaulted a sacred thing, carving the machinations of his seven-year-old mind into the soft, powdery exterior of the living room drywall. It was a carnal act of desperation—thoroughly emotive and thoroughly expressionist in style—reminiscent of the way a younger and less sophisticated Nanak would tramp through the untouched fields of fresh snow in the heart of Canadian winters, desperate to leave his mark. The spoon fell from on high with a logical wrath, an understandable wrath.

"Let's take this fucking shot," Toucan says, and yet again the iron comes to mind. It burned before Young Nanak understood cause and effect, when he crawled and groped at a world with fewer distinctions between object and subject. Young Nanak's hand reached out—the same hand which was smacked by the turmeric spoon of logic years later (the same hand that is raised in the portrait of the man he is named after)—and it laid flat, palm side, against the shiny face of the plugged-in iron. For one second, nothing, but then the world turned red, Young Nanak screeched and Biji screeched, and for ever after the iron remained incomprehensible.

"Yo, you gonna take your fucking shot or you just gonna sit there staring into space?" Toucan says, and I do as he says. The Jameson's burns too, but not nearly so much as the iron.

It's a technical problem at bottom, isn't it? Whether all inputs into a closed system will necessarily express themselves? Energy inputs on the pool table are expressed as billiard balls colliding against each other and against the felt bumpers, and energy inputs into arguments are expressed as a poker game of rising stakes with childhood memories as the hands and shots of Jameson as bargaining chips. But what about violence as the input and a child as the closed system? Is the output expressed the same as the input, or is it different? Joe Jackson's violence was ultimately expressed as some of the most beautiful and compelling music of the twentieth century, but the violence in my life was not as carefully directed. It appeared to affect the objects within my electromagnetic field more severely than it affected me.

Half empty plates of food crashed against floors and walls, doors of bedrooms splintered down the centre as they were kicked in, video games controllers were swung round and round like the cowboy's lasso before colliding with television screens and sending shards of glass skittering across the floor.

Perhaps Lindsay H. is real after all and I am just making prejudicial assumptions about users of the chat platform Kik. Perhaps Emil was wrong and, even if we do grant importance to things which have none, existence remains an impractical enterprise. I will never understand why the iron burns so hot. "Rack it up," I say. "I'm gonna get another shot."

1970

Gora was a beautiful ullu da pattha.[23] Akin to those olive-eating Macedonians who crossed the Indus River in 326 BCE, with their alabaster-white skin that made all the Brahmins swoon and cry, "Itne safed gorey kahaan se aye?"[24] In a similar fashion, Gora flaunted his godlike pale skin in village after village, causing the young women to pensively bite their lower lip while their grandmothers vigorously fanned themselves as they calculated potential wedding dowries they might have mustered. But Gora had no interest in the ordinary stock, monochromatic as they were, boring shades of brown set against more boring shades of brown. Greatness covets greatness and the extraordinary demands extraordinary. In all the villages of Punjab, the only creature to match young Gora's beauty was the daughter of the industrious Jat, Gurvaid Sahib—the lovely Grahini. Her beauty lay not in her skin, which was not as shimmering as Gora's, but in her hair, which was streaked auburn and mahogany, and her irises, which were a lighter shade of brown than the commoners (almost what might be considered a shade of green).

By God's grace, one day Gora saw her on the back of her father's wagon as they were travelling to Patti. Gora stood on

23 Son of an owl.
24 Where on earth did such fair whites come from?

the bank of the road, engaged in the grand Punjabi tradition of irrigation, but the sight of her beauty was so great he began to miss his mark. His hose hardened mid-task and the stream flew over the brush! When she saw him, it raised higher still. She smiled and he damn near lost all control of the thing! At last, in place of the ever-thirsty wheat fields, Gora practically irrigated himself! Grahini snickered and Gora smiled dumbly, and there it was, a union of destiny—two butterflies in a land of moths.

Gora was also a sneaky son of an owl. Though not as sneaky as Shinda, the Lubani, the fox. For example, when the youth came together to play Oochi lumbi kockli,[25] Gora snuck away from Ahmedpura to Bagradi, the neighbouring pind, where Grahini waited at the edge of her father's crops, heart beating violently against her chest and chunni wrapped tightly around her face in the fear her brothers might catch her in her indiscretions. But young love is a powerful force, and forbidden relations are more tantalizing than the officially sanctioned kind, so despite the danger, they embraced. And as their bodies rumbled and tumbled under the cover of Gurvaid Sahib's crops, Gora and Grahini travelled in their minds away from this place and its oppressive strictures, away from its commandments against love, to the evergreen valleys of the Swedish mountains, the blue ocean beaches of Bali, the cobblestone streets of Caucasia, and other destinations depicted in the musical montages of Bollywood blockbusters.

It was and would remain, without a doubt, the most joyous time in both their lives. A time when romance flourished alongside their coming of age and each of the lovers' own conceptions of self, forged in relation to the others. Such bonds tended to be lifelong and this one might have gone the distance if not for one inauspicious afternoon when Grahini revealed a grim truth to Gora—the reason she was on the

25 A game played in the wheat fields, a mix between Hide-and-Seek and Marco Polo.

wagon that fateful day they first saw one another, the reason her father had taken her to Patti. Weeping, she collapsed, her face in her hands, and said, "Oh Gora, mere mangni ho gayi ah!"[26]

Gora was dejected. All his happiness was reaped in an instant like when the hand scythe slices through the wheat shaft; his heart was crushed like when the wheat flower is placed between the stones of the mill; and his vision for the future was swallowed whole like when the roti is rolled into a cylinder and gobbled up by the hungry farmer. With no response to offer Grahini, he rose silently and wandered home in a haze. In the days that followed, thoughts of her intruded on him at all hours, but the idea of Grahini blurred and softened like a dream, a fog that would not dissipate and from which nothing tangible could be claimed.

Over the next few days, Kala did all he could to console his relatively gorgeous fraternal twin. "Ja yaar, hor aju giyan,"[27] he said repeatedly, but to no avail. Kala, monochromatic and unshimmering, could never understand what it meant to be part of a rare breed and to find a kindred spirit who existed in the same exalted strata. No, Gora found no solace in the empty words of his brother. What he sought, at the very least, was a sense of closure. He wanted to confront the lovely Grahini, to smell her lovely brown hair, and to rumble and tumble with her one final time in her father's lovely wheat field. This is what he explained to his closest confidants and this is what spurred the four of them into action.

So the mighty band of brothers embarked on the treacherous trail of adventure and love. Sir Gora leading, light-footed and lighthearted, bouncing toward his destiny. Sir Kala following behind, the bulwark against his brother's exuberance. Kala held enough sense for both. Sir Shinda was third, scheming and slippery, sleuthlike and serpentine, savvy and suave. And Sir Kaka at the rear, reliable and full of strength.

---

26 Oh Gora, I am engaged to marry!
27 Come on man, there will be others.

He held his tongue but kept his eyes peeled. He lurked and slinked from wall to wall, and from brush to brush, in between Sir Kala and Sir Shinda, keeping a watch in Bagradi in support of his beautiful, sneaky friend Sir Gora.

The young maiden Grahini's mother had gone to hum hymns at the Gurdwara and her father had gone to Patti to engage in commerce but—keep your wits about you, young lotharios, danger still lurks here!—the three sons of Gurvaid Sahib kept a keen eye on his property, and Grahini was his most prized possession. Bunty, Shunty, and Funty were amateur wrestlers, a three-headed dragon bred on a diet of lassi, desi ghee, and the passive aggressive put-downs of their father. They roamed the dirt streets cocking their heads, grunting and spitting, slapping their thighs and beating their chests, and seeking, in general, a purpose to exert their might. And all the while, Grahini and Gora rumbled and tumbled in the field next to the village.

Had the young maiden been possessed of a softer spirit, the young knights might have slipped away without incident, but alas her passion was too great, too roaring, and she roared like Othello as she tupped her white ewe. So intense were her roars, in fact, that she betrayed the location of her and her lover, and the next thing the lookouts saw was Gora, clothes in hand, sprinting wildly out of the field in his God-given state. The three-headed dragon, who despite its lumbering size was lithe and sneaky, had managed to circle the lookouts to catch the young duo mid-tumble. Mere steps behind Sir Gora, the three heads, each with bared teeth, emerged from the flowing stalks of wheat.

"Oye panchode, ithe ah! Mein tenu kushti dek-hondein!"[28] one of them screamed, channelling his father's expertise at crafting insults. But Gora did not dare stop to address the challenge. He bolted forward and only stopped once in the company of his companions. When the brothers gathered behind him, Gora picked a rock and threw it

---

28 Hey sister-fucker, come here, I'll show you how to wrestle!

at the angry trio, but with so much flapping going on, he pitifully missed his mark. Shinda, on the other hand, had spent many hours throwing rocks aimlessly and as a result had developed the ability to throw rocks with top-notch aim. He cast one across the sky with all his force and it struck Shunty in that holy spot where the bindi sits on the forehead of brides. His eyes crossed and he hit the floor, incapacitated for the moment. But soon he found his feet with an assist from his burly brothers, and together they approached the friends, slapping their thighs and hollering churlish provocations. Gora was the first to react, clenching his fists, extending his arms, and spinning round and round like a whirlybird. The brothers were hesitant to close in on him, but not for the reason he presumed. Too much of him was flapping about still and none were eager to be entangled in all that.

Funty moved around and took aim at the culprit's brother, Kala, heaving him from his feet and slamming him to the ground. Meanwhile, Kaka was advanced upon by Bunty, the largest of the three, and received three solid claps to his head, which sent him crashing to the ground. Shinda retreated a distance and established a temporary artillery station, lobbing rocks on the enemy as quickly as he could manage, though now with less impressive aim as a few of the rocks struck Gora, breaking him from his twirling battle manoeuvre. Gora changed strategies and leaped onto Funty from behind, subduing him (literally) with a rear-naked choke. Shunty attempted to pull his shimmering white body away, but now Kala had found his feet again, and it was Shunty's turn to be heaved from the ground.

Meanwhile, Bunty approached Kaka, who was still on his back. But Kaka was a tenacious bastard even in that position, flailing and kicking his feet as the brute advanced. Then he found his mark and the flat of his foot slammed against the two soft cushions between Bunty's legs. With a mighty groan he collapsed, nothing flapping as his capacity to rumble and tumble became severely diminished. At this point, Gora had successfully choked Funty into half consciousness, and Kala had beat Shunty enough times that he was unlikely to get up from the ground. The heroes rose and revelled in the ecstasy of their victory in unarmed combat. The day was won and the knights of Ahmedpura hauled their asses down the dirt road to return to their homes as champions.

It was a happy day by all accounts. One that Kaka might have looked back on when he was old and tired, fondly thinking, "Wasn't that a swell time!" However, the Punjabi day drags long and this one was not yet finished. The man I am named after was something of a naturalist and he observed the world with an empirical eye. In so doing, he stumbled upon a fundamental axiom of the universe, which wouldn't be formally named until a century after his death—Newton's third law. For every action, there is an equal and opposite reaction. But the man I am named after never applied this law to the physical universe. Rather, he applied it to the cognitive universe: "In this world, when you ask for happiness, pain steps forward." An ominous dictum, which unfortunately holds true in more cases than not.

Grahini certainly learned the truth of this law, because she saw that in her universe a daughter's honour is a more valuable thing than the daughter herself. She paid the price for the cardinal sin of craving happiness, and perhaps justly so, because it is such a crude and ephemeral thing to crave. And perhaps Kaka did not ask for happiness per se, but in his naivety, he allowed himself to feel it. As he walked back with his friends, step-in-step, arms slung over each other's shoulders, he did not resist when his lips stretched to the sides of his face, he allowed his cheeks to redden and burn as they bloated with laughter, and he welcomed too easily that warmth that waved over his heart. He was oblivious to the fact that the universe had taken note of all this, but it had, and it demanded balance, and to that end we will now witness the pain that stepped forward.

Kaka approached his home at dusk. The setting sun cast a deep red glow across the village. All the villagers had crowded outside his home. No, not his home, the field that abutted his home—his grandfather's field. He pushed through the crowd and saw his mother. She stood with her back to the crowd, arms crossed. She looked down at him. She didn't care that he was bleeding and bruised. The tree in the field with the large heavy branches, which he climbed when he was younger...

The wind moved across the field, gently bending the tops of wheat shafts.

The wind came from the west, where his grandfather had looked nostalgically.

His mother said, "Rassi nu bacha ke rakhi, kum aju gi."[29]

The wind moved the wheat and grazed against the soles of his grandfather's feet.

---

29 Save the rope. It will be useful.

2000-2005

Biji was the Viper. Her posture was rigid, her lips pursed, and her sentences terse. She moved from room to room surveying inconsistencies and rectifying them with verbal lashings. Her interactions with the world were imbued with boundless dissatisfaction, as if reality itself had failed to live up to the standards which she had set. Only her will was of such force and her morality so self-assured, that we who lived in her presence silently questioned whether reality was to be trusted over the authority of Biji's word.

She craved warmth, not in any metaphorical sense, but like a viper weaned on eternal sun, her blood required external heat to remain fluid. When the snow fell, she refused to interact with it. The First Man and I trekked into the subthermal weather to fill plastic recycling bins with chopped timber each night. Der Vater cut trees down each morning to ensure there was always more chopped timber to burn. Even while next to the fire, wrapped in blankets, she grimaced.

She needed prey. Something to attack. Der Vater spent all waking hours working, moving his feet, so she could not reach him. So the First Man bore the brunt of her poison. He didn't eat enough, "Pathala jiya!"[30]; his legs were bowed,

---

30 Too skinny!

"Sidha tur!"[31]; his lips protruded too much, "Bulard jiya!"[32] I evaded, I hid, I pushed the First Man forward whenever she approached. Children are foolish and too full of fear, but as we grow, and as we learn, we notice the tenderness behind the scorn.

"Corrupted Sanskrit," akin to "vulgar Latin," Punjabi is a limited language, specific in what it affords the speaker. Born of the pragmatism of the working class, commissioning orders is its smoothest operative function. Reflective thinking and communicating emotions are more difficult. I will still try to translate as best I can.

"Pathala jiya!" *Eat more my child. I have seen too many young boys with bloated bellies and my heart still aches that there was nothing I could do for them.*

"Sidha tur!" *Walk without slouching and with your head held high. This world will try and take everything it can from you, but you mustn't let it take your pride.*

"Bulard jiya!" *Don't show too much of yourself to other people. Don't wear your heart on your sleeve. Only you should know the contents of your own mind.*

What a grand thing life would be if such lessons could be absorbed through words alone. But wisdom of this magnitude can only be earned through active erring and then retrospective analysis of one's own mistakes. It was how Biji had come to acquire the knowledge herself, and her lessons were undoubtedly more hard-earned than mine, but the stories of those lessons cannot be told because the mind that learned them no longer exists.

Her consciousness degraded from the pressure of trying to straighten out the inconsistencies in life. When I finally came to understand the depth of Biji's love, I saw her wander from room to room aimlessly instead of with intention. I saw her yelling admonishments at figures on the TV as if they could hear her. I saw how she mumbled to herself, trying to conjure

---

31 Walk straight!
32 Fat lips!

recipes in her mind that were once intuitive. I saw how she forgot our names. I saw how she forgot her own.

She no longer called out to the First Man but glared at him from afar as one does to a stranger one is wary of. When I approached her with a plate of food, she slapped it from my hand and backed away. She no longer desired even the fire. Her lost memories controlled her cold-blooded body and made her step out into the frozen snow with no shoes. She trembled and trembled, but even when we found her and pulled her back toward the fire inside, she wanted nothing of it. No one knows what to do with a viper that rejects the sun.

Something changed in Der Vater's demeanour. He was not as quick to rise in the mornings and not as late to return in the evenings. The fury of determination in his eyes had dulled and was replaced with the softer fury of regret. As Biji beat on his chest and screamed "Tu kaun ah?"[33] he endured it and embraced her as gently as he could manage, hoping that it would do something to remind her of who she was. But there was no way to bring her back because in the final count, reality always asserts itself as a greater force than our desires. In the final count, we are left as idle witnesses to the slow erosion of a human being.

Punjabi is a limited language, specific in what it affords the speaker. Though if it weren't, if by chance it provided Der Vater the tools to express his sorrow, perhaps he would tell us that the reason his feet moved so endlessly was to show something to the first person who ever held him closely. And now they had slowed because that person could no longer see him.

---

33 Who are you?

1970

On the day of Kaka's birth, a baba rode his bicycle into Ahmedpura to discuss old grievances with an old man. It was a discussion of great relevance as the grievances of the old man were indicative of a larger cultural wound, one the baba had a stake in healing. Not yet an elder, yet not still a young man, with slightly wrinkled skin and slightly greying hair, this baba had a graceful stride, an easy posture, and an austere expression. But it seemed to be a pretense, almost as if he was imitating the sculpture he believed would one day be erected in his honour. Even still, it was a compelling aura, one that would be put to use on this day to officiate the funeral ceremony of an old man who could no longer bear the weight of his old grievances.

Kaka had spent the day hauling timber from the wood merchants in Patti. Gora, Kala, and Shinda had sacrificed their time to assist. They stacked the wood in a grid, six-feet-long and two-feet-wide, and they stacked it up until it reached their chests. As he worked, Kaka examined the faces of those who had congregated to pay their respects. Many were familiar, hailing from one of the eighty-seven houses in Ahmedpura. They idled around in groups, all clad in ceremonial white, politely acknowledging Maher's few virtues before quietly conjecturing who would assume control of his land now that he was gone.

Noticeably absent from the day's affairs was Maher's son, Kaka's father, who served as another topic of gossip for the whispering masses. Why, after all, would a son not be present at the funeral of his father? In Kaka's imagination, the answer looked much like a man who was too burdened by his work, by the responsibilities of providing, at the least, the assurance of food on the table for a family he ached to see. In Kaka's imagination, his father worked tirelessly, without ever lying down to rest his head, so that one day Kaka might be afforded the privilege of leisure himself. So none of the gossip bothered Kaka, not even that of a group of mysterious and grim-looking sardars who had huddled around the baba (who was also something of a mystery to Kaka). Their whispers were quite a bit louder than the rest, and they seemed concerned directly with the taboo circumstances of Maher's demise.

With the assistance of some of Maher's close relations, Kaka moved the body, wrapped to the neck in white cloth, to the funeral bed he spent the morning building. Then the baba took his place before the pyre and turned to the scattered crowd. He cleared his throat to gather their attention and began the Ardaas[34]: "Waheguru, Waheguru, Waheguru." He roped the words together, so it sounded like a single guttural utterance instead of three distinct chants. It was a solemn affair so there was little cause for theatrics, but even still, he shifted the tone of his voice, adjusted the timber, and paused meaningfully. He watched the crowd and the crowd watched him, and he reacted as the leaves of a tree react to rays of sunlight, making subtle rearrangements to ensure the focus of their attention remained on him as much as possible.

As it happened, the baba had spent many hours on his bicycle throughout the years, riding it out of Amritsar to various surrounding communities. He had lived his entire life in Amritsar, so Cyril's line stole nothing from him. But he was a studious man and had taken an academic interest

---

34 Funeral Prayers

in the affair. When he rode his cycle around, he heard the voices of the villagers and learned that just as the rivers Beas, Chenab, Jhelum, Ravi, and Sutlej cut deeply into the earth of Punjab, there were grievances that cut deeply into the hearts of his countrymen. The baba was also an ambitious man and though he never lost anything to Cyril's line, he quickly realized there was much to be gained from it.

There are many stories in the history of the Khalsa[35], and like all beliefs, they can be used to unify or divide. The baba knew these stories by heart and they afforded him a certain kind of power and influence that had an intoxicating effect on him. There were some new faces among the circle that day, which meant more minds to turn to his cause. The baba was wise, so he knew that the distinction between unification and division was a false one, for the surest way to unite a group of people was to divide them from some other group. To unify is to unify *against*. The stories he chose to focus on reflected this ethos. They were about conflict, strife, and most importantly, retaliation.

When he was alive, Maher had considered his grandson as little more than a pack mule, so he never spoke with Kaka about anything other than wheat. That never bothered Kaka, because to him, there was nothing terribly enchanting about the old man. His grandfather was a squanderer of fortune, obsessive about the past, and always pathetically emulating the dandyism of British nobility. But as the baba spoke, and as the mysterious crowd focused intently on his words, Kaka found it difficult to maintain his apathy. He saw Maher's life being transcribed into a tale of piety, devotion, and even sacrifice—attributes more foreign to Maher's psyche than a lamb in a field of wolves.

The fire was lit and the flames began to rise. The skin around Maher's neck—blue and green and purple—began to blacken. No matter what tale the baba spun, it appeared one thing about Maher had remained the same even in death: his scowl.

---

35   The community which considers Sikhism it's faith.

1995-2003

The Viper sits crossed-legged on a folded comforter on the floor. The cassette player hums as it churns the audio tape, giving life to a muffled voice droning on and on about things I don't understand, in a language that's only half mine. Her eyes are closed and yet her finger still scrolls across the open page of a book in her lap. Before I could know the scorn of her bite, I reach out my hand to touch the page, to see what it can communicate to a person with closed eyes, but it is immediately slapped away. "Gundey hathaan de nal ki kardein?"[36] the Viper snaps.

The book is beautifully ornamented, blood-red with gold inlaid designs, spiralling fractals and inscriptions in an ancient language. But I have never touched it because my hands are never clean enough. When the Viper is done, she stops the cassette player, closes the book reverently, swaddles it in a small silk linen sheet and then again in a bath towel, and stores it high on a shelf in her bedroom closet, on the pillows that sit on the top shelf. It is too high for me to reach.

In 1606, Guru Arjan Dev was arrested by orders from the Mughal Emperor Jahangir. He refused the emperor's demands that he convert to Islam. As punishment, it was ordered that Guru Arjan Dev be boiled alive in a pot of scalding water. He

---

36 What do you think you're doing with your dirty hands?

endured his fate silently, serenely, and in so doing, he became the first martyr of Sikhism.

The Viper completes her ritual with the book every night before she goes to bed. But she also brings it with her when she takes me to the huge white building with a big gold dome on top that ends in a pointy tip. Here, there is no need for cassette players, because the voices droning on and on about things I don't understand, in a language that's only half mine, are coming from real people—men who sit on podiums at the far ends of great halls. They sit still for inhuman amounts of time, except for when they wave the white fan across the book in front of them. I understand none of this, but regardless, I like it here because there are so many big, empty halls with soft carpets that I can run around and wrestle with the First Man and the Toucan, and even with French Sinatra, if he is visiting. We practice our chokeslams and powerbombs and Crippler Crossfaces until we exhaust ourselves, and afterwards the Viper takes us to the room where the pots clang and we get to eat dal that tastes much better than the stuff that gets made at home.

In 1675, Guru Teg Bahadur resisted the imposition of taxes on the Kashmiri pandits by the Mughal Emperor Aurangzeb. He further resisted the emperor's impositions on the growing Sikh community in Punjab. This resistance resulted in an order for public execution. Guru Teg Bahadur was held in a cage to watch the horrific torture and execution of three of his devout companions, Bhai Dayala, Bhai Mati Das, and Bhai Sati Das, before he himself was also beheaded.

The sermon has been going on for what seems like forever and my legs are cramping up from being crossed. The man at the podium has not even moved to scratch his nose, and my legs feel as though they might fall off at any moment. For relief, I stretch them out in the direction of the canopied podium, where another beautiful red book, like the one belonging to the Viper (though much larger, and more intricately decorated) is being fanned by the man reading from it. From behind me, a different man wearing the same holy uniform yanks my shirt, jerking me backward. He hisses, "Luthan dus-rey passe kar!"[37] Coincidently, this is a rare occasion where I understand what is being said by the man at the podium. The sermon of the day relates the time that the man I am named after travelled to Mecca. Once, he stretched his legs toward the holy Kaaba, and when a Muslim cleric admonished him for it, he retorted that God is in every direction, so it matters not where you stretch your legs. I think the man who yanked my shirt must not have been paying attention.

Guru Gobind Singh realized he must organize and milita-rize to have any chance of resisting the tyranny of the Mughal Empire. His two eldest sons, Ajit Singh and Jujhar Singh, took up arms in support of this cause. In 1704, during the Second Battle of Chamkaur, they were among a diminished and severely outnumbered company of Sikh soldiers. Both sons were killed leading a charge against the aggressors, a last-ditch attempt to provide more time for the fleeing civil-ians of Anandpur.

I listen and I try and grasp the meaning of the droning again and again, asking the men in uniforms, but they just say, "Ja seva kar!"[38] and when I ask the Viper she snaps, "Chup karke sun!"[39] Over time, I begin to decipher some of what is said on my own, but instead of clarity it only rais-es more confusion. I learn that this beautiful red book and these beautiful white buildings exist because of the man I am named after, whose portrait sits at the top landing of the staircase in the homestead. I also learn that that man was an infamous questioner, never satisfied with shallow answers. But if both of those things are true, then why can't I ask questions in this building of all places? I begin to think that people who wear these uniforms, who treat this book with so much reverence, and who treat a curious child with so much

---

37 Aim your legs elsewhere! (Not in the direction of the Guru Granth Sahib).

38 Go and do service!

39 Shut up and listen!

contempt, are not very curious themselves. Then I grow and think that perhaps my questions exceed the capacity of that beautiful red book.

In 1704, Zorawar Singh and Fateh Singh, the two younger sons of Guru Gobind Singh were discovered by Mughal forces following the sacking of Anandpur. They were offered safety and protection on the condition that they convert to Islam. Following the tradition of their forefathers, they refused and were ordered to be sealed behind a brick wall and left to die. Zorawar was nine years old. Fateh was five.

Now, I am less fond of the place called the Gurdwara. I don't like wrestling anymore because I've learned that organized wrestling on the television is scripted and staged, and too much of this place reeks of the same betrayal. So now the large, empty rooms are useless, except as a metaphor for what is to be found in these buildings. Now when I come here, I no longer seek answers, but only an escape from the grim-faced men in uniforms who seem preternaturally disappointed in me even though they don't know my name. They have a collective tendency to harangue me about my supposed duties and then they task me with some chore or other that's meant to illustrate my devotion, "Ja seva kar!" they order, handing me a mop and bucket, pointing to the basement bathroom that smells overwhelmingly like piss. If this is where God is to be found, then I can do without God.

Banda Singh Bahadur, the unofficial eleventh Guru, was handpicked by Guru Gobind Singh to continue the war against the Mughal Emperor. He led several successful campaigns before he was eventually captured in 1716. As great a nuisance as he was, his execution was a unique spectacle. His eyes were gouged, his limbs were quartered, and his skin was flayed.

"I don't want to go to the Gurdwara," I say when the Viper comes around in her pristine white salwar kameez and matching chunni. It's as close an approximation to the holy uniform as she can manage. I try to explain to her in the language that's only half mine that I can't understand what they're droning on about. I can't even read the damned book because it's written in Sanskrit. But I can't get my message through to her because the Viper is unwilling to hear it. To her, all these behaviours and habits are beyond questioning. Instead, I seek protection with my Hobbling Guardian and the Viper, having no desire to interact with him, hisses and leaves us be. Bapu[40] has no interest in these metaphysical affairs. He keeps his half deaf ears tuned to the noise of political ramblings, anxiously awaiting the announcement of more lines being drawn across maps.

Ahmad Shah Durrani, of the Durrani Empire in Afghanistan, destroyed the Golden Temple and desecrated the holy waters with the entrails of animals. An act of retribution against Baba Deep Singh, who had interfered with Durrani's pillaging of goods and trafficking of humans back to his own lands. In 1757, Baba Deep Singh, seventy-five years old, assembled a militia force to drive the remaining Afghans out of Punjab. At the Battle of Amritsar, an enemy sword severed his head from his neck. In a final act of divine will, he held his head in his left hand while continuing to swing his mighty broadsword with his right.

Der Vater attends the Gurdwara less frequently than his mother, and only on occasions that are unavoidable (unions of man and wife, departures of the elderly, et cetera.) When he does attend, he sits quietly, but it's too obvious the force it takes for him to remain still. There is a tension in his muscles, his eyes dart around, and he takes forced breaths, slow and deep. This place is not for him, but that does not mean he is not a pious man. He is a proponent of the Kierkegaardian tradition, expressing his faith through personal rituals that are too oblique to understand. He begins with his holy sacrament, a bottle of Canadian Club, or Smirnoff, or on the rare occasion, Johnny Walker Black, and when it reaches the divine half-full quantity, he retreats to his room to bellow

---

40 Grandfather.

as loudly as he can, "Ik Onkar, Satnam, Karta Purakh, Nirhbau…"[41] On and on and on until he slips from consciousness. He is trying to ensure God hears him, I think. He is a pious man.

I, on the other hand, stubbornly evade the Gurdwara's grasp with more and more success until a different iteration of God takes its place. St. Someone Highschool, where these clothes I'm forced to wear itch terribly. Another holy uniform that plagues me, dress pants made more of polyester than cotton, and ill-fitting golf shirts. Every morning, I enter the building wrapped in a cocoon of shitty fabrics and loose threads (another fitting metaphor for the tapestry of religion), and there above me looms the crucifix with Jesus' tortured body. But I am thoroughly unimpressed. I am already too familiar with martyrdom and I understand the marketability of gruesome sagas of death. I understand that the way a person is persecuted will always be more compelling than what that person preached. Jesus Christ was martyred and, as his spirit ascended to Heaven and the Holy Father above, he brought with him all the sins of Christendom. There sits in my heart a convoluted mixture of apathy and envy as I look at the crucifix, for all the martyrs that Sikhism has to offer, none of them ever thought to take our sins with them.

The ornamented book still sits on the top pillow of the top shelf of the closet in the Viper's room, but I leave it be. That infamous questioner and I have much in common, I think, more than just our names, and I ponder and ponder the cosmic irony of how the teachings of a man who detested and ruthlessly criticized religious ceremony and superstition, have evolved to propagate their own set of religious ceremony and superstition. I think the knowledge in that book will always elude me. I think it will always be too high for me to reach. I think my hands will always remain too dirty to touch it.

---

41 Sikh prayer meaning, "There is one omnipotent God, God is truth, God is the creator and destroyer of all, God has no fear…"

1972

It's an idle day, a rarity not considered fondly by Kaka. He rested beneath the shade of the banyan tree whose branches were still under the weight of the heat and humidity. But Kaka's limbs were as restless as ever. The muscles in his legs flexed and released of their own accord. His hands were fisted, fingers pulsing into palms with steady repetition. The beat of his heart felt louder than it should, perhaps faster than it should as well.

In his eyeline was the new owner of his grandfather's brick home, atop the roof—Pinda, the moonshine merchant, who had wasted no time at all in obtaining the rights to Maher's estate. The hope that something positive might have resulted from the old man's demise was firmly put to rest the moment Kaka learned his grandfather had been in debt to Pinda, and that ultimately nothing was altered much in Ahmedpura. At most, Kaka had to now stare at a slightly different silhouette caressing Chekhov's gun, leering down at the world, and he now had to haul and sell a product that was heavier and more desirable than wheat.

All the elements in Kaka's life seemed to have conspicuously conspired to aggravate his anxiety. In the schoolhouse, when his mind wandered from the rote recitations the class was forced to repeat endlessly, "Oorha, aarha, eerhi, ik, tho, theen,"[42] and his heel began to bounce off the floor without him being conscious of it, or his eyes wandered out the window to briefly admire the freedom of the robin flying by, teacher sahib's rosewood metre stick always moved swiftly and violently to correct him. And on the streets of Patti, where he was required to sit still for hours on end, engaged in the tedious repetition of prices and the mind-numbing process of haggling with stubborn customers, always, he was forced to defy his nature. He felt cursed, trying in vain to reconcile the incompatible positions of his heart and his mind: keep moving, and don't move a muscle.

It was all correlated, something he was unable to pin down. A young, waddling boy who loved the feeling of his feet moving forward; an adolescent who roamed endlessly for the same reason. A mysterious internal force, like a language with no meaning, a drum forever beating in his mind, the arm of a clock that marches forward for the sake of nothing—no destination, no conclusion, only to tick for the purpose of continuing to tick. A pointless, unyielding drive, which can only be understood in the abstracted, unarticulated sense, as the desire for *more*. The only thing certain was that nothing would be solved by laying under a tree.

He decided to head toward Patti, which was by no means a bastion of civilization, but it was certainly larger than Ahmedpura, and there he would have a higher chance of encountering something of interest. At the edge of the city, he found a crew of men hollering orders and directives at one another, busy in the construction of a new commercial building. Another rarity, for it was not often that development of any kind found its way this far into rural Punjab. Kaka went closer to get a better view. Close to where he stood a bricklayer slapped a trowel of wet cement on the bricks in front of him. "Oye, tu udhar ki dekh reha ah, idhar ah ke hath de!"[43]

---

42 A, B, C, 1, 2, 3.
43 Hey you, what are you staring at? Come here and lend a hand!

the labourer called, noticing Kaka's interest.

Tentatively, Kaka collected a bundle of bricks from the skid, cradling them in his arms, and walked over to the brick-layer. "Challo, sheti sheti!"[44] he shouted, wiping the sweat from his brow. Kaka handed over a brick and watched as it was put into place. The brick's weight caused the excess cement to spill out from under it, and the bricklayer cleaned it away with his trowel and slapped it back into the bucket. "Inj kyon kardein?"[45] Kaka asked without thinking, and in-stinctively tensed his muscles. Curiosity, he had learned, is usually met with a slap or strike from a rosewood metre stick.

But the bricklayer did not raise his fists in violence. Instead, he explained patiently that the excess cement must be cleaned away immediately, or it would harden and ruin the look of the wall. If too much cement is laid before the bricks, it, too, will start to harden, and it will become more difficult to ensure there is an even layer of bricks along the wall. He handed the trowel to Kaka and urged him to give it a try, further explaining that it takes a delicate and precise touch to do the job well.

As Kaka moved to replicate the process of the bricklayer, he felt the pace of his heart slow down, the muscles in his arms and legs relax and orient themselves to the task at hand, and the drumbeat incessantly ringing in his mind beginning to quieten. The work was directed and intentional, the out-come tangible, and he became not just a witness, but the primary cause of an alteration to the material world, which would have been impossible without his effort. Needless to say, he found it all gratifying.

The bricklayer was also impressed. As the day progressed, Kaka also found himself seated next to the carpenter, learn-ing about kinds of joints and the importance of proper mea-surements. And later, as he hauled pails of water to the metal shop, he watched the welder solder two rods of iron together.

---

44 Come on, quickly!
45 Why do you do it like this?

On this worksite, all Kaka's questions were answered with detailed and thoughtful replies, and his boundless energy was lauded as an outstanding, positive trait. And as the sun began to set over the horizon, all the workers encouraged Kaka to return in the morning, sending him home not only with a newfound sense of confidence, but also a handful of rupees.

2004

Agitation is thick in the air. Mine from having sacrificed fourteen consecutive days—evenings and weekends included—labouring away in the chilly grey confines of the homestead's garage, measuring and drilling slabs of plywood to be constructed into kitchen cabinets; and Der Vater's from having to deal with the ineptitude of his careless son. I'll admit, I did drill holes on the wrong end of the plywood on three separate occasions, but only because my mind was on the more pressing concern of what jump combinations would allow me to clear the secret green-pipe area in Super Mario Bros. 3's Water Land. If only it were plumbing instead of cabinetmaking, I surely would have been a greater asset. "Tun panchode sunda ni?"[46] Der Vater cries whenever a blunder occurs. In response, I opt to give my shoulders a bit of an aristocratic shrug—Medici-esque—as if I were the patron and not the craftsman. It does nothing to improve his mood.

It's nearing the end of the winter season when it's still cold as the ninth circle of Dante's Inferno (the ring of great betrayers) and all the residual snow that's been pushed to the curb by plows repeatedly throughout the season, mutates back and forth from a grey sludge to a calcified grey sludge,

---

46 Can't you sister-fucking listen?

prolific in its indecisiveness. Nobody wants to be out here right now. Not I, not the First Man, and certainly not the Toucan, who was snatched away from his blissful Saturday morning cartoon-watching by an uncle who always has a keen eye for free labour and a father who implicitly concurred with the sentiment when he shouted, "Kush sikh ke ah dungara!"[47]

We pull into the driveway of a semi-detached house in a neighbourhood of aging Italians who are rapidly being replaced by young Asian immigrants. You can tell who's living where by the level of driveway cleanliness in the winter and lawn maintenance in the summer. Italians pride themselves on keeping such things pristine, for the wisdom of Machiavelli looms in their hearts, and he once said, "Men judge generally more by the eye than by the hand, for everyone can see and few can feel."

The First Man and the Toucan unload the last of the cabinets from the cab of the truck and place them next to the finished ones in the garage. I accompany Der Vater to the front door to talk to the recipient of my hard (if unenthusiastic) work, Ajitpal Singh, the patriarch of a recently arrived family of four. Coincidentally, he and his wife delivered newspapers, just as Der Vater and his wife once did. This process of job usurpation is quickly spreading across the land, and it leaves the parents of adolescent Italian boys quietly murmuring about the "damned Pakis" who are "stealing all the jobs." Machiavelli also said, "Hatred is gained as much by good work as by evil." No doubt Mario—who is generally disliked throughout the Mushroom Kingdom—would have agreed.

Ajitpal is glad for the quick construction of his kitchen cabinets, and he walks to his garage with us to inspect the final batch. He doesn't want us to install them because he has that plucky do-it-yourself attitude that one finds in people living just above the poverty line. But he also has that hesitancy to separate with cash that one also finds in people

---

47 Go learn something you lazy dog!

living just above the poverty line. He hems and haws while inspecting the carpentry, pointing here and there to perceived blemishes and inconsistencies. Now, I'm no master craftsman, and none of my religious prophets was a carpenter, but I assure you that these cabinets were not of a low quality. I endured many angry tirades and volleys of obscure Punjabi insults that attest to that fact. Still, Ajitpal seems unsatisfied. "Tooteh pajeh lagdeh ah, yaar,"[48] he says, nudging the one the Toucan and the First Man have just set down. Der Vater is grinding his teeth and clenching his fists, and my coworkers and I have the good sense to back off. Ajitpal continues to circle the cabinets, arms folded across his chest, eyebrows furrowed, and entirely obliviously he barks out a sentence that seals his fate. "Mein nahi tenu paisey de ne."[49]

Yes, the spirit of Machiavelli does loom large on this day, but Der Vater has no time to engage in such political superfluities. He does not heed the great Italian's advice: "Never attempt to win by force what can be achieved by deception." No, it is the philosophy of Mario the plumber that wins out: When a thing is to be done, you don't talk, you get to doing. Der Vater takes hold of the nearest cabinet from opposite corners and lifts it, an impressive feat as it's an unwieldy thing. He heaves it at the concrete wall of the garage. It shatters into its constitutive planks, some of which also crack in half, and they crumble to the floor. The First Man, the Toucan, and I are silent and still, as one should be when encountering the Malebranche of Dante's eighth circle (the ring of great fraudsters). Ajitpal the foolish, pale as a ghost, tries to reason with the demon. "Nah kar veer! Asi taan iko desh dein!"[50] But there is no escaping Der Vater's wrath now. More cabinets smash and shatter. A sledgehammer is retrieved from the cab of the truck, the shards are shattered, and even the concrete of the garage is cracked into. In the end, all evidence

---

48   They look busted up, man.
49   I'm not going to pay you.
50   Stop brother! We come from the same motherland!"

of a once completed set of cabinets has vanished and Ajitpal's spirit has been flattened, much like a Goomba that comes beneath Mario's mighty foot.

An extreme response perhaps but backed by the solid logic of primordial commerce: you don't get the product, if you don't pay the price; don't stiff a man you can't take in a fist fight; and, most important, a man's labour does not belong to any other, no matter what banner of brotherhood you claim it under.

The ride home through the grey sludge landscape is notably less agitated. A serene, meditative calm falls over Der Vater, who seems to have travelled to some mysterious place in his mind, away from us, while we, giddy with young boyish excitement at having witnessed such a carnal act of destruction, keep our smiles tight and our laughter stifled, but we glance at each other conspiratorially, as if to say, "That was fucking awesome."

1977

There was no ceremony on the day Kaka left Punjab. No long lines of well-wishers or naysayers. Nothing to portend good tidings or ill omens. It was, rather, a quiet, unpronounced, and even sombre sort of event. Not much time was spent packing, for there was not a lot to pack. In a small, underused schoolbag, Kaka had placed his two extra sets of clothes, along with his passport. The only theatrics were performed by his sister, who spent the day crying, though she may have been more dismayed at being left alone with their mother, than of her brother leaving.

Gora and Kala had also come to say their goodbyes, though Gora seemed too distracted to be much invested in Kaka's departure. In fact, he seemed to be perpetually distracted of late, and surprisingly, not by women. He appeared to have abandoned his fascination with the fairer sex, and replaced it with a fascination of the history of Punjab, taking frequent trips to Amritsar, and never passing up the opportunity to mutter something about "justice" or "fairness." Kala, on the other hand, was invested in Kaka's departure, warning him again and again to be cautious and diligent, and to only keep one eye on the horizon and the other on his feet, to make certain he was always moving toward it. "Ussi fir milan gay, Kaka ji,"[51] Kala said.

---

51   We'll meet again, Kaka, my friend.

Shinda was present, though not to say his goodbyes. On the contrary, he was the catalyst for this journey. On one of those long Indian evenings, under a red sky, when Kaka was feeling particularly disenchanted with his life—that proclivity of the young to feel uniquely persecuted by the universe—he had confessed to his friends, "Mein ithon jaana chahundein, yaar."[52] At that time, the comment was received with silence, acknowledged by all with another sip of daru, but days later and, unexpectedly, Shinda returned to Kaka sporting his characteristic wolfish grin. He said, "Mein Delhi vich kise nu jaandein jo sanu Iran lehja sakda. Othe kam haiga."[53] Of course, it didn't take long for Kaka to leap at the opportunity.

In Ahmedpura, Shinda was one of a few rare creatures afforded with the luxury of carelessness. He lived in a house made of brick. He had more money in his pocket than Kaka and less apprehension at its loss in his heart. He didn't pursue any course of action by means of necessity or even ambition, but simply out of curiosity. But just because the road behind them was different, it didn't mean the path ahead couldn't be the same.

Kaka's mother stood at the threshold of the mud hut with her arms crossed. She was statuesque, stoic, de-cathected, and unwilling to admit any emotion. "Ja paisey kumah,"[54] she had said, bluntly. As far as she was concerned, banal platitudes were worth as much as their weight, and whatever final advice she could have offered to him before he left should have already been firmly cemented in his head through his upbringing. It was her opinion that if he hadn't yet learned that the world was not a kind place, then her saying so would not shield him from any pain. The boy was either prepared, or he was not, and that was for the world to decide.

The train pulled into the station, and for the second time in his life, Kaka stepped foot in Delhi, only now his mind was

---

52 I want to leave from here, man.
53 I know a guy in Delhi. There's work in Iran. He can take us there.
54 Go make some money.

developed enough to take it all in. And what he witnessed was the Ship of Theseus, landlocked. The constituent parts had eroded, decomposed, died, were replaced, died again, and replaced again, but the soul of the place never faltered. It was maintained by the densely composed and evergreen scent of manure that sat heavy in the streets, by the screech of auto horns, curses of rickshaw operators and stall vendors, the pleading of limbless, hungry children, the sermons of clerics with different headdresses, the labyrinthine architecture—all coalescing with the heat to produce that mystifying haze that still lingered in Kaka's memory.

At the station, Kaka left Shinda to deal with his connection. There were two things he had resolved to do in the capital of the country, and he headed out to accomplish the first. He walked his way to an upscale shopping centre a few kilometres away and into a Sikh-owned jewellery shop. All told, Kaka had saved $600 USD through his life, and that in painfully small increments. Four hundred dollars of that would soon be used to pay for a plane ticket and travel visa to Iran. And Shinda had informed him that the customs office only allowed travellers to bring $13 dollars in cash with them across the borders. So, Kaka counted out what remained after subtracting those sums and slapped it on the counter saying, "Mein soney da kara leyna."[55]

Kaka had never worn a kara before; piety being in many ways a form of opulence. But now the band would serve a practical purpose, because the price of gold generally appreciates, so he could transport his money to Iran, not only free of charge, but in fashionable style, which produced a profit. And though he was not a superstitious man, it felt like a good omen, a token of prosperity. Nearly every cent he'd ever earned was spent in a single day, nay, a single afternoon. But it was a simple calculation in the end: $600 in hand and a life in Ahmedpura, or the risk of losing it all and gaining everything else worth having. Smiling, he slipped the kara on

---

55 "I need a gold kara." – A kara is a Sikh religious bracelet.

his wrist and headed out into the city to complete the more meaningful of his two resolutions.

The apartment complex was smaller than he remembered, but he was smaller then, too. It was one of the buildings he would waddle past with his mother when they would go to the market together. Definitely more than eighty-seven homes, more in the range of hundreds, and all condensed into the area of a single city block. There were children laughing and running through the courtyard, not much older than he was when Maher first lashed a bale of wheat across his bare back and told him to start walking. He remembered how the cord of rope cut into his flesh. In the courtyard, there were mothers cradled in their husband's embrace, smiling at the careless exploits of their children. Nobody had ever embraced his mother, and she had never smiled.

The apartment was unexceptional as well, barely the width of two men, barely the height of one. No kitchen to speak of but for an oil stove burner in the corner, and a communal bathroom on the ground floor of the building. Kaka stood at the threshold. There was no door. There was no need for one because there was nothing to steal. What he saw was an image more jarring than Maher's limp corpse, dangling from the banyan tree. His father, on a cotton rope munja, face turned towards the wall, peacefully asleep.

The sun had not yet set. Kaka watched his father sleep. For as long as he could remember, Kaka had slept in the dusty corner of a mud hut, never on a surface elevated from the floor. His father was asleep in the light, and Kaka had never closed his eyes while the light shone. That, he knew, was a luxury for people with brick homes.

He felt rage. He knew what he wanted—an answer to the question of how a father could live without his son. All his life he had assumed that answer would take some form that he recognized, something familiar to his own character. Here was a man who he imagined worked tirelessly, and now he watched as that man slept like all the drunks and idlers in Ahmedpura. He looked at a stranger.

He decided it was not worth the trouble to disturb the old sleeping man. Whatever the mysterious force that lived within him, it clearly did not live within his father. The sun was still up and there was work to be done. He turned around, more sure than ever that leaving India was what he wanted.

1997

My head didn't hurt, but through the powers of neuroticism and self-delusion, I convinced myself that it did. I wanted to avoid school because I did not like it there. Unmanageable swells of anxiety plagued me as I sat in that vice-grip like plastic desk-chair hybrid. And all those eyes that glided around the room, like they always had access to my deepest and darkest inner thoughts, I could not bear. Luckily, my pleading and aimless pawing of my forehead were convincing enough, so I was granted reprieve from the torture of the classroom, at least for the day. "Ghar reh fir, Bapu de naal,"[56] Der Vater instructed as he left in the morning. This was fine by me, for I had an affinity towards the father of my father. He was a kindred spirit, opting to remain silent in most situations, allowing the world to exist as it was instead of trying to force it to exist as he wished.

However, I might have been positively inclined toward Bapu more as a matter of exposure than disposition because through the homestead's diffusion of responsibility, my care fell primarily under his purview, just like the First Man's fell to the Viper. When I was hungry, it was Bapu ji who I would turn to. I would ask him to make me a "butter sandwich." There were not enough native English speakers in my house

---

56   Stay home with your grandfather then.

to correct me or to inform me that what I actually wanted was "buttered toast." It didn't matter to him though. He only heard the phonetic sounds of the words and they signified in his mind "Mere potey nu bhukh lagi ah,"[57] and he hobbled to toast some bread.

Bapu remained quiet when Der Vater issued his commands to me, but he had plans of which I unwittingly became a participant. When Der Vater had left, Bapu turned to me and said, "Coat pallah, puth,"[58] and then he hobbled to the door. We made quite a pair, me waddling behind him as he hobbled in front. In this way, we went to the bus stop on the main road to board the bus that would take us to the central terminal where the shopping mall was. Bapu had arranged to meet an acquaintance, one who coincidentally had skills of a mystical quality that could help with my headache.

Bapu ji hobbled everywhere he went. He hobbled because he was exhausted from sprinting from Lahore to Amritsar, watching the world burn after Cyril drew his line. But he pretended he hobbled just because his knees hurt. "Mere godey!"[59] he cried whenever he rose from a chair or a couch or a bed. He hobbled to the community centre to sit in silence with other old men who wore turbans, who might have also had to run as he did. He hobbled to the park to feed the birds in silence. He hobbled behind me as I walked to the bus stop for school, and to the video store to rent movies and video games, and to the park that was farther off, so every time the First Man and I went there it felt like the first time. He hobbled behind me as my silent guardian.

He knew many people through some mysterious mechanism I had never witnessed. When I walked into the Italian bakery next to my school with him, all the nonnas behind the counter laughed joyously when they saw him. "Buongiorno!" they would say, "your nonno is a lovely man!" and they forced

---

57 My grandson is hungry.
58 Put on your coat, my boy.
59 My knees!

a slice of pizza into my hands, free of charge. Any bus driver who pulled up at the stop near the homestead smiled broadly when they saw Bapu hobbling along, and they ushered him in without ever demanding the fare be paid.

But in terms of duration—that is, absolute time—these sorts of experiences were short-lived. His hobbling was not endearing to everyone, especially not to those who he spent most of his life around. Der Vater and the Viper detested it. They never lent a hand to help him up, and they rolled their eyes when he cried "Mere godey!" The lovely doting geriatrics in TV sitcoms and commercials did not resemble my reality in the least. My Guardian slept in the basement; two floors separated from his wife.

At the bus terminal, Bapu ji spotted his acquaintance, a man I'd never seen or heard of before. He claimed to be a mystic healer, but nothing about him appeared exceptional or even out of the ordinary. He was older than Bapu, but they both wore turbans tied in a similar style, both navy-blue, both with the slight Amritsar tilt. He had a long white beard like Bapu but his was loose and reached way past his chest, whereas Bapu's was tied into a knot and tucked beneath his chin. "Sat sri akal, Sardar ji,"[60] Bapu said politely, folding his hands together and bowing slightly. The man returned an austere nod. "Mein apne potey nu naal leh ke ayein. Eh da sir peed kardeh,"[61] Bapu explained, gesturing toward me. The old healer stepped closer and leaned to inspect my face.

Bapu's acquaintance placed his hands on the sides of my temples, blew softly against my forehead, and muttered a prayer under his breath. Then he stepped back and Bapu knelt and asked me, "Sirr ajey vi dukhdeh?"[62] Here, I found myself between a rock and a hard place, because I was not willing to admit that my complaints of a headache were not entirely genuine, and that I had abused the goodwill of my

---

60 Hello, sir.
61 I have brought my grandson along. He has a headache.
62 Does your head still hurt?

friend and ally, my Hobbling Guardian. But I also did not know how much the dignity of this shaman man meant to Bapu ji, and I did not want to spoil the relationship if it was important to him.

But Bapu ji was a kindred spirit, and though he did not say so explicitly, he sensed that I had not been entirely honest. He leaned so his ear was next to my mouth and pretended to hear something I never said. Then he turned to the shaman man and nodded to indicate that his incantations had successfully altered my brain chemistry. We continued on with the day without saying more. He hobbled and I waddled, and together we watched the shaman man blow on the aches and pains of various superstitious hopefuls. Some of them nodded reluctantly after he was done, tentatively suggesting an improvement, while others were more enthusiastic. But my Hobbling Guardian retained a look of skepticism through it all.

He was not superstitious and, unlike the Viper, he did not go to the Gurdwara. So, I wondered to myself, what was it that had taken us there on that day, shadowing a mystic healer whose power came from muttering to God? God, who didn't hear Der Vater when he screamed, but for some reason listened to this unexceptional man's mutterings. We did not speak about it when we arrived back at the homestead, but I could see a disappointment in my Guardian's eyes. He sat on the couch sighing as the weight of his body was released from his knees. He turned the radio on—static-infused ramblings of doomsayers and cynics—and his face grew more and more weary as he listened. He had seen more pain and death than I ever would, when he had to sprint across a country in flames. I think that is what the day was about—searching for something, anything, that could indicate that there was a way to heal the world.

Revolutionary Roads

1977

Nations are more well-defined than humans. This is because, spatially and temporally, they remain more resistant to change than humans. Or, at least, they aspire to a kind of permanence that eludes living creatures who move around unpredictably and often die without much warning. In this, nations partly resemble geometric shapes, defined necessarily and sufficiently by the lines drawn around an empty space. Pakistan, for example, did not exist until Cyril drew his line in the east, dividing Punjab in half, and 54 years before Cyril ever picked up his pen, Mortimer Durand began the task, drawing his in the west.

But it is not merely a border that defines a nation—that is a necessary condition, but it is not sufficient. Because within those lines is more than just empty space. Within those lines there are many of those strange, undefinable things called humans, with all the resentments and anxieties that plague them, and that must certainly factor into the definition of a nation. For example, just as Cyril's line left Maher scowling on the roof of his house, Mortimer's line had left the ruler of Afghanistan, Daoud Khan, scowling as he paced back and forth in his office. The native Pashtuns of Afghanistan (like the native Sikhs of India) did not look fondly on the arbitrary borderlines of Pakistan. Mortimer's line is just one of the things that Daoud had promised his people he would rectify in his reign, and in attempting to do so, he turned to the behemoth Russia for aid. But the Red Mother was too self-interested to have any concern for the well-being of brown-skinned desert-dwellers, so the relationship had soured. The people of Afghanistan began viewing Daoud's efforts as ineffective and they whispered behind his back about what the nation might look like without him, seeking as it were, to change the definition of their nation. As a result, Daoud paced back and forth, evaluating his life as movements on a chessboard, his vision clouded by paranoia.

Meanwhile, not far off, Kaka sat in a small hotel apartment in Kabul with Shinda and eight other men. They were an odd collective, a veritable hodgepodge of desperation, all prompted to leave their homes by the promise of gainful employment. Among them: Amarjot Singh from Ferozepur, a single brother among eight siblings, the burden of future dowries heavy on his conscience; Kamal Bhagvan, a Hindu and son of a Delhi real estate baron who did not believe in providing an easy life for his children (rather the opposite Kamal discovered when his father dragged him from their home by the scruff of his neck with the instruction to "go make something of yourself"); and a man shuffling in the corner of the room who meekly identified himself as "Grewal." Hardly a man, to be honest; his cheeks were puffed out like laddus and his eyes were as wide and innocent as a newborn doe.

The city itself was familiar and alienating all at once. There was nothing of Delhi's frenzy and nothing of the agrarian camaraderie found in Patti. The buildings resembled those of Ahmedpura most closely, loose assemblies of mud blocks that sprawled out endlessly, and on the horizon in every direction was the black silhouette of wide rocky hills and jagged mountains. An eerie feeling permeated the streets. Onlookers did not gawk openly, or innocently, but in cloaked glances of suspicion. There was distrust in the air, a stale resentment of the powers that be, and a stagnant, unspoken tension between those who desired a slow and thoughtful revolution and those who desired a fast and bloody one.

A similar feeling sat in the room with the ten men, for they were little more than strangers to one another, and trust was too valuable a currency to be squandered easily. Not to mention, none of these men had expected to be sitting in Afghanistan at all. That was an unwelcome piece of news quickly spat out by the organizer of this expedition, Jeet Singh, who by all appearances did not inspire much confidence at all. A profoundly circular man and profoundly sweaty. He moved about with a frantic quality that was also mirrored in his eyes, as if he had just lost something of great importance a moment ago. He had a voice to match, high-pitched, quick, and prone to repetition. "Shoti ji, shoti ji, koi gal ni, bilkul koi gal ni,"[63] he had said, after explaining that due to some bureaucratic red tape, he had been unable to attain travel visas directly to Iran. Instead—and he assured the party that nothing about this was out of the ordinary—they would have to spend just a single evening in Afghanistan, where entry from India was freely permitted and travel visas into Iran were more readily available.

Jeet Singh had left earlier in the day, apparently to visit the embassy to handle the business of travel visas. He promised that he would return by the next morning at the latest, leaving the strangers to eat dinner and to suppress their anxieties by speaking idly of uninteresting things, "Vekho, pishab beth ke kar de, jinanian vangu,"[64] Amarjot remarked, tearing a piece of naan bread from the communal stack and sticking it into his mouth. "Lund katt ke rakhe ah, es karke beth de ah,"[65] Kamal added, as though he had some clinical experience in the matter. Grewal remained silent just as he had for the entire voyage, and strangely Shinda had also decided to remain mostly quiet.

---

63 Very small, very small, nothing to worry about, nothing at all to worry about.
64 See how they piss squatting, like women.
65 They have their dicks cut, that's why they sit.

The Lubani, who always had some wisecrack or smart remark, sat with his mouth shut, looking a bit paler than usual. Kaka thought nothing more of it than premature homesickness, so he returned his focus to his dinner.

It took him some time to find a vendor who was selling food he could eat. Metal skewers with camel meat and dripping beef were plentiful, but the former was too expensive and too exotic for anyone's palate, and as for the latter, sacred cows remained sacred, even in strange lands. More difficult to find was the man selling dal, and what Kaka did find could hardly be called that. It was mostly water with a few lentils stewed in, but for lack of any other options, it had to do. He reached forward to tear another naan in half, and the kara he had bought the day before slid out from under his sleeve and dangled against his wrist. Before he pulled his hand back a few pairs of narrowed eyes got a glimpse of it. Kaka cursed himself silently and pulled the thing back up, cranking it sideways so it stayed lodged firmly against the flesh of his forearm. Desperate measures are fine and well for desperate straits, but caution and reservation serve better in the company of desperate men.

There were still a few naans in the stack after everyone had eaten their share. "Passe sut la," said Amarjot, yawning and reclining into a comfortable slouch. "Sverey nikal jaa-na."[66] The man closest to them tossed the leftover naans to the corner of the room and stretched his feet out as well. "Luxurious," as Jeet Singh had put it, was a generous word for the accommodations. There was such little space that all ten men would have to sleep head to foot, side by side. The heat in the room was intense. They inhaled dust as they breathed, leaving their mouths dry and hoarse, and their minds were restless, focused as they were on the uncertainty which lay before them. Naturally, there was not much sleep on this first night away from home.

However, with the dawn light came a disconcerting development, something to justify all their private, suspicious

---

66 Just toss them to the side… We'll be out of here tomorrow morning.

musings: Jeet Singh had not arrived. The time devoted to yawning and rubbing eyes was cut short as this realization settled on the group. Quickly, they adopted a collective attitude—equal parts alert and brooding—a grinding silence, like the axe head being placed against the sharpening stone. Kaka watched Shinda tap his heel rapidly against the concrete floor. "Shinda, tera banda kithe giya?"[67] he whispered, and Shinda replied, "Pata ni."[68] He seemed nervous, his eyes slowly scanning the ground, refusing to make contact.

The day pressed on and their agitation continued to stew and thicken in the heat of the desert. Kaka remained as calm as he could, but his stomach growled, which did little to elicit positive emotions. The naan from the previous day did not fare well in the heat. A group of flies skittered around them and debris wafted in from the window, coating them with a thick layer of dust. Kaka picked up a naan, brushed it off as best he could, and chewed it solemnly. Some of the others who noticed, grimaced and recoiled, believing that they were witnessing an act of premature desperation, but they had never had the lessons of pragmatism beaten into them as Kaka had.

"Ah ju ga. Ah ju ga,"[69] Amarjot muttered to himself off to the side. The self-assuring mantra succeeded only in summoning an angry hotel owner who screamed in Pashto while waving his hand toward the exit staircase. No one had the linguistic capacity to argue back, and none were eager to chip away at more of their precious thirteen dollars, so they gathered their belongings and headed down the stairs. "Maa chode motte ne bund mar li!"[70] Kamal growled and received a few approving nods from the group. They debated the options before them in a rather unstructured manner, the loudest voices taking precedence over the rest.

---

67 Shinda where did your man go?
68 I don't know.
69 He'll come soon. He'll come soon.
70 That mother fucking fatass screwed us up the ass!

"Vapas ja ke, motte da sirr paad dein ah!"[71]

"Nahi yaar, ithe rehne ah, aju ga."[72]

"Mein nahi ithe raina, panchode sah vi ni onda."[73]

Needless to say, sentiments did not align, and the group fractured. Three men, Kamal Bhagvan among them, formed an impromptu lynch mob, cutting their journeys short in favour of returning to Delhi to dole out some vigilante justice. The rest retained their faith, at least for the moment. They split up to find lodging suitable to their respective comfort needs, with an agreement to reconvene at the hotel in the morning to wait again for Jeet Singh. That night, Kaka and Shinda found refuge under an alder tree in a public park. Alone now, Kaka sincerely asked his friend whether this Jeet Singh was a reliable person. Shinda shrugged. "Hai taan banda sahi lagda, par pakka nahi keh sak da."[74] He still made no eye contact.

The morning of the second day arrived and as Shinda and Kaka returned to the hotel, they found that the Afghani night had stolen away the ambitions of two more men. Now only five remained. Again, they waited for Jeet Singh. And again, he did not show. The day passed in silence, each man quietly contemplating what course of action to pursue. Kaka performed some mental accounting to see how much longer he could afford to wait and do nothing. Thirteen dollars, and from that he had paid for two meals a day since he had arrived, four in total so far. Even though $1 was equivalent to roughly nine rupees and a single rupee was equivalent to roughly four afghanis, Kaka's coffers were slowly eroding.

Shinda slinked over to Kaka and, for the first time, whispered retreat into his ear. "Vapas chaliye, Punjab nu, kam lub ju."[75] But Kaka was not to be deterred. This was a small obstacle; the journey could not end so quickly. He would

---

71 Let's go back and split the fatass's skull!

72 No man, let's stay here for the night, he'll show up.

73 I'm not staying here. You can't even fucking breathe in there.

74 He seems like a good guy, but I can't say for certain.

75 Let's go back. We can find work in Punjab.

not allow it. He would not go back to Ahmedpura, where he slept on the floor with no bed, having lost what small fortune he had to begin with. The drum in his head beat ferociously if he even considered turning back. It simply was not an option. "Mein marju ga, par mein vapas nahi jaana,"[76] he affirmed, more to himself than to Shinda.

As the second day in Afghanistan came to a close, the sun moved beyond the western mountain range and the red glow in the sky dissolved to black. Amarjot Singh returned to his seven sisters, rehearsing a speech to explain why there would be no nuptials in the foreseeable future. Two others took flight with him. Now only three remained: Kaka, Shinda, and Grewal. This time, they did not split up, spending the night together under the alder tree. Grewal blinked his innocent eyes, communicating nothing, while Shinda squirmed in discomfort.

On the morning of the third day, in defiance of folk fables across the globe, nothing different happened. Jeet Singh still did not materialize. Shinda, however, seemed to have urgently lost his faith and no longer pleaded but demanded that Kaka return with him. There was nothing more to be gained by standing idly outside a hotel, so Kaka humoured him and agreed to go to the bus station nearby. Once Shinda had purchased his ticket to the airport, Kaka took him by the shoulder and explained that he was not going back.

"Ki yaar, vapas chal mere naal. Ithe ki labna?"[77] Shinda urged.

"Patha ni, par mein piche ni ja sak da. Othe mere vaste kush nahi haiga,"[78] Kaka replied. "Je tun Jeet Singh nu lub leya, mera paisey kol rahk lein. Mein tere te bharosa kardein."[79]

Nearly $10. Ninety rupees. Three hundred and sixty afghanis. Likely not enough to overcome the bureaucracy of a government embassy but probably enough to bribe a

---

76 I will die before I go back.
77 Come on man, come back with. What are you going to find here?
78 I don't know, but I can't go back. There's nothing there for me.
79 If you find Jeet Singh, hold on to my money. I trust you.

disgruntled border guard. Enough of a probability, Kaka figured, to warrant travelling to the border and giving it a shot. And if that failed, he would be in no worse position than he was now. He still had the gold band on his wrist, which if sold, might afford more opportunities to continue, and if that proved untrue, then he might begin to consider turning back. But not until every stone he was capable of lifting was overturned. Not until every avenue had been exhausted. Shinda realized there was no convincing Kaka out of his plan. He had known him long enough to know the look in his eyes meant there was nothing to be gained from arguing. He embraced his friend and boarded the bus.

Now only two remained. Silent Grewal looked at Kaka with his puffy laddu cheeks and innocent, childlike eyes. He did not appear to be the most formidable ally, but he stuck around longer than anyone else, and that showed some gumption. At the least, they spoke the same language, and that was not without its uses. "Aja, chal mera nal. Mein border val chaliyein,"[80] Kaka said, waving for the boy to follow, and without a word, he did. Together, they boarded the bus headed for the border town of Islam Qala. Kaka eased into his seat and watched the country float by through the window. It had been three days since Kaka had arrived, and Daoud Khan still paced anxiously in his office.

The highway across Afghanistan was desolate. At times, it weaved through narrow passes between towering rock cliffs and hills pocked with slate. The terrain seemed to defy erosion, and this landscape had left its mark in the hearts of the people who lived in it. They were resistant to Daoud Khan's edifices, his increasingly authoritarian progressive policies. That sounds like an oxymoron, I realize, but it describes an accurate state of affairs. Daoud wished to see his country modernized, to provide more opportunities for women, to see them liberalized in the fashion of developed Western nations, but he pursued that end with an iron fist. Through the

---

80 Come on. I'm going to the border.

window of the bus, Kaka saw women in black burqas carrying water back to their villages, content in their traditions. Daoud was committing an error, one made by all who wielded the power to materialize their dreams. He was myopic, squeezing tightly what was already in his grasp, while ignoring what slipped through his fingers because of it; straining his eyes to work out the details of grand vistas in the distance, while the things right before his nose were ignored.

For two days the vehicle moved, two drivers switching out at four-hour intervals, stopping only intermittently to meet the needs of stomachs and bladders, until finally the bus pulled to a stop in Islam Qala. Hardly more developed than Ahmedpura, the town served mainly as a gateway for the border crossing into Tayabad, Iran. To that end, there was a hotel and a military encampment in addition to the loose collection of homes. Kaka and Grewal dismounted the bus, along with the few other travellers that stayed for the duration of the journey. When the passengers dispersed, Kaka tugged at Grewal's sleeve, urging him to follow.

The town was quiet, and there were few people in the streets. Kaka walked toward the border, Grewal lagging two paces behind. Kaka did not know what he'd say to the soldiers who patrolled the crossing, but he marched on regardless. Something would come to him. He would be able to explain, human to human. The necessity and urgency would be communicated without words. Gesticulation would do the trick. Moving on past the edge of the town, past the last set of watching eyes, something in Kaka's mind perked up. He felt a forgotten sensation, a budding optimism that something good lay ahead. The same feeling as when he took his first steps in Delhi, the drum quieting, and clarity emerging. He forgot his anger toward Jeet Singh as his anticipation rushed ahead of him.

Daoud Khan would not become aware of his error in time to amend it. Too focused on his vision, he ignored the people who were plotting against him; he overlooked their desires and motivations. He saw enemies where there were none and did not properly address the ones right in front of him—those who once aided him in his conquests but now conspired with the Red Mother to remove his influence from Afghanistan indefinitely. One year hence, these people would storm Daoud Khan's home and assassinate him along with most of his family, effectively altering the definition of the nation of Afghanistan. These events would become known to the rest of the world as the Saur Revolution.

"Chal, sheti!"[81] Kaka said to Grewal, not looking back. The border gate was in view now and he quickened his pace, nearly jogging. The light in the guard house was still on. They were still there—

The world snapped out of his vision and a high squeal shot through both of his ears. His knees had hit the ground. No, his back. He was on his back. The world blurred for a fraction of a second. Grewal stood above him, a rock dripping blood held in his right hand.

Then everything went black.

---

81 Come on, hurry!

1993

The mountain towered over little Nanak, four, perhaps five times his size. But he had resolved to conquer it, and not only to conquer it but also to plant a flag of conquest—in the form of his favourite toy—on top. There was no logic to the desire. The toy did not even lend itself to the act of planting. It was a plastic tricycle produced by the Hasbro toy company, so it may be more accurate to say he wished to park it on top of the mountain, like the victorious Greek army parked their wooden horse in a conquered Troy.

Many a time had he attempted the task and many a time had he failed. In some instances, his pudgy legs slipped against the grass, wet with dew. In others, his pudgy hands, slippery with sweat, lost grip on the plastic seat of the tricycle. But failed attempts had done nothing but strengthen Nanak's legs and hands and fortified his determination to succeed. That day, the sun shone true and strong on his face and the wind pressed reassuringly on his back. That day, failure was not an option.

He placed his hands on the back of the tricycle seat and leaned his weight into it. His fingers gripped the plastic with as much force as they could muster. His feet pushed into the ground, leaving the indented footprints of a boy who would soon become a legend. The initial change in slope required the most effort to overcome. He knew this from experience. So, he sprinted toward it with tremendous velocity and watched in ease as the world changed its orientation.

Now the onerous part. The momentum of the sprint was gone and Nanak's will was put to the test. He tightened his brows and grit his soft baby teeth. The weight of gravity he felt against his tiny chest was mighty, but from within his chest he felt a mightier force—the protean will to power, the godlike drive that pushes all life to fight against an unco-operative world for the right to exist. And the world would know Nanak existed once his tricycle sat atop the mountain of heroes. And he was close now, closer than he ever had been before, so close that the single front wheel of the tricycle cleared the crest of the mountain and then... it turned.

Not slightly, not in any way salvageable, but a complete ninety degrees, placing it perpendicular to his efforts. Nanak pushed, the wheel dug in, and he stumbled. From that close to the crest of the hill the fall was greater than it ever had been before. He tumbled and bounced all the way down; scratches and scrapes and bruises adorned his pudgy body. And then the tricycle followed his path, and as he looked to find his feet, it crashed into him with tremendous force, sending him sprawling back to the ground.

For a moment, Nanak was spared from the pain by the adrenaline, but then it descended on him all at once. It radi-ated through every tendon of his body, along with a deeper, more potent pain in his mind and heart—the pain of failure. He wailed and wailed, until finally, Der Vater (seated on the park bench nearby) acknowledged the boy's anguish. He put down his newspaper, raised a hand over his eyes to shield them from the sun, and watched Nanak squirm and cry. But rather than scoop him up and coddle him, rather than ex-tend a hand of comfort, or give a reassuring pat on the back, he stayed seated and simply shouted, "Chup kar ke uth ja!"[82]

---

82 Shut up and stand up!

1977

One hour.

Kaka's eyes opened and he struggled to determine what he was looking at, or rather, what direction. He faced the ground and was behind a rocky outcrop on the edge of the town. Dry blood caked the side of his face and the dirt beneath his head had absorbed what had shed, leaving it black and muddy. A wide, continuous line of perturbed earth indicated the path on which he was dragged. Every compartment of his backpack had been turned over, and the contents were scattered around him. What remained of his $13 was gone, as well as his kara, but more concerning than that, his passport was nowhere to be found. He found his feet, at least, and with a throbbing head and blurry vision, he dragged them back into town.

Eight hours.

Kaka's stomach growled, a familiar sound, a familiar sensation. There was no cause for concern just yet, but the wound needed to be cleaned and tended to. Not many people were out in the streets, which he was grateful for, because his pride was more wounded than anything and he had no desire to be viewed as weak or in a helpless state. He walked through the town looking for an unsupervised well to pull water from. He found one, used by locals to water mules. The wound stung as he poured water from his cupped hand onto it but he clenched his teeth and scrubbed the dried blood away. He loosely covered the wound with a clean turban sheet that had not been stolen from him. Then he drank. The water was gritty and tasted of iron, but his parched tongue was grateful for every grey drop.

Three days.

Kaka could not sit idly by but was forced to do so. Already, he had attempted to approach the border guards and explain his way past them, but they enforced their mandate with the blind obedience of trained soldiers. He had no means to make the journey back to Kabul, and if he did, what good would come of it? There was no one to go to for aid, no one to call who could send him any funds and, besides, he was cursed with a tyrannical pride that would see him die before prostrating himself before another. He resolved instead to find gainful employment, however humbling the work may be, and to that end he moved from door to door explaining as clearly as he could that he was willing and able to work, that he had skills that were useful, and a keen mind that was able to learn quickly. But Islam Qala has little to offer in the way of opportunity and those who called the place home had grown leery of foreign drifters, so he was turned away by the inhabitants of every house he approached. His stomach no longer growled but clawed, sending lancing pains across his abdomen. But he would not be held hostage by the whims of his body. The image of his father lying comfortably on a manja, while the sun still shone rested firmly in his mind, and it granted him the fortitude to keep moving.

One week.

Kaka had walked the road from Islam Qala to the nearby ancient city of Herat, a twenty-four-hour journey by foot, which took him three days to complete. For just as long, he had wandered aimlessly through the maze-like streets, unknowingly moving in circles, following the shadow cast by the Citadel of Alexander. His body had reduced superfluous functions, and an acuity of sensation emerged—sharper vision, more discreet hearing—and the division between the conscious and subconscious eroded as the whole mind focused on the achievement of a single outcome: food. But this narrow focus was not conducive to achieving its goal, because it operated without the aid of reason, and impulse absent logic left him stumbling after mirages in the desert.

Two weeks.

Driven by delirium, Kaka dipped his hand in a gutter, believing it to be a stream or some other natural source of clean water, and he raised his cupped hand into his mouth to drink. Not long after a shigella bacterium found its way into Kaka's stomach and began to replicate. He developed dysentery and every swallow of water he consumed rapidly left his body, taking with it layers of his stomach and intestinal tract. He found rest beneath an alder tree much like the one he and Shinda had slept under on the second night of their arrival. His muscles seized from dehydration, and he saw the feet of his grandfather, swaying before him as they did against the wind in Punjab.

One month.

Kaka moved through the streets, hardly upright. The world blinked in and out of existence. Thought had dissolved. Desire had eroded. The flesh moved by primordial animalism. There was nothing to move toward anymore. He blinked. He felt the fall but not the crash. There was nothing anymore.

1999

I sit on the recliner couch with my leg slouched over the arm-rest. The First Man is splayed out on the adjacent love seat. In my school bag is a ham sandwich in a plastic Ziploc bag, made fresh that morning by Der Vater. Normally, this task fell to my Hobbling Guardian, but he has fallen ill as of late. Der Vater wakes up before me, naturally, but now earlier than he is required to. He stands in the kitchen and lays two slices of ham on a toast-ed piece of bread, one slice of processed American cheese—the generic kind, not the brand stuff—then a squirt of ketchup, and finally topped with the remaining piece of toasted bread.

This is entirely wrong. I don't like the bread toasted, and the ham slices can't be laid one atop another like they were in the package. Each slice needs to be separated, folded in the centre, and then laid next to the other, overlapping ever so slightly. The cheese is acceptable, but it has to be squared up properly. If a cor-ner pokes out on any side, it's no good. Under no circumstances does ketchup belong anywhere near this sandwich. Mustard per-haps, but I like mine dry, so the bread doesn't become too soggy.

By the time lunch comes around, the sandwich has been in the bag for hours, and it's not refrigerated, so of course it's a mess. The meat is room temperature, and the ketchup leaves the toasted bread soggier than untoasted bread would have been, and the cheese is kind of melted and dripping out the side, and it's just utterly inedible.

The kids around me have Lunchables and Dunkaroos and Snack Packs and other foods advertised on daytime television. They have thermoses with chicken noodle soup and insulated lunch boxes that keep the cold things cold and the warm things warm. There's no way I'm taking this sandwich out and eating it in the face of all this luxury. I don't care if I go hungry; this is unacceptable.

So, at the end of the day, as I'm slouched over the recliner, the sandwich remains in the bag. I take it out and huck it at the First Man, as a gag.

It splats against his face and I laugh. Der Vater is sitting across the room, looking at the mail. He is dimly aware of our existence at the moment.

The First Man hauls the sandwich back at me and now we've started something.

We throw the bag from him to me.

It's all fun and games, you see!

This activity finally catches Der Vater's eye. He sees what we're throwing back and forth.

He warns us to stop.

He's always yelling, so I take no heed.

I hold it by the corner of the plastic and wave it tauntingly at my father before I send it back over to my brother.

He charges me like a bull charges red. His hand is raised and reeled back and clenched.

I freeze.

He glares at me, more ferociously than I've ever seen before. An avalanche of rage held back by a single flake of civility.

He turns away from me, toward the wall.

He drives his fist into the brick mantel of the fireplace.

A dull thud.

A few chips of brick hit the floor.

His hand is broken, two fractures down the knuckle of the middle finger.

He doesn't make a noise.

He leaves the room.

The Good Pakistani

A certain man was going across from India to Iran, and he fell among men of ill will who beat him and left him destitute. For thirty days the man went without food and without shelter, and on the thirtieth day he fell from exhaustion. By chance, a certain Imam was going across that way. When he saw the collapsed man, he passed by on the other side. In the same way an Afghani also, when he came to the place and saw the collapsed man, passed by on the other side. But a certain Pakistani, as he travelled, came to where the collapsed man was. When he saw him, he was moved by compassion. The Pakistani lifted the man up and bore his weight on his own back, and brought him to a hospital, and took care of him. In the evening, when he departed, he took out all the banknotes in his possession, gave them to the nurse, and said to her, "Take care of him. Whatever you spend beyond that, I will repay you when I return."

Saleem Ali walked through the dimly lit market. The hustle and bustle had fallen silent and he wondered to himself if he had done the right thing. The voice of his father rang in his head, endlessly repeating, "Saleem, tera dil bohta narm ah."[83] If he was being honest with himself, Saleem could not argue the opposite. He did have a soft heart. He was easily moved by another's anguish, and he would rather have it that way than to feel nothing at all. However, this situation he was in was unique from any he had been in before as well. The Quran warrants vengeance in proportion to a wrong committed, and Saleem was not above feeling justified anger when it was warranted, but the abstracted wisdom of the Quran was always more difficult to apply to the concrete aspects of one's own life. For instance, how does one determine who committed the wrong in a case like this? And how does one determine what is proportional in a case like this?

Saleem lingered outside the lodgings he had rented for the evening, basking in the cool breeze of the night, listening to the soothing voice coming from the window of his dear wife Amira. She tended to sing only when he was not around, convinced that she was no good at it. To Saleem, her singing was the sweetest sound on Earth, but he wasn't ever able to convince her otherwise. But even this he did not mind, because her stubbornness was one of the things that endeared her to him, and he preferred to hear her sing without her knowing about it. That way it always felt more like stumbling on some secret of nature that simply couldn't help but be beautiful, like a morning bird calling to its mate, or the whisper of a gentle stream.

He stayed there for a few moments, preparing himself for the conversation that would inevitably follow when he entered. He tried to derive answers for the questions she would undoubtedly ask, questions he undoubtedly did not have answers to. "Jaanu, tusi kithe si?"[84] Amira said as she noticed her husband enter the room. "Koi banda dig gaya si," he replied. "Mareya lag da si, mein hospital shud ke ayein."[85]

---

83 Saleem, your heart is too soft.
84 My love, where have you been?
85 There was a man who fell. He looked half dead. I took him to the hospital.

His wife gasped and asked for more clarification, but Saleem had none to offer. The man had been unconscious, so Saleem knew nothing more about him. Nothing but what was plainly obvious from the man's appearance.

"Mira, banda Sikh si,"[86] Saleem confided, and Amira, normally so full of chatty exuberance, became solemn and quiet. She came from the same place as him and she had witnessed the same things that he had, so of course she was burdened with the same painful memories. Not all were painful to be fair; many were joyful. The home he had grown up in was not a lavish place by any means, hardly more than a few dozen square metres. But from the roof, the gleaming peak of the Golden Temple was visible, and he would stand in awe at how it appeared to make the sky even brighter than it already was, like a second sun sprouted up from the Earth. It was on that roof that he had spent long evenings talking and debating with Amira, and in his mind that was where he truly began to love her. He recollected these things with fondness, but then the memories of losing it all followed close behind, and with them, a potent pain. The memory of her hand in his as they ran for their lives. It was many years ago but it was a day he would never forget.

He took a seat next to his dear wife and wrapped his arm around her. "Papa har valey kehn da si, mein bohta narm ah,"[87] he said. To which Amira nodded her agreement and replied, "Par eh koi kharabi nahi. Es karke mein tenu pyaar kardein."[88] He forced a weak smile, knowing as well as she did that there was a time when his father's assessment had been wrong. He had harboured a violent rage for so much of his life, for so long, that he seemed to have exhausted the impulse in himself. It's a young man's game to be resentful at the world, but now his hair was white and his belly plump, and he had no anger left in him.

---

86 Mira, the man was a Sikh.
87 Father always used to say I was too soft.
88 But this is not a flaw in you. This is why I love you.

Would it have made a difference, though, if he had been violent and angry when it might have counted, when all the world seemed to be violent and angry all at once? But what had come of all that resentment? It was the reason he had lost his home and the reason he had lost his father. It was resentment that birthed Pakistan and caused him to have to leave his home in Amritsar. It was resentment that caused the group of Sikh men to use their sacred kirpans to cut down Saleem's father in the streets during the Partition.

He sat in silence with Amira. She had lost loved ones as well during that time. Everyone had lost something. How then could Saleem have left the man, who was too young to have been born during Partition, to die on the street in some misconstrued act of justice? Many long years he had contemplated what had happened, and he could only arrive at one certainty: that the sins of one man may not be laid upon the head of another. He remembered the prayers resonating from the Golden Temple in his youth, the words of Guru Gobind Singh Ji: *The sword is never to be struck in hatred or anger or the spirit of revenge.* Saleem said to his wife, "Mira, mein saun chaliyein, sevareh hospital vaapas jaana, oh nu vekhan."[89] And his dear Amira pressed her lips to his forehead and replied, "Tusi sahi keeta, jaanu."[90]

The next morning, Saleem awoke and left for the hospital without breaking his fast. The nurse from the previous day was just finishing up her shift and was heading out as Saleem approached the door. He called to her and inquired about the fallen man's status, and she informed him that he had come to in a confused state and was speaking in what she presumed was Punjabi. However, none of the staff was able to speak Punjabi so they were not able to learn anything about the man. Saleem smiled, thanked her, and went into the hospital.

---

89 Mira, I'm going to bed now. I have to return to the hospital tomorrow morning to see him again.
90 You did the right thing, my love.

As Saleem entered the hospital room, the man sat up quickly and looked to have dizzied himself in the process. "Ki haal ah?"[91] Saleem asked. "Tuhana Punjabi aundi ah?"[92] the man replied in a hoarse voice. Saleem explained that he could speak Punjabi fluently as it was his first language. He also explained to the man that he was born and raised in Punjab and that Amritsar had once been his home. The man took a moment to process Saleem's words before asking, "Meinu ki hoya?"[93] Saleem explained patiently how he had found the man passed out on the street and how he had brought him to the hospital. They continued to talk for some time and Saleem learned the man's name was Kaka, as well as the events that brought him to Afghanistan and his ultimate goal of reaching Iran.

A nurse approached them with a tray of food and placed it before Kaka, and he looked at it hesitantly, asking Saleem if it was beef. Saleem nodded his head. "Ithe hor kush khaan nu nahi hega,"[94] he explained. Apparently, Kaka did not need much convincing, as he was already halfway through chewing a mouthful of the beef kebob by the time Saleem finished speaking. He asked Kaka what he planned to do and Kaka simply shrugged his shoulders, "Paise nahi hai ge, passport vi chori ho giya. Hun patah nahi ke kar sakdein."[95] He was clearly, and understandably, focused on the more pressing demands of his stomach at that moment. Saleem took a seat in the visitors chair next to the bed. After the pace of Kaka's chewing slowed and he appeared to be relatively satiated, Saleem said to him, "Mein Mecca ja rehein, Hajj karn li. Tu mere nal aja, mein tenu Iran leh jaaneh."[96]

---

91 How's it going?
92 You can speak Punjabi?
93 What happened to me?
94 There is nothing else to eat around here.
95 I have no money and my passport was stolen. I don't know what I can do anymore.
96 I am on my way to Mecca to complete my Hajj. Come with me, and I will take you to Iran.

Kaka stopped chewing and blinked in confusion. Saleem went on to tell him not to worry about the passport situation. Ever since the Partition, he had little regard for borders, and the one separating Iran from Afghanistan was poorly enforced. He had crossed it many times before with no issue whatsoever, and there was plenty of room to spare in his Jeep. Kaka's expression did not change as Saleem spoke, remaining thoroughly incredulous. Finally, he asked, "Tu meri madat kyun kar rehein?"[97] And Saleem replied with a piece of wisdom that throughout the years had given him solace. A passage from the Holy Quran that never struck him as too abstract. *"Whoever takes a life, it will be as if they killed all of humanity; and whoever saves a life, it will be as if they saved all of humanity."*

---

97 Why are you helping me?

2003

A gust of wind pulls my shirt tight against my body and a single tear streams down my face. Is it in anticipation of the blood that will be spilled this day, or has some plant debris wafted into my eye? I do not know. To my left, Toucan Sam. To my right, the First Man. French Sinatra stands with us as well, along with half a dozen other sons of the Khalsa, born and bred on the thick syrup of Canadian maples and the questionable contents of American fast-food cheeseburgers. The First Man has been accused of unholy relations with Lindsay M. by her dearly beloved, the sinister Abdul Mohammed. He stands across us with his legion, the pathetic wispy mutton chops on his pimpled cheeks wafting in the wind. We have come in support of the First Man, to defend his boundless honour.

But there is more beneath the surface here than can be cleanly described. Just as the assassination of Archduke Franz Ferdinand served as a tidy headline to summarize the conflicts of the Great War, so Lindsay M.'s chastity veils the deeper reasons for our mutual antipathy. Across us is the ancestral enemy, the last of the line of Abraham, the pilgrims of Mecca. They are the Mughal hoard that harassed a peaceful Punjab, the Afghani Empire that burned down Sri Harmandir Sahib. Those fires still burn in our pubescent hearts, and rumours from across the pond fuel the flames higher. The Toucan has heard through the reliable vine of vague familial relations (cousin-brothers and the like) that in England—the crown of the Commonwealth—the religious tensions between Sikhs and Muslims has reached critical mass. The Muslims march into the Gurdwara, douse the Guru Granth Sahib in gasoline, and set it aflame. The Sikhs answer in kind by storming the Mosque with a dismembered pig's head in tow and slapping the bloody porker onto the Holy Quran.

And if our blood was not pumping fast and hot enough on that account alone, then it should not go overlooked that both armies here today have recently completed the required reading of S. E. Hinton's *The Outsiders*, mandated by the Peel District Educational Schoolboard, and now each side considers themselves akin to the noble Greasers, facing off against the treacherous, snobby Socs. Each side stands tall, knights of unerring faith, ready to wage a neo-crusade on the freshly fertilized outfield of the River Grove Community Centre baseball diamond. Though by now, I've garnered some significant animosity toward the faith I was weaned on, I knew—as all theologians and battered spouses do—that that devil you know must always be defended against the one you don't.

Abdul Mohammed steps forth, brandishing a forgotten-looking cricket bat. "Yo, why you messaging my girl on MSN, bro?" The First Man smoulders silently, a psychological battle tactic to strike fear into the hearts of his enemies. The Toucan is not so subtle. He slams the tip of his chosen weapon—a forgotten-looking field hockey stick—into the flourishing turf. "Yo, my cousin never talked to yo' ratchet-ass bitch." As it turns out, this is a vague interpretation of the truth, as all gathered here are well aware that the First Man's unscrupulous text-messaging fingers may well have tapped their way into Lindsay M.'s MSN chat box. But that is beside the point, for this is a battle not of love, but of faith, not of the heart, but of the soul.

Abdul Mohammed is incensed. "Fucking dildoheads!" he calls, a nuanced derivative of the more general "raghead" to specifically isolate the juda, the religiously mandated hair topknot worn by Sikhs. To this, we retort, "Fucking half dicks!" Not as nuanced, but an accurate accusation of the required circumcisions in Islam. Next, they call out, "Cowfuckers!" which relies on the tenuous connection between Sikh dietary practices and the superstitious reverence of milk-producing mammals throughout India. And our rejoinder, "Inbred sister-fuckers!" A hyperbolic reference to the proclivity of Muslim majority countries to have higher rates of consanguinity than would be deemed appropriate in the West. That seems to stagger them for a moment, and someone on our side takes the opportunity to land an additional killing blow with, "Fucking sullah!" [98]

You see, it is not the guileless whites who possess the most barbed tongues. Those careless boobs are hindered by their ignorance and can summon only lifeless and impotent anatopisms such as "sand n——." The great insult here is having to interact with an imagination so atrophied. How refreshing it is to verbally duel with sophisticated minorities, especially those who hail from slightly different geographies along the same latitudinal line, and who are able to harness the knowledge of subtle ethnic differences to sculpt the most admirably severe derogatory attacks. As Sun Tzu says, "To know your enemy, you must become your enemy."

But now the time for talk is done. Jagbir, the quietest among us, the one who has spoken no insults, is the first to leap into battle. He pounces toward Abdul Mohammed's second in command, a stout Iraqi called Isa, and thumps him on the side of the head with a red-knuckled fist. They both go tumbling to the ground, and the Muslim force begins to beat on Jagbir's back as Jagbir beats on Isa's front. "Oye Panchodeyo!" [99] the Toucan bellows. To the Sikh contingent, nothing short of a battle cry. Limbs and retired sporting goods clash in a cloud of grass blades and upturned earth. An old Caucasian couple gasps from the path abutting the field

---

98 A derogatory Punjabi word for Muslims.
99 Hey you sister-fuckers!

of battle. Italians perhaps? Germans maybe. There's no way to tell for sure, as my head is currently locked in the sweaty crevasse of lanky Iqbal's armpit. I snarl and chomp my teeth, hoping to get them around some vulnerable halal meat. The elderly woman's voice approaches and grows louder. "Oh my, stop that young man! You'll hurt each other, my goodness! What's the hubbub all about!" No one stops to acknowledge her; the colonizer's interference will have no sway in this barbarian blood feud. "Herbert! Herbert, call the police! These boys will tear each other apart!"

"Yo, this crazy buddhi[100] is about to call the popo," cries a combatant from within the fray. "Let's fucking bounce, guys!" It is unclear who spoke the sage advice but it is well-heeded. I am released by lanky Iqbal, and before my eyes have time to refocus, he's fifty yards away, hauling up the waist of his oversized pants as he clambers over the chain-link fence that separates the baseball field from the wooded bike path.

"Yo, split up! Someone grab Jagbir!" A casualty on our end! Jagbir limps toward us and is braced up by the First Man and the Toucan, but an eye for an eye is served because, off in the distance, we see stout Iraqi Isa being dragged away by three of his compatriots. The battle concludes but the war goes on. Two faiths, forged through war, will remain locked in their eternal struggle for terrestrial superiority. But just as Joseph Smith updates the software of Christianity to place Zion in Far West, Missouri, our Holy Land is the River Grove Community Centre in the Mississauga suburb of the Greater Toronto Area. This day, the new Jerusalem has been christened by the blood of our brother and the blood of our enemies.

A post-battle feast is convened at Ozmos Authentic Shawarmas, where a general consensus emerges that regardless of how villainous the Islamic axis is, they sure do know how to make a delicious sandwich wrap.

---

100 Old lady.

1977

Here is a descriptive passage: Kaka was slouched against the window of Saleem's Jeep. His head bounced against the glass as the tires bounced over rocks and into shallow ditches. His body was exhausted and still recovering from near starvation. The journey from the border town of Tayabad to Tehran was twelve hours by road. Saleem, his dear Amira, and Kaka made the trip in two days. As the clouds were painted red by the setting sun, the skyline of Tehran came into view.

Here is another: Kaka was grateful for Saleem's help, but he thought Saleem talked too much and wished he would be quiet. He wondered how his mother and sister were faring, whether Gora and Kala were still jostling each other, whether Shinda had returned safely to Punjab and what he would tell the rest of Ahmedpura about their journey. Most importantly, as he moved toward the horizon of Tehran, he believed he moved toward his dreams and aspirations. He believed he moved toward opportunity.

External versus internal, the difference is important. The first leaves little room for ambiguity, how human flesh interacts with earthly strata, and given that both things described are "objects," the words align more closely to an "objective description." The second attempts something much more daring, something impossible perhaps. Because the natural existence of thoughts cannot be classified as "objects" per se. What are thoughts besides electrical currents in the mind, sensory experiences superimposed on the noumenal? As such, they are too slippery to pin down with "objective description". They are larger and foggier than the words used to describe them and they always escape the definition in some way or another. They bleed and bend and weave and break and collide and dissolve and evaporate. Trying to capture them in a still frame is like trying to capture the platonic ideal of a thing.

Why does any of this matter? Because the same thoughts, the same ideas (or at least the same interpretations of a single idea) that compelled Kaka toward Tehran, were compelling thousands of skilled and unskilled workers toward the same destination. Mohammed Reza Pahlavi, the Shah of Iran, saw this influx as progress. In fact, he saw everything he did as progress. Perhaps it was, in a certain sense, as foreign governments began to take an interest in the Iranian boom. Western pundits predicted Iran's evolution into a "First World Nation" within a single generation. In Punjab, the blood of the land flows from the five rivers, but here in Iran the blood is black, and it swells from the barren ground, and in place of wheat crops and sugarcane, it grows steel structures and weapons that fire lead in clouds of black carbon.

But not everybody agreed with the Shah. He measured his conception of progress only with corporeal things: the erection of skyscrapers, the production of automobiles, the stacks of bank notes that could be attributed to the product of Iranian labour. But he had lost sight of the thoughts that gripped the minds of Iranians. Not people like Kaka who had come from faraway places to share in the Shah's vision, but the ones who had always been there, who had learned to weave fine carpets by the steady hands of their grandfathers. These people now watched the destruction of the textile industry as Henry Ford's factory model slowly replaced the weavers' skilled hands with the efficiency and artless precision of machines. The Shah had lost sight of those slippery things that animated the soul of his people.

Here again we stumble into Guru Nanak's dictum, the third law of thermodynamics applied to the realm of cognition. The pendulum swings too far in one direction and ideas will emerge that pull it back the other way. The idea that rose against the Shah's dream was that of *Gharbzadegi,* the "Westoxification of Iran." Iran need not become a puppet of the godless West to prosper, said Ruhollah Khomeini, as he sat in the holy city of Najaf in the neighbouring nation of Iraq. The Shah had banished him there because he had gained too much influence and he spoke his ideas too loudly. But ideas are slippery things, and even from 1000 kilometres away, Khomeini's whispers retained their hold on Iran's soul. For now, it was still a silent grasp, one the Shah did not sense as he threw lavish ceremonies to honour himself. The idea was spoken about only by intellectuals in universities and by clerics in religious institutions, and it had not bled openly into the streets.

The ideas of a place are as important as the geography. Indeed, they are more important. But let us leave philosophizing alone for now, because it appears that Kaka had just entered the thriving city of Tehran in pursuit of his fortunes.

2009

It was the age of Kid Cudi's *Man on the Moon*, an auditory experience that had captured Nanak's imagination much like the visual experience of the same name had captured the world's in 1969. Nanak sat in an undersized chair in a university lecture hall for a course called "Media Studies." With a third of his attention, he wondered whether such a course needed to exist, given that the study of media tends to happen in real time when it is consumed. With another third, he concentrated on Lindsay T. in the next row down and a few seats over. And with the final third, he recited the opening line of Kid Cudi's "Soundtrack 2 My Life," which succinctly captured the essence of his experiences in the realm of courtship.

Nanak took the course with the lascivious aspiration of squeezing into the child-size lecture-hall seats next to Lindsay T., so his prickly, hairy, brown arm might rub against her velvety soft arm with invisible downy blond hair. But his efforts were thwarted by a brainless, unevolved brute who had already squeezed into the seat next to her. He was named Harminder or Garminder or Charminder or something along those lines.

Now Nanak was forced to endure an undergraduate's most loathed and reviled activity—paying attention in class. The professor, a progressive young lady of ambiguous ethnic origins (but dark enough to qualify as a minority), had a six-foot image of Apu Nahasapeemapetilon displayed on the projector. For a moment, it blissfully transported Nanak back to his youth, waiting eagerly on weekday nights with the First Man as the clock crept closer and closer to 9 p.m., so together they could revel in the glory of those iconic yellow bubble letters emerging through the cartoon clouds.

Quite a ceremony it was, Nanak recalled, as only a single tubular television occupied the homestead, so access to it was severely limited. He also recalled that it was a finicky device, as he once was struck with the not-so-brilliant idea of trying to clean it with a glass of freshly squeezed orange juice. An imitative practice spurred by the childish urge to be seen as important, the way the Viper was seen as important when she cleaned things. The logic was impressive for a toddler—citric acid being a powerful disinfectant. The result was less than ideal as most operating buttons became fried and the method for changing channels devolved to sticking a straw into the desired button cavity and jabbing in just the right direction. (It bears noting that Nanak became very proficient at this task, a talent he wanted desperately to share with the lovely Lindsay T.)

It was preordained what usage time belonged to what demographic. Saturday mornings, hotly contested, oscillated between low-budget Punjabi talk shows (usually consisting of forty minutes of textile and jewellery advertisements presented by a sweaty couple in front of a low-resolution green screen of the Bahamas, interjected with austere religious ramblings from prominent gurus with well-trimmed beards) and Saturday morning cartoons: Marvel Comics' *Spiderman* and *X-Men*, the golden age of 90's television.

Meanwhile, Charminder was squishing ever closer to Lindsay T., and as Nanak snapped out of his nostalgic daydreams, he became nauseated and infuriated all at once. They were splitting the headphone buds protruding out of his laptop. He had her attention tuned to a YouTube comedian that resembled the young professor at the front of the room in appearance, but the lady on YouTube was contorting her face in exaggerated ways, and donning turbans and chunnis, creating sketch parody comedy of her immigrant Punjabi parents. The subtitles were visible. "Ju go do homeverk eediot!" read the caption, as the young lady waved a turmeric-stained wooden spoon in front of her baboonish expression. Nanak couldn't bear to watch as Lindsay T. tried desperately to stifle her laughter, grasping Charminder's wrist as she did.

He resorted to focusing ever harder on the lecture produced by the young lady professor. She was ardent, animated, and flailing her limbs about, but then she reeled them in when she came to the conclusion of a point, making sharp, measured movements and furrowing her brow as a serious person might do when they are speaking of serious things. It was all terribly rehearsed and was lacking that aura of spontaneity and unpredictability that is present in all good entertainment. (In this the professor could learn a thing or two from her YouTube doppelgänger). But Nanak paid attention all the same, and he began to suspect that the professor did not share such nostalgic flashbacks of those four-fingered yellow folk. "Problematic," she said. "Racist tropes," she said. "Orientalist view of first-generation immigrants, lacking any and all nuance," she said. Could it be? Was that lovable Kwik-E-Mart operator not as great as Nanak remembered?

He contemplated putting his hand up. But miss, what about the sensitive portrayal of the anxieties and pressures surrounding arranged marriage in the episode "The Two Mrs. Nahasapeemapetilons?" What about the demystification of veganism and Eastern diets in the episode "Lisa the Vegetarian?" What about the torrid love affair with the squishy girl who looked like Lindsay T. and the complex marital troubles that ensued between Apu and his spicey wife Manjula? Do not these count as examples of a nuanced, three-dimensional character? But alas, Nanak kept his hand down as his attention snapped back to Charminder, whose wily arm slithered its way around Lindsay T.'s shoulders.

Nanak stared daggers at the back of Charminder's five-dollar garage fade, and he soon became mesmerized by those uneven and unfaded bands of hair. He peered for too long, and much like the afterimage of an optical illusion, a revelation emerged in Nanak's mind. This YouTube comedian—who relentlessly parodies her hapless immigrant parents, and in all likelihood shares the progressive, anti-colonialist attitudes of the professor—does she not deal in the same problematicism and racist troping us culturally aware, high-minded, second-generation Westerners are supposed to denounce? As she produces her sketch comedy, rife with stereotypes crasser and more damaging than anything poor Apu ever managed, are we to laugh and applaud her efforts? Can only the brown-skinned portray and play with the concept of brown skin? And if so, are we to accept the unacceptable portrayals that they may produce, lacking any and all nuance?

The conundrum rattled through Nanak's brain as he watched the postmodern deconstruction of Mr. Nahasapeemapetilon, while simultaneously watching the stratospheric rise in view count for the cringe-inducing creations of an Internet hack. He witnessed disapproval directed at a three-dimensional character produced in two-dimensional space, while approval was showered on a two-dimensional character in three-dimensional space, and all this grounded in some amorphous philosophy of identity.

Is a cartoon character less *Dasein* than a bad Internet comedian? What would the midwife say about Nanak's predilection to view drawings with unwarranted humanity? Should people across the globe douse their entertainment devices in freshly squeezed orange juice? Would Nanak ever squeeze next to Lindsay T. and show her his proficiency at changing channels? Was this whole thing some ultimate occurrence of galactically ordained juxtaposition, or is this just a contrived literary device by an uninspired writer trying to make a point? Join us next week to find out!

1977

Saleem was a chatty man, made more so with the opportunity to speak his native tongue with someone who shared the geography of his youth. Common roots lend an intrinsic connectiveness, no matter where the leaves sprout. He asked about the state of the Golden Temple, whether his various favourite dhabas were still in business, and the current records of local kabaddi teams. Kaka answered as best he could, having visited the Golden Temple only a handful of times, not ever having had the luxury to visit any restaurants in his life, and never having much of an interest in organized sports. All the same, it was a revealing conversation. Kaka had only heard stories about Partition from a single perspective (one which painted the other side as uniformly villainous), and now listening to Saleem reminisce, romantically as it were, about a place which Kaka had only ever considered as entirely ordinary and without much charm, he was forced to re-evaluate the nature of the conflict and who was affected by it.

More practically, Kaka also took the opportunity to extract what value he could, learning phrases and words that would be most useful for everyday exchanges. Saleem spoke Dari, which is similar enough to Farsi for a person to get by for a few days in Iran. Persia appeared to have nearly as many languages and dialects as India, which was a comforting thought as it increased the chances that vendors and employers would have more patience for all forms of nonverbal communication, hand gestures, facial cues, and the like.

It was late afternoon when Saleem's Jeep pulled to a stop in front of the recently constructed Shahyad Tower in the centre of Shahyad Square—a monument of progress, commissioned by a Shah who was too fond of patting himself on the back. Kaka stepped out of Saleem's vehicle and thanked him for the ride. Saleem asked, "Hun ki karunga?"[101]

"Kum labunga,"[102] Kaka replied, and Saleem nodded, unsurprised. Then he reached into his pocket and produced a handful of folded banknotes. "Chal fir, asi chal de ah. Ah leh, te roti kha la,"[103] he said, holding the money out to Kaka. Kaka kept his hands down, already feeling as though he was too far indebted to Saleem. Saleem then pushed the wad into Kaka's chest, after which a kind of awkward wrestling match of pride ensued. Saleem continued to push the cash toward Kaka more forcefully, and Kaka ducked and dodged the attempt for as long as he was able. Finally, Saleem managed to get a hold of Kaka's arm with his free hand and pressed the money into Kaka's palm, closing his fist around it.

There ended the debate, if ever there was one, because before Kaka could open his mouth to protest, Saleem had already waved it shut. He offered his parting advice, loudly and cheerfully. "Challo Kaka ji, teri jindegi shuru hogi. Jad tu ameer ho geya, rab da naam na bhulein."[104]

In the distance was the racket of the city, the chatter of pedestrians walking around, and the smell of gasoline from the vehicles speeding by. Kaka tried to focus his attention on anything at all to distract from his shame. A petty emotion, to say the least, because gratitude should always be freely

---

101 What will you do now?
102 I'll look for work.
103 Alright then, we're going to be off then. Take this so you can get something to eat.
104 There you are Kaka, you're ready to start your life now. When you're rich and famous, do not forget God.

expressed, not smothered away. But he was not yet mature enough to understand that any opportunity to give thanks when they are truly deserved should be seized greedily. And it had not yet dawned on him that Saleem Ali was one of the rarest kind of people one could encounter, the kind most deserving of thanks. A man possessed of a superhuman selflessness, one with a true understanding of morality, akin to what the Buddhists call *Maitri* (loving kindness), a practitioner of the Christian "Golden rule," and perhaps even an example of Kipling's "Thousandth Man." In short, Saleem was a good person. And in the face of that, the only weak-voiced reply Kaka was able to summon is this: "As-Salamu Alaykum, Saleem."[105]

Saleem smiled broadly and replied, "Sat Sri Akal, Kaka."[106] And then, as nonchalantly as could be—as if he didn't just save a man's life, or as if it were a regular thing for him—he hopped back into his Jeep, kissed his wife on the cheek, and like the hero at the end of an American Western film, drove off into the horizon with the sun on his back, never to be seen by Kaka again.

Kaka turned and blinked. He had no idea where to begin, but he drank this new world in as he did when he left the womb, with hungry glances. Immediately, it was clear that Iran was full of promise. The place was unlike Afghanistan, certainly, but different even from Delhi. All around, young people roamed in the latest fashions of the West: men in bell-bottomed jeans and form- fitting half-sleeve button-down tops, and women in skirts and turtlenecks and checkered blouses, all awash in rainbows of pastel. Displays of abject poverty were few and far between; wild animals were not roaming aimlessly and defecating where they wished; and there even existed an adherence to basic traffic conventions.

Kaka wandered into the cavernous pass beneath the Shah's tower, curious to see what was on the other side, when a voice called out, "Oye, tu kam labdein?"[107] Kaka flinched,

---

105 Peace be upon you, Saleem. (Islamic greeting)
106 Truth is God, Kaka. (Sikh greeting)
107 Hey, you looking for work?

startled at hearing his mother tongue so unexpectedly. He looked around to identify the speaker and it was immediately clear who had yelled out. The man wore a peaked turban in the Punjabi style and his beard was untrimmed. He had darker skin than Kaka, but he undoubtedly was a Sikh. He was leaning against the wall, chewing on an orange wedge.

Kaka didn't reply. He kept a reserved distance. His muscles were tensed. A still tender and scabbing scar on his head had led him to recently adopt the sensible opinion that familiar people were more dangerous than strangers, and this stranger was acting far too familiar. The man approached with his arms open, placatingly. "Badeh onde ah kam labun, par kum karn valleh nahi hunde. Tun lagda meinu kam karn valla,"[108] he said, pointing his finger at Kaka and grinning broadly. Kaka narrowed his eyes and nodded, not wanting to squander an opportunity if one truly existed. The man said, "Challo,"[109] gesturing with his head to the opposite side of the tower, toward a large, paved road that extended as far as the eye could see. They walked, but Kaka maintained his position behind the orange-eater. When he slowed, Kaka slowed, when he stopped, Kaka stopped short of him. The orange-eater talked a great deal. He talked quickly. And he was happy to keep speaking without an engaged interlocutor.

"Let me tell you, many people—many Punjabis, too—come to Iran looking for work, but they stay for two days max before they haul their lazy asses back to their comfy cotton beds in the wheat fields. Mothered too much if you ask me, sons of owls the lot of them. You don't look the type to me to be mothered too much, and I'm a good judge of these kinds of things, which is why the bossman lets me take a longer lunch, so I can come to the tower and pick up new arrivals like you. You don't look like a complainer to me either, and I hope I'm not wrong on

---

108 Many people come here looking for work, but they're not keen on working when push comes to shove. But you look like a worker to me.
109 Let's go.

that account, because I don't like being embarrassed in front of the bossman, because he doesn't like excuses, and neither do I for that matter. And believe you me, I've heard every goddamn excuse in the sister-fucking book. 'Oh, I'm not getting paid enough!', 'The hours are too long!', 'Iranian food gives me the shits!' I swear one son of an owl told me the dogs look at him funny over here! Let me tell you, I've heard it all. I just want you to know that. But let me say this as well, whatever shit's bothering you is bothering all the rest of us too, but you're not gonna hear any of that kind of hollering from the real workers. In fact, that's what separates the real workers from the lazy asses, the ability to shut their fucking mouth and get to it. I hope you got some skills in that serious looking head of yours, pal, because these guys who come over thinking I'm gonna hold their hands, teaching them this and that, no way, I got my own work to keep up with. Hey, are you paying attention? Ohh yeah, you got yourself mesmerized by these olive-skinned Iranian women already, huh? Well, let me give you some advice right off the bat—they don't have eyes for you! Western-educated is what they're looking for. Hell, Western-educated is what they are! And don't take no offence to this, but buddy, you don't look Western-educated to me. Haven't even said a damn word in Punjabi since we met, so I'm not expecting you to know how to quote Shakespeare in the Queen's English, no sir, I am not. I'll tell you what you can do though, and this is a goddamn human universal. Get yourself a lot of money. Then it doesn't matter how educated you are and it damn well doesn't matter what direction the education came from either. By the way, I never got your name back at the tower. Come to think of it, I never gave you mine! Well, there's something for you. You can call me what everyone else calls me, and that's Gill."

Kaka nodded at various points in Gill's speech, but he was also looking around and absorbing his new environment. The road that went on forever was called Eisenhower Avenue, and as they moved deeper, he saw a mixture of people wearing the traditional tunics of the Bakhtiari and Qashqai, the bur-qas and salwar kameez of the nomads of Afghanistan and Pakistan, and, most surprisingly, the three-piece suits of Western men with white faces. However, the disparate appearances did not appear to stop or slow interactions and engagements. Having witnessed only cultural homogeneity (along with the incurious spirit it fosters) until this point in his life, Kaka watched the comingling with intrigue. English was spoken openly and fluently by as many people communicating in Farsi. The blood of Iran had clearly been lucrative for more people than just those that reside within its borders.

A construction site came into view down the road and Kaka spotted more turbans tied in the style of Punjab, sitting atop faces with untouched beards. They were all busy in frenzied movement, different tradesman: bricklayers, carpenters, welders, and more. They seemed to be erecting a building of some kind, not of antique, brittle mud, but of sturdier stuff, stone and steel being brought together in contemporary designs. There was a feeling of warmth in the pit of his stomach, a sense that perhaps Kaka had finally reached the company of his kinfolk. Not merely the kinship derived from a common birthplace, but in the deeper sense one that emerges from encountering kindred spirits, souls that contained enough fire to burn past the endless fields of Punjab. Men with ambition.

Gill led Kaka into the worksite, walking past half a dozen labourers who seemed to have no interest in the new arrival. The bossman Gill was referring to was an Iranian. His hair and beard were cropped short and speckled grey. He watched his worksite with an iron glare from beneath bushy eyebrows on a prominent forehead. He was short of stature but clearly a commanding presence. Those near him were visibly working with greater intensity. As Gill and Kaka approached, he addressed them in flawless Punjabi, "Tenu kehre kam onde?"[110]

Dumbstruck until Gill nudged him in the back, Kaka

---

110   What skills do you possess?

related what he had learned so far from his unofficial internships in Punjab, embellishing where he could as all hopeful employees do. The bossman's name was Dariush. He kept his head still and his arms crossed during Kaka's speech. When he finally did move, there appeared to be no superfluous movements. He turned to Gill and gave a single nod, and then Gill grabbed Kaka by the arm and dragged him to a pile of construction debris. "Ah dubbey vich sutke ah,"[111] he ordered. Grunt work, but Kaka welcomed it. It was something to do, after all, and for that he was deeply grateful. For the first time since he had left Ahmedpura, the pace of his heart slowed, because at last he appeared to be moving away, instead of toward, his self-imposed proviso to die rather than return home empty-handed.

Not long after he started hauling trash, the workday concluded. Gill returned to collect Kaka and took him to the place he had secured for Kaka to stay—the apartment complex where many of the workers resided. It was single military cot among dozens, in the conference room of a roach-infested two-star hotel just off Eisenhower Avenue. Compared to the room in Kabul—or for that matter the dusty corner of the mud hut in Ahmedpura—the spartan accommodations were luxurious. Excuse the pun, but anything off the floor was a step-up.

Unfortunately, as Kaka lay down and shut his eyes, hoping to find some rest, paranoia kept him awake. He tossed and turned for most of the night and, though he no longer had anything of value, he kept his backpack clutched close to his chest. His mind turned over, again and again, tediously rehearsing all the things that could go wrong. He did all he could to quiet it, but the war waged on, the battle between the optimism of the hopeful unknown and the pessimism born of lived experience, and he remained awake as a combatant on both sides.

The next morning, he rose earlier than the other men. His stomach growled but he ignored it. Having familiarized himself with the various stages of starvation, he was better able to

---

111 Take this waste and put it in that bin over there.

gauge when his body needed nourishment and when it was simply whining. He was hungry only to move again and now he had a place to exert himself, even if for weeks he would do nothing but haul materials here and there and dispose of construction waste. It was of no concern. The movement is what mattered. It slowed the furious pumping of his heart and dampened the incessant drumbeat in his mind.

His effort quickly made an impression. Gill, who prided himself on being able to spot the workers was now worried that he had spotted one that worked too hard. He said, "Holli kam kar yaar,"[112] half in jest, but Kaka didn't slow. Dariush watched with his penetrating gaze and soon the privilege of more important work was granted to Kaka. The duties of hauling waste fell to the newcomers, many of whom fled soon after by citing one of Gill's excuses. Their departure motivated Kaka all the more, the singular pride that rose from the knowledge that he had done something others could not.

As the months progressed, Kaka's hands mastered new skills. Dariush had short patience for slow learners, but in those he saw potential, he freely poured his seemingly limitless fountain of knowledge. Kaka learned the creation of steel and ceramic cookware. The craftsmanship of working with wet clay he found particularly enjoyable, and it was the first time he realized that aside from brute pragmatism, there was beauty to be found in the construction of things. Marble cutting, where he encountered the potential of heavy machinery and its ability to bring life to marvels of human architecture that in eras bygone would have taken hundreds of men hundreds of years to complete. Most of all, however, he fell deeply into the primordial science of metals. The heat of the torch, the blinding sparks, the smell of melted ore. To Kaka, there was something deeply satisfying about working with elements of the Earth and transforming them into artifacts that withstood the touch of decay and persisted through the transience of life—perhaps a salutary effort in pursuit of that all too human desire for immortality.

---

112 Take it easy, friend.

2001-2016

"Hello this is Nick calling from—"

Der Vater generally takes no interest in the career outcomes of the First Man and me. He sometimes speaks vaguely of the desire to see his sons in positions of prominence, but nothing specific. He bucks the trend of immigrant parents who have little regard for the opinions of doctors and lawyers, paradoxically pushing their children toward doctorships and lawyerhoods. Instead, there is a kind of passive scrutiny, spectating our exploits from a distance to see what we might achieve in our isolated, yet privileged circumstances. There are many avenues open to us, but any guidance to the correct path is woefully absent.

"Hello this is Nick calling from DWB Technologies, I was wondering if you had a moment—"

This is not to say that he is unequivocally uncaring. His interest merely depends on context, specifically, whether the product of our labour manifests as something tangible, or at the least, that we exert ourselves in some physical, sweat-inducing manner. The flexing of muscles, effort expended toward the rearrangement of objects into more useful objects—all this he understands. But he peers with curiosity through the slightly cracked bedroom door when I say, "I have homework to do." This is not to confirm whether I am actually studying, but to investigate how the concept of "work" can be associated with slouched postures in comfortable chairs, or on occasion, lying prostrate on a soft twin-sized bed with a book nestled under my face.

"Hello, this is Nick calling from DWB Technologies. Do you have a quick second to speak about a revolutionary new service that will simplify your life immeasurably—"

The assignment questionnaire poses the following: "What is the purpose of the gravedigger scene in Shakespeare's *Hamlet*?" The obvious answer, "To dig a grave," will not satisfy the teacher, who has just graduated from her accelerated Masters of English Literature program, and consequently, has an unquenchable thirst for deep analysis and explanation of subtext. On the television, rosy-cheeked high schoolers do their homework with their friends of the opposite gender, with their sneaker-clad feet on the couch, and when they hit a hitch, they ask their parents who are fountains of knowledge about the Western canon and all its subtexts. At the homestead, quality time with the opposite gender is for one purpose alone, and I am not of age to explore said purpose, and the flat side of my sneaker would certainly be slapped against the flat side of my head if it progressed past the foyer, and Der Vater, if presented with *Hamlet*, might consider it some kind of pork-infused egg dish.

"Hello, this is Nick calling from DWB Technologies. We specialize in streamlining and expediting the process of sanitation and waste removal produced—"

Der Vater may not be an expert at deciphering archaic lines of Elizabethan-era playwrights, but when it comes to measurements, he is otherworldly. Unfortunately, this is of little assistance when the subject of mathematics takes centre stage in the classrooms of my youth. Yes, he can multiply and divide two-digit numerals by three-digit numerals with ease. He can convert inches to centimetres to feet to yards at the drop of a hat, and he can even conduct Pythagoras's theorem without ever having heard the name Pythagoras, but Der Vater is only able to do all this inside the confines of his alien brain. "Show your work," the teacher warns—a principal that Der Vater has proven time and again to tacitly agree with. But, apparently, not in this case, for when I place the question sheet in front of him for assistance, only answers appear.

"Hey, Nick calling from DWB Technologies, gimme a quick minute and I'll change your life forever! How, you ask? Well—"

Der Vater doesn't speak of things called passions or hobbies. Most of the things that float before his mind's eye are swallowed back up before they materialize on his tongue. But silent as he is, Der Vater is still skilled at accumulating wealth. To that end, he is like an automaton, whose programming only permits movement in pursuit of capital returns. A quiet, furrow-browed, mechanical entity, who if he deigned to speak, might only do so to voice the philosophy of the poet-warrior Wu-Tang Clan, solemnly murmuring, "C.R.E.A.M." before swinging his hammer at another nail.

But sometimes that deeply hidden humanity peeks through the cracks of the façade and a more sincere motivation emerges. Sometimes, when the work is done, and his energy expended, we drive home through the city and he points to a building I've never stepped foot in and says, "Mein ithe tilan laiyan si."[113] Or a house on the preposterously luxurious Mississauga Road. "Mein es ghar di deck banahi si."[114] He speaks with no detectable emotion, but pay attention and you may sense some cues that betray a quiet pride: his frown relaxes and his posture is not so hard. In the contemplation of things he has built, he realizes that this place we live in is more than it used to be, that because of him people's homes are made comfortable and beautiful, their workplaces safe

---

113 I put the tiles in here.
114 I built the deck at the back of this house.

and functional. He realizes that some of what is great about the architecture of this habitat is directly due to his work, and through that he achieves the solace of knowing he is a valuable human being.

"ThisIsNickFromDWBTechnologiesWeCanHelpYouSave TimeAndMoneyPleaseDontHangUp!—"

I learn to walk, I learn to decipher instructions, and soon after I am holding a hammer. Der Vater allows me to hammer my fingers a few times, so he need only recite the lesson on where to place them once for it to take root. Next, I am learning to operate a drill. Always hold the drill at the same angle as the screw and start slow, applying even pressure until it stops wobbling, but pull away as soon as the screw is in, otherwise you risk stripping the head or digging too deep into the wood. Choose straight 2x4s when building frames by closing one eye and peering down its length to check for warping. Measuring and cutting drywall, a gentle practice because the sheets are prone to crack if not properly handled. Mudding and taping—keep your plaster the consistency of pancake batter and your life will be easier. Laminate floors are faster to install but not as durable as hardwood. Tiles are the most durable, and the cement beneath the tile needs to be even or the tile will crack when it's dried—and keep your cement much thicker than pancake batter or your life will be difficult. Measure twice, but if you still manage to fuck it up after that, develop the habit of always cutting on the outside of your measurement because you can always shorten later but you can never re-lengthen.

Der Vater teaches everything he is able to teach and he does so with uncharacteristic patience and kindness. It is what he knows best and he wants his child to appreciate how humble work can transform a life. It did for him after all, taking him from a shack made of mud halfway across the world to a house of brick. But his children are raised in a world where humble work is not as transformative. Every house is already made of brick in his world so the markers for success are strange and ill-defined: thread counts in bed fabrics and towels, percentages of lead in gasoline, branded symbols on clothing and accessories, and the scents of perfumes and shampoos which effectively terminate the rugged stench of humanity for hours on end. And people who achieve these heightened strata of existence do not do so by way of manual labour. They must study hard in the domains of technical, euphemistic languages, and learn to understand neo-hieroglyphics such as B2B, B2C, EBITDA, CXO, ACCT, EPS, COB, EOD, Q3, and BS. They don custom-fitted suits, enter buildings that require giant machinery to erect, and speak in intelligent ways, to intelligent people, about intelligent things.

He should be happy that his children do not need to work as hard as he did to earn a living. But something about this holds the implicit admission that the work he has done is not as important as what his son is doing. If he had ever read Heller, or had known what a catch-22 was, he might consider himself in one—to desire that his child live an easier life than he did while simultaneously understanding that it is only through the toil of a hard life that meaning and self-actualization can be found. So, it is with bittersweet sentiments that he watches his son don a custom-fitted suit, enter a building that he could not have built with his own hands, and speak in intelligent ways to intelligent people about intelligent things.

"Hullo. This is Nick calling from DWB Technologies. Do you have a moment to talk?... You do? Ahem, excuse me. Well then, I'm calling because my company specializes in providing a sanitation and waste disposal service geared specifically to entities in your house that would qualify as of the non-human variety... Aha, yes, of course, I can clarify. You see, DWB has developed a proprietary system to radically simplify the method in which you deal with the waste material produced by your pets... Mhmm... Mhmm... Yes, it's very interesting! We begin by auditing your personal sanitation needs. To receive the most personalized service possible you would just need to visit our website and fill out our short Needs Survey, which would be followed by a call by a DWB Needs Consultant who can provide a full breakdown of the custom package that would suit your needs... Yes, of course, ma'am, I can see how that's unclear. In fundamental terms what DWB strives to accomplish for its clients is to remove the stress and hassle of pet waste from their lives... No... No, no one will actually come to pick up your pet's waste for you, but what we offer is the next best... What are you subscribing to? Well, in addition to receiving everything you require for your pet's sanitation needs on a rolling basis, you will have forty-hour a week access to our specialized consultants... What was that? What do we send? Well, we have a large suite of products from scented bags to scoopers to... Mhmm... Well, ma'am, I would say we do more than merely mail you dog waste bags. If I can just schedule an appointment with one of our consul—... What does DWB stand for?... Yes, I'm still here ma'am... DWB stands for Dog Waste Bag—"

1978

What, so far, has been revealed about Kaka's appearance? Recall that he has features crowded toward the centre of his face, like his father. They are sharp features like his mother, not soft like his grandfather. He was born in the Punjab state of India from which we surmise dark hair, black mostly, but maybe some brown mixed in, and in the right light of the sun, maybe even some red. Admittedly, not the most thorough description possible. But the vagueness is somewhat intentional so as to accommodate both the imaginative readers, who will create whatever image they desire in their minds, and unimaginative readers, who are likely to get bogged down and fold themselves in half trying to decipher overzealous poetics of eye shapes and lip quivers. But there is one important dimension of Kaka's appearance that has so far been unaddressed. What, for instance, immediately indicated to Saleem Ali that the beaten-down, half-starved man he encountered in the ancient city of Herat, was a Sikh?

Saleem Ali, born and raised in the holy city of Amritsar, knew clearly what a Sikh man looks like, and he would tell us that a devout Sikh is required by the tenets of their faith to adhere to a well-defined list of visible markers—five, to be precise. Now these five requirements are adhered to in varying degrees. For example, when travelling internationally it is difficult to retain an ostentatiously ornamented dagger strapped to your outfit, and a shiny gold kara won't do the trick if it's recently been stolen. Neither can you easily examine what kind of underwear a man is wearing, not unless you've got a skill for seduction. But hair is less troublesome to border guards, and it is often the first thing you're able to see on a person, whether you've seduced them or not. So, if asked how he knew the beaten man was a Sikh, Saleem Ali would have pointed to the thick knot of hair peeking out beneath a bloodied and loosely tied turban, and to the dark, full, untrimmed beard, not easily pierced by the light of the sun. Both imaginative and unimaginative readers would do well to keep this detail in the front of their minds as we proceed.

Throughout the ensuing months, Dariush accepted contracts all across Iran. He took his team to Babolsar on the north shore, where Kaka felt the breeze of the Caspian Sea, and to the south to Bandar Abbas to work in the shipyards where he saw massive freighters break through the unimaginable waves in the Strait of Hormuz. They migrated from large, developing cities to small, rural hamlets, and from temperate, smoggy geographies to dry, arid ones.

Kaka found himself well-suited to the travels. The constant change of scenery reflected the restlessness of his appendages. But travelling so far and so wide and so often, presented a set of challenges distinct from staying stationary. In Ahmedpura, the luxury of sanitation areas, in the form of a stream, or well, or an irrigation system reservoir, were always accessible. In the deserts of Persia, he lacked regular access to these things, and the mud and dirt began to accumulate on his skin and beneath his turban. In his thick topknot of hair, he began to feel a relentless itching.

It was in Abadan, near the southwest border in the corner of the country, where this problem became unmanageable. Dariush and his crew had been commissioned to build homes to house the influx of Western expatriates who were travelling to Iran to capitalize on the economic boom. Here was the truth of the universally consistent irony that the people who build lavish homes can never afford to reside in them themselves. Dariush and his crew were camped near the outskirt of the city in a tight collection of individual tents and lean-tos. At the close of the workday, Kaka went back to his tent and hastily unwrapped his turban so he could better reach his scalp with his fingernails, and against the deep blue fabric of his turban he saw dozens of rapidly skittering lice. With no quick remedies available, he decided to tie the turban against his scalp again to contain the vermin. Then he laid his head down and tried to rest for a few hours before he was called back to work.

A person who dies for a belief is called a martyr, but a person who lives for a belief is not called anything. Another man, in similar circumstances, might never have made it to Iran at all. He might have died in Afghanistan, believing till his final breath that sacred cows must remain sacred, but Kaka never had the luxury of such convictions. He swallowed the meat of a sacred cow believing that he could do more with another breath.

Survivors are not those who have more courageous hearts or more resilient minds. They possess a simple thing that is a rarity among most people: the ability to reevaluate a fundamental moral precept in real time. Survivors do not withstand; they adapt. Kaka was raised on sermons of Gurdwaras that sang the praises of martyrs, but, somehow, he got a hold of the idea that maybe in some cases it was as noble to choose life as it was to choose death, because life is always the harder choice. Now he was asked again to choose, perhaps not between life and death, but progress and tradition, and it was all too fitting that this should happen to Kaka in a nation that was asking itself the same question.

When the housing project in Abadan came to a close, Dariush gave his crew some time off before the next job. Most of the workers took the opportunity to visit the far outreaches of the city where there was no infrastructure and the desert sprawls out endlessly past the horizon. Here could be found Iranian women who were not educated in the West's leading institutions but had nonetheless developed the same liberated spirits and promiscuity that such institutions were thought to instill. "Ik din di kamai naal, raqs vehk sak dein!"[115] Gill said enticingly, swaying his hips from side to side, mimicking the women who belly danced wearing nothing but a hijab.

It had been long enough that Gill had earned Kaka's trust, and the feeling was reciprocal. Dariush's crew had become something of a family under his keen eye. Seeing as how he only tolerated competence, there was a mutual respect between all who'd made the cut. But even still, Kaka refused Gill's good-natured offers. He was not keen to spend his money on such frivolous pursuits. Even if he were overcome with an overwhelming urge to see a "belly dance," he did not carry enough money to pay for one. He wired most of his pay back home to Ahmedpura as soon as he received it, and kept only what he required for his necessities, and even that he kept hidden along the inner seam of his underwear waistband. He was hesitant, even in his condition, to spend money on a barber, so when Gill came to convince Kaka to go to the belly dances, Kaka replied, "Mein vaal kutaney ah. Tu mere li kar sakdein?"[116]

Gill became taciturn and looked at Kaka with a penetrating gaze. Gill had kept his hair and retained his faith, but like Kaka, his ambitions were large, and he knew how tight the constricting grasp of convention could be. And he had been dealing with the burden of keeping his hair much longer than Kaka. It was not the first time the thought had crossed his mind, but it was the first time that the prospect of a friend sharing the experience along with him was on the

---

115 For one day's wages you can see a "belly dance."
116 I want to cut my hair. Will you do it for me?

table. "Challo, mein ve kutah loon ga,"[117] he said after a long pause. Heresy was better done with a friend by your side.

So that night, the two men found a pair of scissors, a pack of disposable razors, and a few gallons of Iranian wine. A bonfire was lit in the camp, and the family of Dariush's work crew gathered to witness the ritual. Some were Sikh who had their hair cut; some were Sikh who had not. Some were Iranian who had grown to understand the importance of the kesh;[118] some were nomads from across Persia and the Arabian Peninsula, and from the north of Africa, who were witnessing something they had never seen before. All had gathered respectfully in support of a thing they knew was difficult to do: to let go of the past.

Kaka cut Gill's hair first. He took the long strands, which went down to Gill's waist, and he tied them into a knot. Then he picked up the scissors, heavy ones, used in the construction of denim clothing. He placed the open blades as close to the base of Gill's neck as he could and slowly pulled the handles together, watching as they sheared through a thing which had always remained whole. Gill smiled softly as he took hold of the thick knot of severed hair. "Kam hogya, yaar, hun teri vaari ah,"[119] he said.

They switched positions and now Kaka sat cross-legged in front of the fire. In due course, he felt the cold metal on the back of his neck and heard the scrape as the blades grinded against one another. Then, when the metal fell silent, he felt the tangible weight of the hair fall from his head. Gill handed him the knot and he took hold of it. He was overcome by sentiment; he could not help it. When you become used to a thing, even an anchor, its loss is always felt remorsefully. This particular thing was imbued with all the significance of his youth—memories of his mother, usually so surly and

---

117 Alright, I'll cut mine too then.
118 One of the five Ks of Sikhism, specifically, the custom to keep hair uncut and don a turban.
119 The deed's done, friend. It's your turn.

retracted, gently running a comb through his hair, rubbing in oils squeezed from almonds and coconuts, and tying a strong knot on the top of his head.

The fire before him danced and he looked into it, his eyes watering from the intensity of light, but he looked harder still, because he saw the prophesy of better things and the sacrifices required to achieve them. He threw the knot in and it flamed up ever so higher. At once, a heavy burden lifted and a ritualistic rebirth. Burn the past and let it light the way forward.

And then Kaka grabbed hold of a gallon jug of wine and drank deeply, those around him hollering and applauding. "Oye panchodeya, mere li vi bachaa!"[120] Gill chided as he threw his knot into the fire alongside Kaka's. A flash faded to a flicker and the evening proceeded into an uproarious celebration. Motivated by Gill and Kaka (and a few generously poured glasses of Iranian wine), a few of the other Sikhs also found their place under the blade's edge. Laughter and song and exuberance was born in the haziness of drink and company of respected peers and loved ones—brothers. Even Dariush, who usually kept his mind sober, and his face perpetually frowned, was seen with a glass in hand, and some witnesses attested to the fact that from the right angle he may even have been seen smiling. In this fashion, the night passed, innocent and regretless, with good men and good wine and good fortunes.

As the sun rose the next day, it did so on a face that was entirely unrecognizable. The features still crowded toward the centre, and they were still sharp, but you must now imagine a different man. A jaw line was visible, not especially prominent but well-defined, as there was too little fat to conceal it. A faded silver scar on the side of his head, behind his right ear, flashed in the sunlight as he stepped out of his tent. He went to the pond nearby to view himself. The water rippled and a deadly hangover blurred his vision, but when

---

120 Hey you sister-fucker, save some for me!

it all became still, he took some time to absorb the new man before him. Through his spine he felt a whisper of the temptation of Narcissus—a young man, a handsome face. He felt a shallow kind of pride, but pride all the same. Finally, he pulled his gaze away from the water's reflection.

Before long, Dariush asked the men to gather, because hangover or not, the work didn't stop. Most of them were groggy and dishevelled, and they chuckled and elbowed each other as they remembered the night's shenanigans. "Ah ki hunda peya?"[121] Gill asked with bloodshot eyes and a hoarse voice, gingerly holding the sides of his freshly shaven head. Next to Dariush, there were a few newcomers who were hoping to join the crew. Dariush lined them up so they might introduce themselves. "Naam devo,"[122] he ordered.

At first, Kaka was uninterested. His brain hurt and his stomach growled, and he was dealing with the petty regret one had when they were in a sorry state and have a mountain of work to look forward to. The first two newcomers who rattled off their names did so without any interest. But when the third man said his name, Kaka's world snapped into focus. Everything else became peripheral. A towering rage bubbled up in his stomach and provided a clarity he had never had before in his life. The third man in the line of newcomers had cheeks that puffed out like laddus, and his eyes were large and innocent, and when he spoke, his voice was meek and quiet, and it softly said, "Grewal."

---

121 What's going on here?
122 Give your names.

1958-1977

Shivani was a rambunctious young woman. Born in Pathankot, the northernmost city of Punjab, which sits in the foothills of Himachal Pradesh, she spent most of her time daydreaming on the bank of the Chakki River. The river ran down from the Himalayas and became a tributary of the Beas River. Most people who came to Pathankot did so as they were passing through to the more northern, more scenic states of India. But Shivani had no interest in going north, where it was cold and underdeveloped. Like the current of the river, her thoughts took her south, where the water eventually poured into the Arabian Sea and then crashed against the shores of Mumbai.

Often, she skipped from the gate of her home with her chunni not properly wrapped around her head, so it flew behind her like the tail of a comet. Her mother yelled at her, "Sudhar ja, ladki!"[123] but to Shivani these warnings just rang away like the fading echoes they were. So, she paid no heed, and each day she skipped through the town, attracting the attention of everyone with eyes to see, just as a comet might. It was no secret that it was her greatest desire to be seen by all the people in the world, just like the starlets of Bollywood. It was an exhilarating feeling to be seen. When she sat by the

123   Straighten yourself out, girl!

river, she imagined herself being carried away to Mumbai and washing ashore to fame and applause.

She was not like the other girls in the city who listened to their parents and averted their eyes when strangers looked at them. Rather, Shivani looked back, sometimes proudly, sometimes mischievously, sometimes defiantly. And why should she have been blamed or shamed for such an impulse? A person who wishes to be seen by the world should not shy away when looked at. They should embrace the attention, revel in it. And that was precisely what Shivani did as she skipped through town. When all eyes she passed began to follow her and watch her, she looked directly back into them.

One day, Shivani sat by the river and got caught up in her daydreaming for longer than normal. The sun began to set, and the hustle and bustle usually present around the bank began to peter out. The monks doing yoga returned to their temples, the wives washing their families' laundry returned to their homes to hang them for drying, and the ashes of the dead had already floated down the Chakki and into the Beas. Shivani rose to her feet and looked around. The world was dark and only forms were visible. A pair of eyes appeared in the darkness but she could not see who they belonged to. They were large and innocent. She looked back at them, curiously.

Shivani continued to look into them, though the curiosity quickly faded. It was replaced by paralyzing dread and suffocating horror. She was numb, unable to move, unable to look away. For the first time ever, she wanted to look away but she wasn't able to. She couldn't understand how eyes that appeared so innocent could have done what they did. How could those eyes have been capable of such evil? And how could she have been the one to endure it? Shivani never found answers to these questions, and even though she did not deserve it, what she received was blame and shame.

Her father had no words for her when she limped through the gate of her home. He turned his head away. Her mother had a few words for her, but they were spoken remorselessly.

"Yahaan se jao. Vaapis mat anaa."[124] She was unable to skip. Her body was in pain but she didn't feel it. She was divorced from her body, as if floating above it. She didn't want to feel her body again. Never. She walked until her legs were no longer able to carry the weight of her body. She collapsed. She never wanted to be seen again.

Nine months later Shivani was no longer in Pathankot. She sat in Jaipur, the pink city of kings. Now a new face blinked up at her and the eyes were all too familiar. They had haunted her dreams since the day she fell from exhaustion. The nurse asked, "Aap uska kya naam rakhna chaahti hain?"[125] but Shivani just shook her head. She refused to name the boy. She could hardly bear to look at him. Her heart turned cold when he grasped at her finger, and her mind fell into a fog when he cooed to get her attention.

Many nights passed with the child's wails going unanswered, and when they were answered it was only because the landlord demanded the new mother do something to stifle the noise. Shivani fed the child her milk but only to relieve the pressure in her breast, and she covered his face with her kameez as she did. The nameless boy grew older. His mother referred to him as "Munda"[126] and others referred to him as "Shivani ka ladka."[127]

The boy was beaten relentlessly. He was beaten for reasons he did not understand. The beatings were so regular that he began to consider them as a kind of necessary price for his existence. As more time passed, and the boy's understanding matured to grasp the meaning of motivations, he sought to find a reason for his mother's actions. He concluded it must be from affection. What else could be the reason but affection? When his mother's arms tired from beating him, and she ran out of breath, why else would she begin to smile?

---

124 Go from here. Do not come back.
125 What do you want to name him?
126 Boy
127 Shivani's boy.

The landlord knocked on the door to their apartment once a month and his mother said, "Ab yahaan se chale jao."[128] So, the nameless boy wandered aimlessly through the dusty slums of Jaipur. Month after month, year after year. Quiet and alone, the boy grew into a young man, but every month, when the boy returned home from his wandering, the landlord was always leaving, always smiling, always sweaty. His mother was on her bed, beneath her blanket, a vacant look in her eyes.

This made the nameless boy uneasy. He did not like to see others smile when his mother did not. She was the only one who cared for him and he was the only one who cared for her. He did not like the landlord and that smile on his face. So, when the next month came around, and his mother told him to leave, he sneaked into the shadows, staying close by. He remained quiet and lurked near the window to the apartment.

He heard the landlord grunting. And then a sound he had never heard before. His mother's laughter. He wanted to know what was making her so happy. He could not imagine her being so happy. He peeked over the bottom ledge of the window to see.

Shivani turned her head. Her eyes floated around the room. They glossed over the window where she saw something—the eyes that haunted her dreams. Again, they peered at her through the dark. Again, they had no form. She screamed and closed her eyes. She screamed louder and began crying. The landlord's face contorted in confusion.

The nameless boy saw his mother screaming and crying. He blamed the sweaty landlord who was pressing his weight down on her. He grasped a loose brick from the ground. He kicked the door of the apartment open. His mother was still wailing. She had her palms over her eyes. Her voice was shrill and it cracked. The veins bulged in her neck from the exertion of her screams.

---

128   Get out of here.

133

The landlord turned to see who had entered. His eyes widened as he saw the nameless boy. He shouted as he saw the brick in his hand. He climbed off the boy's mother and turned to the boy with his hands up.

The boy walked up to the landlord and swung the brick as hard as he could. It collided with the landlord's temple. Blood pooled.

Shivani had stopped screaming. She looked at her son. She was numb. Vacant. She remembered her mother. She remembered what had been said to her. She said, "Yahaan se jao. Vaapis mat anaa."

The nameless boy left the apartment. He left the slums he had wandered through all his life. He left Jaipur, the pink city of kings. He had no destination in mind, so he followed the path of the largest highway out of the city. He would go as far away as he could because it is what his mother wanted. He remembered the sound of her laughter. He remembered the name of the landlord, the man whose blood pooled around his head, the man who was able to make her laugh.

His name was Grewal.

1978

Within the first few hours it was clear that Kaka was un-recognized. Grewal glanced at him once but gave no signs of alarm and didn't seem concerned by him since. He'd been directed under the supervision of Rajbir, a hulk of a man who spoke rarely, and even then, no more than single words softly spoken. Dariush had accepted a new contract to erect a warehouse for the Abadan refinery. The first thing to be done was to square away and flatten the earth where the foundation was to be laid. Kaka watched Grewal and Rajbir from the corner of his eye, from behind the mound of dirt he had piled up, cautious to not draw any attention to himself. "Oye Kaka!" Gill yelled, approaching from the opposite direction. Almost instinctually, Kaka tackled Gill to the ground and jammed his hand over his mouth. Gill tried frantically to push Kaka off him, shouting curses that were muffled by Kaka's palm. "Tu panchode pagal ho giyein?"[129] he said incredulously.

Kaka furiously shushed him and pointed to the scar on the side of his head, which succeeded in calming Gill down for a moment. With the same finger, Kaka then pointed to the newly arrived, laddu-faced worker. Gill looked back and forth between Kaka and Grewal until realization dawned

---

129   Have you gone sister-fucking insane?

in his eyes. "Panchodeya,"[130] he muttered under his breath. Gill had heard the story of the scar before, as had many of the crew. And Kaka had heard stories equally harrowing and more in return. These stories emerged around campfires under starry skies while sipping whisky, an alchemical procedure which transmutes all traumatic experiences into something lighthearted, entertaining, and even amusing. In fact, so honest was the dialogue among the veterans of Dariush's crew, it was common knowledge that even Silent Rajbir, usually so humble and acquiescent, harboured a near murderous resentment toward thieves, though he had never explained in any detail why.

But stories around the campfire only seem diverting in their effect because nothing can be done about them. These men had divorced themselves from those experiences and now used them as a thing to laugh at because that was the only value to be extracted from them. None had ever been afforded the opportunity to right a wrong committed against them, to change the ending of the story. But now the opportunity had presented itself, and since the men were bonded as brothers, the pain of one of their wounds was imprinted on all their bodies. "Aja, maariye ohnu,"[131] said Gill, but Kaka shook his head, still watching Grewal through the corners of his eyes. A confrontation would lead to justice, but justice was not the ending he wanted from this story. Justice was not thematically resonant. This story must end in the same callous, vicious, and violent way that it began. Kaka wanted revenge. In his mind, he devised a plan.

Meanwhile, inside the city of Abadan, hundreds of Iranians were planning to spend their Saturday evening at the cinema. Screening that evening, at the amply seated Rex Cinema, was *Gavanzha*, The Deer, a seminal film exploring the themes of friendship, loyalty, and redemption, starring the acclaimed Iranian movie star Behrouz Vossughi.

---

130 Sister-fucker.
131 Come on, let's kill him.

Gill approached Rajbir and his new ward. He slapped the hulk on his back, a friendly gesture of camaraderie. Gill was on good terms with everyone. With his characteristic charm, he introduced himself to the new worker. "Grewal? Wadiya, wadiya. Challo, tun mer naal aj raat ohna, raqs vehkan. Nikka jia rivaaz ah,"[132] Gill said pinching his index finger against his thumb. Grewal accepted Gill's offer rather emotionlessly, nodding his head but a single time. Rajbir, the Silent, remained silent, but he furrowed his brows in confusion. He had been a part of Dariush's family for as long as Gill had, and he knew of no such tradition. Gill gave the hulk another slap on the back and said, "Tun mere naal ah palvan ji, Dariush ne gal karni ah."[133] Rajbir shrugged and followed Gill out of Grewal's sight, where Kaka was waiting.

Movie-goers flooded through the doors of the theatre and found their seats, laughing and chatting loudly before the film began. The theatre was located in the working-class district of Abadan, so it was a rare treat for many of the people attending that night to be able to afford a ticket. Those who had come to watch for the first time were eager to see if the film lived up to the hype, and those who had come for a second viewing were there because they knew it did. The chemistry between the lead characters, Seyed and Ghodrat, expressed in the strength of their shared history and the tension of their current situation, was undeniable.

The workday came to an end, and in high spirits Gill came to collect Grewal to make good on his promise. It was a clear night and the humidity was low, so the air was crisp and refreshing. On the edge of town, the last concrete house made way for the first canvas tent, and behind that was an entire commune of debauchery. Gambling, drugs, and prostitution, all hidden in plain sight and ready to pack up at moment's notice. Not that the law ever saw need to flex its

---

132 Grewal, you say? Good, good. Listen, you're going to come with me tonight to watch a belly dance. It's a little tradition we have for newcomers.
133 You come with me, big guy. Dariush wants to talk.

authority here, as those sorts of institutions were recognized as a necessary consequence of liberal progress.

"Eh Amaya ah,"[134] Gill said, introducing Grewal to the dancer he frequented most often. Raven-haired and raven-eyed, she was undeniably beautiful, and she shared with Gill a relationship that was more honest than most marriages, mediated as it was by the almighty dollar. Besides that, she found Gill rather charming, as most people did, and at his request (along with the promise of a healthy tip) she was willing to assist him with nearly anything. With the little Persian that Gill had acquired in his time in Iran, he told Amaya to show the young man a "good time," whatever he wanted, he said, adding a charming little wink. Amaya smiled, nodded, and led the young laddu-faced man into her tent. Gill's easy manner slid away, and he hurried to meet with Kaka and Rajbir, who had been trailing unseen since they left the worksite.

The lights in the cinema had dimmed and the film was well under way. The story was so magnetic that not a soul left their seats. Outside, a group of four men pulled cowls over their faces. Their motivations were clandestine but their plan was simple. They moved around the building with cans of airplane fuel and splashed the walls and floors. When the cans were empty, they convened at the entrance and locked the door, wrapping the handles with steel chains and rebar.

Kaka and Gill approached the flaps of the tent as silently as possible and peeled them back an inch to peek inside. "Ah ki panchode kardeh?"[135] Gill whispered, struggling to comprehend what he was seeing. Grewal was lying prostrate on the ground with his trousers off; Amaya stood above him, swinging the leather tip of a belt repeatedly against his exposed backside. The young man's eyes were closed and he looked to be trembling, not in pain or fear, but in ecstasy. Amaya saw Gill peeking in and took that as her cue. She sat

---

134 This is Amaya.
135 What's this sister-fucker doing?

the young man on his knees and pulled his hands behind his back, reassuring him with gentle coos that he wouldn't regret allowing her to do so. She took the belt and weaved it around his wrists, and then pulled the end tight so the bind was secure. Then she moved in front of him and began to sway her body sensually. Grewal's eyes were locked on her movements, and his cheeks flushed red. Kaka let the flap fall and turned around to wave Rajbir over. He had been briefed about the situation at hand, and more than insisted that he be made a part of the evening's proceedings.

Gavaznha ended in a violent shootout. Both of the lead characters were held up in a building and they chose to face their fates together. In this final act of brotherhood and loyalty, each character was redeemed in his own way, one from a life of crime and theft, and the other from the hollow pursuit of drug use. However, not a soul who entered the cinema on this day would witness this ending. As the audience sat, transfixed by the screen, four matches, lit by four hands, fell to puddles of gasoline on four sides of Rex Cinema.

Rajbir rushed in through the flaps of Amaya's tent. Amaya moved back and Grewal blinked his giant, innocent eyes. Rajbir pulled Grewal to his feet by the throat, squeezing to ensure he didn't call out. Then he dragged him out behind the tent, into the cover of darkness, where Kaka and Gill were waiting. Grewal didn't make a sound, and he showed no emotion when Kaka brought his face close and tilted his head to reveal the scar on the side of it. Gill hissed curses and demanded to know where Grewal kept his stolen goods, but Grewal said nothing. Rajbir slammed his mighty fist into the boy's kidney, driving the air from his lungs, but still not a word. Then Grewal was stripped of his remaining clothing and searched. Amaya found the hidden seam on the inside of Grewal's kameez, and in it they found Kaka's kara and passport, and even now, caught red-handed, the young boy remained quiet. He did not plead, or protest, or cry out, or curse, or even offer an explanation.

Grewal remained silent because he had endured pain for his entire life. It was more familiar to him than anything else. As humiliating and degrading as his punishment was, it affected him not in the slightest. But if for some reason it did, if for some reason he were inclined to scream out, it would have made no difference, because every authority of Abadan was standing outside the towering inferno that had engulfed Rex Cinema. Kaka could have never factored this into his plan, and indeed, he did not care about potential repercussions when he devised it. But serendipitously, the flames on the horizon flickered bright, and like a moth, the country's attention was drawn to the fire, and the fire alone. The universe had declared this an evening of carnage and had orchestrated to make it so. Callousness, viciousness, and violence. Not justice, and certainly not redemption.

Grewal looked ahead placidly.

Kaka and Gill rained their fists down on the boy—brutally, relentlessly.

Between flashes of red, between the fists that crashed against his face, Grewal could see the horizon glowing orange from the fire.

Over four hundred people would perish trying to escape the cinema.

The motivations of the four men who threw the matches would be investigated and argued about for decades to come.

Nobody would ever care what happened to Grewal as his blood soaked into the sand of the Iranian desert.

2008

The Earth's axis is tilted 23.5 degrees. When the tilt leans toward the light of the sun, the soil in the place where I stand softens, the flora thrives, and my father and his father begin to measure out a patch of grass in the backyard of our home. I am not forced to assist as I usually am when there's manual labour to be done. They go silently, and for this reason, I curiously trail after them.

The harvesting season is short in the northern hemisphere. When something is available to you at all times, it can become a tedious enterprise, but if you are limited in your exposure to the same thing, it can become imbued with metaphysical significance. Bapu ji points to a place in the grass and his son drives a stake in to mark the spot.

He is old, my Bapu, and his knees ache. He does not leave the comfort of his bed for frivolous things. He takes hold of the chipped handle of a rusted pickaxe. He raises it above his head and heaves it into the ground. The vibrant green of the manicured lawn is upturned to reveal deep brown soil, moist and teeming with life. My father takes the hoe and begins in the opposite corner.

These two do not speak to each other, ever, and in this activity, it is no different. Words are not exchanged but a different kind of communication is taking place, one mediated by the essence of the earth and the genetic memory of farming in both of their hands. Bapu ji returns to the hundreds of acres he oversaw before he started running, and my father lives the life he would have if he never had to run.

I am acknowledged silently when Bapu ji waves me over and hands me the pickaxe to continue tilling the ground. It resists my first bow, which makes me realize how much power still resides in my Hobbling Guardian's old bones. He doesn't offer any instruction, opting instead to watch me fumble through it, to work harder than necessary, so the effort stays in my mind long after the task is complete.

The earth is tilled, the topsoil is scattered, and with the utmost care we three push our hands into the earth and place the seeds of bygone life: *matar, hari mirch, gajar, tamatar, palak, muli.*[136] When the time for harvest comes, these will be transformed into dishes served alongside home-fermented yogurt made from decades old bacterial cultures, and fresh rolled-rotis. The grocery store carrots never made my mouth water, dull orange and devoid of flavour as they are. But these, near red and so sweet, are as if farmed on another planet.

This process is too difficult for me to understand. Seeds are planted and time moves on, and the seed is fed and shaped by the soil it is in. But it grows by the guidance of a genetic code forged by lives it has never witnessed. The life of the plant is a fragment that surfaces for a brief moment, but its purpose was determined centuries ago. Is the same true of us? Is a human life discretely meaningful or is its purpose tied to something greater, beyond the fragment of time it is permitted to surface?

My father and grandfather move to the front of the house and I witness something even more surreal. My father, a man who handles his body like a battering ram against the universe, carefully curates the bloom of flowers in the garden. I have only seen him apply a violent praxis to the hurdles of life, but here he uses his ever-moving hands with gentle ease. There is no use for the cultivation of flowers but for the

---

136 Peas, birds-eye chilies, carrots, tomatoes, spinach, radish.

beauty they briefly offer, and I have never known this man to cherish beauty. I sense in him an emotion during these moments, something not often seen. He seems remorseful. It is as if he is atoning for something.

In moments of extreme emotion, time stretches out forever, but in moments of quiet contemplation, existence stretches out forever. It is difficult to say which moments are more formative, but this yearly ritual may be an example of both occurring at once. The hatred between father and son is diminished for the short time that the tilted earth faces the sun. Transcendence is achieved through interaction with dirt.

1978

Kaka had developed a taste for Iranian kabobs, though he still opted for the ones made from lamb rather than beef. Conventions had been broken, yes, but there was no reason to brazenly spit on his upbringing. He stood with Gill on Eisenhower Avenue, a few hundred yards away from Shahyad Tower. Having cut their hair, they fit into the crowd more seamlessly than before. Kaka had even purchased some new clothes in the style of the West, shirts with tighter sleeves to keep his kara from falling loose at inopportune moments. He was hoping these changes might have led to the eyes of those pastel-skirt-wearing, Western-educated Iranian women lingering on him longer than before.

But lately, a different atmosphere had fallen over Tehran. The ashes of Rex Cinema had travelled far and wide and had now cast a dark cloud over the nation. It was not clear who set flame to the cinema, but all were eager to place the blame on those they considered enemies. The Shah claimed the act was perpetrated by the most violent of his detractors, and his detractors claimed it was the Shah's secret agents who burned the theatre to drum up anger that could be directed falsely onto them. In any case, the fact that Kaka and Gill no longer stood out in the crowd was a good thing, because in times of turmoil, outsiders are always the first to bear the brunt of blame.

The attitudes and attires of the Westerners previously common in the streets were conspicuously absent now, especially for women, and white faces were nowhere to be seen. Men were out and about and the few women who joined them were clad head to toe in heavy black fabrics. The flow of pedestrians was uniform, moving down the endless presidential road and stopping at the Shahyad Tower. The crowd's common cause was evident from the banners held up displaying the image of a regal man with black eyebrows and a clean white beard. He wore his black turban in the style of Persian nomads, flat on the top with ears unveiled. "Estiqlal, Azadi, Jomhuri-ye Eslami!"[137] cried a group of young men as they passed by Gill and Kaka.

"Ah ki fir baqwas boli jande ah?"[138] Gill said, annoyed at his lunch being disturbed. These sorts of demonstrations had been occurring more and more frequently. Huge swaths of protestors congregated around the Shah's self-congratulatory tower to denounce his westernized concepts of "progress." This was mostly of no concern to Dariush and his crew, but now the animosity toward those who did not appear to be Iranian had been dialled up. Dariush had taken verbal abuse from young, overzealous academics who berated him for not hiring his own kind. They claimed immigrants were stealing the jobs of true-blooded Iranians. Some of the workers who kept their hair and tied peaked turbans in the style of Punjab, such as Rajbir, had left the country. Others, with darker or lighter skin than the general populace, had done likewise. Gill and Kaka were the few remaining. "Challo, vekhiye ki hundeh,"[139] Kaka replied, swallowing the final bite of his lunch, and starting off down the road.

Thousands upon thousands of Iranians crowded before the Shah's tower, erected to mark the 2,500th year since the foundation of the imperial state of Iran. Now it had become

---

137 Independence, Freedom, and the Islamic Republic!
138 What's this bullshit, again?
139 Come on, let's go see what's happening.

a forty-five-metre tuning fork, ringing out a tone that attracted those who detested the Shah and the general excesses of the ruling class. The West and its influence were seen as parasitic by these people, a disease which they thought had infected the Shah. A great irony, for if the West's influence was seen in a more favourable light, perhaps technologies of crowd control which were used against civil rights and anti-war protestors in the Americas would have made their way to Iran. Perhaps then, these Iranian protestors would have been afforded the privilege of facing only rubber bullets and water hoses. Kaka and Gill watched the congregation in astonishment, and both men entertained the idea that perhaps Iran was not the land they were promised and that their journeys did not end here. At midnight, on that day, the Shah would enact a ban on public demonstrations. The next time these people stood in defiance of the king, they would face the carnage of live ammunition.

The Grand Inquisitor Returns

He closes his eyes in Seville, Spain, at the horrible height of the Spanish Inquisition, when fires blazed every day to the glory of God, and now he opens them again in Tehran, Iran, on 8 September 1978. He does not know the reason for his resurrection, but he welcomes it, because for the past five centuries he has been drowning in the burning lakes of hell, so deeply enveloped in flames that he has been forgotten by God. He appears quietly and no one takes note of him, but even still he stalks the streets with a smile of infinite cruelty. His posture still tall and straight, his face still gaunt, his eyes still sunken, but now the glitter of a spark is replaced with the raging fire of a tortured soul. He is donned in his magnificent cardinal's robes, and those who see him, view him as if this is all too appropriate, because the day is his. He is here to view the consequences of his philosophy.

"Still, you refuse to speak to me?" the Grand Inquisitor whispers to the sky. "Still you remain silent? Good, let us together observe the soul of humanity. Let us see that

I was right, so you may remain silent forever." He walks through the city, angry protestors hurdling here and there. He comes to a place called Jaleh Square, where many have congregated, and he reads their signs and listens to their chants, and he looks at the face of the man on their posters. He speaks to the sky again. "What have you brought me here to witness? You think these people are rebels, do you? You think they desire freedom just because they say so? Look at this man whose ideas lead this so-called revolt. His name is Khomeini. His name is different from mine, yes, but his heart is mine and his mind is mine. This man is I, and I am him. He believes as I do that freedom is nothing but a burden, wretched as we are, ignoble as we are, feeble as we are. We possess neither the constitution of body nor spirit to endure the pain of freedom. This Khomeini steps forward as I did to assume that horrible burden, a burden far greater than what you carried. Freedom weighs more than sin ever will. You are too divine to understand, too far away from the reality of us; you are too perfect. But the moisture of your kiss still sits on my bloodless lips, and by that I am made just divine enough, just perfect enough, to be the one to whom these wretched rebels turn to surrender their freedom. The kingdom of Heaven has no entry for their miserable souls. But my kingdom, here on Earth, with earthy bread to spare, has room aplenty. And who in the end is more worthy of praise? You, with your unachievable perfection; or me, whose heart reflects their imperfection? You, who saves only the worthy, the godly; or me, who has saved the vast majority, the unworthy, the wretched and miserable, the sinners? You, who demands piety and nobility in the face of freedom, or me, who provides freedom from the misery of freedom?"

The crowd grows in size in the open square and soon the Grand Inquisitor is surrounded by shouting protestors, and their cries fortify him, because though they may appear to cry for an Independent Iran, he understands that they are

148

crying for him, just as humanity has always cried for him and him alone. On the edges of the square, armoured vehicles with mounted machine guns—the sacrificial fires of the post-industrial age—move around the crowd. "Is this your purpose then? To have me witness death. Me, who burned one hundred blasphemers in a single day and did so in utter ecstasy! Let these men die. Let them go to hell to experience your infinite mercy. You starve them here on Earth and you will burn them afterwards. Still, you do not understand what moves men to action. You know not how much the bread of the earth means to a creature with a ravenous stomach. That is what we are, creatures with ravenous hearts and ravenous bellies, and in your infinite wisdom, you deigned to keep them both empty and you call this freedom. No, I reject your wisdom. I fill their bellies with bread and their hearts with authority, and by giving this I ensure their happiness. You crawled into the alleys of Seville and you stayed there. I entreat you to stay there now, you coward, stay there and remain there, because this day is my day, and these people are my people. I will take their cries for freedom, and I will give them what they truly desire."

A hail of rocks erupts from the crowd and shower down on the police and military personnel. The Grand Inquisitor smiles wider, bearing his decayed teeth. "So, you have brought me back to die again, is that it? Yes, it must be. You have come to learn the pleasure of cruelty, I see. So be it. I will endure your games, but understand that my heart is full knowing you have failed and I have succeeded. Kill me as many times as you wish, I will always return, now as Ruhollah Khomeini, and again afterwards in another mortal form. It matters not what name I take, or what tongue I speak, or what doctrines I espouse. I will always come back, because the minds of human beings are forged for my eternal manipulation. I will always exist as you have always existed, because the consequence of the freedom you grant is singular. When these miserable wretches called human beings are granted an ounce of freedom, they will always come and lay it at the feet of men like me."

The crack of machine gunfire breaks through the shouts of protestors and the cries for freedom are transformed into cries for life. One bullet leaves the barrel of a soldier's rifle, and as if divinely ordained, it finds the single unobstructed path through the limbs and heads of thousands of protestors to kiss the lips of the Grand Inquisitor, just where he was kissed five centuries prior.

1978

The exact casualty count of "Black Friday" has never been accurately assessed. Some historians marked the number in the hundreds; others in the thousands. Whatever the case may have been, the event was universally recognized as a pivotal moment in the Iranian Revolution, crystalizing the rebel cause and destroying any chance of peaceful reconciliation. In the months following the massacre at Jaleh Square, Kaka remained holed up in the hotel conference room with Gill and the remaining members of Dariush's crew. As the weeks went by, they had been dwindling to fewer and fewer numbers. Dariush himself had stopped accepting new contracts, partly because there were none, but also because the country's workers, led by the oil refinery industry, had begun a mass strike. Since the Shah's soldiers opened fire on the protestors, the city had descended into chaos. Skirmishes between the most militant rebels and the military were breaking out throughout the city and unwitting pedestrians were being caught in the crossfire.

Kaka was sitting cross-legged on his cot, deep in thought. He was earning good money here in Iran, but the sociopolitical situation seemed too tumultuous to be sorted out in any short time. Even if it was resolvable quickly, it was growing more unlikely by the day that the side sympathetic to his residency in Iran would win out. They waited for Dariush, who had informed them that he had news. When he entered the room, he appeared dishevelled, tired, worn out. He was of the land; his blood was the same as the blood that was spilled on the square and was still being spilled on the streets. Once apathetic to the political jockeying between the Shah and his ideological enemies, he was now sympathetic to the rebellion and supported the worker's strike. But he was a man of conscience, so he cared for the outcast family he had created. When he spoke to other Iranians, he knew this place was no longer safe for outsiders. "Ithon nikil jao,"[140] he said in his flawless Punjabi.

It was distressing news for the group to be sure but not surprising. Most had already made arrangements to return to their homes and now they packed what remained of their scattered belongings into bags that they could carry on their backs. Only Kaka remained seated. Gill nudged his friend. "Khatham hogya yaar, challo, vapas challiye."[141] The words sounded as though they were spoken by Shinda, but Gill was not the Lubani. His will was much stronger. He merely lacked the imagination to overcome this challenge. But Kaka had no intention of turning back. He approached Dariush, whose respect he had earned many times over now—with the mastery of new skills and with the iron-clad determination to complete a task no matter how difficult. "Mein ni vapas jana,"[142] he said to Dariush, just as he had said to Shinda at the bus stop in Afghanistan. Back then, it was spoken out of naivety and youthful hubris, with no knowledge of how dangerous unknown paths were, but now he spoke with more authority because he had tangible experience of the unknown and had proved himself capable of meeting its challenge. Dariush had deep bags under his eyes and the eyes themselves were almost completely red. His mind was pulled in several directions by the cords of potential futures for his

140 Get out of here.
141 It's over, man. Come on, let's go home.
142 I'm not going back.

country, but even in this state, the fire of a determined heart cheered him up. He smiled, clapped Kaka on the shoulder, and said, "Nahi, vapas ni. Tun agay ja!"[143]

Meanwhile, the Shah watched the developments in his country in horror. With the closing of the oil industry, his legs had effectively been cut out from under him. The protestors' chants, once banal proclamations for an Independent Iran, had shifted violently to cries of "Death to America," and "Death to the Shah." Like the immigrants who came to Iran to share in the Shah's vision, the Shah himself now began to look for ways out of his own country. Ruhollah Khomeini finally rose from his seat in Naraj, Iraq, and inched his way back to his people.

Dariush told Kaka and Gill to stay put as he lobbied his various connections in government to attain visas out of Iran. A process that usually takes months was shortened to weeks, though it still felt an eternity to Kaka and his restless limbs. Much of the time was passed by playing Bhabi with a worn-out deck of cards (a miserably uninteresting game to play with only two participants), throwing pebbles at cockroaches scurrying through the room, and eating hotel meals which made Kaka look back on his experience of starvation in a gentler light. Finally, Dariush kept his promise. "Turkey thani, Bulgaria nikil jao. Fir tusin goriyan de desh paunch jana,"[144] he explained as he handed Turkish visas to Kaka and Gill. Never one to say more than needed, he offered his departing advice without sentiment. "Tusi tej haigey ah, sara kush patha tuhanu. Kam karo jor naal. Zindagi jeeyo wadiya."[145]

Not long after, Kaka and Gill sat on a bus approaching the Turkish border. As the front wheel of the bus rolled past

---

143 No, you're not going back. You're going forward!
144 Go through Turkey and get through to Bulgaria. Then you'll be in the white man's land.
145 You're both quick studies, and you know your business. Work hard. Live good lives.

the chain-link fence that marked the division of countries, the front wheel of the Shah's private plane lifted from the tarmac of the Tehran Airport. Attaining the historically unique moniker, "the Last Shah of Iran," he would go on to find a home among the ancient pharaohs of the fertile crescent, fittingly, the land where dead kings erected the greatest monuments in the world to honour themselves. Mohammed Reza Pahlavi would never step foot in his country again.

Two weeks later, Toronto-born journalist Peter Jennings sat with the world's press aboard an Air France flight to Tehran. When the mic reached his hands, he asked, "Ayatollah, would you be so kind as to tell us how you feel to be back in Iran?" The question was answered by Khomeini's aide, Sadegh Ghotbzadeh, who responded, "Hichi." He feels nothing.

Shortly after Gill and Kaka left, Shahyad Tower and Eisenhower Avenue were renamed *Azadi*, which means freedom. A pregnant idea, one which attracted ambitious minds across the continent to meet and to cooperate, to build something more than was thought possible, was aborted. An experiment, which sought to prove that in a historically lagging geography an empire could be created to rival any of those in the developed world, was cut short. The noble virtues of the human spirit that strove toward these ends, were overcome by the vices of the human spirit, and the dream, which was too fragile to begin with, shattered under the pressure of our corrupted nature. In place of new life flourishing, blood was spilled. Babylon was not to be reborn.

Promised Lands

1978-1979

The Bosporus Strait, which connects the Black Sea to the Sea of Marmara and splits Asian Anatolia from European Turkey, produces two currents. The major flow moves from the larger Black Sea westward into the Sea of Marmara, but deeper down, a heavier saline countercurrent flows in the opposite direction. On the bank of the Bosporus, The Hagia Sophia sits majestically with its four pillars piercing the sky, oscillating between its historical designations of mosque and church. Secular by name, but as Kaka wanders the alleys of the Grand Bazaar, whispers of "Kafir"[146] trailed behind him. Kaka had had enough of nations that could not decide what they were. He continued north.

The Byzantian architecture persisted but the faces paled. Kaka fell asleep in a train station in Sofia, Bulgaria, and a police baton slapped on the floor in front of him. "Sŭbudete se! Ne mozhete da spite tuk."[147] He awoke and moved on. Next, he went into the regions of the southern Slavs, held together in a tenuous collaboration called Yugoslavia, where white-skinned people had devoted themselves to the cause of proving that they were just as capable of hating one another as brown-skinned people were.

---

146 Unbeliever.
147 Wake up! You cannot sleep here.

Then further into the eastern bloc, the rounded domes against city skylines retreated in favour of the needling spires of the gothic era. Budapest during the Hungarian thaw, "the Happiest Barracks," yet far from happy. The disgruntled disposition of the populace found a metaphor in most of the cars on the road, rusted and sputtering black fumes into the air as they reluctantly groaned toward their destination.

As he moved further north, the climate turned more frigid and when he stepped onto the stone streets of Prague's Old Town, for the first time in his life Kaka found cause to purchase a heavy winter coat. It was nearing the end of the year and here in the land of Christian devotees, one would expect lavish celebrations in honour of their messiah's birth. Christmas was ostensibly the happiest day of the year for the Western world, yet no such celebrations appeared to be taking place. Alone and in the quiet, Kaka stood in the orange glow of the streetlights and pulled the collars tight around his neck and stared up at the black silhouette of the cross atop Tyn Church, thinking his private thoughts.

Through this entire journey, not a single cent was earned. Opportunities for outsiders were nonexistent. The only value extracted was in the realization that there were a few universal declarations, which if learned, would allow one to exist among people of any tongue: "Which way?" "How much?" and "Toilet?" An additional culture shock struck Kaka. Moving from place to place and viewing the minimalistic and generally deprived standard of most people's lives, he realized that perhaps Dariush saw the world outside his own through rose-tinted glasses, and that Maher's stories about "the glory of the white man" were nothing more than nostalgic embellishments. Because these people walked with the familiar posture of those who had been pushed down upon for too long—they were too slow to smile, and the echoes of laughter were too absent from the narrow stone streets.

The adage of green grass always being where you are not was proving particularly true at that moment. How could it be, Kaka wondered, that the people who had erected such magnificent buildings and durable roads were the same ones as those who silently shuffled through the streets, peering suspiciously at strangers? He knew what pressures had pushed down upon Punjab to make the people so, and he had watched in real time the pressures which transformed the people of Afghanistan and Iran, but here he had stumbled upon the outcomes of a mysterious history—a confluence of war and ideology—the roots of which sprung from the Red Mother in the north. We need not linger on this history, because Kaka was only passing through, and this was merely a passing thought, but the impression of those frozen paradises would linger in his memory for many years.

1997-2012

The Teachers' Union of Ontario declared a strike! We pick up with our hero in an old house in the forgotten suburbs of the Greater Toronto Area, where vagabonds and layabouts abound. Der Vater was in his element, deep in the process of restoring a dilapidated thing through the movement of his hands and the application of his mind, and Young Nanak— six years old, let's say—was far out of his element, forced to labour under the authoritarian eye of a more competent being than himself. His task was to paint the baseboards that had been freshly installed by Der Vater—a hopeless endeavour. Young Nanak was a notorious scribbler, you see, incapable of keeping things within lines and boundaries. His colouring books were ghastly, and his returned geography mapping assignments permanently resisted the coveted top marks in whatever form they took (the As, the 4s, and the 80+s). The First Man shook his head at Young Nanak's shoddy, perfunctory work, for the First Man's geography mapping assignments were impeccable and his colouring books a marvel of steady-handed proficiency.

The hour for lunch arrived and passed. No one said a thing; all were busy at work. All but Young Nanak who was silently aghast. He knew Der Vater was hungry, so why weren't they stopping to eat? It was unconscionable! Nanak dreamt of Adam's Paradise—the sweet, naked garden with gastronomic delights galore—but instead, he received Adam's dictum, which said he shan't receive his dinner from the benevolence of Der Vater. Young Nanak devised a plan, a strategy to move the day's focus from the work at hand to a fresh hot meal. Taking inspiration from the Teachers' Union of Ontario, he marched up to Der Vater and proclaimed, "I'm going on strike!" At first, it seemed to have the desired effect; Der Vater lowered the paint roller in his hand and stared down at Young Nanak. But no, a hitch in the plan! Der Vater was not as gutless as the government, and he wouldn't be cowed by the political manoeuvrings of an unexceptional six-year-old, whose skills as a baseboard painter were as wanting as the teaching skills of a member of the Ontario Teachers' Union. "Panchode, mein tenu dusdein strike ki hundi ah."[148] Der Vater said darkly, "Ja, baseboard nu paint kar. Aj asi roti li ni rukna."[149]

The battle was lost. Nanak's stomach remained empty, growling at him angrily as if to ask, "How could you let this happen to us?" But the young revolutionary remembered the pain of that day. Humbled but not defeated, Nanak lay in wait like a snake in the tall grass. When he came of age, he attended an institute of higher learning and filled his fangs with potent venoms: discourses, deconstructions, critiques, treaties, essays. He became proficiently trained in the art of explaining complex political and philosophical theories he didn't understand in language more abstruse than originally presented. He rehearsed his arguments with Teaching Assistant Lindsay G., who wore the attire of the working class—$16 Old Navy leggings that accentuated her plump thighs and sturdy buttocks (the lower abdomen of the proletariat)—and she nodded along, not daring to admit that she, too, had no deep understanding of the course-mandated content she was required to teach. Now, he was older, more articulate, stronger, and eye to eye with Der Vater. The war was not yet lost, and the worker's revolution still lived on!

---

148 I'll show you a sister-fucking strike.
149 Go paint the baseboard. We're not stopping for lunch today.

Now, transformed into a man—and also evolved from the third person to the first—I come into the kitchen where Das Kapitalist is seated for lunch. Years have passed but still the baseboards are shabbily painted, still my stomach growls in anger, and still, I have the flame of a lazy heart burning deep in my chest. I gather his attention and he assaults me with a familiar and violent look. But I am steadfast, for I've already eaten and there is nothing he can deprive me of. Without fear of consequence, I lay out the case, so obvious, so clear: "Don't you see? The dialectic that Hegel originated of the Master and Slave dichotomy is brought to its zenith with the work of Marx, and the true material manifestation of the Hegelian synthesis can be nothing but the Marxist 'Classless State.' This is no utopian dream, good sir, but the necessary outcome of the evolution of economic systems. It is freedom incarnate. It is the emancipation of the masses!"

How many times had I listened as Der Vater expounded his love of the German nation, the efficiency, the workmanship, and yes, even the sublime beauty! A mysterious infatuation brought out in the most peculiar of situations, sitting with whisky glass in hand in front of the soft roar of a fire, with a cracking sentimentality permeating his voice. Speaking as though the place were a lost love or some such thing… Well, given all that, is it any surprise that I expected him to wholly embrace the Deutschland's greatest philosopher! But no, just the opposite! Der Vater lowers his head and shakes it, as if I'm exhausting him. Can you imagine? Me with the revelation of a century and he is uninterested.

He shoves a hearty bite of an aloo paratha into his mouth and says, "Menu koi panchode Marx Morx da ni patah, par jithon tak mein vekhya, banday kam karkay nahi raazi."[150] Before I am able to rebut, he raises a condescending finger to prevent me from speaking, and then he takes another bite and continues. "Aapne val vekh. Tun apne bed tak vi ni

---

150   I don't know about this sister-fucking Marx guy, but as far as I've seen, people are not eager to work.

banonda. Koi kam vi karn nu raazi nahi hega."[151] The most bourgeoisie of concerns! How could I ever explain to him the liberated chaos of a free mind that desires—nay yearns—for an untidy bedroom! Of course, I cannot, so I allow him to continue. He picks up the fresh paratha on his plate and, as if to taunt the exploited workers of the world, waves the thing in front of my face. "Bas, ik bhukh kam karondi ah, fir vi bohat saray lok khushi naal bhukay mar jaande ah."[152]

So my protestations fall on deaf ears. He has said his piece and he has offered guerilla logic born of that pesky, inarguable thing called "life experience." It's simply too much for me to overcome. I put down my hammer and sickle that day and resign myself to live the life of a good Canadian citizen, like my comrades, the educators, the members of the Ontario Teachers' Union, to perform my work half-heartedly and to complain relentlessly to anyone willing to listen. The final lesson here should be spelled out clearly for those not paying attention: never bother a hungry man when he is working, and never bother a working man when he is eating.

---

151 Look at yourself, you won't even make your bed in the morning. You're unwilling to put the slightest effort toward anything.
152 Only a person's hunger will motivate them to work, and too many people are happy to starve before they lift a finger.

1979

Charlotte Dietrich was born on August 13, 1959. On her first birthday she blinked her cherub-like hazel eyes at her father, Wolfgang Dietrich, as he hammered a nail into a floorboard beneath the kitchen dining table. On her second birthday, with her lovely golden curls bouncing up and down, she waddled next to Herr Dietrich because he had agreed to take her to the sweetshop down the road for ice cream, a gesture of parental love that would prove to be an exceedingly rare occurrence. But even in this instance, dear Charlotte was tragically barred from getting her ice cream. As she waddled toward the sweetshop, a man in a long grey coat with rifle slung over his shoulder stopped them. "Kehre Sie um. Die Mauer wird hier gebaut,"[153] he said, and with no argument Herr Dietrich collected his daughter and turned around. Over her father's shoulder, she saw another man hauling a cinder block to the centre of the road.

Wolfgang had a secret nobody knew and he wanted to make sure no one found out, which is why he put up no fight and turned around quickly. He especially wanted to make sure that the *Ministerium für Staatsicherheit* didn't find out his secret. His secret was hidden beneath the floorboard of the dining table in his kitchen and took the form of a pair of smart black

---

153 Turn back. The wall is being built here.

shorts and a beige shirt, and most secretive of all, a red-and-white striped armband with a sharp black swastika printed on it. It was a souvenir from the happiest time in Wolfgang's life, when he served as an *Obersharfuhrer* in the *Hitlerjugend* of the glorious Third Reich. Wolfgang had a seething hatred for Communists, as he was taught under the kind guidance of his instructors. He hated them even more because when Marshal Georgy Zhukov and his men broke the German lines and entered Berlin on that cool spring morning all those years ago, they lined his entire troop up against a brick wall and summarily executed them. Wolfgang survived because he was urinating behind a tree, the greatest regret of his life, for if his bladder were even slightly more voluminous, he would have died a hero instead of being a lone survivor of a lost war, burgeoned with taxes, a mortgage, and the lacklustre responsibilities of parenthood. Now Herr Dietrich remained quiet, and he clenched his jaw and grinded his teeth, and when he was spoken to, his eyes flicked involuntarily toward the floorboard under the kitchen dining table.

Charlotte learned to ride a bike and the cinder blocks were stacked to the height of a full-grown man. She came into the kitchen and said, "Papa, ich habe Fahrradfahren gelernt!"[154] and Herr Dietrich clenched his jaw and flicked his eyes toward the floorboard. Charlotte got the top marks on her high school math examination and the cinder blocks were replaced with large grey cement slabs the height of three men. She came into the kitchen and said, "Papa, ich habe die Bestnoten bekommen!"[155] and Herr Dietrich clenched his jaw and flicked his eyes toward the floorboard. Charlotte got a job at the neighbourhood coffee shop and the wall had barbed wire running along the top and the guards held the leashes of growling German shepherds. She came into the kitchen and said, "Papa, wo ist meine Schürze?"[156] and Herr

---

154 Papa, I learned to ride a bike!
155 Papa, I got the best marks!
156 Papa, where is my apron?

Dietrich clenched his jaw and flicked his eyes toward the floorboard. Her apron was on the hook by the front door. Charlotte put it on and walked to the coffeeshop, her curly golden hair bouncing up and down, her hazel eyes blinking against the sun. She had an insatiable craving for ice cream and a mysterious attraction to men she was unable to communicate with.

Now entered our protagonist. Now with a little money in his pocket and more on the horizon. Now with bell-bottomed jeans and trimmed ebony locks flapping in the wind. Now with wide shirt collars flared and buttons unbuttoned to reveal a virile, hairy chest, toned by countless hours of manual labour. Now with the freewheeling sexual liberation of seventies American Rock 'n' Roll in the air. He entered a café; it was empty except for the blond with hazel eyes whose lovely curls bounced when she turned to look at him. He sat. She approached. He waved his hands stupidly before him while mouthing the word for coffee in languages he'd learned, none of which were German. She smiled charmingly and slowly enunciated, "kaffee." He had the smell of forged steel and Iranian kabobs, and she, the smell of vanilla, nutmeg, and German efficiency.

"Eiscreme?"[157] she asked, and he—not knowing at all what he was agreeing to—nodded vigorously. She brought him a scoop and watched him eat, biting her lips in desperate restraint as the sweet dessert plopped from the cone into the hairy musculature of his manly cleavage. His eyes rose slowly to meet hers. Time lapsed. They were both in freefall now, the hallucinogenic effects of desire and attraction dizzying their brains. Oxytocin, serotonin, and dopamine smacked against their skulls like a boxer's flurry. Paris and Helen, Romeo and Juliet, Heer and Ranjha, and now Kaka and Charlotte. The torrid love affair followed the pattern of those of yore. Set against the decayed backdrop of post-war, Soviet-controlled East Berlin, the doomed lovers licked each other's ice-cream

---

157   Ice cream?

cones in every square inch of Kaka's discount hotel room, oblivious to the inevitable *Diabolus ex Machina* that would tear them apart forever.

So it was, that fifteen years after one US. president declared in his nasally, transatlantic accent, "Ich bin ein Berliner!", and nine years before another shouted for all the world to hear, "Mr. Gorbachev, tear down this wall!", Kaka walked down a street in East Berlin. Already he had acquired enough experiences that would bestow him with a lifelong infatuation with Germany, but greedily he pined for more. He was headed to a bank to withdraw money for ice cream with Charlotte, but the bank he was going to was a peculiar one, one that was built into a peculiar wall...

2004

A brief intermission to our story of lovers. Astute readers will have noticed, no doubt, my slippery avoidance of speaking plainly on the topic of "rumbling and tumbling," or of "belly dancing," or of the "eating of ice cream." If you're still unclear about what I'm talking about, let me try another euphemism. Channelling the striking iconography of the 1967 Flower Child, allow me to suggest, "Sticking your flower stem in the almighty gun barrel." Too confusing? I admit, I can see how it could be, with all the antiwar baggage such an image conjures, not to mention the whole "flower" metaphor resting on, shall we say, the opposite foot here in the West. But it's an apt one for Eastern outlook, for there the flower belongs to the possessor of the flappy parts! And woe to him who sullies the sanctity of his flower stem by shoving it into gritty, carbon-ridden gun barrels. Not to mention dangerous! For the wrong gun barrel, not properly oiled, or shoddily assembled, might blow not only your stem apart, but the whole of the petal as well! —All right, perhaps this analogy has reached the limits of its usefulness. Let me try something else.

Familial movie watching is a difficult thing in the homestead. Western movies are strictly off limits. The risk of the aforementioned topic coming up unexpectedly or being spoken about casually is too great. Greater still is the risk of an actual depiction of "rumbling and tumbling", "belly dancing", or "eating of ice cream." Bollywood was safer up to a point, but they've become precipitously less wholesome lately. I blame the sultry gazes and suggestive hip thrusts of the early aughts starlets, including but not limited to Aishwarya Rai, Priyanka Chopra, and Bipasha Basu. But, of course, the case could be made that the industry completed its moral bankruptcy with its embrace of Sunny Leone, that wholly Canadian-born purveyor of smut. I shall not be too harsh on her though, for at least she had the decency to conceal her Sikh heritage beneath a plausible, spaghetti Western alias...

All right, I think I've had enough of this. No more beating around bushes; let's just get right into the beating of the actual bush we're after here. SEX! My, how liberating to just come out and say it. A breakthrough for me really, as many brown-skinned readers may be able to relate, the universal response to any reference, conversation, depiction, or portrayal of sex in my youth was unequivocally—"Challo, band karo bakwas!"[158] A young Caucasian couple getting too comfortable at the park—"Challo, band karo bakwas!" Pouty lips and fluttering eyelids foreshadowing the inevitable on the tubular TV screen—"Challo, band karo bakwas!" The vigorous thrusting and panting one is bound to witness as they pass a dog park—"Challo, band karo bakwas!"

In fact, so averse was my family to discussions of sex, that I was incapable of introducing Lindsay F. to any of my relatives throughout the entire course of our relation. "But whyyyy Nick?" She would whine, "Whyyy can't we just go hang out at your place?" I might have replied, "Well, of course, Lindsay F., just as soon as the Viper and my Hobbling Guardian have met your grandparents to discuss the particulars of our life together, vetted your extended family and their medical histories, and I've received a dowry equivalent to the approximate cost of three dairy cows, then you're more than welcome to snuggle up on the couch next to me

---

158 Go on, shut down this nonsense!

to watch the tubular television." But I did not say that, for I was not keen to subject the mating rituals of my peoples to Lindsay F.'s scrutinizing Western liberal eye. However, wary as I was in bringing members of the opposite sex into the homestead for fear of offending ancient customs; paradoxically, there exists a certain point (incapable of being isolated by any living being) where the instruction of every Punjabi grandmother switches from "Kuriyan taun bach ke rahein!" to "Koi changi ji kudi ghar ley ah!"[159] Nobody knows when this switch occurs but because of it, for much of my youth, I wallowed in a state of sexual quantum indeterminacy—Schrödinger's cat battling the dangling vial of horniness!

So given all that, can you imagine the excitement, the anticipation, the thrill in Nanak's thirteen-year-old heart when Der Vater agreed to install an eggshell-white Dell XPS Desktop computer, preloaded with Windows 2000, in the privacy of the bedroom I shared with the First Man! How my heart flutters even now as I think back to that sweet, screeching dial tone loading up the America Online Internet service, listening for creaks in the floor that might indicate someone approaching my precariously lockless bedroom door, clicking the mouse on the blue-green pixelated globe of Internet Explorer, and the clacking of the keyboard as I Ask Jeeves with nauseating elation to "show me boobs and girl butts." (Though my memory is hazy on this, Young Nanak might also have typed "cartoon" in there somewhere, because the idea of real life, flesh- and-blood boobies and girl butts were entirely too overwhelming for his young mind to process. The midwife, no doubt, would have claimed such depravity was the direct result of my name being inspired by something as inauspicious as a cartoon cereal mascot, but her knowledge on such topics far exceeds my own.)

What happened next you ask? The flappy part loses its elasticity! This may be a medical emergency; I should inspect

---

159 "Stay away from those harlots!" to "Get off your ass and bring a nice girl home!"

by feeling around down there... Yes, all right, everything seems to be in order. A few more minutes of harmless, innocent medical examination and—Oh my! What's this? It bleeds! No, Sweet Mata Tripta, such a heavenly feeling! Keep your secrets Guru Granth Sahib! Stay tucked in your bedsheets and bathing towels, I've found Nirvana here between my legs! Ahem—excuse me, sometimes I get carried away in my reminiscing. What I mean to say is simply that Doctor Sahib, Nanak has healed the loss of flexibility of his flappy part, a medical miracle, of course, and cause for celebration.

But now Young Nanak must clean up the operating site. Spillages and the like were unavoidable, you see. So, I stood and peeked out of the door. The coast was clear. To the bathroom down the hall! But before I reached the destination, he saw me! The highest highs are met with the lowest lows. There was the holy portrait of Guru Nanak, raising his mighty right hand—the hand which pushed into and imprinted the boulder at the Gurdwara Panja Sahib, demonstrating his divine power—as my hand dripped with the sticky residue of my shame. It burned as when I touched the iron, a cursed sinful limb it was, compelled to torment me. And those placid, serene eyes on the canvas locked on to my soul, to say, "Bole So Nihal, Sat Sri Akal!"[160] and I sneaked about like a vagrant! A scarring experience to say the least, the trauma of that day has cemented itself in my psyche. His eyes haunt me still, for from that day forth, I have conducted all my medical examinations with my left hand.

Challo, band karo bakwas!

---

160 Shout aloud in ecstasy! Truth is God!

The Wall

K. walked down the alley toward the bank that abutted The Wall. His mind was thinking about Charlotte and other pleasant things. It was just to be a quick stop to sort out his finances and to withdraw some loose bills to purchase ice cream. The guard outside the bank had prominent features, a large brow and a dimpled chin, and his helmet rested comically far on the back of his head. He didn't acknowledge K. as he entered the bank.

The bank itself was peculiar, K. thought, because one side of the room, the one where he stood, was much larger than the other side. And on the other end of the room there was a door, but it was not large enough to allow a man to pass through standing. One would have to crawl on their knees to pass through that door. It invited the question: What purpose could such a door serve? All in all, a peculiar bank indeed. K. approached the bank teller.

"Hello," said the teller, "How can I help you?"

"You speak my language?" K. replied, astonished.

"Of course. We speak the language of our customers," the teller said.

"And what language is that?" K. asked, skeptical that such a claim could be true.

"The language you are speaking, sir," the teller replied. He appeared to be growing irritable now, and K., not looking to make a fuss, and eager to leave so he could purchase some ice cream with Charlotte, left the point alone. He went about withdrawing some money and, once the teller had handed K. his bills, he turned to leave.

"Oh, you can't leave through that door," the teller warned. He pointed to the narrow side of the room, toward the door that looked as though you had to crawl through to exit, "You must take that exit there."

"But why?" K. protested.

"Sir, it is the bank's policy that a person who has withdrawn the number of bills that you have needs to take that exit there."

"What sense does that policy make?" K. said angrily. He wasn't keen on crawling on his knees as he had just had his trousers washed, and he had no idea where such an exit would place him. Charlotte was just down the street from the larger exit and that's the exit that he entered from!

"Sir, I cannot debate the bank's policy with you. If you refuse to depart through the correct exit, I will have to call the guard," the teller warned. K. was incredulous but he did not want to fall into any kind of legal trouble. Afterall, he was in a strange country where people did not speak his language.

K. began walking toward the narrow side of the bank, and the ceiling began grazing against his head, and the walls began grazing against his shoulders. It was smaller than he had imagined and by the time K. had reached the door, he was crawling on his belly. There were no handles or doorknobs and it stayed stubbornly in place when he pushed on it, so he resorted to knocking, but there was such little room he had to awkwardly pull his arm back and jab at the door like a boxer.

The door creaked open and light poured in from the other side. Relieved beyond measure, K. crawled through and found himself in a setting not dissimilar from the one on the other side of the bank. Encouraged he could find his way back, he turned around and was immediately dismayed. K. was standing before a wall that was the height of three men and extended as far as the eye could see in either direction!

There was a guard, likely the one who had opened the door for K., standing against the wall. He had prominent features, a large brow and a dimpled chin, and a helmet that rested comically far on the back of his head. In fact, he appeared to be precisely the same guard who stood outside the larger entrance of the bank.

"Excuse me," K. said, approaching the guard, "How do I make my way back to the other entrance of the bank?"

The guard, not moving his head to look at K., replied, "The other entrance is on the other side of The Wall, and there is no crossing The Wall." How could such a thing be true, K. thought. He had just crossed the wall and he needed to get back quickly. Charlotte was likely already waiting at the sweetshop for him.

"Excuse me, but I need to go back through that door. I need to get to the street on the other side of the bank," K. said urgently.

The guard slammed his rifle butt on the floor in frustration. "Sir, you can't cross The Wall! It is the rule. So, it must be the case that you couldn't have crossed The Wall to begin with, so you must always have been on this side of The Wall. But if by some illegal manner, you've crossed The Wall once, then you certainly can't cross The Wall again. It would be unthinkable!"

"Sir," K. said calmly. "It was you yourself that opened that door, was it not?" K. asked, pointing to the little door he had crawled through. The guard nodded. "So, it was you yourself that allowed me to cross the wall."

"That door is reserved for bank clients who have withdrawn a particular number of banknotes. There is no other way to exit through that door. Its function is not related to The Wall," the guard explained. As he spoke, his helmet fell even further back on his head, exposing an abnormally large forehead.

"What on earth are you talking about?" K. yelled. "How can a door in a wall not have any relation to the wall in which it is placed?" The guard stared at him blankly. "Never mind that then, how many banknotes do I need for you to open that door again?" K. inquired.

"Sir, I cannot discuss the bank's policy with you. If you would like to ask these sorts of questions, you'll need to go back and talk to the teller," the guard replied.

"Yes, that's fine," K. said eagerly. "How do I get back there?"

To which the guard replied threateningly, "You. Can. Not. Cross. The. Wall."

K. backed away, distraught. He found a bench on the side of the road and sat down, collapsing his face into his hands. This was a catastrophe. Why had he listened to that horrid bank teller in the first place? He should have just run back through the larger entrance, policy be damned!

"Hey," whispered the man seated next to him, "Hey, I heard you arguing with the guard over there. Look, you're better off on this side of The Wall. That other side of The Wall is a damned mess. I say you're better off over here." K. straightened up and surveyed the whisperer. He wore a trench coat and a wide-brimmed hat that sat low across his face, making him appear conspicuous. K. strained his sight to try and see the man more clearly and he thought he saw eyes that were black and bulging, like a beetle or insect might have, and was that a moustache or were those feelers? "Hey," the whisperer whispered again, "Hey look, if you want to get out of here so badly, and I don't know why you would, I can tell you how."

"How?" K. inquired.

"You can go to the train station and get a train to Frankfurt," the whisperer informed him, "But I don't know why you would bother, it's much preferable here."

"I don't need to get to Frankfurt," K. cried. "I just need to get on the other side of that damned wall."

"You can't get to the other side of The Wall, man. You're better off here, I say," the whisperer said.

"Are you mad? You just told me I could get to Frankfurt. That's certainly on the other side of the wall!" K. shouted. He was growing angry now.

"Look, here's the long and short of it. There's no way you can get on the other side of The Wall, because you can't go from west to east. But you can go to Frankfurt, because then you'd be going from west to west." The whisperer explained.

K. took a deep breath and pointed at The Wall, "Look there. That's west. I just need to go west far enough to get on the other side of that wall."

"Are you even listening to me, man? That's east! Everything on the other side of The Wall is east. Except Frankfurt. Frankfurt is west enough that it's truly and properly west. Do you see now? Though like I said, I don't know why you'd bother. Just stay here. It's better here, I say." The whisperer finished and stood. The sleeves of his coat fell flat as it seemed there were no limbs to fill them, and the coat bulged around the midriff as if the whisperer had an abnormally large ribcage. K. was perplexed. He watched the whisperer float away as if he walked on tiny little legs instead of the legs of a full-grown man.

K. stood and began walking toward the train station. He was deeply confused about what had just transpired, but one thing was certain beyond certain—Frankfurt was preferable to this place.

1979

Ah ki kut khana si?"[161] Gill inquired, seated on a train speeding toward Frankfurt. I must admit, I am inclined to agree with him, for even with the assistance of this all-omniscient hindsight, it's difficult to make head or tail of that peculiar monument called The Wall. What was the point, after all? How could brick and mortar ever have succeeded in sealing in the slippery, fleshy vessels that are human bodies? Or perhaps it's simpler than I'm making it out to be (as things usually are). Perhaps, it's not so peculiar that people with certain beliefs want to wall themselves off from those with differing ones. Perhaps, what's more peculiar is that there are not *more* walls.

In any case, this particular wall holds a position of significance in my mind, for were it not for what transpired there, I, your humble narrator, might well have been relating this tale in German, and I might well have inherited Charlotte Dietrich's hazel eyes and lovely blonde curls, instead these woefully monochromatic features centred toward the middle of my face (albeit more intelligently than my father's are centred toward his). I imagine that some aspects of my childhood would have been greatly improved were this the case. At the least, there might have been fewer occasions in which Der Vater oddly inserted his dewy-eyed admiration for Germany

---

161 What the dog-fuck was that?

into a conversation where it didn't belong. Although, on the other hand, I'm not sure that old jaw-grinding Nazi, Wolfgang Dietrich, would have been preferable as a grandfather to my sweet, Hobbling Guardian. But enough of hypotheticals. Bygones are bygone. Now let's return our attention to the man of the hour—Gill.

You were wondering where he was this whole time, no doubt. An oversight on my part, one I will remedy now, posthaste. Picture this—retroactively if you will—in all Kaka's exploits from Turkey to Berlin, imagine Gill in the periphery somewhere, chewing on an orange wedge, for that is what he was doing. The train rattled toward Frankfurt and Gill chewed his orange wedge, trying in vain to cheer up his friend Kaka, who had just experienced his first real heartbreak.

"Oye, oulu de pathe, German vich agey asi!"[162] Gill said, tossing an orange peel at Kaka's head. Kaka returned a forlorn look: the wretched glance of lost wanderers, a dead-eyed, pitiful stare, like a child's when the last shred of innocence is torn from them. There's no Santa Claus, Easter Bunny, or Tooth Fairy. All the magic of your youth was naught but easy lies uttered by lazy parents. And now add this to this list as well: the most passionate love you'll ever experience will one day crumble in your hands like a piece of calcified horseshit.

Gill tried again to lift Kaka's spirits, wiggling his eyebrows up and down, saying, "Sir chak le, yaar, hor vi Charlottean hon giyan!"[163] but to no avail. Kaka sighed and returned his forehead to its resting place against the rattling train window. He stared listlessly at the passing landscapes, remembering how lovely the combined smell of nutmeg and vanilla was. So be it, Gill decided. He wouldn't allow another's dour mood to spoil the rising swell of anticipation in his heart as the skyline of Frankfurt came into view.

He had come a long way. Quite literally farther than Kaka, as Ludhiana was farther to the east than Amritsar. But in a

---

162 Hey, you sunova-owl, we made it to fucking Germany!
163 Lift your head up, pal, there'll be other Charlottes!

more important sense, he'd managed to cross an unbridge-able delta, an imaginary geography designed by the narrow-est outlook of the human mind, and which operates like prison for those who are placed inside. Most never attempt to escape. Indeed, most don't even consider themselves im-prisoned, at least not as far as Gill had witnessed.

"Chuhra" was the first word he ever remembers hearing. A woman behind a gated fence had screamed it at his father before swinging a broom at his head. Thereafter, it was all Gill ever heard anyone call his father. Not Boota, which was the nick-name he preferred, but Chuhra. Another peculiar thing that hindsight didn't help to decipher. An entire people made from the feet of Brahma—the great creator (who apparently thought less of his feet than of all his other appendages). Religion is the opiate of the masses, indeed, but it depends on what religion and it depends on what masses—an opiate for some, nothing but a poison for others. Here was Gill's experience:

- Always carrying a steel glass and plate with him when he was spending the day out because he was not allowed to use the same dishes as all the people who weren't Chuhra—or rather, they did not want to use the same dishes as him.
- Seated at the back of the room, hand always raised first, answer always firmly in mind, and yet the school-teacher never calling on him.
- Separate wells for water.
- The slow migrating shuffle of seated congregants at the Gurdwara when he and his father sat down (while the baba up at the front preached about the grand his-tory in Sikhism, from Guru Nanak to Guru Gobind, of abandoning caste and favouring equality).
- Spit landing at his feet, always, everywhere.

It was not the events themselves that finally caused Gill to leave India (though with time they might have). It was the more insidious hold that these ancient customs had on the people in the country—people like his father. Like Plato's allegory of the cave, they stared at a wall of dancing shadows and imagined that it was all there was, so devoted to their captivity that they wouldn't even turn their heads to glimpse the light of the sun shining behind them. For Gill, the great disgrace was not hearing his father being called "Chuhra," but that his father accepted it as if it was the way things were supposed to be. An intolerable acclimation, so much so, that the last encounter Gill ever had with Boota was to push him up against the mud wall of their home and growl in his ear, "Teri koi nahi izaat karda, fir mein kyun karaan?"[164]

But again, bygones were bygone. At least, that's the ethos Gill operated under. In Punjab, he was a Chuhra and that didn't suit him well, so he went to Iran, where he became an Iranian. That did suit him well, but it was also destined to pass. Now the train pulled into the station at Frankfurt and a German is what he would become next. Because the next moment is all you're afforded and the past is often nothing more than a sorry collection of fragments—meaningless and sharp-edged—and the only result of holding on to them is cutting yourself.

---

164 Nobody respects you, so why should I?

2002

Human beings are a single race and our unity is evidenced by our similarities.

Lamar shouts down the hallway as I stand before my locker. "Yo, Nodick, I heard brown people wipe they ass with they hands. That true bro? That why y'all smell like shit?" All eyes in the hallway fall to me.

Tupac Shakur, the greatest poet who ever lived, died in 1996. MTV plays his work as tribute on the tubular television, and the Viper snaps, "Ah ki kaliyaan de gaaneh laye ah? Band kar!"[165]

My Hobbling Guardian wakes before the crack of dawn to prepare my lunch for school. Two rotis and a Ziploc container of daal. When the time for lunch arrives, my heart beats fast and hard, because I know the class will scrunch their noses and Lamar will make a remark.

In his song "Changes," the greatest poet who ever lived stressed the importance of looking past differences and coming together as brothers.

---

165 What is this Black music you have on? Shut it off!

I sit next to Chen Zhang because his lunch smells as much as my lunch, and I do not like the smell of his, and he does not like the smell of mine, but everyone else dislikes the smell of both of ours, so we sit together.

"Nanak" pronounced Nah-Nick. Nick rhymes with Dick, and then, with one more slight alphabetical alteration, Nodick. Then, "Nodick the Paki! Nodick the Paki!"

I look more like them than Lamar does—closer in skin tone and more similar features. But he talks the way they do; he dresses the way they do; he eats the same food they do; he prays to the same God as them. His differences are accepted. My differences and Chen's differences are too different to accept easily.

Can Biji be forgiven for not understanding the words of the greatest poet who ever lived? Her world was black and white. She did not hear the words, not because she wasn't able to understand, but because she saw the black face that spoke them and decided not to listen. But I will forgive her, because even people who had a face like his, and pretended to listen, still never heard what he was trying to say.

Every brown-skinned person is a Paki, but Pakis from Iran did not like foreign Pakis coming in to steal all the jobs, and Pakis from Turkey whisper "kafir" when they spot a Paki who is not Muslim, and Pakis from Israel are the most loathed by all other Pakis, especially Pakis from Palestine, and Pakis from Pakistan definitely do not want to engage with Pakis from India, so much so, in fact, that there would be no Pakis at all if they did.

I refuse to eat my lunch until my Hobbling Guardian learns to make ham sandwiches that do not smell. With his old, gently creased hands that shake slightly, he learns, and then, at the break of dawn, he makes ham sandwiches instead of rotis and daal.

Chen Zhang is braver than I, and he is prouder than I. He responds to the teasing and name calling with a blank stare—one so severely uninterested that it smothers all attempts at mockery. I still sit with him at lunch because he shows me how to fold paper into beautiful shapes, and he shares his dumplings with me when I refuse to eat my own lunch. They no longer smell bad to me. On the contrary, they are delicious.

The largest similarities that unify human beings are their shared penchant for vindictive pettiness, their comfort in ignorance, and their capacity for transcendent stupidity.

My face flushes. "You hear what I said, Nodick? You Pakis wipe your asses with y'all hands or what?" I think of Bapu ji, who hobbles up the stairs—two flights from the basement—with his broken knees that ran across a continent on fire, with his broken knees that stood in the shit of millions of people. Because I was too young and unable, he cleaned my backside with his old, gently creased hands that shook slightly. I think of Bapu ji and I feel shame.

The greatest poet who ever lived said, "Everybody's at war with different things. I'm at war with my own heart sometimes."

1979

The train came to a stop and the two men disembarked. Immediately, Frankfurt appeared to hold much of the promise that was unfulfilled so far in their journey. There was no litter collecting on the banks of the roads, no emaciated or impoverished persons clamouring for food and money, and mechanical things were operating as they were designed to operate. Gill looked up to the large digital clock at the train station and was amazed to see that it displayed the same time as that promised on the ticket in his pocket. They approached a strange set of stairs, constructed from what appeared to be black rubber. Kaka lay his foot on the bottom step and the entire staircase began to propel upward. He fell back in terror, his eyes breaking from their morose slumber for the first time since Berlin. Instead of laughing, Gill leaned forward to inspect the marvel of engineering.

Twenty-four hours in Frankfurt proved an overwhelming delight for both men. As it turned out, Dariush and Maher both may have been reserved in their praise for the Western world. Everywhere they saw a citizenry that appeared to have respect for the obligations of social contract, rather than the latent hatred one sees when nothing seems to work as it should. Politeness from the pedestrians, cleanliness from the streets, dignity from those with authority, humility from those without, and architecture that managed to seamlessly blend durability and beauty. Clean, crisp beers and spirits that respect the integrity of one's esophageal tract. Scores of beautiful women with hazel eyes and bouncing golden curls. Only the food did not meet the standards set forth by the rest of the city; as both men agreed, more spice would have done well to improve the flavour. But all the same, they drank heartily into the night and wandered the streets with their destinies in mind.

On a bridge crossing the Main, where lovers wrote their names on padlocks and bolted them to the railing, was where each man decided his respective path forward. Gill decided he had come far enough; something about the soul of this city spoke to him. The dim afterglow of the greatest conflict on Earth had left the place docile and capitulated. In place of national pride and racial hubris, there was a quiet self-flagellation in the form of relaxed immigration policies and a collective work ethic that bordered on masochistic. Gill came from a life of racial discrimination to a nation that had learned the hardest way possible what an error such a manner of thinking is. He was the naturalized son of the true nation of the Swastika, and an adopted son of the true nation of Aryans, and now he had come to the place that had forever tainted those concepts. Here was the union of a man who was never given an apology and a nation which would never be forgiven.

And what of Kaka? On the bridge crossing the Main, in a city that displayed the potential that exists in the world, he had an epiphany. Perhaps finally, a glimmer of understanding of that mysterious force that propelled him forward. An understanding which would stay with him long after he left the bridge, one he would look back on and remember as a pivotal and defining moment in his life. A moment of self-actualization that triumphed over any tawdry romance enacted in cheap hotel rooms. And though it occurred here, in Germany, it was the spirit of a different civilization that took hold of his soul, the one which used to tell stories of heroes who rose above the petty exploits of mortals. Icarus, who flew to the sun—but why do you suppose that is? Do you imagine it was only to see how far he could go? Or was it simply the feeling of soaring that kept him aloft? Perhaps, but I think Kaka would tell us that it was nothing so quaint as that.

Prometheus stole fire from the gods and gave it to humankind, changing our trajectory forever. Icarus took inspiration (despite the Titan's grim fate), flying in pursuit of a glory known only to gods. He felt the heat, the way it seared his body, and the feathers on his wings began to blacken. He knew his fate long before it was actualized, but that was part of the motivation, a secret, savage, unrestrained desire for self-immolation. Icarus craved the flames because he wanted to burn, and he wanted the world to burn along with him. But not in a destructive sense, rather to make it brighter, hotter, and generally greater in every way—to increase what is noble and admirable in the human condition.

And that is why Kaka could not remain in Frankfurt. He had to move forward. Like Icarus, he had to edge his chin upward and continue to fly until he fell in flames, until the drum in his heart finally quietened its beat, until greatness was achieved, no matter the cost to himself.

On the bridge crossing the Main, the water rumbled beneath and the faint muffled sounds of car engines emitted from the banks. The stars above were blinded out by the artificial light produced unendingly from lamps and apartments—a vast, matte-black canvas. But below, the artificial lights cast their thousands of reflections against the ridges of the moving water and produced a mesmerizing ballet. Here, in silence, Kaka and Gill decided their fates. By doing so, together, they ushered in a new age of civilization: The Fourth Reich. A nomadic empire held together by no creed, no religion, no political ideology, but unified by the unfathomable tenacity of the human spirit. The ones who do not believe that their destinies are carved in stone, but those who know they hold the chisel, they are the sculptors, not the sculpture. No bolt locks were used to seal this covenant, fragile as they are when compared to the alloy of an *Übermensch's* resolve.

2016

Up and down and side to side and up and down and side to side. The rural roads of Ontario stretch out forever through a hilly, wooded landscape. You are lulled into a hypnotic state, meditative, reflective, and with the assurance of guaranteed universal healthcare, you feel secure in taking your mind off the road long enough to come to mighty epiphanies and realizations.

Not that this is desirable in any sense. The opposite, I realize one sunny afternoon, as Der Vater stares idly out of the passenger side window. It's my fault, as I've commandeered the radio system. No longer could I bear the static-infused ramblings of Punjabi political pundits. But because of that he has no choice but to be brought into confession by the meditative road, or perhaps his mumbling is spurred by his intolerance of Adele and operatic pop music, or perhaps it is the opposite, and Adele possesses some quality of nostalgic recall that transcends language barriers. Whatever the reason, he mumbles, but loudly enough for me to hear. "Mein papaji nu kush nahi keyha jad oh mar rahe si."[166]

Now I've stepped into it, that gurgling, goopy ectoplasm of regret. No, I'll have no part in this! As Adele belts "Hello," I say goodbye to her and good riddance. I dial the radio back to something staticky and political to distract Der Vater's

---

166 I never spoke to my dad when he was dying.

attention. But lady luck abandons me again, and to my great consternation, the voice of our Dear Leader clearly cracks through, saying, "My fellow Canadians…" and now it's my turn to mumble, but loud enough for Der Vater to hear. "This fucking guy…"

"Pehla Trudeau bohat wadiya banda si,"[167] Der Vater muses, seemingly eager to move on past his confession. But with this remark, he brings us the gurgling, goopy ectoplasm of hypocrisy! For by what right does Der Vater acknowledge the father of this cloying wretch on the radio, while never showing even a modicum of concern to my Hobbling Guardian, who lived his life ever so quietly and ever so humbly. Why the regret now, when every opportunity to help him up off the couch was met with scoffing and eye rolls? But wait, is there some connection between these two remarks of his? And now I must hold still and let the wobbly road do its magic because Der Vater is onto something, but it's locked behind his pragmatic language and he can't communicate it with any specificity. Let's review the evidence:

Dear Leader on the radio, Justin Trudeau, an auspicious debutant who made an auspicious debut. The prodigal son. The apple who fell too far from the tree. The heir apparent. The first Canadian political legacy. But not much more than that it seems, as the rationalism, vision, and well-defined policy agenda, which constituted the legacy, are all woefully absent. Charismatic, yes, but only in that engagement tracking and social media selfies sort of way, that only concerned with image and not action sort of way, that speaking endlessly and saying nothing sort of way, that profoundly disingenuous sort of way, that thoroughly twenty-first century sort of way. No, there's not much to work with here, so let's round this bend to a new hilly vista and keep thinking.

What about "Pehla[168] Trudeau"—Pierre as he's known. The legacy maker, the passer of "The Official Languages Act,"

---

167 The first Trudeau was a great man!
168 The first…

188

a monumental piece of legislation, which had the practical outcome of forcing Anglophones to print Francophone instructions on their shampoo bottles, and vice versa. But Der Vater has long since lost his hair and has no need for shampoo... Think harder dammit! Why is Pierre so great? Well, of course, Canada under Pierre had also tacitly endorsed the Fourth Reich, and it welcomed those scrappy nomads from across the globe, freely granting citizenship to people who were equally baffled by both the English and French directions of the nation's shampoo bottles. And that brings us to the one line that sums up the legacy: "Pierre, the man who went the furthest in fostering a "shared Canadian Identity.""

There it is, the subject we're after, the one Der Vater is poking at but can't seem to spear—the gurgling, goopy ectoplasm of identity. He regrets not speaking to his father, even as he was dying, because it is a lost opportunity to understand who he is himself. Because, as much as we are loathed to admit it, fathers define sons. If not by a process of imitation, then certainly by a process of opposition. Admiration or hatred, whatever the motivating emotion, it lives in the son as if it is a part of him, and when the father dies, something of the son necessarily dies with him.

"Tu vi Trudeau nu vote payi, ke nahi?"[169] asks Der Vater, appearing to have abandoned his melancholic rememberings (or rather having telepathically transmitted them to me, the wily bastard). "Yeah, I did," I mutter, as I leave the rural road and merge onto the Highway of Heroes, where I see the sun beams glistening off the thousands of ripples of Lake Ontario. It would be a nice place to get high, on the bank of that lake, which ostensibly is the reason I voted for our Dear Leader, with his promises to legalize that sticky icky. I am a descendent of Punjab, after all, and I have had instilled in me from a young age the importance of supporting local agricultural efforts.

Although perhaps there is a deeper reason... I'm on the highway now and the meditative stupor of the roly-poly roads

---

169   You gave your vote to Trudeau as well, did you not?

is quickly evaporating, so I'll have to be quick to work this one out. Justin, Justin, Justin, I can't be so harsh on our Dear Leader, for though his life is plenty more auspicious than mine, we are brothers in a more profound sense. Because, like Justin, I know too well what a burden it is to carry the weight of a name I did not earn and will never live up to. To live in a shadow that is too large to escape. Legacy, what a thing, perhaps even a gurgling, goopy ectoplasm in itself. Our identities, Justin and mine, appear to be formed by all the things that we did not do.

And then there's this place we both call home, with its "shared Canadian Identity" promulgated by The Official Languages Act, but all who live here know no such thing exists. Whatever identity bonds the true North, Strong, and Free, is not shared but shattered. It is not a result of amalgamating two languages but two hundred. It is the fallout of the Fourth Reich, the yearning for opportunity, along with the ever-present itch to shed any constricting and narrowing definitions that might be hoisted onto us (which are nothing but anchors to weigh us down). Not definition, not identity—but freedom from it. And if we ever fall into confusion or isolation because of our collective lack of identity, then we can take solace in the fact that there is one thing that every person who calls themselves a Canadian will have to do at one point or another. We will all have to do as the late, great Pierre Trudeau once did, and take a walk in the sno—

"Oye panchode, vekh ke gadi challah!"[170] Der Vater hollers. I slam my foot on the brake. The car comes skidding to a halt and stops short of the bumper of the vehicle ahead by a few centimetres. All my aimless ruminating is out the window in an instant, and here the true identity of Canada slaps me in the face much harder than any rural road epiphany ever could. This is home to the most congested fucking highway in fucking North America, and I am going to die some miserable fucking day sitting in stupid, fuck-ass traffic with a bunch of mouth-breathing, moron, dipshit fuckers...

---

170 Hey you sister-fucker, watch where you're driving!

INT - AIRPORT CUSTOMS - DAY

KAKA disembarks from his flight into Pearson International Airport, in Mississauga, Ontario, Canada. After a lengthy wait in line, he eagerly approaches the customs agent. An impatient BUSINESSMAN taps his foot from behind, next in line.

CUSTOMS AGENT
(Blankly)
Passport and visa.

KAKA hands over the requested documents. The agent scrutinizes them for some time.

BUSINESSMAN
(Angrily)
Would ya hurry it up, pal. My wife's waiting outside for me already!

CUSTOMS AGENT
Calm down, sir.

The CUSTOMS AGENT gestures to KAKA.

CUSTOMS AGENT CONT.
What is the purpose or your visit, sir?

KAKA
(Confused)
Burpuss?

CUSTOMS AGENT
(Annoyed)
Purpose, sir. This is a temporary visitor's visa, so are you here for business or pleasure?

KAKA nods his head knowingly, and points to the visa in the CUSTOM AGENTS hand.

KAKA
I cum bisit Canedah.

The CUSTOMS AGENT stares blankly at KAKA.

BUSINESSMAN
(Agitated)
He's asking why you're here, pal. Come on. My wife's gonna kill me, hurry it up!

KAKA focuses on the words he is able to interpret and smiles slyly, confident that he has formed the perfect response.

KAKA
I cum vatching ass huckey.

CUSTOMS AGENT
(Clarifying)
Ice hockey?

The BUSINESSMAN chuckles from behind.

KAKA
(Reiterates)
Jess, ass huckey.

CUSTOMS AGENT
Pleasure it is then. This is a two-week visa you have, so you can't stay longer than that. Here you go and enjoy your visit.

The CUSTOMS AGENT stamps KAKA's passport, hands it back, and waves the BUSINESSMAN forward.

EXT - AIRPORT ARRIVALS GATE – DAY

KAKA exits the automatic door and steps his foot into snow for the first time. A covered patch of black ice causes him to slip, and he tumbles backward comically. The BUSINESSMAN exits the door shortly after and sees KAKA flailing on the ground.

BUSINESSMAN
(Joking)
Gotta be careful, pal. The ass is slipperier than you think!

END SCENE

1979

The Americas differ in their constitution in many ways from the great continental European cities. There, history is cemented in the streets and the architecture speaks of the rise and fall of dynasties and eras. Not so in the New World. The first thing that struck Kaka were endless expanses of untouched land. He had witnessed open vistas before, even Punjab has its share of them, but they exist because the earth has been plowed and seeds have been sown—conscious effort to a directed end.

Canada is still a product of nature's decree, and where the hand of man is present, it takes inspiration from the philosophy of late English utilitarians. Buildings are constructed from durable materials and they are shaped into symmetrical blocks with strange and uninspired names like "Canadian Tire." It is evident that it was not the artists and dreamers who were compelled to explore and colonize the New World, but the less poetic sort who merely wished to keep the cold off their backs as they went about their humdrum work and to have a single place to shop for all their consumer needs. But this suited Kaka fine, because he liked being warm and he had no qualms with buying his frying pans from the same place where he bought his garden shears. In fact, he found it quite convenient.

But for all these differences, there was much that was similar as well. Canada shared with India the status of "England's bastard child," and perhaps, for this reason, pilgrims of Punjab had been drawn to the Queen's Colony for decades. As Kaka explored his new environment, the familiar clanging bells of the Gurdwara sounded out. In keeping with the tradition of ugly Canadian architecture, it was an unceremonious building, a plain white cabin that abutted a group of industrial parking lots. Scattered about were old tires, empty trailer beds, and decommissioned eighteen-wheelers. But sardars in clean white kurta pyjamas still scurried around, attending to their holy duties. God's will did not differ from the land of five rivers to the land of five lakes. Indeed, the humble size of the Gurdwara actually befitted the religious mandate better, as proceeds of a Gurdwara are meant to service the community, not to build towers of Babel.

As Kaka entered the foyer of the small building, he was intercepted by a curmudgeonly old baba. As Kaka began to explain his situation, the baba cut him off and immediately fell into a rehearsed speech. "Bas ik raat reh sakdein. Factory de vich kam haiga. Svehar ton tu othe ja ke kam lub."[171] The baba kept his eyes narrowed as he spoke, and they scanned up and down Kaka's body, treatment one would expect more from an airport security agent than a cleric. He barked his sentences out as orders and then pointed to the back of the house and added, "Ja seva kar!"[172] Abrasive as he might have been, the baba was still something of a welcome sight. His presence ensured that the hurdles of settling in experienced in other nations would not be so difficult to leap over here. At the least, Kaka could have all his questions answered in his native tongue, and if prayers had any sway in the realm of mortals, then at least he could mutter a few here that were understood. And after Kaka had spent a few hours sweeping and serving meals, he sat and enjoyed a hearty bowl of dal and roti fresh off the stove. It was a nostalgic gastronomic

---

171 You can only stay for one night. There's work in the factory nearby. Tomorrow you will go there and find employment.
172 Now go do some service!

195

experience that took him back what felt like decades—before Germany, before Iran, and before Afghanistan, to the mud hut in Ahmedpura. Home, it turned out, is where the stomach is.

In the evening, Kaka sat in the prayer hall for some time, reflecting and thinking. Here were the questions that were cycling through his head: Have I done right by leaving Germany? Should I have just stayed put? Is this impulse that always keeps me moving a *good* thing? These questions were given extra bite as he watched the baba read from the Granth Sahib. He was young—younger than Kaka even. His voice was resolute, however, and he moved through the prayers with a soothing musicality. Kaka watched him, curiously, enviously. So youthful and already having dedicated himself to this single, eternal thing. A book. Contemplation of words on a page. On second thought, not eternal at all, but painfully fleeting. Once the words danced off your tongue, they were gone to the wind and you were left with nothing. How could it satisfy any life to be devoted to a thing that offered so little in return? Ultimately, what broke Kaka from his reverie were not the answers to these questions, but the piercing gaze of the older baba who sat across the room with his eyes locked on him.

At night, Kaka yet again slept restlessly. Although by now he was coming to terms with the fact that he was just no good at sleeping. As a child, the dusty corner of the mud hut was not a comforting place to rest, and conditions hadn't seemed to improve much since then. The mattress beneath him was lumpy and smelled of mould, and the room was poorly insulated. But comfort was not the issue at hand. For his entire conscious life, "sleep" was more often than not a process of watching black splotches shapeshift against whatever ceiling he was staring at until morning arrived. Abjectly, he took to the same task now. This was the part of the proverbial life of adventure, of treading the path untrodden, that he loathed more than all others—the mundanity, the things you can't outrun, the invariable traits of life, the functional routines of biology, and what you expect to happen always proving true. In other words, what he hated most of all was that no matter where he went, he was never able to get away from himself.

Then, like a flick of a switch, the twilight hell ended. The rising sun broke through the dull grey clouds and shone a blinding ray of light directly on to Kaka's eyes. Not a moment later, the old baba barged into the room and handed Kaka a scrap of paper. It was a note for the foreman of the nearby factory, explaining Kaka's circumstances. Along with the note, the baba barked some directions at Kaka and then, not so subtly, encouraged him to get moving. He stood at the door, watching Kaka with folded arms as he got up and collected his things. Then he paced lockstep behind Kaka as he made his way to the front door. When Kaka opened the door and stepped outside, he was blinded by the sun glimmering off a fresh sheet of snow—a novel and thoroughly unpleasant experience. Before his vision adjusted, the baba was already pressing against his back to usher him outside. Kaka took a tentative step but missed the stair and fell forward into snow for the second time since he'd arrived in Canada. Behind him the baba snorted and slammed the door shut.

Now, as he lifted his head out of the powder, he was able to see more clearly. The snow had fallen in flurries during the night, not noticeable against the black sky. It was more than Kaka had ever seen in his life, enough to clog the sidewalks and roads, and where it had been cleared away by plows, it was piled higher than the height of a full-grown man. His hands and face (exposed skin) began to sting as the snow melted against them. A cheap winter jacket may have been enough to guard against the molesting winds of Prague's Old Town, but Kaka learned that thicker stuff was needed here. He closed his hands into tight fists and jammed them into his pockets, but it made little difference. The off-brand jogging sneakers that carried him through Europe were proving a poor match against the shin-high snow. Lugubriously, he continued his march to the factory, a few gruelling kilometres away.

Shivering and miserable, with soggy cold socks, Kaka eventually pushed through the doors of a large concrete block with the words "Precision Technologies" plastered across it. Here he experienced for the first time one of the small joys that all Canadians have come to appreciate, that palpable moment of relief that comes after escaping the withering cold. Instinctively, he began rubbing his hands together and huffing lukewarm breath against his fingers. The reception desk was unattended but a small bell sat atop the counter. Kaka hit it and, before long, a slouchy man made his way unenthusiastically toward the desk. No, "slouchy" does not capture the essence of this man's posture. His spine appeared to curve in more ways than it seemed possible, and on the front an impressively spherical potbelly protruded. He sported a moustache but it was in a style that Kaka had never witnessed before. Instead of curled ends like the shop owners of Delhi, or the neatly tapered moustaches of Iran, it was more of a goatee with the chin shaved off, and sideburns kept preposterously long.

"How's it, pal? You from the old farmhouse then?" the man enquired. Kaka handed over the paper the baba had given him and watched as the man read it, scratching at his sideburns while he did. "Yeah. All right then. I'm Jerry," he said, waving for Kaka to follow. They headed through a narrow corridor onto the work floor. Suddenly, Kaka's senses were consumed by an all-encompassing racket. Manufacturing, the last frontier of manual labour, the very thing the soul of Iran rejected, and now it was not so mysterious why. The charm of the worksite was absent, human limbs were visible here and there in between black and grey pieces of groaning machinery.

Jerry, the foreman, had already tacitly hired Kaka, as the paper he was handed merely reiterated a standing arrangement that Jerry had with the Gurdwara. He need not pay

Kaka the salary and benefits that he would be required to in the case of a full Canadian citizen, with all the thorny rights and privileges that come along with that designation. Immigrants from India (Punjab, in particular) were eager for work, and they were willing to do so at a discount so long as too many questions were not asked by employers. In this regard, Jerry was an enterprising fellow, one who did not ask too many questions. The situation he had devised here ensured he could continue taking naps throughout the day with no drop in productivity and no one the wiser.

"Indian, eh?" asked Jerry, rubbing his naked chin. "Well, Chris is Indian, too." Then he cupped his hand over his mouth and yelled, "Chris, getcher ass over here and show this new guy the ropes." The man purportedly known as Chris emerged from the bowels of the machinery. It was quickly apparent that Chris was not Indian, at least not any kind Kaka had ever seen. Not unless he was from the north where the influence of Genghis Khan's genetics was much more pronounced. But Kaka abandoned that idea when he realized Chris didn't speak any of the languages of India. He was rather unloquacious; in fact, introducing himself solemnly as "Christopher" and stalking off back to his work area. He was, in many respects, a visual antithesis to Jerry. His posture was straight and tall, a full half head taller than Kaka even, and with thirty more pounds of hard muscle. His face was smooth and the hair on his head was shaggy and matte-black. His skin was tanned but not as deeply as Kaka's.

"Go on with Chris," said Jerry, "he'll show ya, eh." Just as Kaka turned to leave, Jerry called out one more time. "Hey pal, what's yer name again?" Kaka answered and again Jerry resorted to scratching his strange sideburns while trying to interpret, "Huh? Kuckyeah? Whassit? Eh? Speak up now, pal." Then he threw his hands up, seemingly in defeat. "All right look, I'll just call ya Kev, that all right? All right then. Go on with Chris then, eh."

Though Christopher kept his mouth shut, it quickly became clear that he was communicating more directly with the movements of his body. He looked Kaka in the eye before he performed his duties, and when he executed an action, he did so in exaggerated fashion, to clearly demonstrate methodology and purpose. Pick up a rough, unfinished machine part and place it on a conveyor belt or in a larger machine, inspecting for defects as you do. Nothing about the work was complex, or even intriguing, so the informal training period didn't last long. But as the days piled on and Kaka—Kev— clocked in and clocked out, he began to feel as though eight hours of this kind of work was far more taxing than twice as long at a job with Dariush's crew. It had little to do with the fact that no one seemed able to pronounce his name, which was a minor annoyance compared to the quality of work life offered by Precision Technologies. It was an insidious and hardly noticeable kind of dehumanization, but once he tuned into it, he could hardly prevent his brain from pestering him with a new and much more pressing question: "What's the point?"

Cat in the Hat(e)

Listen here, listen now, for the tale of an age,
Of a boy who was forced to exist in a cage.
'Twas a strange kind of thing for a boy to endure,
For this cage did not close, had no gate, nor a floor.

The cage was a name that was not of his choosing.
If the choice were his choice, another name he'd be using.
"Nick" was the name that denied him his fate,
The cage that enclosed him, the cause of his hate.

It began one day with a creature called "teacher."
Reading names off her page, she was stumped by a feature.
Her face did she scrunch, and she hummed and she hawed.
At her chin did she paw, with her gremlin like claw.

This creature called teacher wore powders and paints.
Like a circus attraction, nothing was faint.
And what she did next is something quite shameless,
Something that left our good boy rather nameless.

Her best did she try, but it was no use,
She tangled her tongue, then let it all loose:
"I can't for the life of me figure this out,
So Nick's what I'll call you!" she said in a shout!

And it wasn't the last time he ran into beings,
Who were less than familiar with what they were seeing.
The place he was sent was a school that was high,
But as it turned out, the name was a lie.

More creatures called "teachers" and something much worse.
Teenagers with attitudes—callous and terse.
Like foppish flamingos they ambled about,
Picking on Nick, the dastardly louts!

And there's more to Nick's sorrow, to his aches and his pains,
No shortage of heartache and nothing to gain.
In this world where he lived, and was forced to exist,
He spoke in a language, foreign to his.

English it was—a tight way of speaking,
Subject-predicates, and verbs, like a pot with no leakage.
A good way to speak when you've things that need saying,
But what about when you are dancing and playing?

For the soul and the heart call for something more vivid.
Something that grips you and something not rigid.
What that thing is, was lost as a hobby,
A remnant of youth, which was known as "Punjabi."

But Nick left it behind, like a boot that had rot.
He looked far ahead, 'twas success that he sought.
He agreed to be "Nick", and English he spoke
He did all that he could to be one of the folks.

But more trouble emerged in Nick's strange reality.
For agreeing to "Nick" was an informal fatality.
Among his own kind, his cousins and kin,
They teased him endlessly, for his strange sin.

"He's a whitey!" They shouted, not without scorn,
Ever Nick wondered, "Why was I born?"
Betwixt two worlds, both seemingly false,
Nick was still nameless, yet he still had a pulse.

A dark gloomy boy, with a horrid complexion
He angled his head in a newfound direction,
His mind did he lend to bookish pursuits.
What it offered to him, was a refuge from youths.

And his reading all led to a place with more promise.
A university where he was sure he would not miss.
No creature-like teachers, and flamingoes not foppish.
They were rather unreserved, open-minded, and honest.

But even these people, so clever and dashing,
Found it within 'em, to give Nick a good bashing.
His learning, you see, was not fondly considered,
And these tidings had left him wholly embittered.

"Why, good sir, do you read about white men?
They are racists and Nazis, and all rather un-Zen.
Look to the East, where there's wisdom galore,
You're a brown-skinned fellow, it'll suit you much more."

So once again, Nick the Nameless was not free of blame.
And the years that remained, were not free of pain.
But he pushed and he finished, like a bone and a dog,
Then he tied up his laces and looked for a job.

But here was the truth, so sad and so dismal,
Life is a bitch; it's rancid, abysmal.
Listen here, listen now, there's no rhyme this time,
The prose which follows hath no simmer nor shine:

"We're excited to have you on board. You've got some exciting ideas and we can't wait to see what you'll do with them. But I'm going to level with you… A great number of our clients are based in the southern states of America and many of them are old, white men who harbour insufferable prejudices. I won't force you to do anything you're uncomfortable with, but I'm telling you now your job will be easier if you use a Western nickname. I know, I know, I feel like a racist asshole just bringing it up, but you expressed such a fondness for pragmatism in your interview, I thought I'd be straight with you…"

What could Nick do, so nameless and dumb?
All of the world had him under its thumb.
So, he looked to the left, and he looked to the right,
And a path opened up, albeit quite tight.

The answer he found was very sublime,
Indeed, he had had it all of the time.
The answer he found was to shut the fuck up,
Let the world keep on turning, don't muck it all up.

What's a name after all? Just a sound from an ape.
No reason at all, to get bent out of shape.
So, he kept his mouth shut, and as a result,
He lived well enough, a clean somersault.

But beneath all his silence, something remained.
An unscratched feeling that he was betrayed.
What he wanted was small, not riches and fame.
Just the desire to have a real name.

The betrayal was his, he let himself down,
And now he was cursed, to live as a clown.
Like an unending yawn, he would go on.
Less than a human— more automaton.

A wish that's ungranted, a wheel with no spokes,
Always a struggle, yet what was his yoke?
Never here, never there, our Nick was a ghost.
He didn't exist, a laugh with no joke.

1981 / 2001

Kaka stood before a machine that accepted a palm-sized cylindrical piece of metal through a door made of shatterproof glass. For fifteen seconds it whizzed and burred and then it returned the same cylindrical piece, but now with two grooves shaved into the sides. Then Kaka took the piece and placed it on a conveyor belt where more whizzing, burring, and shaving occurred. It was unclear what purpose this piece of metal served.

Nanak sat in the constricting grasp of the elementary school plastic desk-chair hybrid. Marketed as ergonomic, it's true purpose appeared to be to keep children of a certain age just uncomfortable enough to discourage creative thinking, to keep their spirits dampened so their young minds were more susceptible to the lifeless droning of an uninspired teacher.

The process was so atomized, so compartmentalized, that Kaka could not understand what significance his effort had to the outcome of the final product. He did not know what happened to the piece before it arrived to him, or what happened to it after it left his hands. In fact, he scarcely knew where in the factory he was standing.

Nanak's foot slapped against the beige floor like a piston. He strained his eyes at the chalkboard, trying to focus on the lesson of the day. There was a feeling—a swelling in the chest—that he felt when he was running in open fields, outpacing the First Man and the Toucan. He was not running now but the swelling in his chest persisted. In the open field this feeling felt good. Trapped at the desk, it did not.

This job demanded constant movement but it was of a hollow and unsatisfactory sort. In Tehran, Dariush's crew was responsible for the construction of a new empire. The world was changed by the movement of Kaka's hands, and the merit of an individual's labour was recognizable through the process. Now it was merely mechanical. The human body intervened only where automation was still impossible.

"Nick, will you please sit still!" Nanak did as he was told, because he did not like eyes dwelling on him. But now when his mind wandered or he attended to the lesson, his body moved of its own accord and the piston fired up again. The teacher glared at him until he realized his foot was not sitting still. He pressed his palms down on his knees, holding his feet against the floor, and the swelling in his chest grew.

He did not rest for the entire duration of his shift, moving faster and with more precision than all other workers, but even still, he felt like he was not moving at all. That forgotten feeling of listlessness that was omnipresent in Ahmedpura returned, though with added force, because he did not know where he could go to escape it now.

With his foot held in place, he had lost the small pressure release valve he had available. The kinetic force that would have been released radiated through his body. The amygdala was telling the prefrontal cortex to move, but the prefrontal cortex offered nothing in response.

He needed escape. From what? Nothing, it appears, but he

felt it was necessary. Escape was necessary or something bad would happen. But what? Nothing, nothing could happen. Nothing. He needed to escape.

His heart was not a strong enough muscle to control the furiously pumping blood and his brain was not a resilient enough organ to manage the chemical stew being released. His central nervous system was frayed and volatile like a cut power line.

The swelling grew exponentially, limitlessly multiplying until it felt as though it had transcended the bounds of his flesh and was now expanding in the world, outward, infinitely. Sounds were drowned out; his vision sharpened and blurred at once.

This was the end. Looming doom, heavier than gravity, so heavy it pushed down on him, holding him in place as his body screamed to move. Impossibly, the torrent of energy remained contained. Impossibly, he was held still. Impossibly, he lived.

The bell rang. Clarity emerged as the eye of the storm. He left as quickly as possible.

1983

Kaka leaned his torso over the sticky bar top, waving a hand that was clutching a fresh five-dollar bill. The bartender—a man older than he looked, and attractive in a blatant and charmless way—was purposefully ignoring Kaka. Instead, he was chatting up a young woman who was doing everything in her power to look older than she was, garish in her attempt to make herself more desirable. Never in Kaka's life had being drunk been as unsatisfying as this. Pinda was never so shortsighted. None of his customers ever had to wait more than a moment for a refill because as keen a sinner as he was, he knew that greed was always to be prioritized over lust in the hierarchy of sin. Of all the people in the world to miss, it was Pinda the desi daru moonshine merchant who took the prize that day.

Christopher was waiting at a sticky table in the corner of the bar. He didn't speak much but he liked to drink. And Kaka had been drinking a lot lately, near daily, because the mechanistic routine of the factory reminded him too much of wandering aimlessly through Ahmedpura, counting houses. It wasn't long, then, until he also remembered the balm of intoxicants against that encroaching ennui, the feeling of numb limbs and shaking moons and blinking stars—the feeling of uncoordinated, undiagnosed happiness.

So, the two men had come together to engage in that strange, eternal relationship that exists somewhere between an acquaintance and a friend, known colloquially as "drinkin' buddies." When Kaka finally returned to the table with the order (two Canadian Rye Whiskys that were too watered down for a real kick), they both partook in the sacrament of disgruntled factory workers and swallowed the whole drink in a single go. After five more rounds Kaka felt loose and lucid enough to express his dissatisfaction in broken, slurred English. "Verk no good... Vant build something... Vant use hand." He shook his hands in Christopher's face and then tapped his skull, "Vant use head."

He didn't know now, nor had he ever known, that what he was actually railing against in his inebriated tirade was how his brain operated in the face of mundane stimulation. When Kaka's mind was not engaged deeply in some challenging task and had free rein to roam as it pleased—as it did when he stood in front of the whirling and burring machines of Precision Technologies—it only went to places he didn't like, ruminating on potentially dreadful outcomes: ditches he might die in, graves he might come to fill, and other generally morbid scenarios. Were he born a few decades in the future, under the comfortable umbrella of first-world medical experts, he might have been told that he suffered from an "anxiety disorder." But, being born when and where he was, his mind was nothing but a perfectly rational product of its environment. Anxiety was a useful tool for keeping one alive, after all.

"Might find work like that out West," said Christopher, "Alberta, BC maybe." Often, he went days without saying a word, so Kaka was surprised and sat back in his chair. Then an unexpected swell of drunken camaraderie overtook him, an urge to move beyond "drinkin' buddies" to outright pals. "Ju come vith me!" he shouted, pointing at Christopher with one hand and slapping the table with his other. Given the quantity of alcohol consumed, such an offer should have been presented and accepted as one of those pseudo-agreements that occurred on the border of blackout drunkenness, and then never thought of after the event. But something in Christopher's demeanour changed. There was a clarity in his eyes, a tenseness of posture. Kaka wasn't aware that for a long while Christopher had been thinking of making the journey out West. So, he considered the proposition seriously, emptied his sixth glass in a single swallow and, after a moment, he nodded.

When the blinding light crept over Kaka's eyelids the next morning and jolted him awake, he was in a sorry state, groggy and miserable and generally unresponsive. Having thoroughly forgotten the events of the previous night, he walked toward Precision Technologies with a gloomy dread, in no way prepared for the seemingly endless eight-hour shift that awaited him. And when he arrived at his destination, he saw Christopher leaned against his '69 Ford Ranger, with a giant grin that looked entirely out of place on his otherwise stoic face. He clapped Kaka on the shoulder as he approached, which startled Kaka's queasy stomach enough to produce a mouth full of bile that he begrudgingly swallowed back down. Everything about Christopher was rubbing Kaka the wrong way at that moment. That is, until he said, "Talked to Jerry about leaving. He ain't happy about it, but he's got your last paycheck inside."

And then the scene came back to Kaka like a swift kick to the head—kind of. Was it after the eighth or ninth drink, or what came before, that devilish concoction where they dropped their whiskys into their beer pints and chugged them down? That might have been the closest Kaka came to replicating Pinda's daru since he had left Punjab. In any case, the deleterious aftermath of binge drinking immediately lost some of its sting as Kaka imagined the glory of the open road ahead.

Kaka headed inside and collected his cheque from an unhappy Jerry and then returned to his temporary abode to pack his belongings. He was still making do with a single backpack, the same he had left India with, and Christopher had a pair of retired military issue duffle bags. They loaded the luggage into the bed of Christopher's '69 Ford Ranger. A reliable vessel, rusted body notwithstanding. Christopher's bolt-action hunting rifle was a third passenger, crammed between the cushions of the driver and passenger seat. An involuntary smile emerged on Kaka's face, and Christopher was so elated he even managed to chuckle. The key in the ignition was turned and the engine roared to life...

Fear and Loathing Across Canada

We hit the tarmac with the blazing, blue sky grinning on our asses. Der Vater took the wheel and slammed his foot on the gas like he was mad at it, and we peeled back in our seats because of it. We had the centre seats torn out of the caravan and laid out a couple of wool blankets from the ol' country. In the back was a freezer full of bacon, eggs, and milk, and boxes stacked on boxes of the mounties bounty—Canadian Club whisky.

And right off the bat the First Man kept on saying, "Keep on your fucking side, kid, or you'll get a smack from me." The three-year gap between us gave him an edge, bigger fists which came down like brick hammers when he wanted them to. Even at eight, I was a hardheaded hell-spawn, and I was conjuring up the fortitude to reply, but then Der Vater growled like a damned beast from the front and we all shut up.

Everything that was familiar started to retreat in the rear mirrors. Everything that was new was savage and barbaric. A phantasmagoria of titled power line poles and rusted pick-up trucks painted in '60s colours of forgotten pastels. Town after town, the same sights, until we hit that Bay of Zeus where the greatest Canadian who ever lived was frozen in stone at the spot where he ended his Marathon of Hope. It was a shaggy fucking place to have to call it quits.

On the Atlas page the highway was like a lead pencil laid straight across the globe, but the actual concrete monster was more serpentine than that. It swayed like a charmed snake, and we rode its scaly back all the way to the prairies. We entered the home of the frozen plains' cowboys at noon on the third day and found them flirting with the pot stains of Communism. A young upstart with a virile moustache and wearing ripped jeans, named Jack Layton, had seduced them.

I was just about to sock the First Man in the lip for waving his rotten feet around my side of the van when the lights hit us. The ol' red, white, and blue—upholding the freedom loving American capitalism of the South, I bet. They must have known I was ogling Layton's strong Russian jawline in my mind, which is why they dragged us over.

Der Vater slowed the ride and gave us a stern look, as if to say, "Keep your traps shut or else." The copper waddled up, a black cyclops silhouette with his shades glinting and the lights flashing behind him. "Licence 'nd registration," he said, leaning his swollen belly against the door. He was an oozy bastard, the way he spoke and the way he moved. He gave me a chill and a grumble in the gut. I thought I might vomit, but I swallowed it and took the lead. It was a sinful impulse.

"What seems to be the problem, officer?" I asked.

"Now you jus' sit back there, kiddo. I'm chattin' with yer ol' man."

"Right you are, officer, though I'd be entirely remiss if I didn't mention that the Queen's English isn't his mother tongue. He hails from the ol' country, mighty older than this one I might add," I said. The cyclops peered at me over his shades with both eyes and they buckled down on me, and I felt the vomit swelling up again.

Then Der Vater swatted me back like I was a promiscuous insect and said, "Ve go slow." The oinker's eyes peeled open a bit, some kind of wild, manic desire, and then I saw Der Vater slide a sealed bottle of CC Whisky out the window and into the oinker's hands.

"Well, well, ain't that some generosity. Welcome to the prairies, folks. Just a reminder to keep yer speed down now," he said, pulling the whisky bottle close and into the crotch of his navy-blue trousers. I reckon he planned to make love to it when he got it alone. I also reckon Der Vater's been around and he knows a thing or two, and maybe I should use my mouth solely for swallowing vomit from here on out.

We hit the road again before the oinker got back to his two-wheeled wagon, foot to the gas like a lead hammer, and I peeled back into my seat again. Manitoba to Saskatchewan next, and somehow the planet got even more flat and squared away. The tiny God in charge of shaping this part of the world was a damned lazy bastard.

We whizzed by dusty neon signs screaming things like "BAR!" and "MOTEL!" The Canadian air snuck into the cracked window and cast a creepy moist blanket on our skin. It was a sticky goddamn time, and stickier still when we stopped for slumber in the hellish sovereignty of discount campsites.

I couldn't sleep at night for a damn because the First Man was even more covetous of our shared tent than he was of our shared back seat. So, I headed outside to cool the welts he laid on me. It was two in the night, and I saw Der Vater with a whisky in one hand and, in the other, a frying pan with eggs over a dim fire, hovering like a wobbly UFO. The man's hunger was stowaway on our voyage.

He shook the vialed ichor at me with a little wiggle of his head, and I took up his cursed challenge. I gripped the amber throat and tossed my head back and the pale fluid hit my tongue like a sack of magma. I coughed it out on the fire and the heat blazed up, shooing me back. "What kind of hellish ogre blood is that?" I demanded to know, and Der Vater cackled like a depraved madman to the sky.

The next morning, we were off again. Der Vater was driven to move by some internal demon that made his eyes red and his knuckles white. Across the plains, the sun beat us down harder than normal, like we were peeling through the Sonoran Desert instead of the frozen plains. It was to be expected, of course, because July still sizzles like a hot samosa, even in Canada.

The rest of them have a constitution for sunbeams, but I'm a vampire. It split my vision in two. So, when we came up on those impregnable Rocky Mountains, I thought they stretched out forever like a satisfied lover. And at Lake Louise an axe must have cleaved the world in half—two times—once from above to cut the mountains in the sky, and once from below to do likewise in the emerald water's reflection.

We stopped there to sup. Again, we had our eggs and our bacon and some whisky for the inclined. I wasn't after the esophageal thrashing I received, so I went for the milk. By now it had a green hue to it and went down bitter. The corrupted stuff sat heavy in my gut, but I kept it down because it gave me a kind of snarling high. The First Man's borders in the car didn't seem so oppressive when the ceiling of the old van started to wave and the clouds over the BC coast started to jig.

But my constitution was a fickle bitch, and the heavy feeling in my gut migrated to press against my anus. "Panchode, kiniyan tuttiyan kar niyein?"[173] Der Vater shouted, after pulling over at the third gas station in three hours. Indeed, in the end it turned out to be a bout of diarrhea that finally found us lodging in an amply toileted establishment.

I was too twisted up to think, so I ran up to the concierge—the night shift mixture of apathy and misery plain on her face—and I said, "We need a room, quick as you can manage! Spare no expense, ma'am! This grim fellow is Der Vater. He'll deal with the billing on the morrow!"

---

173 How many sister-fucking shits you gonna take?

The clerk's face was placid and unreadable and horrid. The First Man pushed me aside and said to her, "Don't listen to my associate. He's only eight years old and he still wets the bed. And you can bet your ass he'll wet a bed he's comfortable in, so maybe don't make his bed so comfortable."

The looming terror of betrayal set upon me like a hound. I wanted to claw his eyes out, chew on his liver like the crow and Prometheus. I wanted to shout out that it was shit they needed to worry about, not piss! But then Der Vater slammed both our heads together like coconuts, and when I woke up, I was coiled up in the freshy pseudo-clean sheets of a Motel 8.

I moved through the next couple of days in a fever dream. I remember the daisies in the Vancouver flower garden, winking like horny teenagers before sex. I remember we saw the island off the coast named after some royal English lass, whom Canadians honour by launching fireworks into summer skies once a year. Cars entered the caverns of ferry boats like festering maggots, but these ones were taking pictures with disposable cameras.

And then I remember being on the other side of the nation, the sea-salted air wafting into my nose, blistered and red and drooping. I thought to myself that the Atlantic must be bigger than the Pacific—bigger than any goddamn thing for that matter—but I only thought that because the people over here were smaller and paler and they spoke nicer. They ate lobsters like it was a poor man's food, but it never touched our mouths because Der Vater didn't go for meals with antennae.

And before that, the blue and white, the fleur-de-lys, the sub-subcontinent. Der Vater in restaurants and gas stations bellowing, "Bonjo! Bonjo!" because he couldn't get his mouth round enough to draw out that "ooouuuur." I committed a sacrilege there when I declared shredded cheese superior to curds on the poutine, and we had to hightail it out before they recommissioned the guillotine for me.

I was too twisted up to remember if we hit both coasts in the same summer, but we might have. That demon inside of Der Vater was a hell of a driver, and the rest of us were a gang of unholy bandits, chasing our slice of the Canadian dream.

We didn't know it wasn't gasoline propelling us across the polite nation, but years of restrained agitation from sitting still for too long. We were rolling on the rocket fuel of rage: it's the only blessed way to travel. And, at the end of it all, as the homestead came into view, Der Vater slid in broadside in a cloud of smoke, and we were all used up, totally worn out, and loudly proclaiming, "Fuckin' eh!"

1983

Go West, young man, go west and grow up with the country.
An evergreen promise. But in this case, the country to the
West had already grown—prematurely in a sense—sprung
forward through the sticky growing pains of development by
the lucrative lubrication of an oil boom. Development was
in full swing, like the pulsing, steady growth of a tumour,
the cities of Calgary and Edmonton edged ever larger. New
roads, new buildings, new hopes and dreams! Destiny (of a
sort) had manifested in the Canadian prairies, but soon came
the aftermath. Like the hangover of a stupendous cocaine
binge, witness the fallout which optimistic futurists conve-
niently omitted from their utopian projections!

It was all familiar territory for Kaka. He learned in Iran how
flimsy a thing oil was to build a foundation on. It made everything slick, most of all the limbs of those who dealt in it, but they
shook hands with one another regardless. Promises made with
slippery hands are hardly promises kept. All the same, droves of
hopeful entrepreneurs streamed into Alberta just as they did in
the Middle East, seeking their fortunes. And here, just as there,
the demand for housing increased because of it.

Yet again, Kaka's hands were put to the task of creating
homes he could not afford to live in. Christopher negotiat-
ed a position for both men under a foreman for a development company. His posture was horrifically slouchy, he had a

219

large, rounded potbelly, and he sported a peculiar moustache with overgrown sideburns. And though it may be difficult to believe, this man's name was also Jerry. Remarkable coincidence, I know, but I assure you this is no narrative fabrication, nor is it an attempt to make a point by simplifying recurring characters into a single, laughably caricatured stereotype. It so happened to be the case that whenever Christopher and Kaka went searching for a job, they always came into contact with some beady-eyed, half competent, oafish buffoon whose name was always Jerry. Blame Canadian hiring standards if you wish, but do not dare doubt the veracity of this telling…

Anyway, the work they were commissioned to do was framing and framing alone. The atomizing influence of the factory model had infected every industry, it seemed. A single project was contracted out to multiple crews specializing in different areas of construction: concrete pouring, framing, bricklaying, drywalling, et cetera, et cetera. None could construct a home from start to finish on their own, at least not of the quality and grandeur of those they created together. Time was itemized to the minute and workers never saw the ones who did the jobs that preceded or succeeded their own. The dry-waller never met the framer; the tiler never met the plumber; the roofer never met the bricklayer; and nobody ever met the electrician. It was a charming arrangement that allowed everyone to come to the unfalsifiable conclusion that anyone involved in working on the house—except for themselves—was an incompetent jackass.

Suffice to say, there was not much camaraderie—nothing at least like the family that Dariush had curated. This crew was larger, to be sure, but none had risked their skin to be here. None had travelled from faraway lands, leaving the comfort and security of their homes for a shot at a better life. No, these workers were of a kind with the farmers in Punjab who were content to live and die with what they were born with, perhaps with small aspirations to accumulate a little more. Comfort and security, not the irascible itch for *more*. The quality and intensity of their work reflected this ethos, many taking long lunches or "going for a smoke" when particularly toilsome work came up. It was a philosophy of taking the path of least resistance, of which nothing could be said against, but with which Kaka had nothing in common.

Christopher was the exception. Whatever Dariush saw in Kaka, Gill, and Rajbir, and dozens of the other men he hired to work for him, it certainly existed in Christopher as well. He was quick, efficient, strong, and clever. He did not complain or drag his heels. He set to work like a metronome, mechanically reliable. But there, beneath the physicality of it all was that quality, indescribable but recognizable, a quiet fury—the alloy of resolve. It was almost like looking into a mirror for Kaka, except that it remained a mystery what drove Christopher to work so hard. Still, he had not uttered a single word to explain why he abandoned a well-paying job to come out West. A strange motivation, but even more strange was how Christopher was perceived in this new environment. More accurately, how he seemed not to be perceived at all. Kaka appeared to be the only one who was aware of Christopher's value. No one else recognized it; indeed, they all went so far as to ignore it. Not an active disrespect but more of a concerted effort to disregard, to not notice, like an artifact conjuring regret that you prefer to lock away rather than look at. It was a passing observation that Kaka gave little importance to. So long as he was paid fairly, he was content, and Christopher appeared to be of the same mind.

These circumstances persisted for some months, well into the summer when the world began to thaw and the grey sky finally faded away. Singing birds and blooming buds, the green of the boreal forests opened up and breathed slow and deep, far and wide. It was a time when Canadian optimism should have been at its highest point, when the slick handshakes of oil men finally paid their dues. But, instead, the marketplace decided to rear its head in the opposite direction. The houses that Kaka built remained empty, and others built even before them were left abandoned. The buses, which such a short time ago brought hundreds of eager, grinning people to Alberta, began to arrive empty, and the buses leaving had long queues of disappointed faces waiting outside them.

You see, aside from Kaka, the tremors of the Iranian Revolution had also crossed the Atlantic, and had slowly been exerting their influence on the Western economy. The violence was of a quieter sort, effecting most strongly the indecipherable conjectures of Wall Street prospectors, who clammed up or broke down every time the leader of one of those oil producing countries threw a rock over the fence at their neighbour. The cause of this world recession was in part due to Khomeini's squabbles with the person who granted him asylum when he was banished from Iran—a shrewd and ironfisted man named Saddam Hussein.

Of course, Jerry knew none of this. He was not a keen observer of the world affairs portion of the daily newspaper. Once in a while, with a finger poking vigorously into a nostril, he glanced at the comics, and when no one was peeking over his shoulder he flipped to the personals to read over propositions of lonely single women (his fingers were poking vigorously elsewhere in this case.) But Jerry didn't need to be aware of the acute political manoeuvres of Middle Eastern dictators to know the contracts for new housing developments were not coming in anymore. It was not his fault then when—reclined comfortably in a maroon swivel chair—he called Kaka into his office and casually said, "Sorry bud, can't keep ya on no more." Via an entirely objective process, Christopher received the same news a few minutes later. A conspiratorial thinker might come to conclude that Indians, regardless of the type, had been discriminated against here, but that is a bag of worms this narrator has no desire to dig through.

Instead, we will follow Kaka and Christopher as they bounced around the province between short-term employment opportunities: odd jobs on worksites and in warehouses, general labour on the last major contracts whose funding was yet to be pulled, cutting the grass of beer-drinking oil executives who had lost the will to maintain their own yards. When they were hired, the Jerrys in charge were always impressed by their work ethic and competency. "Thought Indians were a lazy bunch of fuckers," they said, which Christopher knew was more a reference to his kind of Indian than Kaka's. But impressed as they were, none of these employers had the means to keep them on for any length of time. In the '69 Ford Ranger, they went north, making their way up the province until they landed in a quaint little town supported by a large pulp mill, called Grand Prairie in Alberta.

It was a vibrant locality, seemingly insulated from the oil bust plaguing the rest of the cities in Alberta. Kaka and Christopher got their hopes up. But, as they inquired about open positions, a visibly less affable Jerry who oversaw the mill expressed himself with an unprovoked candour. "The fuck you Pakis keep coming from? Ain't no jobs up here all right. Now fuck off!" Christopher furrowed his brow at the unfamiliar slur but Kaka—who felt seen for the first time in a long while—slapped the Indian on his back reassuringly. "Paki ij me," he said, as they walked back to Christopher's truck.

The summer sun was sinking low beyond the western horizon. This far north, the moon was already high and bright in the violet-red sky. The brightest of the stars had managed to begin their display as well, piercing the heavenly fabric with darts of silver. All the celestial objects hovering there at once—in times past, perhaps an omen of something. "Now vat?" Kaka asked.

Christopher stiffened. He had his eyes trained somewhere far out of view, watching the last tendrils of light as they passed into darkness. West, where Maher used to look, remembering a place that was lost to him. The quiet fury in Christopher pronounced itself in the heavy veins on his forearm, the clenched muscles of his jaw, a tightness through him like wound coil, and then all at once he released. A slow gust of wind pressed against them from the east and Christopher said, "I'm going home."

1955-1975 / 1846-1893

Christopher was the only name he remembered. "It is a good Christian name," Sister Judith would tell him after she whipped him with a yardstick. But the child before Christopher—the child with a forgotten name—remembered the blurry scene of a home and the retreating faces of crying people he once called parents. He stayed as still as he could, but the distance between them grew larger each moment because the man from the government gripped him tight and walked with a quickened pace. Now he was whipped when he refused to use his Christian name. He was whipped when he refused to speak the English tongue. He was whipped for all manner of things. Sometimes, he was whipped when he thought back to those crying faces. He did not know how Sister Judith knew what he was thinking, but she seemed to be able to. So, he trained himself to not think of them anymore, and now Christopher was the only name he remembered.

At age seven, Duleep Singh sat on the seat his father had sat on. His mother stood next to him, her hand resting reassuringly on his shoulder. She was a strong woman and a cunning tactician, and her word was respected among the throne's political advisors and military generals. But even her loving council was not enough to prevent the British East India Company from breaking the army of the Sikh Empire at the Battle of Aliwal. Duleep did not know why everyone around him looked so sad. He did not know his mother had just received news that the commanders of the Sikh army had refused to surrender and that their forces had been decimated by the merciless Englishmen.

"Jesus Christ is your lord and saviour," Sister Judith would say each day. She did not say "Hello" or "Good Morning," but every day she would say, "Jesus Christ is your lord and saviour." But the remark confused Christopher endlessly. What kind of saviour would send him to this place where he was told to scrub the floors in rooms he had never stepped foot in, for hours on end? To scrub until his arms were numb and the skin on his knees was scrapped raw. What kind of a saviour would endorse Sister Judith's methods, how she whipped her yardstick until the welts on Christopher's back opened and poured blood? What kind of a saviour would allow the priests to drag children younger than Christopher to the broom closet and inflict wounds that were too deep to see? Why didn't his lord and saviour help him to escape from this place, which was the only thing he needed to be saved from?

Duleep began to see his mother less and less, until one day she vanished completely. Instead, the hand that rested on his shoulder belonged to one Dr. John Login. When Duleep inquired about his mother, Dr. Login waved his hands around, or pretended as if he could not hear Duleep, or when the child was being particularly obstinate about the topic, Dr. Login said, "You'll see her in due course, my boy. Now sign your name here, will you." Duleep didn't read the pages he was asked to sign. There were so many of them and all he wanted was to see his mother again. With his mind on her, he scrawled his name on the bottom of a page which read, "*His Highness the Maharajah Duleep Singh shall resign for himself, his heirs, and his successors all right, title, and claim to the sovereignty of the Punjab, or to any sovereign power whatever.*"

Christopher had never heard of "*The Act to Encourage Gradual Civilization of Indian Tribes in this Province and to Amend the Laws relating to Indians*" but it was the reason Sister Judith was in his life. There was a goal that Sister Judith was striving to achieve and it had something to do with this idea called "civilization." Apparently, Christopher was still not civilized because his pronunciation of certain words was not correct, he forgot to say his prayers to his unlistening saviour at night, and some stubborn part of him remembered fondly that place the child with the forgotten name was taken from. Christopher did not know of Sister Judith's motives. He did not know Sister Judith prayed to God each morning for the courage to "kill the Indian in the child."

Dr. Login was not a cruel man. In fact, he was very nice to Duleep, but he never left him alone. Duleep was not allowed to go anywhere Dr. Login did not permit and he was only allowed to speak to people who Dr. Login allowed and read what Dr. Login assigned. Gradually, English soldiers took the places of Sikh generals; Gurus were replaced with Saints; and the holy text of Punjab was pushed aside in favour of the King James Bible. His title as Maharaja was quoted less and the confused honorific "Black Prince of Perthshire" was used more frequently. The strategy was simple—remove the child as far away from his home as possible. Remove him from the savagery of his heritage and place him among the refined sensibilities of the civilized world. And where is more civilized than the court of Queen Victoria of England, the First Empress of India? When Duleep was brought before her, she peered down at him and remarked to her court of ogling servants as one might of a zoo animal. "Those eyes and teeth are too beautiful!"

Christopher grew old enough to finally be released from the tutelage of Sister Judith, and he was excited to finally join this "civilized world" he had been told about. When he tried to, though, he was treated in much the same manner that Sister Judith treated him. Whatever it meant to be civilized, clearly Christopher was incapable of achieving it. When he went searching for a job, he was turned away without a thought. One proprietor of a grocery store vocalized what all the others preferred to remain silent about. "You lazy Indians ain't good for working." Another time, as Christopher was simply walking down the street, he heard someone mumble from behind him a term he had heard countless times from Sister Judith: "Savage-blooded."

Queen Victoria was enamoured of the idea of "noble blood." So enamoured, in fact, that she married her cousin, who looked much like she did. Noble blood needed to be preserved, not diluted with the commonality and barbarism of savage blood. But Duleep was not sure what about the Queen's blood made it so noble. Her eyes were beady and her teeth were not so beautiful, and even her son Leopold seemed sickly. His noble blood seemed to be in an awful rush to leave his body. Perhaps, that was the mark of noble blood, Duleep thought to himself, that it is ever eager to leave its noble body.

Christopher grew weary of the civilized world and thought back to the home of the child with a forgotten name. He thought he might find some vestige of happiness there, so he followed his memories, and his feet carried him. But when he arrived, he saw a place that was nothing like the memory which kept him warm through the coldest parts of his life. He saw a great many things he did not remember seeing before.

Dilapidated houses with boarded windows. Cracked and un-maintained roads. Heavily intoxicated men and women lying lethargically in front of their houses or stumbling around. Everything he had learned about "civilization" was screaming to him that this place was anything but. But then, from a distance, he saw the faces that had cried when he was carried away. As he approached, they turned to him and cycled through a multitude of emotions until realization emerged. In his heart, Christopher knew that they remembered him as he remembered them. He was embraced, and his mother and father began to speak to him at the same time. But Christopher no longer understood what they were saying. As they spoke that language of the child—the Indian who was killed—Christopher only remembered Sister Judith's yardstick cracking against his body. His father shook him by the shoulder and said something, to which Christopher whispered, "I'm sorry. I don't understand you."

Thirteen years after he last saw her, Duleep was granted permission to see his mother. The young, headstrong woman of authority no longer existed. A weary and half-blind entity had taken her place. But deep within, something of her fire lived, and slowly she reminded Duleep where he came from and what he was. The son of a Sikh king who was stolen away from his throne, stolen away from his faith, and stolen away from his mother. But she gave him back some of what he had lost. Even when his mother died and Duleep was refused permission to take her body back to their ancestral home to perform her cultural burial rights. Even when his efforts to research the wrongs committed against him were thwarted by the Queen's advisors. Even when he died and his body was not sent to its birthplace, but burned and discarded in the land of his captors, he still was reminded, even if slightly, even if only for a moment, that he was the trueborn son of Ranjit Singh, the Lion of Punjab.

1983

The Peace River begins its journey in the frozen tips of the Rocky Mountains and flows east across British Columbia to Alberta. Fort St. John sits north of the Peace River, just before the Pine River to the south feeds into it. In the space between where the rivers converge is a vast forest. Christopher's ancestors called this place home as the waters on either side were carving their veins into the earth.

In this forest, Kaka and Christopher spent two days stalking a buck. Long stretches of silence atop grassy knolls and rocky outcrops, scanning the hillsides and tree lines for movement. Slow hikes investigating perturbed earth and following the wafting scent of fresh excrement. All until Christopher gently pushed his hand back into Kaka's chest, ushering him to stop. He pointed forward and, two hundred yards away in an open field of grass, the buck snapped and straightened his head.

Christopher lay flat on the ground and pulled the rifle butt tightly into his shoulder. Kaka lay next to him. Christopher found the buck in his sights and focused on his breathing, taking measure of the slow rise and fall of the reticle. A final slow release of breath and then the trigger slowly retracted behind the weight of his index finger. The firing pin shot forward and struck the back of the bullet casing. Gunpowder ignited, and the bullet was torpedoed through the barrel, obtaining a steady clockwise spin from the barrel rifling. The crack of the bullet leaving the barrel broke the silence and all that was visible of the rifle's work was the casing erupting in a puff of black carbon and steaming as it seared the grass.

Two hundred yards away the buck's head snapped in their direction. It staggered, kicked its hind legs and galloped forward two leaps, and then collapsed into the brush. Christopher leaped to his feet and hurried over to inspect his shot. Kaka followed close behind. The buck's eyes were wide—pain and horror clearly visible. Legs twitching and laboured breathing. Christopher loaded another round into the chamber of his rifle, cocked the bolt, and directed the barrel tip to the side of the animal's head. When he pulled the trigger, another crack broke the silent air, the buck relented in its dying spasms and, though the eyes remained open, all life faded from them.

Christopher employed Kaka in field dressing the animal, instructing him to make cuts along all four legs above the hooves, and then down the leg, down the belly, down the sternum. Peeling the skin back and making short, measured cuts only where the skin sticks to the flesh. When the internal organs were exposed, Christopher pulled the heart aside along with the lace-like caul fat that lines the innards. He made a gesture, raising his pinched hand to his mouth, and Kaka interpreted that this would be their dinner for the night.

Evening set upon them slowly, graciously giving them enough light to set up camp and start a fire. Christopher wrapped the deer heart with the caul fat and pierced it with a sharp branch from the edge of their camp. He hammered the branch into the ground, so the heart hovered over the heat of the flames, and eventually, rendered fat began to drip and sizzle as it hit burning wood. A bottle of whisky was opened and was passed back and forth. They sat in silence, quietly regarding the beauty of the night.

They were unable to speak to one another in any depth, but what might they have said were they able? Would they have spoken of how it was they came to sit by this fire? Christopher, whose forefathers travelled west to east, across the Bering Strait, untold centuries prior, battling against a merciless natural world; and Kaka who went from east to west, navigating the tumultuous geography of an increasingly global and industrialized world, contending with all the evils inherent therein. Would they agree that regardless of the route, regardless of the hurdles, both were searching for a better life? Would they discuss the peculiar moniker, "Indian," derived from the Indus River, which neither man had ever seen or stepped into? Or would they discuss that tainted aqueous humour they were both imbued with, that "savage blood"?

Let's dispense with the theorizing. Let us give them voices and hear what they discuss under the blanket of an infinite sky of stars, in the basking glow of a roaring fire, the smell of venison permeating the air, and a breeze from the western shore cooling the heat of the whisky in their throats. Savage-blooded heathens, both, philosophizing south of the Peace River in British Columbia, Canada.

"You are fortunate to have been born in a land of such opportunity," Kaka says. "Canada is an amazing place."

Christopher, quiet and stoic in his demeanour replies, "What kind of opportunity are you referring to?"

And Kaka clarifies, "Look around you. This place affords so many possibilities. The land is fertile and vast and cheap, and industry is accelerating here. With enough effort you could easily afford a durable house made of brick and eat three square meals a day. You could build a business, make a name for yourself, and create a lasting legacy for your family."

"Of what importance are these things? Houses made of brick and industry and legacy?" Christopher muses. He pokes at the fire, and a circle of flaming ashes rises into the black sky.

"They offer security," Kaka answers. "Freedom from the fear of starvation. And beyond that a purpose to pursue in life. An opportunity to create something that persists through the ages. What else is there?"

"I do not know," Christopher replies, "but this seems to me to be the wrong way to see the world. It assumes that something lasting can ever be created, and this feels untrue to me. And it also imposes a burden on the person who believes it to be true, for how can you pursue a thing that can never be attained?"

· "You can only pursue a thing which cannot be attained," Kaka asserts. "It is precisely this desire for the impossible that makes life worth living, for what would be the point if you could achieve all you wanted? Your soul would wither and die. Your heart would ache for the ache of desire."

Christopher reflects, allowing a significant silence to pass before he replies, "Your soul may not wither and die, but it will never find peace. Your heart will not ache for desire, but it will never be full."

Without pause, Kaka says, "Yours is a philosophy born of abundance. Mine is a mentality born of scarcity. I will worry about these things when my family and I no longer need to worry about starvation. When my belly is full, I will be happy to speak with you about the fullness of my heart."

"I think you will do great things in your life, but I fear you may never understand that you do not need to for your life to have meaning," Christopher says, trailing off as he looks to the sky above. And Kaka does not reply. He knows, somehow, that Christopher is right, because a man cannot fight his nature, or if he can then he is not strong enough to win. After a moment Christopher says a final thing. "You are right, though, Canada is an amazing place." He does not bother to explain why, because his early memories of stories around a campfire remind him of the importance and impact of silence on a discourse—how things unsaid are often louder than those that are said.

Kaka places a heavy log on the fire and its weight crumbles the embers beneath it. The fire crackles and the fresh log hisses as steam evaporates from its pores. The two men sip their whisky and quietly contemplate the quintessence of Canada—a stubbornly elusive thing.

2008

I'm in the back cab of the '97 Ford Ranger with the First Man and the Toucan up front, and we're flying down the highway and every gentle manoeuvre of the ship sends me sliding back and forth. We're young and stupid and intoxicated, the three of us, and we're chasing immortality in all the wrong ways. Trees whizz by in my peripheral vision on either side, and the sky is black and naked and beautiful, and the air is crisp and clean, and I can't stop grinning up at it, because all I can think is that the '97 Ford Ranger is the best thing ever created. On the sheer, vast, untarnished canvas I splay out my thoughts and compose my ode. Here it is:

The school's named after a Saint, St. Someone or other. The building's a hideous, uninspired, utilitarian concrete block. Kills your imagination before you step inside. But when you do step inside you learn the following:

Jatts don't like the other Punjabis, like the Shimbas, and the Khatris—but all Punjabis don't like other Indians, the Hindus and the Christian Goans and the Christian Tamils. And some of these feelings are reciprocated, like the Muslims who dislike all other religions. But what is most true is that all Indians do not like West Indians. The national moniker is already shared with the American Indians and it does not need to be further diluted. Punjab is as far west as you can go as an Indian.

The Viets don't like the Flips (that's Filipinos for the layman), but both hate the Chinese. Koreans are sometimes the arbiters of these feuds. But woe to him who confuses followers of Confucius, with followers of Buddha, with followers of Christ, simply because they all eat noodles.

The Canadian Blacks don't like anyone, except the Muslims if they're black enough, which mostly means the Somalians born in the west. But they especially don't like the African Blacks born in Africa and the feeling is mutual. Also notable: the Canadian Blacks who live on one side of St. Someone High School deeply detest the Canadian Blacks who live on the other side of it. (Everyone likes the Caribbean Blacks.)

Most of the whites do not have explosive grudges, but keep in mind that the Italians aren't fond of the Portuguese. And don't ever in your life seat a Croatian next to a Serb. Don't even think about it. The Polish are not friendly, but they can sit anywhere they like.

The whites—and I mean the whitey whites, with their parents happily divorced and remarried, who are happily doing kickflips in the parking lot, with their dirt-brown hair matted against their foreheads, and who say, "brooo suuuppp?" with their faux deep voices that are projected unnaturally from the back of their throats—are painfully inoffensive and are welcome nearly everywhere but they prefer the company of other whitey whites.

I imagine that this is the case in classrooms and cafeterias of all ugly brick buildings across the nation.

But none of this true.

Because I only see Dao the Viet in the parking lot, sitting on the edge of the back cab, shuffling a deck of playing cards originating in the Tang Dynasty of China, speaking fast and loud, "Five dollars a game, five dollars a chop, if you don't know how to play, please kindly fuck off," pitching his voice high on the last word before each comma or period. Polish

Daniel, Arabic Zain, and Isiah from the Ivory Coast each slap down a crisp blue bill with bald Willy Laurier staring solemnly up into the crisp blue sky. Taneesha and her sassy henchman approach from the Italian bakery run by the nonnas who love Bapu ji—pizza slices in hand—peering over the side of the cab, heckling the losers. Chen Zheng, Josh Ming, and Tony the Tamil are munching on deep fried samosas from the New India restaurant across the main road—three for a dollar—waiting for their turn. Tony is actually Sinhalese, but everyone calls him a Tamil because it gets on his nerves. The wheezy voice of Louisiana's own is pounding from the open cockpit windows. *Da Drought 3*, the hottest mixtape of the summer, and the next one besides. Universally loved are pho and shawarma, but only the thoroughbreds can stomach the suicide sauce on the wrap, and with scorched tongues they earn the right to call the rest of us "fucking pussies." Craig (the whitest of the whitey whites) astonishes Arabic Zain, Zain from Pakistan, and Maryam, by wolfing down an unprecedented double suicide shawarma. Dao says, "If you wanna play for free, go and talk to Tommy." Tommy is Dao's cousin and is parked to the side in his German made '95 BMW 525i. Tommy lets you know you can play a free game if you buy a half-quarter of homegrown purple haze, and Gurvir and Amandeep are haggling with him, trying to trade a bottle of garage-brewed desi daru for a quarter. It's made by Gurvir's chacha[174] who lives next to the 401, so the fumes are a pleasant pick me up for the commuters contemplating gridlock suicide on the Highway of Heroes. The daru is slowly peeling away layers of plastic from the water bottle, so time is of the essence. But then Luca Bianchi offers to buy the bottle for the same price as a quarter of Tommy's kush, because he likes how the daru reminds him of a stronger tasting sambuca. Everyone gets what they want. The back lip of the cab is down and Abdul Mohammad and Cindy Ngo and Tayshawn Jackson are passing a blunt rolled with Tommy's

---

174 Uncle, specifically your dad's younger brother.

kush back and forth, and it's straining the suspension of the truck, but it's worth it. Luca joins them with the moonshine. Isiah says, "Passe ca ici" and Tayshawn says, "In English you fuck," and there's a collective chuckle at Isiah's expense, but he still gets the blunt and he's grinning now, too. Dao slaps a chop down on Daniel's hand and Taneesha shouts, "He just shoved a Kolbassa right up yo ass!" and Chen Zhang nearly chokes on the crispy folded lip of his last samosa. Now the freestyle from the track "Seat Down Low" enters the portion that sticks in the collective imagination. Tommy shouts out his window, "Yo jack the volume up!" Lil Wayne's wheezy voice splits the air and everyone is singing along. Dao allows a pause in the game—a rare thing reserved for sacred occurrences—he mouths the words too. Taneesha clasps her dexterous fingers together, contorting them to spell out "blood" and continues the verse. Tayshawn inhales deep and recites the last part, and then he exhales a thick white cloud of kush that happily pollutes the air around the truck. Dao is the first to say "Bomb track!" and directs the attention back to the game of Big Two, where he slaps another chop down on Arabic Zain, who responds by saying, "Fuck you, habibi." Bellies are full with Indian samosas, Turkish shawarma, Italian pastas, Vietnamese pho, French Canadian poutine, Russian potato salad, Portuguese barbeque chicken, American hamburgers, Southern American fried chicken, Indo-Chinese hakka noodles, and desi daru drinkers wince and pound their chests, and blunt smoke wafts in the air, and we worship a pantheon of monotheistic deities, and we are unified through rituals of sin, and the universal language of laughter fills our hearts, and the '97 Ford Ranger is the best thing ever created, because the cab of a '97 Ford Ranger is the most Canadian fuckin' place on Earth.

1983

The urban world is a simulacrum of life, but the representation offered is unidimensional. Narrow brick alleys and cracked, congested roads and buildings and houses in dizzying arrays of symmetry and repetition. Artificial lights shining in the colour of urine, blinding out everything worth seeing and revealing what it is not. Sounds that screech and grind incessantly against the eardrums, and air infused with unseen black carbon, slowly suffocating everything that breathes. Most of all, too much of humanity exists in cities and not enough of anything else, which leaves one with the impression that life is abrasive, unsentimental, and competitive. But seven days in the forests of Northern Canada had shown Kaka that life could be a much quieter thing, a much gentler thing.

In Punjab, Kaka was surrounded by farmers tilling the earth. This exposure led to an understanding of nature's operations that were necessarily instrumental, that they exist *for* humanity. The weathered hands of hundreds of workers ran through the dark soil and then, months later, the same hands reaped the crops which grew. A profound relationship between man and earth, but it could never be properly divorced from its economic underpinnings—the seasons churned onwards, and the next harvest was always looked toward as a new goal.

But now he pondered something paradoxical. Here, where nature determined its own course, divorced not only from human economy, but also from human scales of time—did any of it have value in the absence of human consciousness? Ancient Douglas firs with moss-peppered bark, breathing out life as they stretched their authority ever higher into the heavens; the steady rumble of mighty rivers, a slow accumulation of godlike power through the counterproductive method of avoiding obstacles; and the ever-present whispers of wildlife, a symphonic harmony of life and death and codependence that quietly rang out with no justification. All of it undeniably beautiful. But that ability to experience, remember, reflect, and project—to see something as arbitrary as a flower sprout and to find meaning in it as a metaphor for existence itself—is a thoroughly human endeavour. Would it matter at all in our absence?

The question had no answer; it presupposed consciousness. *Cogito ergo cogito*, the value of the thing-in-itself (if such value exists) can never be separated from the person who is doing the thinking. In fact, even the person can be doubted. Only the existence of the thought can be proved—therefore valued—and nothing besides. But all the same, Kaka decided that even if he had never witnessed it, the world would be a poorer place if these woods did not exist. He found a sense of peace in the act of contemplation for the sake of contemplation, and when it was time for him to leave the forest south of Peace River, he went with bittersweet sentiments.

He would have stayed if the weight of other people's expectations did not sit so heavily on his shoulders, but they did—he was tethered to those who relied on him by a rope woven equal parts from obligation and love. Christopher was not so burdened. Indeed, he agreed to Kaka's original proposition to travel west because he wanted to return home, and for him, home was a solitary place. "This is the end of the road for me, my friend," he told Kaka, and, of course, revelling as he was in the serenity of this place, Kaka understood.

Christopher offered to take Kaka to Fort St. John and, for the final time, they climbed into his '69 Ford Ranger and headed north, crossing the Peace River.

In 1783, Alexander Mackenzie, seeking a path to the Pacific, floated in his canoe by the land that would become Fort St. John. Two hundred years later, the tradition of passing the place by was upheld strongly by the majority of commuters who drove through without more than a glance. The town was not much to speak of; a few two-lane roads arranged in a grid pattern, cut through by Highway 97 (the Alaska Highway), which finds its termination point at the continent's end.

The houses lining the street were not impressive either, most of them foregoing brick exteriors in favour of the cheaper and more quickly assembled laminate siding. Nothing grandiose or opulent, the whole town appeared to have been erected for the sole purpose of pulling oil from the ground, as evidenced by the fact that most of the inhabitants were men, and there were many buildings bearing the words "oil" and "drilling." The place was designed under the auspices of greed and environmental exploitation—first the fur trade and now the black gold. Also striking was that out of all the other cities he had seen in Canada, here there were more people who looked like Christopher, at least superficially. The same lightly tanned skin, the same matte-black hair, but where Christopher stood tall, with a focused stare, many of these others were slouched and withered, and they stumbled through the streets with glazed eyes. The sight of them made Christopher visibly tense. He gripped the steering wheel tight and clenched his jaw. He knew better than most the consequences of unmitigated greed and exploitation.

All in all, it was a woefully unromantic place.

Christopher pulled to a stop on the corner of 100 Street and 100 Avenue. He reached his hand out, and Kaka was overcome with a kind of emptiness, the same he felt when he left his family for Afghanistan, Saleem Ali for Iran, Dariush and his adoptive family for Europe, and Gill for Canada. It was compounded by the essence of this place, which felt smaller and more far removed than any other place before it. At least in the other cases he had moved on under the impression that a greater world lay ahead, but now he felt like he had come to the end of it. Were the Earth flat, the vast ocean would pour over the final edge, and at the bottom would lie Fort St. John. He shook Christopher's hand all the same. In unfamiliar territories, it was natural to fall into familiar modes of behaviour, and no behaviour was more familiar to Kaka than moving on.

Christopher rumbled off in the '69 Ford Ranger and Kaka turned his attention to the most pressing task at hand—finding employment. Luckily, the town was small, so it was not a great burden to walk on foot to potential employers. Unluckily, the town was small, so there were not a great number of potential employers. The respective Jerrys who were managing the first two oil companies that Kaka approached informed him that they were fully staffed. But the third Jerry, looking a little disgruntled and agitated, said, "Yeah, I just got a spot open up; had to let someone go today." Kaka cleared his throat and gave his practised, reliable pitch, simple and straight to the point. "I good verker," he asserted, slapping his chest, and then added the more important clause, "Verk cheap." Jerry furrowed his brows and rubbed his chin, trying his hardest to read a book by its cover, and from near the gate of the building someone shouted, "Eh, phuckh ju Jerry, panchode kutiya!"[175]

A quick transition from chin rubbing to temple rubbing and Jerry muttered, "Ah fuck, not this guy again." Kaka strained his eyes against the sun, trying to make out the silhouette of the man who was shouting all too familiar profanities. "You're fired, pal. Just get your shit and get the fuck out of here, eh," Jerry yelled back. "Fucking hell, if I knew you were gonna be this much trouble, I'd have booted ya just

175 Fuck you Jerry, you sister-fucking dog!

when I saw ya!" Kaka continued blinking, not because the sun was obstructing his vision, but because he could no longer believe what he was seeing. The yelling man came close enough to notice Kaka, and now the anger dissipated from his face and a look of disbelief replaced it. "Ah ki panchode kismat ne khich leyanda!"[176]

Shinda, the Lubani, had found a way to trot all the way across the planet.

---

176 What have the sister-fucking fates dragged in over here!

1957-1983

Are villains born or bred? It's an impossible question to answer in many ways. For example, in the case of the young doe-eyed thief Grewal, the answer was ambiguous. A strong argument could be made that whatever prompted him to inflict such violence on Kaka in Afghanistan was a result of the cruelty he experienced at the hands of his mother, Shivani. And perhaps, in turn, her cruelty grew out of the horror of what she experienced when she was a young woman. But, on the other hand, there might have been some genetic germ in her from the start, passed along from her parents, who were too callous to ease the suffering of their child when she needed them most. And with Grewal that possibility was only amplified, given the nature of the man from whose seed he was sprung.

Though in the case of Shinda, the question was even more perplexing. His was not a learned hatred in the slightest, for Shinda's parents were perfectly loving people, with no malice in their hearts, and they provided as much as they could with their humble means. It was, rather, one of those mutations of fate that saw the child born hating the world, imbued with an all-consuming resentment in his heart. When first he crawled and his palms fell upon supple blades of grass, he tore them from their roots for no other reason than to see something wither. When first he walked, his eyes caught the sight of a trail of ants, and the impulse to crush them beneath his heel pulled him forward.

His disposition was less than human, the concept of empathy entirely foreign to him. He was like a fox, with a sense of concern that was short and feeble, so short it ended at the tip of his nose, and so feeble it could only bear the weight of a single entity. This selfishness motivated all his actions in the world. He wanted more for himself, to be above everything, and to take as much as he could, only so there would be less left for everyone else.

But in this, Ahmedpura proved to be a poor sandbox for Shinda. In his youth, he preoccupied himself with hollow mischief, ordering the Chuhra to perform pointless tasks, like moving piles of bricks that needed no moving, or stirring up conflict like when he travelled to Bagradi to inform Grahini's brothers about her indiscretions with Gora, and then when the two parties inevitably scuffled, to hail rocks down on all of them. But these were crass pastimes. Ultimately, Ahmedpura was too small a pond, the people too small-minded, and any rewards to be reaped too small a win. However, when Kaka revealed to Shinda that he was fed up with Punjab and was prepared to leave Ahmedura for greater opportunities, Shinda's chest swelled. Right then and there a plan revealed itself to him. Difficult yes, complicated yes, but if he could manage it, he would be free of this place, once and for all.

Earlier that day, he had just got off the phone with his preposterously fat, dim-witted cousin from Delhi, Jeet Singh, who wouldn't shut up about how "Iran taan Amreecka hi ban geya!"[177] He had called Shinda to convince him to join the latest work expedition he was arranging, a terribly unlucrative enterprise on either side. For the workers paying to leave India, nothing but the promise of backbreaking labour, and for Jeet Singh, a sliver of commission that hardly covered the cost of staying in business. The most expensive part of the

---

177   Iran is like America now!

arrangement was undoubtably the cost of the travel visas. If that could be avoided somehow, a sizable purse would remain. All he needed to do was sway his moronic cousin with the carrot of greed.

It took some convincing, some subtle manipulation, but he managed to bring his vision to fruition. It was agreed that Jeet Singh would arrange for the party to travel to Afghanistan, where entry from India was freely permitted, and once there he would leave under the pretense of buying visas to Iran. Jeet Singh would then make his way back to India, where Shinda would meet him as soon as he was able to slip away without suspicion, and they could split the purse.

Once he managed to slip away from Afghanistan, and his plane finally touched down on the tarmac of the Delhi Airport, he let a wide grin emerge on his face. Was there any remorse in his heart? Perhaps a whisper of guilt expressed itself, a soft tingle that radiated in the back of his skull, but he quickly rationalized it away. The stubborn idiot Kaka had brought his fate unto himself after all, insisting on staying in Afghanistan with no money and no path forward.

And if Shinda did for a moment lose resolve in his misanthropy—like a wayward disciple might lose faith in God—it was restored the moment he reconvened with his cousin, blubbering around in the courtyard of his home, squealing out nonsense like "mera taun ki karaata, Shindeya?"[178] and "paisay vapaas de diye, Shindeya. Rab karke karde."[179] He needed only to meditate on a person like Jeet Singh for a moment, for all his hatred to be restored. A resounding justification of his belief in the ignobility of people, treacherous enough to engage in betrayal, yet too weak to see it through to the end.

No matter, he took his half of the purse and returned to Ahmedpura to pack his bags. It took no longer than a day, eager as he was to avoid a run in with Gora or Kala, or Kaka's

---

178 What have you made me do, Shinda?
179 Let's give the money back, Shinda. For god's sake please.

mother, or anyone who might ply him with unwanted questions for that matter. He hardly said more than few words to his parents about his return, and even less about his imminent departure. As far as he was concerned, this was the last time he would ever step foot in this miserable little village. He left with something less than complete detachment, less than total apathy. He purged his memories of the place and the people who lived in it, and as he walked down the single dirt road out of Ahmedpura, it was as if it never existed at all.

But when Shinda landed in his chosen destination, Ontario, Canada, he was somewhat dismayed to learn that he felt the same as he always had. The people were just as annoying here as they were in India. The head baba at the truck yard Gurdwara, for example, would not stop nattering away. Always smiling, pestering Shinda with questions about Punjab, doddering around behind him in a servile way, saying, "Sub kush teek ah, puth?"[180] And the endless parade of Canadian middle managers, with all their pointless work and orders. Shinda was no Chuhra and he did not appreciate being treated like one.

You see, Shinda was mistaken about one crucial thing. He had assumed his resentment was a result of having been born and raised in a place as pathetic as Ahmedpura. He had assumed leaving and travelling to a place more advanced and more exciting would alleviate the weight of hatred on his heart. Grewal, younger and less keen of mind than Shinda, still had access to a fundamental truth of existence that Shinda was ignorant about. Perhaps because he had endured so much senseless pain in his life he was better equipped to understand, for he knew when he left Jaipur, the pink city of kings, that whatever he found out in the great wide world would not change the contents of his heart. He knew that the world is a manifestation of what we bring to it, not the other way around, and since his was a heart born and moulded by violence, violence is what it brought to the world.

---

180 Is everything to your liking, child?

When one night at the Gurdwara, this realization finally crystalized for Shinda, he decided to do as his nature instructed. When there was no one paying attention, he made away with the Gurdwara's donation box and headed west, where he hoped to find, at the least, more interesting scenery than a burnt-out tire lot. Along the way, he kept his keen eyes open for things of value that could be snatched quickly and quietly. When suspicion began to mount, he simply moved on, conjuring fake names and random samplings of nine digits in place of social security numbers. In this manner he hopscotched his way across Canada: Manitoba, Saskatchewan, Alberta, up to a small town called Grande Prairie, where he managed to pickpocket the car keys of the foreman at a paper mill. In his new automobile, he then crossed the final border of the nation to an unassuming little place called Fort St. John in British Columbia...

1983

"Hold up, you know this fucking guy?" Jerry exclaimed as Shinda embraced Kaka, laughing heartily. "Forget about the job, I don't need any more of this trouble, eh. Just get the fuck outta here," he ordered, and then he huffed off back into the factory.

"Tun ithey ki kardein?"[181] Kaka asked. He hadn't spoken to Shinda since the day at the bus station in Afghanistan. That was years ago. Even on the rare occasions he had managed to connect to someone from Ahmedpura through the international phone line in Patti, he hadn't heard anything more about Shinda than that he one day came back home and quickly left without a word to anyone. It was assumed he had simply found work somewhere in Punjab or another state in India and was too busy to visit. Shinda didn't say much to elaborate on this, answering with a short and scantily detailed story. He was never able to track down Jeet Singh, he said, but his father was willing to provide the requisite funds for a visa and ticket to Canada. It was no meagre sum as Kaka knew first-hand, and he wasn't aware that Shinda's father was doing so well financially. But he didn't press the topic, because such things are uncouth, and besides, Shinda seemed eager for other discussions.

---

181 What are you doing here?"

"Vaal kitalay fir, sullah lagdein,"[182] he said, ruffling his hand through Kaka's hair. Since it had been cut, it had grown back in curly locks, and before Kaka could respond Shinda quickly pivoted to a new topic. "Ithey kam nahi mil da. Mere naal chal, America chaliye."[183] He spoke with an easy manner—the kind which made Kaka feel as though he had just spoken to Shinda yesterday, and that this was the most casual of requests. Kaka took a look around him. His surroundings were charmless, lifeless, the kind of place that one could take full stock of in less than an hour of roaming around. Also, it was clear that Jerry of the oil company had no intention of hiring him and it was doubtful that travelling further north would produce any opportunities more promising. The south, however, was enticing. Kaka currently stood at the tip of the world and what a journey it would be to make his way to the butt of it. And in between, the fabled land of America, where opportunity was never in short supply. Standing there with his old friend, he was washed over with nostalgia, and with it the childlike, heartwarming desire for adventure. The lingering peace and tranquility of the Canadian wild eroded and that incessant itch for *more*, that restlessness of his limbs and that drumbeat in his mind all returned in force. He grinned, which Shinda took as a resounding yes.

They headed over to Shinda's car, parked in the company lot. It was a relatively new '80 Pontiac Grand Am. The sharp lines were a departure from the round, bubbly body of Christopher's '69 Ford Ranger. There were beer cans scattered across the floor and empty fast-food packages on the passenger seat. "Thaley sut la,"[184] Shinda instructed, turning the key in the ignition. The floor already had a small pile of garbage and as Kaka took a seat his feet crunched against various kinds of materials: plastic straws, paper bags, and aluminum cans, and beneath it all something unsettlingly

---

182 You cut your hair then? You look like a Muslim.
183 There's no work here, man. Come with me, let's go to America.
184 Throw it on the floor.

mushy. Shinda told Kaka that he needed to pack his things and that they could take off first thing the next morning. "Aj tan peg sheg leyah, fir tu meinu dus, tu kivan reya,"[185] he said, heading toward his place.

Shinda was living in one of the newly constructed detached bungalow houses with side panelling, and it appears that he had dedicated himself to maintaining a uniform decorative style. Empty beer cans, liquor bottles, and fast-food containers were littered all around, along with a heap of soiled clothes. The beer was imported, the liquor top shelf, the car was new and (aside from being dirty) so were the clothes scattered all around. Kaka had made his way across three continents with all his possessions on his back, most of them from his home in Ahmedpura, using public transportation only when he couldn't walk. This made him ponder two things: 1) If this is how Shinda treated his belongings, what was so important that he needed to pack? and 2) How much did that sister-fucking job at the oil company pay?

"Bethja bethja, araam kar, yaar. Eh tera ghar ah,"[186] Shinda said, slapping Kaka on the back. Kaka moved some of the fast-food debris off the couch and took a seat. Then Shinda took a moment to rummage through his "belongings" and located a recently opened bottle of Canadian rye whisky. He unscrewed the cap and took a long swig, swallowed, winced, and then he grinned, handing the bottle to Kaka. From there it was like old times—loitering around Maher's estate with a glass of Pinda's daru, discussing the same old things and the same old dreams. They passed the bottle back and forth, not bothering with glasses or ice, drinking heavily until the response time of their nervous systems became delayed and that pesky contemplative part of the brain shut up. It was the kind of unbridled intoxication that is achieved only in the company of people you love and trust and who share the turmoil of your youth. And tonight's was of a much more

---

185 Today we'll have a drink or two, and you can tell me about your travels.
186 Take a seat, take a seat. Take a load off. It's your house, buddy.

potent kind as they clasped hands and marvelled at how far they'd come.

Kaka spoke of all the things he'd held quietly inside for the past few years, things he would never dare tell someone he did not have complete confidence in: his near death from starvation in Afghanistan, the revenge he wrought on Grewal in Iran and the ensuing revolution that caused him to flee, his affair with the lovely Charlotte in Berlin, how it was cut short after his bureaucratic entanglement at The Wall, the technological wonders he witnessed in Frankfurt, and then his adventures throughout Canada so far. Through it all Shinda was the ideal audience, laughing where he should, gasping where he should, and staying solemnly quiet where he should. They talked late into the night, until their heavy heads began to bob and their heavy eyelids struggled to stay open. Suffice to say, Kaka had little to no trouble falling asleep that night. On the couch, in Shinda's living room, he was not plagued with optimistic or pessimistic forecasts of his future, but with a conscience wiped clean by Canadian whisky, he was deeply ensconced in the bliss of drunken sleep.

When he woke, however, it was not from the break of dawn and the pestering pokes of the sun's rays, but a peculiar dance of blue and red spasmodically breaking through the living room blinds, projecting across his face and the blank wall behind him. The colours were accompanied by a static-infused radio coming from a car parked in the driveway. "Shinda!" Kaka groaned, his mouth parched and his throat hoarse, while he rubbed at his eyes with the back of his hands. A knock on the door. "Shinda!" he called again. No reply, so Kaka got up and headed to the bedroom to wake his friend. Another knock on the door, louder this time. "Open up!" called an authoritative voice from outside. Kaka peered inside Shinda's room and found it empty. Most of Shinda's belongings were still littered across the floor and the curtains were wafting against the breeze coming through the open window. "We're coming in!" the voice from the door

250

shouted, and not a second later there was the thunderous crack of broken wood.

Before he had enough time to integrate the facts of the situation into a cohesive picture, his face was pressed against the floor, a knee was digging into his back, and the cold touch of steel was wrapped around his wrists. He tried to protest, but he did not know what he was protesting against. He tried to plead, but the men who ushered him out of the house were unwilling to listen. In the driveway, Shinda's Pontiac was nowhere to be seen. Kaka's head was pushed down as he was forced into the back seat. He watched through the window as the officers rifled through his bag, found his passport and his expired travel visa. An expired travel visa in Pierre Trudeau's Canada, a crime which under ordinary circumstances wouldn't have raised an eyebrow, but now, because Kaka had been contaminated by his proximity to the Lubani, became a much graver sin.

"Better than nothing," said the officer holding Kaka's bag. "We'll hand this one over to immigration and follow up on the other one tomorrow."

"That Jerry guy had the same story as the rest of his managers. Took whatever he could before leaving," replied the other.

"Real piece of work this guy. How far did he think he would get in a stolen car?"

Kaka had no reason to say anything anymore. It was not even pain that he felt. It was exhaustion. Numbness. Nothing. Blue and red lights danced on the pavement. His journey had finally come to an end.

2014

I remember the kitchen sink. Der Vater's silhouette, always against amber. In the summer from the setting sun through the windowpane in front, in the winter from the glow of the kitchen light bulbs behind. Der Vater himself is always quiet, but the sounds of his movements tell their own tale. A glass clinks against the granite tabletop. Plastic lid unscrews. The pour. The kitchen tap—loud at first, then dull as the sound of the stream is muffled by the glass. The organic squelch of a single swallow. Finally, the glass against the marble again, but louder, with more force and less care. The image is one of tragedy.

He doesn't have any friends. He moves through the world alone and he views all relations with suspicion. Paranoia at the high end and disregard at the low end. No one comes over to catch up or to tell stories or laugh. Der Vater's stories stay in his head, and he does not laugh, and if he does it is only cynically. The social world only exists outside the walls of the homestead, and even then, it is limited. When his sister insists on a gathering, we gather. But he is still alone, perhaps more so because solipsism becomes more potent in the company of people who only hear you superficially. Idle gossip drives these engagements, and Der Vater has no patience for anything idle.

Liquor bottles are purchased and consumed within days,

and while they are being consumed, they are kept under the sink. There is no liquor cabinet, for such an object presupposes a collection of alcohol, and a collection of alcohol suggests refined drinking sensibilities and a social circle to share it with. Der Vater's drinking sensibilities began with an inner tube and unrefined spirits and drinking for the sole purpose of getting your head to spin. These have evolved to prefer the highest legal percentage of alcohol that Canadian law allows, attained at the lowest possible price. Der Vater's social circles began with drunken layabouts on cotton-weaved munjay offering their pointless musings to an unlistening world. These have evolved to Der Vater muttering his pointless musings to himself, in a dark, empty room.

In the photographs of Edward Sheriff Curtis, tragedy exists alongside heroism. "The Noble Savage," that silhouette of the lone American Indian, sitting atop his steed against the backdrop of a muted natural landscape, the last of a dying breed, is a figure eternalized for all time. Because, as the First Nations writer Thomas King pointed out, Edward Sheriff Curtis—an American Romantic—already had in mind the tragic hero he was looking to find. And to make sure he found what he was looking for, "he took along boxes of 'Indian' paraphernalia—wigs, blankets, painted backdrops, clothing—in case he ran into Indians who did not look as the Indian was supposed to look.".

Never sober, never stoic, Der Vater wallowed in the aimless sorrow of his memories. They welled out of him like blood from a deep wound, like a wolf caught in the hunter's steel, howling in distress. But from the outside I witnessed a kind of beauty in them, the nobility of his suffering. Though, they needed tempering, a process of cold logic to balance out the blazing pain. Heroism is manufactured, because real tragedy is not beautiful to witness. The real tragedy is not the American Indian portrayed as a fading remnant—the noble ideal—but the brutalized remains that limped along into modernity—the Indian of fact. But, of course, reality is ignored because who wants to witness that? And the fiction we indulge ourselves in instead is created through selective omission and selective addition.

So far, you have witnessed my selective omissions and additions, but Der Vater standing at the sink is tragedy without a redemptive element. I would have to manufacture the part about heroism but I am not as skilled as Edward Sheriff Curtis. In this case, I have no wigs, blankets, painted backdrops, or clothing, and no image in mind to aim for in place of the truth. I do not know what to do to make this look beautiful. It is not art. It is the muted background. It is not a noble ideal. It is reality.

The Dying of
the Light

1984

The hot, heavy air washed over Kala's face as he drove his motorcycle to Amritsar. The journey was an hour by highway, rural silence sporadically punctuated by beeping car horns, screaming cyclists, and frustrated farmers nudging their cattle along. On rare occasions, a clean stretch of road opened up in front of him, and when it did, he eased the throttle, coasted, and observed the country around him. Outwardly, not much had changed in the many years he had lived here. Development moved at a snail's pace as most of the construction occurred by way of hand tools wielded by overworked, exhausted labourers. But that didn't matter, because the number of wheat fields, the size of villages, and the heights of buildings were not what constituted the definition of a place.

It had more to do with the sweat on the brow of the construction worker who had been swinging a hammer with aching hands for hours on end; the billows in the bibi's chunni as she worked the dough with her leathery hands before slapping a roti in the tandoor; the gentle way the dairy farmer stroked the neck of his prize cow before he milked her; the soft soles of the young boy's feet hardening against the earth as he followed his grandfather into the wheat fields to learn the way that crops were cultivated. These and thousands of other people, engaged in their thousands of tasks, with their thousands of sentiments—a multiplicity with infinite intersections. Movement and noise: actions that become habits, habits that become beliefs, beliefs that become sacrosanct, and when enough of those are bundled together it produces a constantly emerging denominator known as culture.

In the distance, the beaming dome of the Golden Temple dazzled against the stark blue sky. Kala raised his hand to shield his eyes against it. The definition of Punjab was less mercurial than in other places. It was made intransient by this structure, a building which housed over five hundred years of history and the fundamental moral character of an entire people, intangible things which are transferred from generation to generation like an urn of holy water, gently passed along with the utmost care so as to never spill a drop. So again, the question arises: Has Punjab changed? And if anyone was capable of answering this question, then certainly it would be Kala.

Kala was an observer; he always had been. It was a talent unique to his situation, forged in opposition to that of his fraternal twin, Gora. Now we can understand why the two brothers had spent their youth jostling one another in the heat of the sun. Because Gora was not an observer; he was an actor, and his entire life he had launched himself headlong into situations that were dangerous or counterproductive, without thinking. And for as long as he could remember, Kala had stood to the side, seeing the mistakes before they happened, trying to caution his brother to avoid reckless pursuits. "Soch ke kam kar!"[187] he would urge, but Gora would just push him aside and continue on.

Rarely, however, were there ever serious consequences to these actions, because Gora was the beneficiary of an unspoken privilege derived from his tall height, fair skin, and general excess of visual charisma. So, he would always slide free from the punishments that would be foisted on a normal person. Indeed, Gora had managed to saunter through life without so much as a slapped wrist, and this cultivated in him a kind of self-aggrandized delusion, the erroneous belief

---

187   Think before you act!

that he was important and that his actions mattered. All this was distinct from Kala, who was always forcibly reminded of his irrelevance, and so opted to spend his time watching, thinking, evaluating, and attuning himself to the details that all others overlooked.

Kala made his way into the city, and he navigated the narrow, busy streets of Amritsar, pulling the handles of his motorcycle to the left and to the right, and pulling the brakes frequently as motorists cut him off. There was considerable traffic around these days; it was a change that anyone was capable of seeing. Groups of prideful young men moved through the streets, a defiant look on their faces. An equal increase could be seen in the number of uniformed police officers. The two groups sneered as they entered and exited each other's orbits. The animosity made the air thicker than it already was, like the static in a summer storm before lightning strikes. Kala took a moment to survey the faces of the young men, wondering if his brother might be among them, but he saw no one familiar. When a gap between two cars opened up, he pulled his motorcycle through and moved on, eager to be away from the place.

The last time Kala had spoken to his brother was three years earlier. An argument so abstract, he regretted having ever broached the topic to begin with. But it was inevitable. Through a long process of reflection, Kala had come to the realization that there was nothing he could have said or done to prevent his brother from leaving Ahmedpura. That decision was, in essence, the first one that Gora had ever thought deeply about before acting upon. In fact, the seeds of his decision were planted so long ago—more than a decade—that even with his keen perception, Kala couldn't have had the foresight to persuade Gora differently.

It was the day they had spent the morning hauling wood from Patti to build a pyre for Kaka's grandfather, Maher. Kala was concerned about his friend Kaka that day. He was doing his best to ease the burden of the loss, so he didn't see the way

Gora looked at the corpse with confusion and anger. He didn't see Gora move close to the group of muttering strangers and listen to their conversation and nod in agreement. He didn't see the fire in his brother's eyes as the baba gave his sermon. Thousands of people, thousands of tasks, thousands of sentiments—but a single denominator. So, had it changed or not?

If you asked ten different people the reason the religious capital of Punjab was so activated as of late, you would receive ten different answers, but Kala knew all these answers revolved around a single man. A man who, three years ago, was invited to speak in Ahmedpura by the baba who spoke at Maher's funeral. The man was a young, handsome cleric with an unnatural focus. Though most of his speech consisted of banal moral prescriptions like, "Sharaab te nasheya taun bach ke raho,"[188] he delivered them with such erudition, charisma, and force that it was impossible not to be compelled. That was the last day Kala had spoken to Gora.

When the road opened up again, he hit the gas and flew toward his destination. For too long he'd been overcome with melancholic thoughts, dwelling on could-have-beens, and not having a positive vision of the future to look toward. But, for the first time in a long time, he was excited. Today he would get to revisit the good parts of his past without having to dwell on the bad. Today, he would get to see a friend he hadn't seen in a great long while.

Kala pulled his motorcycle to a stop in front of Sri Guru Ram Dass Ji International Airport and honked his horn. "Oye panchodeya, idher ah! Japhee de meinu!"[189] The face was significantly changed—hair trimmed, jaw more defined, and a pale silver scar across the temple—but it was still familiar. Kaka walked over from the front gate of the airport and Kala embraced him, then stepped back and slapped him playfully on the cheek. "Challo, ghar chaliye."[190]

---

188 Stay clear of alcohol and drugs.
189 Hey you sister-fucker, come here! Give me a hug!
190 Come on, let's go home.

2015

"He was a fucking terrorist, man," I say, which got us rocking, and now we're really fucking rolling.

Nervous system depressed by a litre of Jameson Irish Whiskey.

Nervous system stimulated by a gram of Peruvian Cocaine.

The clock is blinking at 2:57, but it's not right, because I haven't changed it since daylight savings, so it's either an hour ahead or an hour behind, but I don't know which.

French Sinatra has been talking since the clock was blinking 2:52—when I said what I said—but now I'm just chewing my jaw waiting for my turn to talk, and he's saying, "You don't understand, you only see it one way because you haven't looked into it or read anything."

And a tiny flame of rage flickers here or there—or somewhere—because this guy who only reads basketball stats is telling me I don't read enough, so I say, "If you strap a fucking ammunition belt across your chest, you're not looking for peace, man. Dude was a terrorist, plain and simple."

"It's not plain and simple, man. It's anything but plain and simple." The red veins in his eyes are pulsing and so is that muscle in his temple, because he's grinding his teeth as much as I am.

Over on the side, the Toucan is tapping the edge of his credit card or driver's licence against a framed mirror, and little clouds of white powder are puffing up off the surface.

French continues *en anglais*. "Do you know how much injustice was being committed against Punjab back then? They dammed up three rivers and rerouted the water to different provinces. They're farmers, man, what the fuck can you farm if you don't have any water? Indira Gandhi didn't see Sikhs as equal, man, she barely saw them as human."

My brain is whirling but I can only think of unuseful things, words that don't fucking work right and don't make good sentences, and I wave my hand at the Toucan to pass me the mirror after he heaves a gallon of air and some powder through his left nostril.

Then I snort mine and the clock's at 3:05 but that might be 2:05 or 4:05 and I say, "She had to be harsh, man. She was the first female leader of India, and India thinks women are garbage, man, look at how many rapes happen over there. So what she was a little harsh—she had to prove to everyone around her that she wasn't no joke."

The couch is blue as hell, like deep blue, so blue it might be purple.

He says, "Don't make this a feminist thing, man. She was an authoritarian; she was abusing people's civil liberties all across the country, not just Punjab. She was a megalomaniac, and just because she was a woman doesn't mean she should be let off the hook for her human rights violations."

He's fucking learned new words or something, more than three syllables. This alchemical concoction of cocaine and alcohol has turned my lead-brained friend into a golden goose of knowledge.

The Toucan's eyes are just spazzing out, bouncing around through the room like there's something moving aside from the blinking clock, like he's playing quidditch and he's the seeker.

French is fucking right about the feminist thing—why did I say that I don't even believe it?

But I'm more pissed off at the fact that I have to look at that terrorist's face the two times a year I'm forced to go to the

Gurdwara, and the offensively unaesthetic reinterpretation of the ancient symbol of the Khalsa—two curved swords, a double-edged broadsword, and a circular blade—into one with Kalashnikovs and bullet belts, all inspired by him.

I say, "Yeah maybe you're right, but he was always praising people who killed his enemies, like basically sanctioning assassinations and shit, man. And he pretended to be religious while he was fomenting insurrection all across the state."

I see French jam himself up when I said "fomenting." That's a win right there, and it happens when the blinking thing is blinking 3:09.

But he's shaking his head now as he goes down to admire his reflection in the mirror and he snorts, and he's still shaking his head as he comes back up, and he's about to say something to refute me, and I try to think of what that could be so I can refute it back, but he's too quick. "I'm not even going to say all that is unproven and could just be propaganda, because even if it's true, it falls in line with what a Sikh religious person would do, because the whole faith is based off self-defence and whether you want to admit it, Punjab and the Sikh community were under attack at the time, so there's no contradiction there like you think."

He's kicking my ass in this conversation and I don't know what to do to come back, and before I've thought any of it through, I say this thing that feels vaguely true, through some tenuous connection of strife suffered here and strife suffered there, but as soon as it leaves my grinding teeth, I know I've made a mistake. "You're only sympathetic to the Khalistan movement because you grew up in Quebec where those French fuckers have wanted to secede forever."

And he snaps back blindingly fast. "I don't think Quebec should be separate from Canada, you moron, but I think the French natives who came to Canada and established homes before the English deserve to hold on to their heritage, and to have their language reflected in the country they live in. And yeah, I also think that people in Punjab deserve the same thing. That doesn't mean I think they should create a new country."

Beige walls, stuccoed ceiling, and purple couch, and French's shirt collar is flared on one side but not the other.

I have no response to his rebuttal, because he's right, but I don't want to admit that just now, so I think about something else, anything else. "My dad never hit me but I wish he did, you know, because then it would be easier to hate the fucker."

At some point during the last few minutes the Toucan got up and started pacing back and forth, doing a little jig, like shaking his hips and bobbing his head.

French says, "What the fuck are you talking about, man, that's fucked up."

And I say, "Remember at the pool hall when we were talking about that shit? Fuck it, man, never mind."

And he says, "That's some heavy shit, bro, and that's something we can definitely circle back to, but I feel like you're just trying to change the topic on me because you're kind of losing this debate. I mean no offence, man, but you do that a lot and I want to make sure you're not doing that now."

"…"
"…"

Fuck, I think, but I say, "You're right."

Miraculously, the aggression with which I'm grinding my teeth subsides and letting go of this anger toward a conversation I don't have a stake in and don't really care about has immediately improved my mental health and has also improved the quality of my recreational drug and alcohol consumption.

"You're right, man. I don't know why I wanted to talk about this. You know more about it than me. It's a grey topic and I shouldn't try to make it black and white because that's what morons do, but I'm fucked up right now, this is awesome, man. Look at this fucking guy over here," I say. I point to the Toucan because he is really fucking moving now, tearing up the floor, and the blinking clock is blinking 3:15 now.

And it's just now that I realize that the Toucan's jig is co-inciding with the thundering volume of the portable speaker on the table in front of us, which I didn't even know was on but it's playing music loudly, and we are not having this con-versation at a relaxed and calm volume, which makes sense because my throat is hoarse as a motherfucker and the bitter drip from my nostrils is doing nothing to help.

"Yo, don't worry about it, man. I love talking about this kind of shit. Everyone thinks I don't read so no one talks to me about anything interesting, but man, I love conversa-tions like this, man. But yo, you did make one point that's interesting about Bhindranwale. Like in religious terms, it depends on what you think the religion is about, man. Like if you take Guru Gobind's perspective, what he did was right, you know, but like if you look at it from Guru Nanak's per-spective, man, I don't know. Hard to say what he would say, you know?"

The clock says 3:17 and I have heard everything that French Sinatra just said and it's awesomely interesting to consider.

I just can't consider it right now because Kendrick Lamar keeps calling me a bitch and telling me to be humble.

Now I'm standing up too and my hips are shaking and I'm doing this bob with my head and it's all coming together into this awesome jig that's coinciding with the music blast-ing from the speaker.

It would be the most interesting thing in the world to think about what the first Guru would say to the last Guru, like in conversation, like a dialogue, you know.

But I can't think about that right now because I *have to* dance.

Omega: It is an honour to meet you, finally.

Alpha: Why? Who am I to you?

Omega: You are the first of our line, the progenitor of our faith. It is a great privilege to be in your presence.

Alpha: I am nobody, I deserve no honours. You should revere only what I tried to teach, but it is clear to me that you did not "honour" my teachings at all.

Omega: What do you mean? Your teachings have guided every action I have ever taken in my life. I have always strived to live up to the ideal you set forth.

Alpha: No. You have taken my teachings, wisdom earned through sweat and blood, and you have used them for the express purpose they were made to reject. Rather than unify, you have divided.

Omega: You are wrong. I have unified our people. Because of me, we have a common cause; we can cooperate to achieve great things. Empires will rise because of what I did. Because of me, we have strength.

Alpha: What strength? You say "our people" but there is no such thing. All people are one. There is no Muslim, there is no Hindu, and there is no Sikh. Strength gained through separation is no strength at all.

Omega: These semantic concerns are too removed from reality. Evil exists in the world, within men's hearts. You must separate yourself from that evil if you hope to fight it. You cannot be one with a person who does not recognize your humanity.

Alpha: It is clear to me, then, that you have never understood. You were given a responsibility to ensure my message was heard, and you failed.

Omega: Do not dare speak to me of responsibility. You, who abandoned your wife and your young children to carelessly travel the world in pursuit of your own selfish desires. You do not even know the weight of the responsibility that comes from caring for a family, so what would you know of protecting a nation? When thousands of eyes look to you for safety, then you can speak to me of responsibility.

Alpha: A nation of thousands… a nation which should never have come into existence. The realm of politics, that is where you've fallen. Peddling in the small desires of small men. Thinking you understand what needs to be done and providing answers you do not have. The correct course is to remain always a student, always questioning, always thinking.

Omega: These are things which are a privilege of affluence. Questioning is a luxury that comes after your home is safe from intruders, after there is food on your plate. But what would you understand of such things? You are one who was never concerned with the duties that were right before your feet. You believed that by walking far and wide, you would be elevated to a higher realm, but all you did was walk away from those who needed you most. How did it feel to push your son aside when all he desired was your love? You have love for the world, for the ideal of humanity, but for your own son, you have none.

Alpha: He did not understand, just as you do not understand.

Omega: I understand things you never could. What if your sons had died trying to protect thousands of innocents, as mine did? What if your sons were bricked behind a wall for not believing things that were forced on to them, as mine were? Would you feel any compassion then? I have watched my children die. Children, not yet men. They were torn from me, and you expect me to show some kind of abstracted love—to show compassion—to those that did it?

Alpha: To exist is to suffer. We can find refuge in the knowledge that all such suffering is temporal. You can find refuge in the contemplation of the infinite, of the boundless, of the eternal, of things which do not and cannot exist in space and time. What we experience in life is but a blink of the eye, and you are only concerned with what is painted on the back of your eyelids.

Omega: You are wise. Certainly, wiser than me. But for all your wisdom you have never understood the nature of humanity. Our minds are not designed for the contemplation of infinite things. We are bound by the relations of our lives. That is what defines us most. I will not ask my people to abandon their identities and their families for the life of an ascetic. There is as much beauty and knowledge and love to be found within a community than divorced from one.

Alpha: Then I have failed. My mission has fallen into the wrong hands. You believe I abandoned all the things you speak of easily. No, true understanding does not come easily. You think I do not understand what sacrifice means? I sacrificed everything to find something which transcends us. That was the purpose of my life. You have taken my name and attached it to a cause I could never endorse.

Omega: Your name? For such a wise Guru, that is quite the small-minded thing to be concerned with. And what of it? You think you are Socrates. You think you are Buddha. You think you are Jesus Christ. But were it not for me, your name would never have been remembered.

Alpha: Hypocrisy is a constraint of life, and I am not immune. And neither are you brave Guru, for you think you are Leonidas. You think you are Constantine. You think you are Moses. But were it not for me, your name would have never been spoken.

1984

The banyan tree in the field in front of his home remained sturdy and resolute, the wheat shafts around its base still swayed against the wind, and the heat and humidity still conspired daily, but many other things were not as they had been. The home he was raised in was no longer a simple mud hut. It was almost inconceivable to Kaka that he was standing in front of the correct house, but as Kala pulled him forward by his shirt sleeve, he began to recognize the familiar features of the courtyard where he had played with his sister as a child. It was a single room when he left, four mud walls and roof hardly the height of a full-grown man, with no use aside from keeping the sun off their backs. Now those walls were made from brick and a raised ceiling of poured cement, and cement stairs as well, leading to a rooftop terrace. And more rooms besides, with separate bedrooms, a kitchen, and a communal space that opened out into a courtyard surrounded by high stone walls and an iron gate.

He set his bag down and settled on to his haunches, trying to understand how this was possible. The distance between poverty and affluence in his mind had always been too wide, to the point of being unbridgeable. But in his seven-year absence, with most of his income being sent back to this place, he appears to have closed that gap several times over. What he imagined would be a dreary reunion, an encore of dreadful memories, had become yet another novel experience for him. As Heraclitus said, you cannot step into the same river twice. The river is not the same as it was, and neither is the man.

"Kaka," called a soft voice from above. "Ah geya ghar?"[191] Kaka tilted his head up, and there, still with soft features crowded toward the centre of his face, was his father looking down at him. The last time Kaka had seen the man, he had been peacefully asleep in his Delhi apartment. Now he was much older. Another old man on a roof in Ahmedpura, and of those, Kaka had had enough. He had no inclination in speaking with his father, because now, as then, the old man was still doing no work while the sun was in the sky, and he was still seated on a cotton-weaved munja. An amendment to Heraclitus: Some men never leave the rivers they step into.

"Mummi kithe ah?"[192] Kaka asked, tersely.

His father answered, "Bagradi gayi si, teri bhen de naal. Shaam nu ah ju gey."[193] And then a pregnant pause. The old man on the roof seemed to want to say more, hoping perhaps for his son to first show some modicum of warmth. But Kaka had no warmth to give. To him, his father was practically a stranger. He told Kala that he wanted to stretch his legs, and he went for a walk to see what else had changed in Ahmedpura.

Not much, as it turned out. A few more unimpressive houses had been built around the perimeter of the village, bringing the total count to ninety-one. Maher's old estate was still the largest of them all, but now it seemed not as prestigious as it used to be. Kaka wondered if it was because he had stood before some of the greatest architectural achievements of the world that now Maher's estate paled in comparison, or if it was because it had grown shabby with the lack of upkeep. The grass in the courtyard had been allowed to grow of its own accord, an offence that Maher would have considered sacrilegious.

---

191 You're home?
192 Where's Mom?
193 She went to Bagradi with your sister. They'll be back this afternoon.

Pinda was still there, counting a stack of banknotes as he lay on a munja, although it appeared a much slimmer stack than before. He looked more aged than he should have as well, his once black beard now nearly stark white, his once smooth skin now wrinkled and hanging. Most glaring of all, that mischievous and taunting smile he paraded through the streets was gone, and the natural posture of his face seemed to have morphed into a deep frown. He didn't notice Kaka, his attention fully consumed by the calculus of his wealth. Down the street, the Chuhra swept a cloud of dust through the gates of Shinda's home. "Sat sri akal, Sardar ji, saffar kiven si?"[194] he called, setting the broom against the iron gate for a moment.

"Sat sri akal, bha ji!"[195] Kaka replied, approaching him. When he was young, he had accepted the common sentiment that the Chuhra was not to be afforded an equal amount of dignity as those of a higher caste, but that sentiment had been properly eroded in the company of people like Gill, who had shown Kaka that those with a well-developed work ethic and a sense of humility ought to be shown more respect, not less. So, he spent some time speaking of idle things and catching up with the man. Apparently, he worked for Kaka now, as the money he had been sending back to Ahmedpura had allowed Kaka's mother to employ the Chuhra for odd jobs.

Given that he was now earning income from three households, one would think the Chuhra would have been in higher spirits, but he appeared melancholic. He said, "Mare haal vich ah Punjab, Sardar ji. Bohat mare haal."[196] As the Chuhra continued, Kaka learned that he was referring to the skirmishes between central government police officers and followers of Jarnail Singh Bhindranwale. On the one hand, the police had resorted to extrajudicial measures to clamp down on anyone they suspected of supporting Bhindranwale, while on the other, Bhindranwale's most ardent supporters had begun castigating

194 Hello sir! How were your travels?
195 Hello!"
196 Punjab is in a bad state lately, sir. A very bad state."

and even punishing anyone who did not explicitly endorse the new messiah. It was something of a tale of two cities—Amritsar and Delhi—the worst of times as it were, with the noisiest authorities offering no middle ground and insisting on viewing things in the superlative degree of comparison only.

Kaka had heard the name "Bhindranwale" a few times before he left India, but he never imagined a rural religious scholar could have amassed such a large and ardent following in such a short time. Too much of it felt familiar, and familiar in all the wrong ways. He was reminded of the state of Iran at the end of his time there, the tension between a lackadaisical government and the rigid ideology of the cleric who opposed it. The thought of similar things occurring here in Punjab made him anxious. And with the sun setting and no other outlet to relieve his anxiety, he made another stop at Maher's estate, buying a jug of desi daru from Pinda before returning home.

"Ajo bha ji, ajo!"[197] Pinda said excitedly, this time offering his full attention and then some, seeing as he did the banknotes flapping in Kaka's hand. The reason for the decline in his business could also be attributed to Bhindranwale. His lectures on piety had apparently persuaded large swaths of young men to put aside intoxicants in favour of service to family, community, and God. As Kaka was relatively untethered to these things at the moment, he purchased a large jug of Pinda's finest with a clean conscience.

On the road, one must find joy in the small pleasures. Comforting rituals that reduce all the noise, that give you something actionable to do when all else feels outside your control, that collapse all that is unfamiliar into a simple, known quantity. So, it was no surprise that Kaka was grinning with his jug in hand. Unfortunately, small pleasures and ritualistic joys are not an iron-clad defence against life's surprises. As he passed the iron gate into the courtyard of his home, there was another thing all too familiar and not at all in a comforting sort of way—his mother, sharp features

---

197 Come in my good man, come in!

frowned, arms folded across her chest. Beside her was Kaka's sister, whose face beamed as she saw him, and next to her was a person he had never expected to see in his life again—Bunty the wrestler, Grahini's brother, whom he had kicked in the groin nearly twenty years earlier.

"Ja andar, cha bana apne ghar vale li,"[198] his mother snapped at his sister, cutting the reunion short. The two newlyweds about-faced and headed toward the house. And then his mother's attention turned toward him. She stood still and unmoving just as she did on the day he left, although behind that façade Kaka sensed a kind of weariness. Streaks of grey in her hair, wrinkles around her forehead, and her eyes, which were naturally deep-set, appeared even further back from the black bags underscoring them. Of course, his mother would never admit any of this, because introspection and emotional communication were as foreign to her as they were to Kaka. In place of "hello" or "welcome back," she characteristically got right down to business. "Ah geya? Wadiya, tera rohka kar leya. Aja."[199]

The words connected together but they did not form a sentence that made any sense to Kaka. He turned it over in his mind, trying to find meaning in it. But it was only once his mother turned her back to him that he was able to see, understand, and comprehend. As his mother walked away from him, and her silhouette grew smaller, the front of the house came into view. A man and women, older in age, around his parents age, stood on the concrete foyer in front of the door, speaking politely to Kaka's father. And in between them was a woman wearing a vibrant yellow salwar kameez. Her back was to him and her chunni wafted against the evening breeze. His palms became clammy, and a rock emerged, hard and implacable in his throat. Abandon any metaphor of man and river, here was the tsunami.

She turned her head.

---

198   Go inside and make tea for your husband.
199   You're back? Good. I've arranged your marriage. Come on.

Lolindsay

A grumble in the gut wakes me up. Eyes caked with sleep boogers, I struggle to comprehend the blurry display reading 4:47 on the digital alarm clock. It's perpendicular to the sideways orientation of my head. The world basks in a neon-blue glow, that slutty translucence of the night. I grope my way on staggering feet to the bathroom, not daring to turn on any lights, lest I be left blinded and helpless. The black silhouette of the toilet beckons, a silent echo to the continued grumbles of my tum-tum. Unconsciously, driven by the Pavlovian repetition of years of lowering my buttocks to relieve myself, I do so again.

Slowly, my ass falls toward its destination in the familiar parabolic arch, but then, nothing comes to meet it. Only a half inch, but the most recognizable half inch in the entire universe; the toilet seat is not down. The beastly cold touch of the ceramic bowl crawls across the back of my thighs, and then the infinite dread that comes from contemplating the fall into the abyss, the sloppy wetness of the toilet bowl. In this moment, my heart leaps and falls simultaneously. The world is broken into slim fragments of time, and everything is perceived in gruelling detail, each second a lifetime. And through some impossible mechanism I still exist through them, as my cheeks move closer, micron by micron, to the surface of that placid toilet water. Nothing can ever match this feeling of presence, of complete submersion into the qualia of lived experience. Nothing, except the first time I saw Lolindsay.

Convention had nothing to do with our union; a thoroughly twenty-first century affair it was. In the dark we met, both of us awash in that slutty translucence but of a manufactured sort, the kind that nightclub owners have perfected in emulating. The DJ scratched at his table jarringly to make the unseemly transition from The Weeknd's "Can't Feel My Face" to Fetty Wap's "Trap Queen" and there, through the jumble of sweaty limbs and bloodshot eyes was the gentle bouncy cusp of the bottom of her breast, peeking out from under the bottom edge of her custom-cut crop top as she swayed her body sensually back and forth next to the expectation-thwarting DJ table.

She was a sight to behold. Her hair, golden streaks that wafted like the wheat fields of Punjab, and an aura of such exuberance that it filled the room like air in a balloon, near to bursting. Her eyes? Ask me not of her eyes, for they rarely met my own, but contact of that sort is of such an antiquated nature. She kept her eyes focused on the realm of cellular text messages and data-using applications and I kept my eyes on all her cusps, because we are of a generation where the superficial is of the superlative importance, where the cover of the book speaks more than the icky, confusing innards of the thing. But this is not to say that there was no depth of feeling.

To the contrary, it was a cacophony of emotion and somatic turmoil. She stumbled off the elevated dance floor and fist-pumped her way over to me, and like a kick to the head from a deep swig of undistilled grain alcohol, my vision circled before my eyes. Then she placed her hand on my fast-beating chest, and that frenzied elation, that came from the first time I clicked "Yes, I'm over eighteen" when I certainly was not over eighteen, returned. And, finally, when she leaned in and uttered in a hoarse voice, "I'm Lo-*hic*-Lolindsay, bebe. Sss'yerr name-*hic*?" It was as I am now, frozen in time, dangling all that is dear to me over an all-consuming abyss.

But the goddess spared me that day. She proclaimed, "K

bebe, I-*hic*- gotta pee. Add me on IG k?" and stumbled off, abdicating her natural right to the harvest of my soul, and blessedly giving me leave to pursue her attraction as a free man. But what am I—a mere mortal whose features are so monochromatic and crowded toward the centre of my face— in comparison to her and the celestial beauty she possesses? What was I to DM an online persona of such breathtaking magnificence? Beige cusps and curves accentuated against backdrops alabaster-white, a thematically consistent, mesmerizing mirage of flesh. Selfies to be sure, but what else of the universe is worth seeing if she were not part of it?

I open the direct messaging feature of Instagram and compose my ode, writing, deleting, writing, deleting, and writing again. How does one entreat Pythia, the oracle of Delphi, the priestess whose knowledge of my fate is infinite compared to my own? Parsimony is key. "Hey," I say. And my heart catches in my throat as the three dots appear, and it does not beat, and I do not live, until she gives me life again by replying, "Hey bb;)" Soon after, I am rewarded with another chance to see her, this time when her gait is less stumbling and her speech less slurred.

The grand narrative of our relationship is a mystery to me, but such abstractions are of no concern. I live only for the moments in between, the flash photographs of lust and attraction that awaken my soul—or at least, my loins. In the slutty glow of the night, her body against mine, the mores and psychological constraints of my youth erode, and I ascend a sexually liberated phoenix from the ashes of social conservatism. And an emotional rejuvenation, pride—so rare a thing in my life—overcomes me, because I have attained what so many suitors have desired. Penelope had chosen her Odysseus and it was I!

But pride cometh before the fall, and my fall with Lolindsay resembles too closely my three-inch voyage from the rim of the toilet bowl to the murky surface beneath, except for in one great respect. In the darkness of my bathroom, the ever-looming reality of water soon touching my clenched cheeks is foremost in my mind, whereas Lolindsay's impending declaration of "Bebe, I can't, like… do this anymore," was never once fathomed. Yet, being blind to the inevitable does not protect you from experiencing it, and when she does finally step out of my life and blocks me on all social media applications, it is no less discomforting and humiliating than falling into a toilet in twilight stupor.

For weeks, I am utterly dejected. I pray to gods I have no faith in to turn back the clocks, to give me the wisdom or fortitude to find a path out of this hell. But God is unlistening, and time's arrow flies in only a single direction. So, to relieve my pain, I access the seedy corners of the Internet, searching for digital harlots whose features might resemble even a sliver of my lost goddess's beauty, but this is a task as hopeless as turning back time. All I am granted from this is more heartache, now with the sticky residue of shame leaking off my (left) hand.

The First Man parades out his litany of "I told you so's," and Der Vater—who is no bastion of sympathy, and whose own experiences in romance are so far removed from mine—can conjure no response other than passive bemusement. "Real eyes, Realize, Real lies," read the tattoo across Lolindsay's third ribcage. Even when it is before our face, we are incapable of heeding sage advice.

But there is one who steps forth to catch the pieces of my broken heart and to hold them for me until I am ready to weld them back together. The one whom I constantly berate and degrade, throughout my time with Lolindsay and even after. I say to her, "You don't understand Western relationships," and "She loves me, I don't care what you think!" and, most scathing of all, "What would you know about love? You married an abusive drunk!" But she doesn't scream, or yell back, or slap me across the skull as I rightfully deserve. She accepts my vitriol with poise. She listens, and nods, and speaks plainly and truthfully the one thing I am not willing to accept: "Tenu pyar de baare kush ni pata."[200]

---

200 You know nothing about love.

1991 – Present

She has been conspicuously absent in this story, hasn't she? Present at my birth, of course, and there I told you that she does not belong in these pages. On that account, nothing has changed. But the answer to the question of why that is, which I could not answer so early on, I will venture now. Because now you have the general shape of understanding required to see why this piece does not fit into the puzzle of the story.

I remember the cold touch of the winter air seeping through the cracks in the car door. I'm huddled in the back seat between her and the First Man. We are young. We are in an empty strip mall parking lot. It's dark, nighttime, a weekday. Der Vater had yelled, profusely, then things were broken, then we silently filed out the door. His eyes were red like a demon.

But in the car, we are laughing, because she is stroking my forehead and telling stories about places I have never seen and people I have never met. She tells the stories with wit and humour and an illuminating intelligence. She is smiling and she implores us to dream as though we live in a world where dreams might come true.

I remember falling. Many times and always in different ways. From the top of the hillcrest as a boy, and as I grew, in ways less literal than that. Der Vater had only a single piece of advice, simplistic but inarguably true: "Chup karke uthja."[201]

But she never stood back with her arms crossed. She pulled me up and brushed the dirt off my clothes, and she waited until I stopped wailing to explain the more sophisticated truth—that failure is not definitive but formative.

I remember impatience, angry outbursts and curses and agitation and restlessness. I remember a sense of self-reliance that was masochistic, and an empire being built through a will fuelled by pure rage.

But she was immeasurably patient, working equally hard, stamping car doors from giant sheets of metal in the bowels of groaning machinery, an environment which Der Vater could not survive in. And when she returned from twelve-hour shifts, she maintained a household with quiet grace.

I remember the kitchen sink. Der Vater, glass in hand, in the amber light of the dying sun, unheroic, unredeemable.

But I remember the kitchen sink, the yellow light of the rising sun falling gently on her face as she sings with a voice like sweet honey, a hero redeeming everything.

These are fragments. Can you see the problem? The delta of their opposition is too wide; their perspectives too misaligned. Is there any way to reconcile her story with his? Perhaps it would be possible, if it were only a seething hatred between the two, a singular dynamic that could be contextualized and understood. That might have had a place in this narrative. But there is something else, profoundly perplexing. Because their relationship was forged through a process of great pressure, and like all things that endure great pressure, it has grown durable and strong. It is resilient in a way that seems to me otherworldly. There is, undeniably, hatred between them, but also a deep and enduring love, and that is something I cannot comprehend.

Why his story then, and not hers? Because I, like everyone else born with a heart, remember the abrasions much more

---

201 Shut up and stand up.

than the gentle touch. As is always the case, you strive to understand why someone treats you with scorn, but never to understand why another loves you without cause, which is a mystery, because the latter is all the rarer.

Moreover, the arc of her story is one that I do not consider possible to distill. For how do you speak of the metamorphosis from the most disrespected creature on Earth: the Punjabi woman, to the most revered: the Punjabi mother? It is a paradoxical analysis, for the definition of one never escapes the definition of the other, and both are beyond my understanding.

You might say that by omitting this story, I am committing the same sin against her that the history of the world has committed against women *en masse*, relegating them to the position of "the second sex." You are free to hold whatever opinion you wish, and you may be right. But I cannot assume the responsibility of reporting on how the world should be. I can only say how it is. I am not the prosecutor of my own life, merely a witness of it.

In my eyes, the devaluation comes from attempting to confine her, to package neatly the experiences of a person who is more than can be summarized. Because she is not a character in a story; she is a person in my life, the most important. And if you think her voice is absent, you are sorely mistaken, because her voice has shaped me more than all others. If you have read this far, you have done so because of her. If you have laughed or smiled or frowned as you read, you have done so because of her. Without her, there is no story of Kaka, and there is certainly no story of Nanak.

And if still you are dissatisfied with her omission from these pages, then I will leave you with this final justification. You are not permitted to her story, because you are not deserving of it, just as I am undeserving of it. Anything further than this and I must plead the American Fifth. I must say as Iago said to Othello, "Demand me nothing." And I must invoke the unforgettable closing clause of the *Tractatus Logico-Philosophicus*: "That which cannot be spoken about, must be passed over in silence."

Sardar Quixote

In the village of Ahmedpura there lived a gentleman who was much esteemed by his compatriots. He was well-off and he had acquired ample leisure time, his fertile fields handily looked after by a few sturdy-armed Jats. However, it was his deep fascination with the lore of bygone Sikh warriors that truly lifted him above the rabble. Burying your head in the tales and exploits of fictional beings was considered a ruinous waste of time, but if such zeal was to be expressed toward the *nonfictional* beings who graced the pages of historical works and religious scriptures, well, then it goes without saying...

This is how one particular individual, known as Sardar Quixote, came to have the renown and prestige of a most pious man in a most pious state. But to his dismay, Sardar Quixote's fixation on the heroics of Sikhism remained an entirely intellectual affair. Many years of his life migrated away with his only contribution to the faith being the regurgitation of the tales of legendary warriors such as Banda Bahadur and Baba Deep Singh, to anyone who, like himself, had the luxury of time to spare. That is, until the fateful day on which the static-infused ramblings of the political pundits crackled and confirmed that Sri Harmandir Sahib was surrounded by soldiers of the central government, and within the walls of the holy complex was garrisoned the legendary living knight of the faith, Jarnail Bhindranwale.

On this day, without hesitation, Sardar Quixote vigorously leaped from his bed, grabbed hold of his kirpan, and tore out of the gates of his home screaming the eternal battle cry of Sikhism, "BOLE SO NIHAL!" Throughout the village, an uproarious response called back to him "SAT SRI AKAL!" The tales of Sikh heroism were told often and fervently throughout this countryside and had thus cultivated great reverence. The warriors gathered did not do so out of delusions of grandeur, but rather to seize on the opportunity to convert the metaphysical to the hyper-physical, to turn ideas, histories, and mythologies into matters of flesh, bone, and blood.

In the distance, Sardar Quixote noticed one of the young men of the village not congregating in preparation for battle, so he called out to him. "Kaka ji, wherever are you going? Have you not heard the news? A battle has begun at the holy Golden Temple. We all must do our part to protect the faith from heretics!" To which the young Sardar off in the distance replied, "I know, Sardar Quixote, and my heart aches deeply from hearing such ominous news. But look here, Sardar ji, my mother has arranged for me to marry. I must travel to Firozpur this day to meet my fiancé's extended family!"

"I see, Kaka ji. It is well that you go to do this. Marriage and child rearing are holy duties as well! More warriors must be birthed and raised and taught of the plight of our Gurus, but not just their plight, their wisdom too! Take care of yourself, Kaka ji, and hold us in your prayers this evening, for we go to battle, and if blood is spilled, let it only be spilled in defence of the faith!" And with that, Sardar Quixote swung his blade round his head and screamed out again, "BOLE SO NIHAL!" and again the collective reply, "SAT SRI AKAL!"

The warriors hastily piled into the back of the tractor wagon and it began to rumble toward the holy capital. Before long, the brilliant Golden Dome glinted against the sky, but in the tight labyrinthian streets, armed enemy forces glared at the tractor dangerously. Sardar Quixote was struck by a tactical insight, and he said to those in the wagon, "My friends, we must separate here and reconvene within the walls of Sri Harmandir Sahib. This is to avoid suspicion until we join our brothers in arms, and then we can display our disobedience ostentatiously!"

Agreeing collectively that this was the best course of action, they separated. Sardar Quixote wrapped a large shawl around his torso to conceal his kirpan, and he affected a hobble in his leg and dramatized a wince as he stepped, and he watched the suspicion of the soldiers in the streets quickly fall away from him. Thus, he was able to sneak his way inside the Golden Temple and find the awaiting Sikh force standing in the shadow of the Akal Takht—the eternal throne of Sikhism, the highest seat of justice in the faith.

Inside of that building sat the warrior monk Jarnail Bhinderwale, who had fully assumed the position as terrestrial arbiter of God's will, and it sent goosebumps up Sardar Quixote's spine to know he was so close to a living legend. His authority had grown to eclipse all others in the land and for months it was known that any dissenter of his—whether they be journalists, clerics, or common folk—would be dealt with just as those treasonous defectors from the red army were during the Battle of Stalingrad (they would be gifted a sturdy lead round directly between the eyes). Bhindranwale had no formal designations, occupied no offices of government, and yet he had accumulated more influence and power than any person in the state. He was considered the de facto leader of Punjab, and it was to him that Sardar Quixote had come to pledge his allegiance.

It was then, just as he was going to introduce himself and explain the tenacity of his devotion, that a volley of shots was fired by the military forces outside the temple. The bullets cracked against the plaster and the concrete of the walls, and one of the warriors in the Akal Takht, whose torso was too exposed over the sandbagged battlements, collapsed backward as a haze of pink mist erupted from his forehead. No longer a warrior, Sardar Quixote mused, but a martyr.

"Hold! Hold your fire goddamn it!" The man who spoke the words hurried over from across the compound, shouting his orders at the remaining soldiers on the battlements. He was young, tall, strong, and spectacularly light-skinned—a true gabru[202] if there ever was one. "My name is Gora," said the young man, turning to the newcomers. "I've been sent over by the generals to sort out you newcomers. Hurry up, get in line over there to receive your weapons," he said, pointing his thumb toward a building behind him. Sardar Quixote immediately fell to one knee and proclaimed, "Sir Gora, it is I, Sardar Quixote, but a humble man of Punjab, yet a fierce and zealous attender of the faith, and I have come with a steadfast resolve to stand with the noble warriors gathered here against the heretical scum who fire upon the holy city and the pious Bhindranwale!"

"Pipe down Sardar Quixote!" Gora shouted, "I know damn well who you are! We're from the same village if you haven't noticed. Now put away your kirpan, we have British-made STEN machine guns imported from Pakistan! Take one up and assume a position on the battlements where that fellow was just martyred!"

Sardar Quixote rose to his feet, aghast at what he had just heard. "British-made, Sir Gora? Did you say imported from Pakistan, Sir Gora? Are the British and the Pakistani not the enemies, which the martyrs of our faith gave life and limb to defeat? How can we accept their aid now, in this holy crusade?"

"Goddamn it!" Gora shot back. "This is no time for muddle-headed arguments about the ethics of aid-seeking. We could be here all day if we entertain such a discussion. We've got to operate in accordance with that damned quotable strategic aphorism, 'the enemy of my enemy is my friend,' because if you haven't noticed, Sardar Quixote, the enemy is at the bloody gate! Now take hold of a STEN machine gun and assume a bloody post!" Gora marched off to sort out the other newly arrived warriors, and a thoroughly chastised

---

202 A virile young man.

Sardar Quixote turned in his kirpan for a much less romantic STEN machine gun.

Then he approached that precarious position on the battlements of the Akal Takht, where the pool of the martyr's blood was still expanding out, and he kneeled and poked his head over the sandbags to sneer at the enemy. From there he watched what transpired over the next seven hours, as the bullets of government troops continued to ding and kick up dust when they collided with the infrastructure of Sri Harmandir Sahib.

By the end of the day Sardar Quixote counted eight more martyrs who gave their lives in defence of the faith, and a further twenty-five who were half martyrs or quarter martyrs depending on how much importance one would place on various limbs and organs. Throughout it all, Sardar Quixote stayed vigilant, and on the second day of the battle he noticed a conspicuous-looking fellow milling about the ground of the temple. By all outward appearances he seemed to be a bystander, an innocent pilgrim come to pay his respects. But upon closer inspection, it was clear that he seemed inordinately preoccupied with the positions of STEN guns. Just then the warrior Gora crawled up next to Sardar Quixote. "Psst, listen up," he hissed. "You see that bastard down there? I can't prove it but I think he's a spy. I think he was sent by the army to report on our positions."

"But Sir Gora, that man is clearly a Sikh!" Sardar Quixote declared. Gora replied in annoyance, "And what of it? There are plenty of Sikhs in that army out there, traitors who didn't defect as they should have!" Sardar Quixote, unable to prevent his loose tongue from wiggling away, said, "Sir Gora, what is this you say? There are many Sikh warriors out there who stand against us? In no history of the Khalsa have the martyrs stood against others of the faith, which is to say, how can we now, as pious Sikhs, stand in combat against other Sikhs?"

"Would you shut the bloody hell up, Sardar Quixote," Gora barked. "They're attacking the Golden Temple, the holiest monument in Sikhism. Does that strike you as pious?" to which Sardar Quixote sincerely had to think about for a moment, before responding, "But sir, we are here with weapons in this holy place, and could that not be seen as an act of desecration, especially in the Akal Takht?"

Gora collapsed his head into his hands, seemingly out of exhaustion, and then muttered to himself, "I think I will be here for three lifetimes, explaining the nature of war to the man who is holier than us all." Then he turned earnestly to Sardar Quixote and continued, "Look, forget all that for the moment. I've just received orders to sneak out of this place and head to the capital, to take the fight directly to Gandhi. But this bastard army has tightened their grip on Amritsar, and they've sealed all the exits. How the hell did you sneak in here when you first arrived, Sardar Quixote?"

"Why, Sir Gora, I used this shawl of mine to sneak into the complex grounds. Here, take it and go on to do your holy duty!" Sardar Quixote said proudly, handing over his shawl. The warrior Gora took it and wrapped it around his head as a pious housewife would, and he shuffled back until he was clear of the battlements. Then he stood and darted away to do as he was ordered. So, Sardar Quixote was left alone on the battlements to watch what transpired over the next few days.

And many things did transpire. Several days of brutal combat in which the government forces attempted multiple attacks and were repelled. Then, heavy artillery strikes and aerial monitoring with helicopters, which the warriors in the compound deflected by using the pilgrims as human shields. Not an entirely effective strategy, Sardar Quixote learned, as the army had no compunctions about firing through innocent pilgrims to get to the warriors behind them. Finally, tanks were forced into the grounds of the Golden Temple, but they, too, were repelled by armour-piercing grenade launchers, which surprised Sardar Quixote, because he was not aware that they were stashed in the compound where the Guru Granth Sahib rested, and it struck Sardar Quixote as perhaps slightly blasphemous that they were. Upon the closing of the sixth day since he arrived, Sardar Quixote came to the sombre realization that he would be martyred here just as he had prayed, but this realization was much hollower than he had anticipated. He questioned how closely this pickled situation resembled those of the great martyrs, and in wondering these things a great doubt clouded him.

He wished in that moment that he had not traded away his holy kirpan, because he would have preferred to be martyred with that sword in hand rather than the unwieldy STEN machine gun he was holding. There was very little romance in the use of machinery as such, and the dead bodies around him did not look very heroic either. They were strewn about with their limbs comically flailing, and they held expressions that were not noble at all, tongues protruding or brains leaking out. It was all so inhuman. Not at all like the tales he gorged himself on in his idle hours on the farm, where everyone is displayed superhumanly—divinely. But here it seemed that nobody was seeing any other person as a human at all. Everyone was an enemy, a terrorist, the government and the rebels both, depending on where you stood. It was a curious case to witness, windmills tilting at windmills.

And the most important of Sardar Quixote's realizations came too late for it to make a difference. As the bullet that would martyr him sped toward his forehead, he came to understand that a tale need not be fictional to construct a mirage in the mind. To be too enamoured of any ideal—no matter how lofty, no matter how noble, no matter how grounded in real life affairs—is still to view the world in an incomplete way, a way that impoverishes the quality of one's life. For life is such a beautiful thing, full of so many wonderful opportunities if one is just able to keep that little window of doubt open, the escape hatch from certainty, that in any circumstance no matter how dire, allows a person to think "Perhaps I am not entirely right in this case!" and to vacate their convictions posthaste, before they become lethal. That is the last thing Sardar Quixote thought before his brain exploded into a cloud of pink mist.

2017

Two swings, that is all it had ever taken for Der Vater to fully lodge a nail into a piece of wood. The first swing, more of a tap actually, just to indent the nail slightly in place so he could remove his fingers, and the second with full force and no lack of precision, to drive the thing straight down and into place. A deep curiosity it was, then, when I first noticed the third swing. It was off centre, catching the edge of the nail (perhaps with less force as well) and two-thirds of the metal still protruded from the wood after all was said and done. He blinked down at it, muttered under his breath, swung again, true and strong, and then went about his business as though nothing had happened.

Then weeks went by, and the two-swing standard was more and more eroded, replaced with four swings, five swings, whole misses, until one day he threw the hammer against the wall, shouting profanities loudly until he too quickly lost his breath. Next came a trickling away of weight—a sturdy torso, broad shoulders, and an imposing presence, all dwindling away to be replaced by a lank body, bony shoulders rolled forward, and an almost ghost-like presence. On one idle Tuesday evening at the homestead, Der Vater sits, glassy-eyed, in front of the television, arms across his torso, hands loosely clasping the opposing elbow. "How are you feeling?"

I ask. "Teek ni,"[203] he breathes out. It's a unique reply, as most queries sent his direction lately elicit the same response: "Patha ni."[204] He doesn't know what he wants to do. He doesn't know what he wants to eat. He doesn't know if he is cold or warm. He doesn't know what he wants to watch.

On the television screen, reruns of popular prime-time sitcoms, entertainment he does not, and has never had even an inkling of interest in. They are popular, probably because at the close of the episode, everything reverts to how it was at the outset, tranquil and happy. Certainty is what they provide, a tactless enactment of the fantasy that the problems which arise in a person's life can be neatly and handily remedied within a half hour, commercial breaks notwithstanding. Maybe, subconsciously, it's why he stopped clicking the remote on this channel. Grasping at certainty, wherever it's offered, no matter how feeble that offering may be.

I don't know what's happening inside of him, but I can describe what it feels like from the outside looking in. Imagine if a sculpture of a man carved from marble one day broke free of its stasis and walked among us. Surely it would be a sight to behold, an inanimate object become organic. Now imagine Der Vater, ever in motion, ever in action, come suddenly to a screeching halt. That hammer forever in his hand, pounding away at earthly elements for longer than I've been alive, now lies dead and motionless on the cold concrete floor of the garage, the same place it had landed after he threw it the last time he touched it. To me, the two are synonymous, for in each case the subject has defied its nature. Der Vater was designed to move, just as the sculpture is designed to stay in place.

The doctors in white coats and nurses in blue smocks arrive, much to his chagrin. So self-assured when what needs to be done is clear and charted. But now they fold their hands over each other, and dart their eyes to the side, and poke

---

203 Not good.
204 I don't know.

and prod and take vials of this fluid and that fluid, and offer updates like "we just need to do a few more tests," because no advancement in medical science can ever hope to tell you how a marble statue has come to life.

It's all deeply unsettling. As he sits, morose and brooding, he is too easy to behold and evaluate. Too much of him has been lost because of this mysterious ailment, and what remains is all the worst of him. He is like a taxidermy leopard pinned to the wall, all the majesty stripped away, leaving a comical, pitiful, and depressing simulacrum. He seemed like such an unstoppable force, his accomplishments so impossible, but once the hurricane passes, all that's left is wet earth and felled branches. What does any of it mean now? I don't know. There is nothing certain anymore.

1984

Operation Bluestar was a roaring success. Jarnail Bhindranwale is dead. So too are his generals and many of his followers. (There were also collateral casualties of innocent bystanders, who had attended the Golden Temple on June 1 to celebrate the birth of their Guru, numbering in the hundreds, but these lives are inconsequential in the battle against "domestic terrorism.")

Now, the Akal Takht lay in ruins. Following the battle, a clear blue sky illuminated the fallout and wreckage wrought. The dome of the Golden Temple no longer gleamed, as it was dimmed by the debris from bullets and artillery shells. Slowly, the dust fell in circles, and in response, the vapour of steaming blood rose to meet it, just as slowly, mixing together to create a muddy fog.

Outside the holy compound, the military, under order from Indira Gandhi, moved throughout the entire state of Punjab and began a clean-up operation, attempting by force to weed out the last of the insurrectionists. The result: thousands of young men were unlawfully detained and tortured. Another small price added to the tally. Fear not, however, for our protagonist had avoided most of the trouble so far.

During the attack on the Golden Temple, Kaka was in Firozpur, where he sat in silence for three days, watching his mother and father hammer out the details of a marriage with the parents of a woman he had spoken no more than three words to. The news of the attack had reached them, of course, so when they returned to Amritsar, the dismal situation was not a complete surprise. An ominous atmosphere pervaded the whole city. Like a cut powerline in a pool of water, electric flashes of violence flared up instantly and dissolved just as quickly.

Back in Ahmedpura, Kaka kept the new iron gates of his house locked. More than once, posses of grim-faced officers had rattled the gates with their weapons drawn, demanding information about Kaka, his family, and where they were during the days of the attack. Kaka had managed to elude arrest with his matrimonial alibi, but the state was still under a state of emergency, and nonessential activity was being dissuaded by means of random beatings with police batons. All this had resulted in Kaka being locked inside the opulent new brick walls of his home, subjected to the unique psychological torture of planning a wedding with his mother.

"Sheti viah kar lo,"[205] she said, multiple times a day, while puttering around the house with her arms crossed. No doubt, the political tension was partly to blame for her more authoritarian attitude toward Kaka's future. When a person loses freedom in one aspect of life, they squeeze their grip on whatever remains under their jurisdiction. It was all demoralizing for Kaka, who had spent the majority of his adult life roaming through an open landscape of potentialities and was now being told to turn it in for a very definite direction down a very long tunnel. Was the prospect entirely off-putting? In truth, he did not know. It would, after all, be a novel experience, and many long nights had passed when Kaka had wished for a companion, another mind to bounce off his doubts, fears, and aspirations. But the finality of it all was daunting, an obligation with no escape.

The inverse, that solitary outlook, to live with and for oneself, has no place in the conceptual lexicon of Punjab. It

---

205 Let's get this wedding over with quickly.

had only seeped into Kaka's mind as a consequence of travelling through countries and witnessing lives where such an attitude was acceptable, even respectable. Perhaps something of the desire to be alone was inculcated in him from a young age, when he sat in the Patti marketplace as the sun went down and the other merchants went home. Perhaps he inherited a genetic disposition from a grandfather who wanted to be alone, above the world, or a father who wanted to be alone, so he could rest. Whatever the reason, it did not matter. Punjabi custom dictates that a life alone is a life impoverished in a fundamental way, almost to the point of not worth living. It was childish to reject family—a boy was not a man until he took a wife.

Kaka endured the situation with gritted teeth, week by week, through the relentless heat of the summer. Eventually, the state of emergency was lifted and the soldiers and police officers harassing the villages of Punjab eased their efforts. But as the boot lifted off the throat, another quickly took its place. Khalistan loyalists in name, but all the noble actors with a true vision, perished in the battle at the Golden Temple. Now the cause had been co-opted by the vicious and the deluded, thieves, murderers, and those with a general predisposition toward carnage. This new movement entailed less resistance against Indira Gandhi's government and more looting and pillaging by roving bands of gangsters. More fanatical than before, more desperate as their aid from Pakistan had been choked off by the army, they turned their scorn toward the only thing they could—their own countrymen. So, still, Kaka remained locked behind the iron gates of his brick home.

One day, as the temperatures cooled in the autumn months, Kala came to pay his friend a visit. He appeared distressed, thinner, paler, and less well-rested than before, even given the current sociopolitical situation. Privately, in the courtyard of Kaka's home, Kala sullenly said, "Gorey di khabar ayi... Mar geya Dehli de vich."[206]

---

206 I received news about Gora's whereabouts... He died in Delhi.

294

Protests had been taking place in the country's capital since the attack on the Golden Temple. Like the Iranians who marched against their king, the protestors in Delhi were treated to live fire ammunition (but only after the more humane use of water hoses proved ineffective in dampening their spirits). Gora had been attending many of these rallies and protests, even after the initial outrage had faded. He had managed to avoid the bullets that were fired, but he was not treated nearly so well when he was taken into police custody. Gora's family had been contacted by the authorities to come identify and claim ownership of the body, a curious allowance not provided to the vast majority of Sikh men who never managed to find their way home after the protests.

"Mere naal ah sakdein?"[207] Kala asked. Without a moment's hesitation, Kaka was on his feet and ready to leave. Their destination lay 450 kilometres to the east. They broke the journey into two days, stopping at a highway inn for the night, not speaking much, not eating much, and not sleeping much. The next morning, they woke early and made toward the city as the sun rose.

Meanwhile, in Delhi, English-born journalist and film actor Peter Ustinov waited to interview the Prime Minister of India, Indira Gandhi. She walked down a wicker path in her private estate, with her two bodyguards trailing her.

Kaka and Kala arrived in the sprawling concrete jungle. They headed straight to the All India Institute of Medical Sciences, where Kala had been informed his brother's body was being kept refrigerated. Though "refrigerated" is something of an exaggerated term. "Behind the door of a refrigerator" would be more accurate, one that was not prioritized by the hospital's backup generators, which roared to life whenever the city's power shut off (a frequent occurrence throughout the day). The smell of death was overwhelming. Kala stopped and hunched over, gagging. Kaka had a strong enough fortitude to remain upright, but barely.

---

207 Can you come with me?

One day earlier, Indira Gandhi, presciently said during a speech, "I am alive today, I may not be there tomorrow…" As she walked down the wicker path, one of the two bodyguards trailing her, Beant Singh, drew a .38 revolver and fired three rounds.

In the forest south of Peace River, Kaka had watched Christopher load his weapon and fire a single round into a wounded deer's skull. Christopher did so because he respected the animal and wished to end its suffering as quickly and humanely as possible.

As Indira Gandhi writhed on the ground, her other guard, Satwant Singh, aimed and unloaded the entire thirty rounds of his STEN machine gun magazine into her body. Only three rounds missed their mark. Both men surrendered without resisting. Indira Gandhi was rushed to the All India Institute of Medical Sciences.

The body bag zipper was pulled back by the mortician and Kala silently observed his brother's face. It was swollen with bruises, black and purple, contrasting fiercely with his pale skin. The police proved to be adamant in their questioning when they detained Gora. Kaka placed his hand on Kala's shoulder, not saying anything of assurance. What is there to say when someone's worst fears are realized?

One day earlier, Indira Gandhi also said, "I shall continue to serve until my last breath, and when I die, I can say, that every drop of my blood will invigorate India and strengthen it." This was not so prescient, as India would certainly be invigorated by her death, but it would not be strengthened by it.

The thunder of thousands of footsteps rattled through the ceiling and Kaka became concerned. From the basement they heard shouting and cursing. Even Kala was broken from his solemn reverie. "Chal, ithon nikliye,"[208] said Kaka.

---

208   Come on, let's get out of here.

2010

I received my kara when I was twelve years old. It is one of the five signs, the most pragmatic of them. So simple, the craftsmanship is hardly worth noting. Objectively, not worth more than the material made to produce it. When you slip it on though, the weight is all you notice. It pulls your hand to the ground, and you can feel the small strain in your bicep when you lift your arm for routine tasks. And then not long after, it becomes part of you, and on the rare occasion you remove it, you feel its absence acutely.

My father wears one as well, and I imagine that it is a part of him. I cannot imagine it has ever left his wrist. There are no traditions that we hold dear, no celebrations, not even birthdays, but when he handed me that steel band he did so with reverence. "Pah ke rakh,"[209] he informed me, and I noticed, for an instant, that shallow stone veneer over his eyes cracked, and the human well beneath came through. Objects are meaningful only insofar as we imbue them with meaning. The band means nothing more to me than that it means something to my father, but whatever it means to him I do not understand.

Right now, I am doing as much as I can to focus on the band, turning it around, again and again, noticing the glint of the stainless steel, feeling the weight of it, nothing significant,

---

209 Keep it on.

around thirty grams maybe. I'm trying to focus on any feature that might distract me enough from what's happening around me, yet no feature of the kara is able to overcome the smell of peroxide and citrus. It's a nauseating smell, and I know as I sit here that this is one of those times when the details of the experience are too refined, too resolute, and they will cement into a memory I'd rather not carry, but will have to.

My cousin is in the room as well, silent, with a blank look on his face. The night is spinning in his head like a top. He's rehearsing all the hypothetical ways in which he could have made it on time, but none of that matters now, does it? Because we're here now, and the blood is thick, and it refuses to stay put. It prefers to pool on the peroxide, citrus floor. And my brother sags his head, holding the towel—soaked through—against his skull. His eyes lulling, blissful almost. "Stay awake, man," says my cousin. My brother nods, sending more drops of red to the white floor.

What transpired this night does not spin in my head like a top, but moments flash out like the shattering bulbs of old cameras, and between those moments a fog, refusing to dissipate, presents only a vague impression of continuity. The First Man is accused of speaking to a girl, likely the truth. Is that a sin, to speak to another human being? It is when that human being is not equal. A sister—an object whose honour is more coveted than its happiness. An object imbued with the wrong kind of meaning. And that object belonged to someone more familiar than not. Silent Jagbir, with whom I once stood shoulder to shoulder, was now across from me, and dangling from his wrist, the glimmer of a band that should hold the same meaning as the one that I now turn in my hand.

"Relax," I say to my cousin. His fist is tensed so tight I think his tendons might snap, but he doesn't relax and the pressure breaks against me. "Why the fuck didn't you do anything to stop it? Where were you?" he accuses. I was there, but I didn't do anything. My cousin is more accustomed to violence than me. He has endured more of it than most, and now he is unflinching in the face of it. He's a warrior through and through, but I possess only the mind of a warrior. My heart is a coward's heart, and the incongruity between the two is an infinite jest.

My brother slouches forward more and more, until he's about to fall off the examination table. I place my hand on his chest to straighten him and he blinks lazily at me, and when I pull my hand away, it's red. The edge of the band is red too. It is an artifact of warriors, that is what my father had told me. A signifier of people who follow a creed of violence used explicitly for self-defence. But Jagbir was not defending himself when he drove his kara into my brother's skull, again and again. Not thirty grams, much more than that. Thick steel with a clean ridge moving through the centre. And I could not defend my brother even though I wore a kara as well.

A woman enters—the doctor. Her skin is brown, her coat and shirt are white, pristine, almost in a religious sort of way. Stray strands of grey hair kick up here and there against the black, likely dyed, and it's all pulled back in a tight bun. Her skin is wrinkled, her mouth a thin, tight line. Her pants are not white, but grey, dark grey, darker than the stray hairs, and they are too long, bunched up around her black, orthopaedic shoes. Her eyes are vacant, weary, indifferent—irreverent even—and they reveal her humanity so much more than concern ever could. None of these features are relevant, but they will remain in my memory forever.

"Help me hold him upright," says the doctor as she peels the towel away from his head. Everywhere, skin splits apart in thin slits through thick black hair, and as the blood is blotted away, I see the white of bone. The peroxide hits the back of my throat and I taste bile. The doctor raises a surgical stapler and positions the face of it against the lesions. It produces a dull noise when she activates it, and the sharpened points of the staples converge to pull the flesh on his head back together.

My brother stepped forward before me to try and navigate this foreign landscape, to find the footholds that wouldn't break beneath our feet. And he should not have been wrong in imagining that there would be a bond among those who were in the same situation, those whose fathers came from the same place as ours, witnessed the same things as ours, and wore the band with the same reverence as ours. But these bonds are built upon our fathers' memories, not our own, so they are as good as ether. A foundation of nothing. The footholds have broken and my brother has fallen because of it.

Seventy-eight times I listen to the sound of sharpened steel mending torn flesh, and I shake my brother to keep him awake. Each staple weighs a little less than half a gram, so there are just over thirty grams of steel in my brother's head. Medical staples are a good use of steel, worth more than the materials used to make them. "There are no fractures in the skull, but make sure you wake him up every two hours. If he becomes unresponsive or his condition worsens in any way, bring him back here." I nod along as I watch a drop of blood fall to the pool below and the ripples that wave out when it makes contact. The doctor leaves the room, and my cousin supports my brother from one side and I support him from the other.

Objects have meaning only insofar as we imbue them with it. But sometimes it's not in our control what meaning attaches itself to an object. Sometimes life forces meaning onto an object that we rather wish it didn't. What happened in my father's life to make him revere the kara is a mystery to me, and I wish I could inherit the reverence he holds for it. I wish I could look at this steel band as something positive and noble, but to me it's become a symbol of ignorance and violence.

There are thirty grams of steel in my brother's head, holding it together after it was torn apart by someone who should have been unified with us through heritage. But he used a symbol of unity to rip it apart. There are thirty grams of steel in the band I hold. I place it on the examination table and leave it there. Coated with blood, it is too heavy for me to hold any longer. And besides, I figure that there are better uses for steel.

Nineteen Eighty-Four

What need is there to emulate Orwell in diction and prose, when the world emulates Orwell so closely in spirit and function? Of course, not entirely. There are always places where reality sees fit to depart from the Englishman's vision, but never in a way that is less dystopian. For example, the "two-minute hate" is a daily practice wherein the citizens of Oceania are forced to watch a propagandized film depicting various enemies of the state, and to encourage and foster a general hatred toward these otherwise phantom actors. But in India the actors are not phantoms, and the time allotted for hatred is far more than two minutes. You see, there was no need for the central government of India to force-feed hatred into the hearts of the populace. It is much simpler than that. Hatred already exists in humanity's heart, more deeply and more potently than love. All you must do is posit an enemy and the rest will take care of itself.

Kaka and Kala had no idea what the commotion was about, and they had little concern for it besides. Kala was thinking about how he would arrange to transport his brother's body back to Ahmedpura and Kaka was anxiously dreading his forthcoming nuptials. Naturally, they decided that the best course of action was to get drunk. Outside the hospital, Delhi remained as it always was. Obnoxiously loud, obnoxiously hot, and obnoxiously ever-changing. They headed to a bar located near the hotel they booked for the night. It was an unpretentious place in an alley off a main road, owned by a rosy-cheeked Sardar named Motu. His cheeks were rosy because he liked drinking as much as his patrons, but he ran a profitable business because he was the kind of drinker who only got more pleasant the more he drank.

The hours dwindled by as the three men spoke of idle things not related to the turmoil in Punjab. They discussed the prospects of various cricket teams, exchanged funny stories from Kaka's travel and Kala's time in the pind, and they were eventually persuaded to sample Motu's appetizer menu (of which the tandoori chicken proved the most delectable). But maintaining light-heartedness under the circumstances proved to be too difficult. The memory of Gora sat heavy on Kala's mind, and successive drinks provided the clarity to strip away the sorrow, revealing something else lurking beneath—envy. He said, "Kamse kam oh kise kaarn lahi taan khalota si. Mein kade kise cheez lahi nahi khalota."[210]

Kaka had no reply. He knew there was truth in it. It was an inescapable paradox of life, mostly unspoken, that the aimless living will always, in some small measure, remain envious of the steadfast dead. "Shad yaar, tu changa banda heygein,"[211] Kaka finally offered. He filled up their glasses again and raised his in honour of Gora and the nobility of his reckless ways.

In the afternoon, news of the prime minister's assassination began to be broadcast over multiple radio channels. As they drank their sorrows away in Motu's tavern, the radio remained off. Elsewhere, initial reports were met with skepticism and disbelief, but as the news became corroborated more and more, the citizens of Delhi began to absorb the information as

---

210 At least he stood up for something in his life. I've never done that.
211 Drop it, Kala. You're a good man.

the truth. At around 6:00 p.m., Delhi's ever-present racket dialled down to a quiet murmur, and then fell silent completely. It was a tangible sensation, like an eerie fog that entered Motu's restaurant, and it brought the three men inside to a wary alertness. "Ah ki hunda peya?"[212] Kala asked. Motu shrugged, put his glass down, and headed over to his radio. It whined as he dialled it to a news station, and then settled with a few pops and crackles. The broadcaster's voice filled the space and rang out like a hammer against an anvil. "Indira Gandhi kee hatya un ke Sikh angarakshakon ne kee hai."[213]

Motu's rosy cheeks turned ghost-white and his jolly demeanour vanished. Given the boiling animosity between Hindus and Sikhs, a flash point was inevitable, but this was an extreme one. Soberly, Motu told Kaka and Kala, "Tusi ghar jao."[214] They were far from needing to be convinced, so they quickly gathered their belongings and headed back to their hotel. Behind them, Motu closed up his shop and hurried off down the street in the direction of his home.

The lobby of the hotel was empty but for the clerk standing behind the reception desk. A young man who had a turban wrapped around his head, and the wispy beginnings of a beard. He appeared no older than twenty. He looked at Kaka and Kala nervously, desperately almost, as if he was looking to be told what to do. All Kaka offered in return was a gesture toward the exit sign, not daring to stop long enough to say a word. It was not the time to make friends in low places. But the boy took the hint and collected his belongings from behind the desk and scrambled out the door.

Once the door to their room shut behind them, Kala whispered, "Ki kariye?"[215] It was unclear to them both what would transpire in the coming days. There were two concrete facts they had to work with. Indira Gandhi had been

---

212 What's going on?
213 Indira Gandhi has been assassinated by her Sikh bodyguards.
214 You should go home.
215 What should we do?

assassinated, and the assassins were her bodyguards, two Sikh men who had sworn an oath to protect her. The situation conjured the familiar and unsettling churn in Kaka's stomach like when he sat on his bed in the hotel conference room in Iran. Back to when he was an impartial observer amid a revolution. He remembered vividly that beneath the idealistic statements on the revolutionaries' placards, there was a deep yearning for violence, even a celebration of it. There was no reasoning to be found on either side, but the ones who managed to live did so by staying out of sight. That much, Kaka remembered. The only sensible answer he could provide in reply to Kala's question was: "Aj raat ithe rahiye. Jad svehar ho ju, nikle javaan ge."[216]

The silence finally broke, and from the window, the sounds of street mobs crying for blood rumbled up like rolling thunder. The black skyline retreated higher as the orange glow of flames danced against the horizon. A fear emerged unlike any Kaka had experienced before. Not stemming from the known anxiety he had felt most of his life, of having to sit still when he wanted to move, but the inverse, not wanting to move but knowing he had to.

As the night progressed, the flames rose higher, and from places nearer and nearer to the hotel. They were reminiscent of the Cinema Rex fire in Abadan, but they sprouted up in a thousand places at once, burning red spires like the fingers of hell clawing out of the underworld. The smell of ash, searing metal, rubber, and kerosene wafted into the room and Kaka and Kala covered their mouths and noses with bedsheets. They sat on the floor, leaning their backs to the door of the room, hoping to keep it barricaded with their weight. They did not allow themselves a moment of sleep; hardly did their eyes blink. They pressed into the door with the urgent understanding that their lives depended on it remaining closed.

In Orwell's *1984*, "hate week," is a cumulative celebration of hatred directed at the enemies of Oceania. The citizens

---

216 We should stay here tonight. When morning arrives, we leave.

demonstrate their enthusiastic spite through speeches, parades, enactments, posters, and more. During this week they were kicked up into such delirium, Orwell describes, that had these citizens got their hands on their perceived enemy, "they would unquestionably have torn them to pieces." In fiction, this is merely a hypothetical statement, but here again reality departs.

The mob's chants finally faded away. The flames reduced to glowing embers, and behind them the yellow light of the sun began to emerge, but it was obstructed by the grey, oblong spectres of smoke, steadily cascading upward. Kaka and Kala finally relaxed their pressure on the door. Cautiously, Kaka cracked it open and peeked down the hall. It was empty and dead silent. They needed to make it to Kala's motorcycle so they could leave the city but they could not be seen by anyone. Ever since he returned to India, Kaka had relaxed his grooming routines, and his beard had grown back thick. Alone, he could pass as a Hindu or a Muslim, but with Kala that was not an option. His friend had a thicker beard than him, and it swooped down to his navel, and a heavy knot of hair lay beneath his thickly tied turban. Kala was a six-foot target in a city full of firing squads.

Kaka took the lead out of the hotel, cautioning Kala to remain back and out of sight as much as possible. Once outside, it became clear where the smell of burning metal and rubber came from. The carcass of Kala's motorcycle, along with every other vehicle in the parking lot, was smouldering in ruins. The owner of the hotel was inspecting the damage, and upon seeing the two men he immediately warned them to leave, "verna ..."[217] Kala suggested they go back to Motu's bar to see if the jolly man might lend a hand, but when they arrived there, they saw the windows smashed, the goods looted, and furniture reduced to kindling. Motu himself was nowhere among the rubble but a pool of blood convinced them not to linger.

---

217 Or else.

A similar scene emerged everywhere they went. Shattered storefronts and black smoke wafting out of businesses and homes, only now the pools of blood surrounded the bodies they came from. Not a hundred metres passed by without another corpse sprawled out on the street. No discernment between age or sex, but all with clear markers betraying their faith. It was ominously quiet nearly everywhere but then Kaka heard a cluster of voices, and he ducked and hid alongside Kala, behind the counter of a looted convenience store. Like a pack of wolves, a group of men with deranged eyes stalked by, their clothes stained black and red, their hands wielding blunt weapons or carrying canisters of kerosene.

That mystifying haze of the city had evaporated, the sky was a tarnished grey as the ashes rose, and everything was stark and clear. No longer were limbs elongated, but they were severed, the visual spectrum was not distorted, but it plainly offered carnage. These streets, that once he gleefully paraded down, not bothering with the safety of his mother's floating finger, now held him still, paralyzed in a vice like grip.

Kaka looked around, trying to devise an escape plan, but his mind was numb and unresponsive. Even the drumbeat which pressed him forward was dead and silent. He didn't know what to do. Kala grabbed his arm and whispered, "Aja, bus udda chaliye."[218] He nodded and moved alongside his friend as if he was floating through a dream. It must have been a dream. Like when his father had told him how he ran across Punjab as the world burned around him and the blood of innocents flowed red in the rivers. His father ran, and then never wanted to move again. Because his father became numb like he was numb now. That is what this was, a dream from Kaka's father's life. Not reality. A hallucination of life that carries you through it, and all you could do is divorce yourself from what your senses believed they were witnessing and wait until you awoke.

---

218   Come on, let's go to the bus station.

In the broad light of day, the cries and screams of unseen humans echoed through the streets. The black smoke rose from the bus station a mile away. The air was noxious but they went toward it regardless. If there was any way out of the city, it should be there. But as they came closer, they found the source of the screaming echoes. The wolves had descended on the only bus not on fire and Kaka watched as men, women, and children were dragged from it, pulled by their uncut hair. Screaming, a distant sound, as in a dream. He would not wake. Visceral, yet unreal. Experienced, but not remembered. The sight of it would live forever, through the eyes of an unwilling witness. The forgotten deaths he saw. He would not wake.

A blade entered a man's torso and was pulled across his chest, and his disembowelment elicited howls of satisfaction.

A young woman was violently raped on the blood-soaked concrete. A gang of jeering demons circled her, awaiting their turns as her screeching transitioned to muted whimpers, and the life in her eyes slowly faded away.

A father, a young girl hugging at his leg, and a mother, the baby clutched against her chest, were lined against the wall. The kerosene fell on them like heavy rain, and when they tried to move away from it, the lead pipes beat them back into position.

Kaka was pulled away by Kala into the shadows between buildings. They moved on but the carnage continued. All buses and taxis out of the city were being stopped by mobs and checked for Sikhs. The trains fared no better: some had been derailed entirely, set to flames with whole carriages of passengers cooking alive inside. Once or twice, they witnessed Sikhs who stood their ground—resolute expression, with a kirpan pulled from its scabbard—but those few were mobbed twice as hard and butchered with twice as much fervour.

Kala remained vigilant as they went about, keeping off main roads, and dragging his friend behind him, but eventually he realized that to leave Delhi, they would need to expose themselves. Kala saw details that no one else did. He noticed the leaders of the mobs. They were zipping around on motorcycles, and now and again they hopped off them to resupply the mob with more fuel or weapons. Kala wagered that if he could get to one quick enough, they could speed away before the mob caught up to them.

He pulled Kaka to a less frenzied area, where the larger mob had already passed through, and he spotted a smaller gang of murderers. Kala shadowed them until one of the motorcycle leaders pulled to a stop before them. The motorcycle was left running as the group entered a Sikh-run auto body shop to douse it in kerosene. The street was still occupied and Kala could not risk exposing himself. If he was seen, they would both be torn to shreds. So, he pulled Kaka close and told him that they needed to get to the motorcycle that had been left running in the middle of the road. "Ik mint dey, soch ke kam kariyeh,"[219] Kala said, peering out from the alley they were in. He was observing and thinking, looking for ways in which his plan could go wrong before they acted too rashly. But Kaka saw an opportunity, a flash of clarity in the fog of his mind. He bolted out without thinking.

When Kaka had bought the kara seven years earlier, he had done so believing that over time it would accrue in value and be worth more than when he had bought it. He was right. The value of the weight of gold on his wrist had increased by $27.87 USD. As he sprinted to the running motorcycle on the centre of the street, Kala saw the band fall out from under Kaka's sleeve, and the brilliant glimmer of the metal's reflection in the broad light of day. It had been forgotten about by both. They were concerned more with Kala's turban and beard, and never thought about the band on Kaka's hand. It was never thought about in Punjab; it just was a part of you.

Kaka ran to the vehicle but he heard Kala hissing warnings at him from behind. Before he could understand them,

---

219 Give me a second, let's think about how we're going to do this.

someone screamed out at him, "Arey, tum ruk jao!"[220] Kaka stopped in the centre of the road, halfway between the bike and the alley, entirely exposed. The mob leader was glaring at Kaka from the entrance of the shop, squinting to get a better look at him. But before the leader had a chance to approach, Kala ran from his hiding spot and grabbed Kaka by the collar with one hand. With the other, he deftly slid the kara off Kaka's wrist. "Mein tenu kiya si, ruk ja,"[221] Kala whispered to him. There were tears in his eyes but he was smiling. "Hun vekhla Kaka, mere taun ki karaata tun." [222]

Kaka did not understand what had just happened. Kala drove his fist against Kaka's chin and he staggered backward. With blurry vision he saw his own kara glimmering on Kala's wrist and his friend yelling out loudly, "Eh panchodo Hindu kutte ne tenu das na si, mein kithe lukeya si. Par panchodo, mein tuhade saamne ah! Mein nahi lukda! Ajo! Ajo!"[223]

Kaka did not move. His body had reversed every instinct it had ever developed and it held him frozen in position. He watched the mob close in around Kala. Kala threw his fists toward them, knocking a few back and down to the ground. But there were too many. They grabbed his arms and held him still. A tire from the autobody shop was dragged out and pulled over his body. A canister of kerosene was emptied over his head. It soaked into his clothing, into his turban, into his hair. It filled the empty crevasses of the tire and it pooled around his feet. Someone smashed a metal rod against his knee. Kala fell to the ground, still screaming profanities at his attackers.

The leader smirked and lit a match.

---

220 Hey you, stop!
221 I told you to wait.
222 Now look what you've made me do, Kaka.
223 This sister-fucking Hindu was running to tell you where I was hiding. But I'm not hiding! I'm right here! Come get me! Come on!

2018

The light shining from behind the hospital bed drapes over Der Vater in an almost cinematic fashion. Not merely because it paints deep shadows over his sunken eyes, creates contrast in the wrinkles of the limp skin hanging off his skeletal face, and shimmers as it falls on his now stark white hair, but also because I feel separated from him. It's as if I'm watching him die through a high-resolution television screen.

Each year in Canada, blood-red leaves shrivel and fall from anemic branches. And then the world becomes colder and darker. But this precedes a rebirth, when the buds of new leaves unfold and colour the world again. It is an earthly apoptosis—necessary and functionally beautiful. But in Der Vater's body, apoptosis refuses to occur. The dying leaves cling to the branches and they eat away at the rest of the organism.

The tubes and wires snake around him and inject themselves into various places and infuse him with an artificial life that is pale and fragile, born as it is of chemicals and machinery. They groan and beep and display technically precise readouts of the inner workings of his body. In truth, they communicate more than he ever did. He was always content to keep his traumas buried. Perhaps that is what ravages him now—pain and anger calcified into tumours.

But likely not. There's a more malevolent force at play here. Death—that tall, dark, shadowy figure, draped in black

310

cloth, always lurking in the rear, gripping the gnarled, wood handle of his blade. But not stoic, not detached and impersonal as he is with others. No, with us, he laughs heartily. He plays games and toys with us. He does not swing his sickle cleanly at our lot. He fumbles the blade, does not cut deep enough, and generally puts a half-hearted effort forward when it comes to collecting the debt we owe him. This is a scientific observation, backed by empirical data. My microscope takes the form of the light that shines up the pantry staircase from the basement, from the single bedroom where my ancestors were sent to die.

From there I listened as the Viper tried to hold together the remnants of her rapidly deteriorating mind. It was loud. There was crying and screeching and raving. There was anger and confusion and fear. At first, I believed I was witnessing a person who was changing—morphing into something new. But this was wrong. It was a person who was leaving—morphing into something less. What I saw and heard from the basement was the Viper's shed skin, stubbornly imitating the behaviours of life. A stark refutation of Descartes' duality. It is hard to believe in an immaterial soul when you see how closely it is entwined with flesh and blood. When you can correlate the piecemeal destruction of the person you know neatly with degeneration seen on MRI brain scans, you see plainly that there is nothing ethereal about it. Our souls are woven into the hard material fibre of our being.

And then the light from the bottom of the stairs went out, for a time. But when it was relit, putrid odours wafted up with it. He stopped complaining about his knees; they pained him the least of all his aches. Like his son now, his husk could no longer be bothered with the burden of existence, so it was pushed along by different kinds of tubes and bags: dialysis, catheter, stoma. It was quieter this time, because my Guardian was always quiet. But now even the murmur of the radio was turned down, so low I could hear his laboured breathing and hoarse, hacking coughs. Before he died it was clear to me he had finally stopped believing there was anything that could heal this world, and that was a cruel thing to have to witness.

Purgatory is not a place between life and death. It exists as a reality, both in a psychological sense and in a physiological sense. Though what places us there, those things called sins—which are often nothing more than choices, coerced or freely decided; ambitions, failed or achieved; ideals, lived up to or lived beneath; and promises, kept or broken—are not cleansed or forgiven. They are merely rebranded as a "legacy" and passed on to those left behind. No matter the intensity of suffering one endures, nothing is ever absolved.

Der Vater breathes and the translucent plastic mask strapped to his face fogs and clears. His eyes are not dimmed by the litany of nervous system depressants dripping into his bloodstream. They are animalistic. Strained and red and wet, and he wants escape, but no one can give him that, least of all me. I am watching him through a high-resolution television screen. My attachment to this moment is impersonal. I do not feel alive. The tubes and wires enter his body. He is dangling from cords but I am the marionette. Though there is pity, it is of a shallow sort. My heart is gone somewhere. I want him to die, for mercy's sake, but maybe something less defensible than that as well. Maybe something ignoble, maybe something bitter, maybe something unforgivable. But it does not matter, because I am not alive right now.

1984

A withering self-doubt accompanied Kaka as he returned from Delhi to Ahmedpura. As his senses absorbed their surroundings with a dull passivity, his mind was furiously retracing the threads of the past with the hopeless goal of undoing what was done. He knew it was of no use, but there was no way for him to stop it. He did not have supernatural control over the processes of his brain. It was an organ addicted to its own conceit, content to endlessly turn over memories in pursuit of answering that cancerous question: "what if?"

It had been two weeks since he had left. That's how long it had taken the police and the military to tamp down the riots. Their efforts in this task could not be said to be enthusiastic, or even competent. Many officers stood by as the capital burned, both of their own accord and under order of the local district politicians. The human heart is a vengeful thing, and it remains so regardless of the uniforms that shroud it. For those two weeks Kaka found shelter in the less aggravated districts of Delhi, and without his kara, there was nothing left to identify him as a Sikh. When buses began to run without being harassed, he boarded the first one home.

In the meantime, a queer atmosphere had fallen over Punjab. The riots did not spread into the state because the mob had courage only when it greatly outnumbered its enemy. But there was still discord in the place of Kaka's birth.

The two men who killed the mother of India were generally revered as heroes in Punjab, martyrs of the faith, but their actions had done little to unify Sikhs. The cause of Khalistan was still championed and led by the most violent and most deplorable actors. They harassed innocent farmers, looting and pillaging at will, and they'd amassed such a force that even the state police were cowed into inaction.

As he walked down the single dirt road leading into Ahmedpura, Kaka did not see a single soul out in the village or the fields. As he approached his home, he saw the newly installed iron gates were shut and locked with a heavy iron chain and padlock. On the other side, the Chuhra swept the porch. "Sardar ji! Shukar ah Rub da, tusi zinda ho!" [224] he said, running over to the gate and reaching into his pocket to retrieve the key. "Sanu tera fiker si. Sub kush theek thak ah?"[225] he asked.

Kaka had no desire to speak. He wished to go to a dark place and to close his eyes to make it darker. He nodded, hoping it was enough to discourage any more questions, but then his mother appeared at the threshold of the door, her expression as always, dour. She said, "Ageya? Ja fir, aapne dadey de ghar. Jera keemti suman ah, chak leya. Oh kuta Pinda mar geya."[226] Not bothering to argue, and with no stomach for it besides, he nodded and then turned to leave. The Chuhra followed along to lend a hand, and though Kaka was entirely uninterested, the Chuhra explained what had happened as they walked.

Apparently, Pinda had been ambushed by a group of ban-dits as he was making a delivery of desi daru to Bagradi, the pind next door. His body was found a day later in a ditch on the side of the road, stripped of anything of worth. Since he was a solitary man, and had no next of kin, the contents of

---

224 Sir, thank god you are alive!

225 We were worried about you. Is everything alright?

226 You're back? Well then, go to your grandfather's house, and bring back anything that's useful. That worthless dog Pinda is dead.

Maher's estate had fallen to no one. And since Kaka's mother was a practical woman, she has sent her son to the estate to gather what he could before the place was torn apart by looters.

Once upon a time, Maher's estate had been a symbol of everything worth striving for, bricks stacked upon one another to create a palace of prestige. Exceptionalism, at least as much of it as could be achieved in Ahmedpura. Kaka looked around. He saw a soggy pile of wheat in the corner, and it conjured a host of grim memories. Beatings so severe and so unwarranted that for a moment they took centre stage in his mind's eye over the look of agony on his friend's face and the smell of burnt flesh. A bitter taste spread through his mouth and he spit on the stone floor to eject it. "Tun thaley vekh, mein upar vekh dein,"[227] Kaka said to the Chuhra, and headed toward the outer staircase.

The second floor was nothing more than a bedroom suite with a large balcony overlooking the court. Kaka looked around but found nothing of significant value. Just some of Pinda's clothes and a few empty bottles of imported liquor. It was a depressingly solitary place with no decor or images of loved ones. A fitting layout, as neither man who resided there appeared capable of love. He left the room and climbed the short staircase to the roof.

His head crested over the short stone railing bordering the terrace and he blinked against the light. Then, for the first time in his life, he saw the sun setting over that lost Western empire that Maher had spent so much of his life scowling at. Kaka had only ever seen his grandfather stand on the roof; he was never permitted to go there himself. It was a beautiful vista, overlooking the entire village and beyond, extending endlessly outward. The red-and-orange glow of the skyline bled effortlessly into the amber and gold oceans of wheat, making it nearly impossible to distinguish where one ended and the other began. It imparted the feeling that the world was a large place, so large you might never come to the end of it.

---

227 You take the downstairs; I'll check the upstairs.

Pinda's manja sat on the roof as well and leaning up next to it was Chekhov's Lee Enfield rifle, the only thing the English empire had ever given to Kaka's family. He took it in his hands and felt the grain of wood and the coldness of the steel barrel. Cold even as it lay in the heat of the sun. It was a hollow thing. He felt no satisfaction in holding it, but what difference it would have made, he thought, if only he held it two weeks ago.

The irony of this situation did not go over Kaka's head. For years, he had observed his grandfather (not without resentment), standing on this roof. An old man, mulling over old grievances. And now that he stood in the same spot, not yet old enough for old grievances, but certainly with enough time, what would distinguish him from that old man he hated so fiercely? "Sardar ji, kush ni labya. Chaliye?"[228] the Chuhra shouted from the courtyard. Kaka took one more look at the horizon, slung the rifle on his shoulder, and headed down the stairs.

It was nearly dark as the Chuhra and Kaka approached his home, and from a distance he heard his mother's distinct voice. She was screaming, not in pain or distress but anger. "Kuth kanay dungaro, badmasho, jao duffa ho jao ithon!"[229] she yelled. Kaka sprinted the distance, roughly fifty yards, to see what the commotion was about, and as he came closer to the iron gate of his home, he saw a shadowy group of men gathered around it. Their faces were covered with the loosened ends of turbans, or bandanas for those with cropped hair. Without the light he could only make out their forms and could only guess at how many there were—at least half a dozen, maybe more.

"Chup kar haramzadeya! Darvaza kholo!"[230] shouted one of the bandits as he rattled the gate. They were armed with kirpans and various farming tools. Only the one who rattled

---

228 Sir, I found nothing of value. Should we go?
229 You shit eating, lazy donkeys, get the hell out of here!
230 Shut up you whore! Open this door!"

the gate appeared to be holding a rifle. Kaka moved without thinking. The reservoir of despair that followed him back from Delhi boiled into a scalding rage and he stormed forward, slamming the butt of Chekhov's rifle into the head of the bandit standing closest to him. Before the man had hit the ground, Kaka cracked his head again and he went limp.

The leader who rattled the cage turned around and shouted, "Panchode!" and Kaka responded by quickly aiming and cocking the rifle before the other man had a chance to get his up. "Jao ithon,"[231] Kaka warned. The bandit leader didn't move but the rest of them inched back slowly. Kaka saw his father behind the gate shielding his mother, wielding an old pickaxe that belonged to the Chuhra. The bandit grinned, opened his mouth to speak, but before he had a chance, Kaka's mother took hold of the pickaxe and swung it through a gap in the gate, digging the sharp end into the gang leader's clavicle.

He cried out and fell to his knees, groaning in pain. The rifle he wielded fell from his grip and then through the gates, landing next to Kaka's father. The old man picked it up and pointed it at the squealing bandit on the ground. "Hun daffa ho jao,"[232] said Kaka's father with a shaky voice. Two of the henchmen came forward to drag their leader away. The pickaxe was still lodged in his shoulder. Kaka said, "Hatto."[233] They came to a stop, eyes widening. Kaka approached them, placed his hand on the handle of the pickaxe, and yanked it back with as much force as he could summon, tearing it from the bandit's flesh. The bandit cried out in agony and fell backward. Kaka waved for the henchmen to leave and they dragged the howling man away as quickly as possible.

Kaka turned around and saw his father lowering the bandit's rifle with trembling hands. His mother straightened her chunni and walked back to the house, mildly annoyed, as if she had forgotten to turn the stove off. The Chuhra was

---

231 Leave from here.
232 Now get out of here.
233 Stop.

standing awestruck at the edge of the road. Kaka walked over to him and pushed the rifle into his chest. "Je oh vaapas agey,"[234] he said. And then he entered the gates of his home and went searching for a dark place to close his eyes.

For once, he found sleep, the deepest he'd ever known. But with it, dreams that were agonizingly vivid, a patchwork of images pulled starkly from his subconscious mind, a place where memories go to die. That night, they were briefly and violently resurrected. Where once these memories held an amber hue, warm and heartening and life-giving, time and circumstance had ravished it away, and they were now rusted grey and painful to touch.

He saw the day he first tried daru with his three closest friends but the scene was grimly warped. Shinda next to the banyan tree, a fiendish grin plastered across his face, throwing gold ingots, muddied with blood and soil, into a field of dead wheat crops. On the ground, Gora and Kala, young as they were on that day, but not jostling one another in the heat of the sun. They were apart, as if they never touched one another in their lives, and their small bodies were beaten and burned and devoid of life. And in the distance was the silhouette of a man on the roof of a two-floored house. As his face came into focus, an expression of hopeless rage, a black and endless remorse. But the man on the roof was not Maher. It was Kaka.

In the morning he would wake, wipe the cold sweat from his brow, and urge his mother to expedite the wedding ceremony as quickly as possible. He would travel to Patti to visit the real estate offices there. He would place the house he'd managed to build with his money, and the land he'd been able to accrue, up for sale. Even sold at a discount it should be able to cover the expense of six visas and plane tickets. He knew without a doubt that Punjab would not be a home to him. His memories of this place were like cold poison,

---

234 In case they come back.

salt churned into soil, allowing nothing new to blossom. "Home," if such a thing existed, did so elsewhere.

As for Chekhov's gun, that object which had pretended importance for so long, like the British officers who first held it, what became its fate? Once, it was a metaphor for power and authority, but now after years of refusing to do anything but be caressed, it had fallen from those lofty heights. The barrel had begun to rust and corrode under the stewardship of careless men, the wooden frame, cracked and chipping away. The trigger was jammed in place and it was doubtful that it would budge without first being oiled. But even given that, it was still a symbol of something. A relic of that vast and endless ocean called the past, stubbornly moving through the ages, if only to remind the person currently holding it how many had drowned before them. A reminder, that they too would be swallowed by the past. An important thing to remember.

In any case, Chekhov's gun would now remain in the Chuhra's undignified hands—thoroughly unfired.

1992 / 2018

The day is too bright. What right has the sun to shine so arrogantly today? The room I'm in is a large auditorium, high ceilings, and on the far side of the room is a raised podium in front of a glass wall. The white light of the late morning sun is beaming in at a diagonal, and the air glimmers with the crisp, crystalline sheen of spring. Life is speaking outside this room—the playful calls of mating blue jays and the rustle of tree limbs as they dance with the breeze. The casket is open and the silhouette of his face is barely visible, a white marble mask expressing a profound silence. It should be darker today.

There was a tool I had once, a way to block out the light and all the chaos it brings with it. It was just a blanket, a simple and inexpensive thing, made mostly of green polyester, but I still remember the *feeling* of it, what it was like to be without that blanket—naked, exposed, vulnerable. It's hard to remember concrete things from that age in life, when distinctions are still being drawn in the mind, but that blanket I remember as the first distinction my mind ever made, the first line to be drawn, between myself and the world around me. When things became too overwhelming, too much stimulus for my young brain to process, I would crawl beneath that blanket and it would block the world out, darken the light, and reduce the chaos. From there, I would tune into the singular sound emanating from my chest, and all the universe would condense to a heartbeat.

The chatter of the gathered crowd intrudes from all angles and what they speak disorients me. Phrases like "great man" and "good person" and a succession of handshakes, firm and limp, combine to send a wave of vertigo down my spine. There are more people here than I expected. He was so solitary a man, it's difficult to understand why they've all come. Some of them I know but many of them I don't. Unfamiliar faces that make me anxious. It reminds of how when I was young and I would crawl underneath that blanket to escape from the world, people I didn't know would always pull me out from under it. Pull me out and bring their faces close to mine and guffaw and squeal and feel too entitled to a space that was mine. I would cry then, and I remember how he would come to take me away from them.

That blanket, I don't remember exactly how it was lost, but it was. Left out on the bank of the river during a family picnic or something. I don't remember. But again, I remember how it felt to be without it. It was sheer terror. A cold grip from the soles of my feet to the crown of my head, and the world was pressing against me so intensely, like it was falling into me. I felt overwhelmed, I felt like everything that could possibly happen was happening to me at once. I felt like I was experiencing so much life I would certainly die of it. Now, after escaping it for so long that feeling is beginning to grip me again, swelling in my chest like a rising tide.

There are no stacks of logs piled up in this auditorium, nor are there any outside it. This won't be done like how it was where he was raised. Later, the casket will be rolled down to the basement, where an oven built into a cement hole will bake the corpse to ashes with the press of a button. It's an inorganic process, sterile and grey and dead. And though that marble mask on the podium is also sterile and grey, it bears no resemblance to who or what he is. It's why this affair seems so inauthentic, so cowardly. He burned so fiercely in life that it feels a disgrace to shield ourselves from the final flame he will ever produce. We ought to be able to see the fire, to feel it's heat.

What we get instead is the baba solemnly murmuring his Ardaas in front of the casket. For how could the proceedings go on without God, the most unwelcome of guests, who finds a way to be inserted into every situation without ever offering anything in return. But that's a tool for some, I see, to guard against the chaos. They close their eyes and hum the prayers along with the old baba and it steadies their feet against the earth. And who am I to deny them their solace, me whose feet feel as though they float over an abyss?

After I lost that blanket, I had learned to steady my feet, and to block out life when it suits me, but it wasn't easy. The night the blanket was lost was a horrible night for everyone. I wouldn't allow anyone to rest, because I couldn't stop crying. I remember that too, the sharp pain of overstrained vocal cords and the cotton feel in my mouth from dehydration. And when everyone had given up trying to soothe me or calm me down, and they resorted to screaming at each other, casting blame about the lost blanket, he came over and picked me up. He pulled me away from them to a dark room, and he lay down on a bed and cradled me over his chest. I was so small at the time that my whole body fit the distance from his chin to his sternum, and there I sprawled myself open, weeping and crying with my arms and legs stretched out, hoping to grab hold of something that would help me find the ground again.

Then I felt it. The gentle rise and fall of his chest as he breathed in and breathed out, and beneath that the steady pulse of his heart, which drummed through my whole body like an earthquake. There it was, the secret truth that finally quieted me to sleep, the secret truth that I've carried with me ever since. That the blanket held no special importance at all; it was merely something objectively reliable that I could turn my focus to when I wanted everything else to go away. But it was a coward's tool, because it's a false belief that you can make the world go away. Better to face it head on, and that's what I found that night as that heartbeat thud against my body, objective and reliable and seemingly eternal. A much better tool, not a shield to guard me from the light, from the chaos of the world, but a rhythm to march out into it with. I fell asleep that night, because in my father's chest, all the universe was condensed to a heartbeat.

That drumbeat is silent now; that universe no more. My last remaining tool against the world is gone. Soon, the baba will stop his Ardaas, and I will have to roll this casket into the basement of this building that is too brightly lit. I will have to deposit all that remains of him into a stone enclosure. I will have to press a button to start a fire I will not feel the heat of—a fire designed to bring to ashes something I always considered indestructible. And once that is all done, I will have to learn how to turn around and face the world again.

1987

Now we come to the close of Kaka's tale. It took longer than anticipated for him to leave India. The civil discord that existed for years after 1984 acted like a sludge that gummed up the already incomprehensibly slow gears of bureaucracy. But with persistence, he eventually achieved what he had resolved to do. Now for the second time in his life, he stepped out of the sliding doors of Pearson International Airport, into the Mississauga suburb of the Greater Toronto Area. Though this time he was accompanied by the entirety of his family: his parents, his sister and her husband, and his lovely newlywed wife as well. It was spring now, so the snow had melted and the ice beneath had thawed. Up above a cardinal chirped, circling around the smiling group of optimistic immigrants, who were facing the light of the sun, baggage in tow with the wind on their backs. Even the customs officer, normally so terse and unsentimental, was inordinately polite, and he enthusiastically said, "Welcome to Canada!" before stamping Kaka's passport with a hyper-green "approved" stamp. A well-deserved, happy ending for the hero and all those he loved; clichés be damned.

But that would be too simple, wouldn't it? Because it's not really the ending. The hero's journey has come to a close, but what about after that? It is the beginning of something else, when the hero stops doing heroic things. And though it may be comforting to view this happy portrait as if it's frozen in time and will extend out into the future indefinitely, the truth is that the road ahead is filled with as much pain and turmoil as the road behind. That part of life is impossible to escape, but at least the turmoil will be of a different kind, one that is not as exciting. The dangers of the external environment will become less of a priority, but the conflicts that exist within this group that surrounds him will become much larger. Family is something of an abstract concept for Kaka, a motivation always in the back of his mind as he travelled and worked, but not for a long while has he been made to deal with the day-to-day realities that come along with all those loving relations.

Pay attention here and you'll notice some of those conflicts already bubbling beneath the veneer of all this tranquility. A mother who is like a Viper, who has enough scorn to distribute to all the people here, and who will lash out at them given the slightest provocation, especially the man she stands next to, a timid and quiet fellow whose knees constantly ache, causing him to hobble everywhere he goes. And behind them, a sister who is loving and kind, but not terribly educated and somewhat naive about the world that exists outside the village she grew up in. Her integration in this new land will not be a smooth one, made harder still by the man she is married to. He has little patience, as he was trained from a young age to deal with problems by grappling and tackling them, a heuristic that is not fondly considered in the northwestern hemisphere. Not to mention the fact that he still harbours no small amount of resentment toward Kaka from having been kneed in the groin by him nearly twenty years earlier. But who could blame him for that? Such things are not easily forgiven.

And then there is Kaka's own wife, a woman he hardly knows, and who does not belong in these pages. But at the moment she holds a secret that will make Kaka's life a great deal more complicated. Her face is blushing and her belly protrudes ever so slightly. She carries a child, and in a few months' time Kaka will be forced to learn to live his life in a manner altogether foreign to him. That is, that he will have to remove himself 'from the centre of it. Because in all his time on Earth, that is always where he has placed himself—at the centre. Peripherally, he thought of others, of course, as all people do. But their lives were never inextricably tied to his in the way this child's will be.

Though right now, he is blissfully unaware of this reality, so he breathes an easy sigh of relief outside the airport. He thinks to himself that he has had enough of moving around. He thinks he wants to establish a thing called a home, and in theory, the prospect of children is not such a scary thing. He has been to Canada before and he knows it is a good place to make one of those things called a home. He thinks it will give him a sense of peace, to be stationary, to build a place of comfort, free from the dangers and perturbations of the world. But he does not yet know how hard it will be to rebel against his nature. He has sacrificed so much in life already, but never has he sacrificed his autonomy, never has he had to place the needs of another before those of his own, not in any real way. And never has he had to deal with the tedium that comes with a secure and predictable life. In Frankfurt, on the bridge crossing the Main, he was Icarus, chin tilted toward an ever-burning horizon, but now the question poses itself: Can Icarus bear the punishment of Sisyphus?

He will have to, whether or not he is able. He will be required to shed those parts of his character that enabled him to do extraordinary things. Sheer will carried him through the darkest moments of his life, but sheer will is not a useful tool in the challenges that await him. He succeeded because he is an uncompromising man; now he will have to learn how to compromise through the agonizing tutelage of caring for a wife and children.

I have never met Kaka. To me, *he* exists in the abstract. He is an apparition, a ghost who pops up here and there, whenever I need to sympathize with the man I know in the flesh. I only have direct experience with the real person who Kaka will become, and the two are not synonymous. Because right now, Kaka has nothing in front of him except potential, and it can manifest in so many different ways. I hope that they will be positive ways. If I could give him some advice, it would be to let go. Stop holding on to the past. It doesn't have to define you. You're free of it now. But then, who am I to say a thing like that?

2019

I'll tell you where I am. I'm standing on a road, rocky and unpaved—at the end of it I suppose—in a village that bears my family's name. It feels like a place locked in time. Mud houses in a loose assembly, surrounded by oceans of fertile fields on all sides. Laughing children are running barefoot through the dirt roads. Old men sit with grumpy satisfaction next to their old wives, sharing their private silences with one another. A cow's tail swats from side to side, trying to shoo the irritating flies. And the sky is so blue and clear and vast I feel as though I'm falling into it.

But it's also hot, suffocating, and it's leaching the energy out of my body. It makes standing here on the road a trial in itself. I want to find a place to lie down, sit in the shade until the heat subsides, but it's doubtful that it will. Heat is the nature of the place and I am alien to it. I wonder how it is that those who came before me were able to persist—to do anything at all.

From here, my great-grandfather, who I never knew, reigned over an agricultural empire, basked in the prestige of British officers, and fell into resentment and bitterness and scorn for the world when it was all taken away from him.

From here, my grandfather, who I knew only as my quiet, gentle, Hobbling Guardian, began to run for his life when he was hardly a man, as the world burned all around him, and he watched the suffocation of life that comes from hatred, and forever after he sought a cure.

From here, my father, who I knew all too well, inherited a restlessness that drove him across the world, a drumbeat that wouldn't be silenced until he took another step, and a deep-seated anxiety which reminded him always that no matter what he was able to build, something would always be lost.

From here, I stand, and in my hands is a jar filled with his ashes. They seem heavier than they should, but he was made of denser stuff than the rest of us. There's roughly 320 million cubic miles of water in the world's oceans. If I were to upturn this jar into a river that leads to those oceans, or directly into them by standing on some beach somewhere—as custom dictates—then I would be doing him a great disservice. What did custom ever mean to him? The oceans of the world are too small, and if I deposited these ashes into those waters, they would fill the 320 million cubic miles and still be unsatisfied with their depths.

He was a great man, that is uncontroversial to all who knew him. But greatness is a thing defined by extremes, and so a great person is manifested in extremes, both positive and negative. It is not possible to be great in all the ways we admire, without dipping your feet into the kind of greatness we loathe. Hero and villain coiled together, and all my life I've sat in a front row seat, trying in vain to decipher the play I'm watching. That is why these ashes weigh so heavily on me, because they are an ending that makes no sense. The curtains are drawn and, yet, I still wonder, who was that man? Who is he now that he is gone?

A strong westerly wind presses against my back. I take a handful of the ashes and cast them outwards. They'll travel farther this way, carried as they are by one of his own kind—a force of nature. But the weight remains. This I will need to become accustomed to. What I set out to accomplish at the beginning of this telling, to bury this story so it no longer burdens me, I know now is not a possible conclusion. There is no resolution to this story.

I look down the road and I try to imagine the sight of my grandfather running. But he was never young in my life, so he can never be young in my imagination. He cannot run down this road; he must hobble. And it takes him a long time, but I know he is moving for me. He is coming to tell me something I already know but don't know how to do. He is telling me to keep moving forward.

My father was a runner. He ran farther and faster than I can fathom. He ran because he needed to, because his blood was on fire, and moving forward was the only thing that could cool it down. He ran because he wouldn't have survived otherwise. But how do I do what my father did, what my grandfather is urging me to do? I was born at the end of the race and there is nowhere left to run. There are no horizons left, just sheer cliff faces that fall to nothing. And behind me there is no light, because there stand the giants who ran so I never had to. And the shadows of those giants fall onto me, shrouding my world in darkness.

What was I looking to find? What notions of truth, what catharsis? The world they lived through no longer exists. It died with each step they took, with each day that passed, with each memory that was forgotten. All that remains of what once happened now only exists in the meagre confines of my mind, and there it is nothing but a fragile, glass facsimile. Already it begins to crack. Not a slow dissolution, the way that sand falls through the dial, but large shards of life stripped and fallen away into obscurity. There is nothing I can do to hold on.

There is no forward for me. And now, standing here where it began, I see that there is no past either. The past belongs to me no more than the future does, no more than the present does. But it did belong to my father, that man who is too great for my words. This world is no place for me, because it was his world. So, whenever the wind blows against my back, I'll cast a handful of his remains into the sky.

Hopefully, this world will be a big enough place for them.

Acknowledgements

Arun Bedi, for playing the devil's advocate, even (and especially) when I myself was the playing the devil.

Parteek Purba, for reading and humouring my early writing, which was truly awful and beyond redemption.

Daniel Karten, for always offering your honest opinion, no matter how brutal.

Subhraj Riar, for your mastery of the mother tongue, and helping to translate to words what I could not.

Aimée Parent Dunn and Jamie Tennant, for seeing the value of my manuscript, and for kindly guiding it to publication.

PHOTO: TREVOR HALDENBY

Arjun Bedi is a second generation Indian-Canadian writer born and raised in Mississauga. Formally educated in Philosophy, with an eclectic set of experiences to follow, his aim has always been to interact with the world in a way that keeps his curiosity alive. *The Blood of Five Rivers* is his first novel.